WITH LOVE FROM LONDON

WITH LOVE
FROM LONDON

A Novel

SARAH JIO

BALLANTINE BOOKS • NEW YORK

A Ballantine Books Trade Paperback Original

Copyright © 2022 by Sarah Jio

Reading group guide copyright © 2022 by
Penguin Random House LLC

Published in the United States by Ballantine Books,
an imprint of Random House, a division of
Penguin Random House LLC, New York.

BALLANTINE and the HOUSE colophon are registered
trademarks of Penguin Random House LLC.

RANDOM HOUSE BOOK CLUB and colophon
are trademarks of Penguin Random House LLC.

LIBRARY OF CONGRESS CATALOGING-IN-PUBLICATION DATA
NAMES: Jio, Sarah, author.
TITLE: With love from London / Sarah Jio.
DESCRIPTION: New York: Ballantine Books, [2022] | "A Ballantine Books
Trade paperback original"—Title page verso.
IDENTIFIERS: LCCN 2021045072 (print) | LCCN 2021045073 (ebook) |
ISBN 9781101885086 (trade paperback) | ISBN 9781101885093 (ebook)
CLASSIFICATION: LCC PS3610.I6 W58 2022 (print) |
LCC PS3610.I6 (ebook) | DDC 813/.6—dc23
LC record available at https://lccn.loc.gov/2021045072
LC ebook record available at https://lccn.loc.gov/2021045073

Printed in the United States of America
on acid-free paper

randomhousebooks.com

randomhousebookclub.com

2 4 6 8 9 7 5 3 1

Title page art by iStock

Book design by Barbara M. Bachman

For my beautiful nieces

(and flower girls),

Selah and Johannah,

with love from Auntie Sarah

IN THE END,

WE'LL ALL BECOME STORIES.

—*Margaret Atwood*

A LETTER FROM

THE AUTHOR

———

Dear Reader,

Whether you're reading this in the very same year as I'm writing, 2020, or long after these pages have been published, or even after I'm no longer alive (that's the beauty of stories—they live on), I have some stories of my own to tell before you set your eyes on the first page. In writing books over the years—this is my eleventh—I've come to understand that a book is to an author like a baby is to its mother. I'm the mother of three sons, who, at this moment, are fourteen, twelve, and ten. When they were babies, I wouldn't dare think to hand off any one of them to a babysitter without instruction. "He loves pears," I would tell the sitter, or "He gets a little sad at bedtime, so please read him a story." It feels equally strange to place this book in your hands without fussing over it a bit.

In 1992, I was an awkward fourteen-year-old navigating braces, boys, and junior high while also recovering from a bad haircut, and possibly even a horrific perm. That same year, I transformed—from an avid reader into a passionate lover of books. Somehow, I discovered the great Irish author Maeve Binchy and set out to read as many of her titles as I could get my hands on. As I treaded water in the turbulent river of adolescence, her cozy stories were a much-needed life raft. I then vowed that if I ever had the opportunity to write a book, let alone figure out how to publish one, I would attempt to create for my readers cozy places all their own.

I've made this attempt with all my books, including With Love from London. *Halfway through writing this novel, the utterly unexpected happened. Life as we all knew it was turned on its head, courtesy of the Covid-19 pandemic. I battled a fever for more than a month, my boys' schools shut down, and everything came to a weird, screeching halt. But that's exactly when this novel-in-progress became the cozy little world I so desperately needed. At the end of a long writing day, when dogs needed to be walked and children fed, I found myself longing to stay just a little longer in these comforting pages.*

In moments of uncertainty, I thought back to the best of times in the best of places, when my now-husband proposed one evening in 2016, in the most charming spot in Notting Hill (if you adore the movie Love Actually *as much as I do, you'll know exactly where I'm talking about). Just like that, I had my setting,* London.

Some of the places mentioned in this book are fictional, of course, but many I discovered during two research trips. One night, I was lucky enough to be invited to dinner at the storied Royal Automobile Club, which enjoys two scenes in these pages. I can tell you, the RAC was just as ritzy and celebrated as you might imagine. I treasure the memory of that night.

And now I'm handing you my baby. I am forcing

myself to step away, even though I could probably go on and on—and on. With Love from London *and its myriad characters are now in your possession. I'm guessing you'll tuck this book into a beach bag or purse, maybe even pack it on an upcoming trip (to London, even!), or just read it in the comfort of home.*

Wherever you are, and wherever life may take you, I hope you find reading this story to be as comforting as it has been for me to write.

> *With love*
> *from Seattle,*
> *xo,*
> *Sarah*

WITH LOVE FROM LONDON

Valentina

LONDON, ENGLAND

November 3, 2013

———

"THERE ARE FAR BETTER THINGS AHEAD THAN ANY WE leave behind," says the stranger sitting next to me on the airplane—a sixtysomething woman with feathered bangs and a hair tie clinging so tightly to her left wrist that I've spent most of the flight worried it might turn into a medical emergency.

In my years of assorted travel, I've had a long history of questionable airplane seatmates: the ninety-year-old man who touched my leg 3,781 times, then lapsed into a flatulence-fueled nap; the crying baby of all crying babies; the woman who drank too many mini bottles of rum and passed out on my shoulder, drooling.

However, on this particular flight, it seems I've been graced by the "Sentimental Orator." We'd barely cleared the runway, and Chatty in seat 26B had already quoted Shakespeare, Marilyn Monroe, and, if I remember correctly, Muhammad Ali.

My tired, blank stare obviously troubles her, because the corners of her mouth plummet into a disappointed frown.

"You poor child," she says, shaking her head. "You don't know C. S. Lewis? A shame."

"Yes," I say, closing my eyes as I press my head against the seat back, attempting sleep—or, at least, pretending to. "It's . . . *very sad.*"

And it is. I've just been accused of not knowing a quote by one of my favorite authors, though I'm presently too exhausted to defend myself. But what's sadder? The very *quote itself.*

"There are better things ahead than any we leave behind."

My eyes shoot open as the plane begins to descend over London and a burst of turbulence jostles me against the Sentimental Orator who, I predict, will soon start reciting Gandhi, or maybe Mother Teresa.

My mind churns. *What if C. S. Lewis was* wrong? *What if* there *aren't* better things to come? What if . . . ?

The plane rattles again as it slips beneath a cloud, landing gear deployed. A moment later, we're touching down at Heathrow with a thud.

I peer out the window. *So, this is London.*

The Sentimental Orator gasps and fumbles for her inhaler as I take in my first view of England and its seemingly endless gray. A thick layer of fog and dark clouds blend like a muddled watercolor painting—and my own gray mood. Gray on gray on gray.

I sigh as I collect my bag from the overhead compartment and walk numbly ahead. I'm thirty-five years old. This should be chapter thirteen of my life—maybe even chapter sixteen. But somehow, I feel as if I've been catapulted back to the very beginning, or worse, thrust into a laborious rewrite.

"Chapter 1: An American Divorcee in London."

"Miss," the Sentimental Orator says, tapping my shoulder. "I think you forgot . . . your *book*."

She hands it to me and I eye the cover with equal parts humiliation and denial. *How to Get Divorced and Not Lose Your Mind*. I'd only read two chapters, as covertly as possible, but quickly lost interest and tucked it into the seat pocket for the next passenger's guaranteed delight. I mean, what therapist in their right mind would title a chapter: "The Best Way to Get Over Someone Is to Get Under Someone"?

"You poor thing," the Sentimental Orator says, smiling to herself.

Give this model citizen a gold star!

"Are you going through a *divorce*?"

Is it just me, or did she say the word "divorce" several decibels louder? The pair of women to our left look over, their faces beaming pity—for me.

I nod. "Yeah—recently." More nearby eyes descend on me. I might as well have a sticker on my back that reads RECENTLY DIVORCED.

"Remember, dear," my transatlantic seatmate says, "that it takes six months for every year you were together to get over someone."

I'd heard this before—from other well-meaning people—but it always left me feeling confused and, well, a bit terrified. Nick and I were married for twelve years, so by those calculations, will I wallow in sadness and self-loathing for . . . six more? *Who made up this ridiculous statistic, and can we all agree that it's completely bogus?*

It has to be, right?

I sidestep a couple in front of me to avoid the Sentimental Orator's inevitable, forthcoming question: "Do you mind my asking . . . *what happened*?" And then I'd be backed into that awful corner, where I'm required to explain that my husband, an attorney, left me for the twenty-three-year-old paralegal he'd been secretly seeing for months. And yes, I *actually* believed he was working late all those nights. Her name? Oh, it's Missy, who shows off her endless legs and fake eyelashes on Instagram.

My own account is @booksbyval. When I should have been posting inspiration from the novels on my nightstand, I stalked Missy. Guilty as charged. You're wondering: Is she . . . attractive? Smart? Yes, on both counts, though don't you think it should be illegal for someone with perennially pink, pouty lips to also graduate summa cum laude?

They're a couple now. Missy and Nicky. #MadeForEach-Other, or so read one of her recent posts, where she casually hinted at the new love in her life: my husband, or rather, soon-to-be *ex-husband*.

I feel like a zombie as I walk to the passport control area, grateful to have parted ways with the Orator. I scan my passport into a machine, and it begins flashing red and beeping. A moment later, a customs officer appears to tell me I've been randomly selected for further screening.

Of course I have.

"Miss, I'll need you to come with me," he says, leading me to a nearby room, where I hand him my passport. "Here for a holiday?"

"Uh—" I stammer as he fumbles through my bag, my underwear right on top of my jeans, and the old ratty AC/DC sweatshirt I can't seem to part with, even if Nick did give it to me the year we first started dating. "A holiday?" I shake my head. "No."

"Business then?" he continues, as he searches through my carry-on bag with gloved hands.

"No," I say, rubbing my forehead. "Not business."

"Well, then, what is it, miss?"

I swallow hard, deflecting his intense gaze, which feels as if it's piercing into me. "My mother died," I finally blurt.

A tinge of humanity appears in his eyes—only a glimmer, but it's there. Perhaps that's the only good thing about death—that it softens the hardest edges.

"I'm very sorry," he says, returning my passport, then pausing briefly. "You're all clear. Welcome to England."

I nod as he leads me out a separate entrance, then follow the signs to baggage claim, where I collect my two large suitcases on carousel 11 and make my way outside to find a cab. I wave at a waiting driver, who's leaning against his car, smoking a cigarette.

"Where to?" he asks, loading my luggage.

"Primrose Hill," I say.

He nods. "Coming home?"

Now that the divorce is nearly final and the Seattle house sold, Primrose Hill will be my landing place. Still, it's foreign to me.

I shrug. "Sort of."

As he drives off, the raindrops cling for dear life to the window glass. I close my eyes and immediately see my mother's face beaming at me in the rearview mirror. She's singing that old Stevie Nicks song "Sara" and shifting the car into fourth gear. I'm twelve years old. Two weeks later, she would be . . . gone.

I wipe the foggy window with the sleeve of my jacket, remembering how hard it was after she left. Dad had done his best, but he could never fill her shoes. No one could.

Books numbed the pain. Inside their grand adventures I could walk alongside a myriad of characters with lives as complicated as mine.

After college, I got my master's degree in library science, with a particular interest in rare antique books. Call me a first-rate nerd, but I loved spending my days at the circulation desk of the local library, amid the heavenly scent of books, while my ambitious husband finished law school and set out to climb the corporate ladder. The only ladder I was interested in climbing, however, was the one in the vintage book section.

A library is a world unto itself—with its own rhythm section, even, the clatter of hardback books being stacked and shelved, the click of a stamp pressed to a due date, mothers shushing their children, readers tiptoeing from one bookcase to another, discovering unexpected treasures, losing track of time.

Anyway, after I found out about Nick's affair, I took refuge in the library—my favorite little branch in Seattle's Fremont neighborhood—where I could disappear. I raced to the fiction section and sank into the threadbare chair in the far corner and wept and wept and wept. When there were no more tears, I read.

On our last night together, I made chicken parmigiana, and he told me it was the best he'd ever had. Then we watched an episode of *Mad Men,* and when it was over, he kissed me good night. The next morning, I opened my eyes and assumed the empty space beside me meant he'd left early for work as he did so often. But then, on my bedside table, I found a handwritten note that said nothing, and everything.

Val,

I'm so sorry. I always will be.

Nick

My heart sank, because I knew. Perhaps I'd known all along. But there it was, his handwriting in stark black ink. I'd always loved the curve of his *s*'s—with the little squiggles on the tail—but they looked foreign to me now, cruel even, as if they were calligraphic co-conspirators in this grave turn of events. I steadied myself as I let the words marinate in my mind until the reality of the situation finally set in: Nick was leaving me.

When the phone rang a few minutes later, I answered it cautiously.

"Yes, hello." It was a man—with a British accent. "I'm looking for a Ms. Valentina Baker."

"This is," I said, rubbing my eyes as a chilly draft seeped through the bedroom window. "What is this about?"

"It's about your mother, *Eloise Baker.*"

My eyes widened as I sat up in bed. I hadn't heard anyone say *her* name in . . . so long, and it had been more than twenty years since I last saw her. "I'm sorry, what did you say your name was?"

"James Whitaker. I work for Bevins and Associates in London. We're an estate-planning firm; your mother was one of our clients."

"Your mother."

My mother.

It was as if this stranger on the phone had produced a key to a vault of dusty old memories. I closed my eyes tightly, but like meddling ghosts, they demanded my attention. And there she was, my mother, on the last morning I ever saw her. She was standing at the base of the stairs, holding her arms out to me. I studied her beautiful face, with those chiseled features and arresting, crystal-blue eyes. She wore a long, flowy pale blue dress, with a ruffle at the hem.

The man on the phone cleared his throat, and the image disintegrated like a popped bubble. "I'm sorry, but I must relay some upsetting news," he continued. "Your mother . . . she . . . passed away last Tuesday after a battle with ovarian cancer. However, I'm told that her passing was peaceful and painless."

I swallowed hard. My arms and legs felt numb—foreign limbs connected to my despondent body. My heart beat so loudly, it was the only thing I could hear. *How could she be dead?* It seemed so . . . selfish. As if her last breath was a perfectly executed final blow—to me. While it's true I'd long since given up on the idea of our reunion, I suppose a small part of me believed it might happen. Someday. The way it turns out in books, when the pain of the past is miraculously healed in the final pages—wrongs righted with the blot of a handkerchief, heartache mended with a needle and thread. I was supposed to have that ending. But, no, mine would be a tragic one: Nick's letter, and now this. I once read a book about a woman who was struck by lightning three times in one year. It was as if it hunted her.

No, no, no. I blinked back tears. Was I dreaming? Was it all a nightmare?

As Whitaker continued speaking, I fell further into disbelief. I listened, but his words sounded garbled and extraneous.

"Your mother has designated you as the sole heir to her

estate. This includes the property she owns in Primrose Hill—which is a fine neighborhood in London, always holds its values. The building is old, but quite comfortable. There are two flats, on the first and second floors. The bookstore is on the ground floor."

I shook my head, his words finally sinking in. "The . . . *bookstore?*"

Eloise

LONDON, ENGLAND

January 11, 1968

"YOU LOOK PERFECT, EL," MY BEST FRIEND, MILLIE, RE-
assured me. "The question is, will *he* be good enough for *you*?"
She tucked her arm around my waist and leaned her head
against my shoulder, both of us staring into the hallway mirror in our shared flat.

"Maybe I should wear the blue dress. Is red . . . *too much*?
Now, be honest, it's your solemn duty as my friend to tell me
if I look like a tart."

I turned sideways, instantly grateful that I'd skipped tea
today. A scone and jam would have certainly burst the zipper.
I could barely breathe, but I didn't care.

I smiled at our reflection—both versions of us were there
in the mirror: the little girls who had met at age nine, and also
the grown women, navigating the ways of the world. We were
an unlikely pair from the beginning—me, a sprite with blond
hair and pale skin, and Millie, the tallest girl in primary
school, towering above me, with her brunette braids and always a blunt curtain of bangs across her forehead.

Millie had little interest in boys or, later in life, men—but

I was quite the opposite. My collection of schoolgirl crushes and young adult romances was as vast as it was unimpressive. But the storybook dream of love remained firmly rooted in my heart. Like my favorite heroines in books, I longed for my own version of true love, even if Millie thought it was all poppycock.

But Roger Williams—*the Honorable* Roger Williams was hardly poppycock. After my shift ended, he escorted me outside, then asked me to join him for dinner at the Royal Automobile Club. I'd nearly fainted, right there on the corner of Brompton.

True, he ran in upscale circles I might not have been privy to, but it was 1968, not 1928. A girl from the East End could go to dinner with any man she chose, including one from London's highest of societies.

Millie carefully snipped the tag off the side of my dress. It had been an extravagance that had cut way too far into last week's paycheck, but it was a necessity for a date with one of London's most dashing and eligible bachelors. Roger's father, Sir Richard Williams, was a decorated military commander, one of Churchill's most trusted wartime confidants. His mother was a frequent visitor at Buckingham Palace.

"How did you meet him again?" Millie asked, as if what I'd previously recounted was somehow insufficient; she was looking for cracks in my story.

"I already told you—at Harrods. Remember, he was shopping for a birthday gift for his mother?"

"Or his girlfriend," she said with a smirk.

I sighed. "Please, Mill. Can't you just be happy for me?"

She shrugged. "Well, what did he get her, then?"

"A scarf," I said with a smile. "Hermès."

Millie wasn't impressed. "You wait on him, and then he . . . asks you on a date? El darling, I don't doubt that Roger Williams has more charm in his pinky finger than most men have in their entirety, but let's not forget the fact that he's one of the most notorious playboys in London."

"Stop being such a prude," I said.

"I just . . . don't want you to get hurt, that's all."

"I won't, Mill," I promised. "I'm going to meet him tonight, and I intend to have a marvelous time."

Millie looked unconvinced. "What will . . . Frank think?"

I rolled my eyes. "Frank? You're seriously worried about Frank?"

"Well, he is in love with you, isn't he?"

"He is *not* in love with me," I countered. "Besides, just because he's taken me to dinner a few times doesn't mean I *belong* to him."

I stared at my reflection in the mirror a moment longer and even though I was quick to dismiss Millie's concerns, they held weight. Frank, an American businessman I'd met last month at a bistro in Primrose Hill, was a far cry from my usual suitors—earnest, hair a bit askew. After he bumped into me at the counter and spilled my tea, he insisted on buying me lunch, and for some reason I accepted. I don't remember ever laughing as much as I did that day. His suit was in need of tailoring, which I noted immediately, but there was something genuine about him. When he asked me to have dinner the following weekend, and the one after that, I said yes. I enjoyed his company, even if my heart didn't beat faster in his presence.

Millie approved of him immediately. "Finally, you're going out with a decent gentleman," she whispered to me as I slid into his car before our second dinner date. She may have been right about that, but my mind wasn't yet made up on the romantic front. Frank Baker remained a wild card.

A loud thud sounded from the flat above. Shouting, then the cry of a child. Millie and I exchanged knowing looks. In this rough neighborhood of London, mothers were overworked and exhausted, and fathers often turned to the bottle.

Millie had her stories, and I had mine.

My own father turned into a monster when he drank. One evening, when I was no more than ten, he struck my mother's face hard enough to draw blood. That night, she perched on the side of my bed, holding a cloth to her wound as she said a prayer and kissed me good night. "Dear Father in heaven, give my sweet Eloise the most beautiful dreams, and may she grow up to marry a prince and live happily ever after."

"When your mind's made up, El, there's no stopping you," Millie said, brushing a piece of lint off my dress. "But promise me that you'll be careful tonight, and don't blow off Frank. He—"

"He loves me, *right,*" I said sarcastically. And so what if he did? I didn't owe him—or any man—my love in return. I would hold on to that tightly until I *knew.* And, of course, I would know! Just like in all of my favorite novels, there would be a feeling, an instinct. I'd know it immediately. Until then, what was the harm in having a little fun? I valued Millie's concerns, but what did she know about matters of love?

I took a final deep breath, then squared my shoulders. "My darling friend," I continued, beaming as I heard the honk of a horn on the street below. "Don't worry about me!" I kissed her cheek, brushing off the doubt in her eyes. "I love you. Everything will be fine!"

My heart began to race when I glanced out the window to see Roger's car waiting on the street below. A shiny black Rolls-Royce. Last week, when he'd inquired about my address for the car to pick me up, I'd made up a story about the "charity work" I was doing in the East End. "Aren't you a saint," he'd said dryly. "I wouldn't be caught dead in that neighborhood." I smiled knowingly, ignoring the feeling of regret that tugged at my heart. I told myself it was only a white lie—a compulsory invention to gain access to a better life, the one I'd always dreamed of. And just like a character in a book, I could play a part, too.

As Millie stood in the doorway, arms folded across her chest, I peered out the window and waved to the chauffeur standing beside the fancy car. "I'll be right down," I said, the words flowing out of my mouth as if I'd uttered them a thousand times before.

THE DRIVER, A GRAY-HAIRED, serious-looking man, gave me a curious look, then helped me inside the car, which was . . . empty.

I shook my head, confused. "Where's—"

"Mr. Williams has . . . been detained," he replied curtly. "He's given me instructions to take you to the club. He will meet you there."

I nodded. After all, Roger was a busy, important man. If I were to be a part of his world, I'd have to understand that. And, oh, *the club*. I loved the way it sounded, as if I were already a member. Even more, I loved that this private car was whisking me out of my miserable neighborhood—to a better one.

As I gazed out the window, East London looked markedly different from the plush backseat of a chauffeured car. The awning of Lainey's Bakery, where I sometimes stopped for tea, appeared weathered and tattered. A homeless man was slumped over a bottle of booze, and two teenage boys were engaged in a raucous fistfight.

Just over the bridge, the lights of London sparkled like diamonds in the night. I glanced back a final time, feeling an indescribable ache as I watched my neighborhood fade in the distance. All my life, I'd dreamed of getting out of there, and now this car was taking me away.

IN FRONT OF THE Royal Automobile Club, a doorman helped me out of the car. "Good evening, miss," he said, balancing an umbrella over my head as if it was his sworn duty not to let a single raindrop fall on my dress. I had the feeling he might even throw his jacket down to prevent a lady from stepping a dainty foot into a puddle. "Will you be dining with us tonight?" he asked cheerfully, immediately revealing his East End accent—the one I'd worked so hard to disguise.

Before I could answer, the chauffeur motioned from the front seat, and I couldn't help but wonder how often they'd had this very same exchange about Roger's *other* dates. "She's meeting Mr. Williams."

The doorman nodded smartly, his smile momentarily dimming. "Yes . . . of course, sir."

Inside, an attendant took my coat as I gazed up at an exquisite chandelier strung together with hundreds of crystals. I marveled at how such a massive piece remained fixed in place, but I forced myself to look away for fear of appearing like a wide-eyed adolescent gawking at all the finery.

"This way, miss," a man in a white tuxedo said, leading me up the staircase to a dining room fitted with gilded fixtures, ornate furniture, and delicately painted frescoes on the ceiling. The diners were exquisitely dressed—the men in their coats and tails, the women with their long, white gloves and furs draped over their shoulders. I'd left my only pair of gloves, stained, at home, and how I wished I'd had a fur to hide my bare hands when I felt the room's collective gaze. I wondered if they knew it was my first time here. I wondered if they could smell it.

"Your table," my escort said, pulling out my chair. It was not just any table, but clearly the very *best* one, perched on an elevated landing that overlooked the entire dining room. And there I sat, alone.

"May I bring you anything before Mr. Williams arrives?" he asked. "Tea, champagne?"

"Yes," I said, eyeing a chic-looking woman in the distance holding a glass of bubbly. "Champagne, please."

I never drank, but I was in desperate need of something— anything—to quell my nerves. And like magic, a few moments later, a white-gloved waiter deposited a flute of effervescent elixir in front of me, before vanishing, it seemed, into thin air.

Painfully aware of the other diners' eyes on me, I fiddled with my pressed, gold-stitched napkin and studied the polished cutlery, fretting about which fork corresponds with which course. Was it left to right, or right to left? My heart beat faster when a nearby table erupted in laughter. One of the women, in a dress far nicer than mine, and wearing gloves, naturally, cast a sympathetic smile in my direction. *Does she feel sorry for me? Do they all feel sorry for me?*

When I finished my champagne—in three sips—the waiter poured me another, and then another. I eyed the enormous gold clock on the far wall as it ticked off twenty minutes, then forty-five. With every passing minute, my heart sunk lower. *Where's Roger?* I began to lose track of time, and the number of glasses of champagne I'd consumed.

When a jazz band began to play, I felt light and floaty. I made up stories in my mind about why Roger had been detained. His mother had been ill, and he went to check in on her. An important business meeting had run late. He'd stopped to help a stranded motorist. One day, I told myself, years from now, we'd lovingly recount the unfortunate story of our first date to family and friends, laughing about Roger's late entrance and how he'd spent the next month making it up to me.

But while my fictional version was charming, and forgivable, his real-life entrance a few moments later was not. The dining room erupted in a chorus of whispers as he walked in—with a woman on each of his arms.

"I'm sorry," Roger said, disregarding me as he turned to a nearby waiter. He was close enough that I could smell a waft of booze on his breath. "Why is my table occupied?"

I cleared my throat nervously. It was all so inconceivable. Had he not asked me on a date tonight? "Roger, it's Eloise," I said meekly, hoping this was all a simple mistake he could easily explain away. "Don't you remember?"

"Who is *she?*" the woman on his left asked, sizing me up with a long look of displeasure.

"Your cousin from the country?" the other woman said with a giggle.

My cheeks burned. "I'm Eloise Wilkins," I said. "His *date*." My embarrassment soon morphed into rage. "Roger," I continued, sitting up in my chair. "Surely you remember sending your car to get me earlier?"

Both women looked up at him with pouty eyes as he expertly extricated himself from the two sets of arms entangled in his. "Why yes, of course," he began. "Eloise. You'll have to forgive me. I ran into some . . . old friends."

I stood, reaching for my purse as my napkin fell to the floor. Millie had been right, if only I'd listened to her. "Don't let me keep you," I said. "You three clearly have a lot of catching up to do."

Everyone was watching. And why wouldn't they be? A circus show with three women in the ring was better than anything on the telly—and it was all happening right before their eyes. This was Roger Williams at his finest. A jewel for the gossip columns. There was even a poor girl from East London! (Cue the laughter.)

That's when it hit me—a sudden and intense urge to *run*. My eyes darted right, then left, until I located the nearest exit. I couldn't bear the idea of making the walk of shame through the enormous dining room to the main entrance, so I chose the nearby French doors that appeared to lead to an adjoining balcony. With any luck, there'd be a staircase that led *out of here*.

I darted ahead, making a beeline for the exit, but then the heel of my left shoe caught on the carpet and I lunged forward, colliding with a waiter carrying a tray of plated entrées under polished silver domes, sending steaks and their garnishes flying through the air.

With a broccoli floret in my hair and béarnaise sauce smeared on my sleeve, I burst through the double doors and onto the balcony. To my great disappointment, there was no staircase, no exit. I was, in a word, trapped.

The cold air settled on my skin and I shivered, wrapping my arms around myself as I leaned against the railing and gazed up at the night sky. I was a fool for thinking I could fit into this world.

I sank to the ground, tucking my dress over my knees for warmth—unladylike, but I didn't care. But a few minutes later, when the balcony door creaked open, I stood up quickly. *I had company.* Cigar smoke clouded his face and top hat.

"My dear, what on earth are you doing out here? It's cold enough to snow!" he exclaimed, the smoke parting to reveal his tall frame and distinguished face. He was older than me, perhaps by ten years or more. "Where's your coat? You'll freeze to death."

I nodded as I steadied myself. "I . . . just needed some fresh air."

The man eyed me curiously, his mouth forming a slow smile. "Or could it be that you're hiding from someone?"

I sighed, eyeing the béarnaise sauce on my sleeve. "Obviously you saw what . . . happened in there." I turned away from his gaze. "Please, sir, just leave me alone. I've already endured enough for one night."

"I don't have any idea what you're talking about, but if you don't come inside soon, you'll die of exposure." I shivered, which is when he suddenly slipped off his tuxedo jacket, draping the exquisitely cut garment over my shoulders, its fabric still warm from his body.

"Thank you," I said, straightening the collar so it covered my neck as it released the aroma of pine and some other familiar yet elusive note.

"So, you really didn't see the . . . debacle in there?"

As he shook his head, there was something disarming about his expression, so I began to relay the series of unfortunate events that led me to the balcony. I pointed to my sleeve with a sigh. "And for the record, this is béarnaise sauce."

He laughed, but not in a mocking way. "Well, you wear it quite well."

"It's all the fashion these days," I replied, bolstered by his kind eyes.

He cocked his head to the right curiously, as if trying to place me. "I don't think I've seen you here before. I can assure you that if I had, I would not have forgotten you." His voice was deep, and he spoke with a disarming confidence. "Wait," he said, as if struck by a memory. "Were you here last weekend for that ridiculous soirée that the old viscount hosted?"

"Yes," I said quickly. The lie flew out of my mouth with such speed, I was stunned by my own brazenness.

"That speech he gave!" he said. "Could it have been any longer?"

"Or *any duller*?" I added, trudging deeper into my deception.

He smiled. "Why have we never met? You're . . . different than most of the women here."

My cheeks flushed.

"I meant that as a compliment, Miss . . ."

"Wilkins. Eloise Wilkins."

"Miss Eloise Wilkins," he said, taking another puff from his neglected cigar as he glanced through the window to the dining room. "The women in there are—well, how do I put this delicately?" He paused, then nodded. "They're rather . . . forgettable—all the same, down to their gloved hands."

At first, I assumed his words were a veiled commentary on my own gloveless hands, but the thought vanished when he reached for my hand and kissed my bare wrist ceremoniously. "How do you do?"

"Well, I'll admit, I've had better evenings. . . ." I withdrew my hand and tucked my arms back inside the warmth of his jacket.

"Tell me," he continued, smiling, "has your family been members here for a very long time?"

I nodded tentatively. "My father was a . . . very private man. He . . . kept his name and his business interests far from the public eye. After he passed . . . it all went into a . . . trust for my mother and me."

"Sounds like a smart chap," he said, "and an admirable one."

If only he knew how far from the truth that was.

"Well, look at us, standing in the cold outside the stuffiest club in London where it apparently has taken us a lifetime to meet."

"And what brings you here this evening?" I asked, attempting to deflect his attention from my past.

He grinned at me curiously, rubbing his chiseled jawline. "Your turn to sum me up, I see?

"Maybe," I said, playing along.

He shrugged. "The answer is simple. My father made a name for himself in the car business, and membership was a necessity." He sighs. "And to your question, why am I here? Simple: I'm a good son."

"What do you mean, exactly?"

"Well, Miss Wilkins, you see, when you're the eldest son, and you've just turned thirty-four, as I have, without a marriage prospect on the horizon, your family, naturally, becomes obsessed with finding you a wife." He took a puff of his cigar. "Tonight is my sister's latest, and worst, attempt."

I smiled. "So, I gather a proposal isn't imminent, then?"

He walked closer to the window, motioning for me to follow. "See the woman at the table in the middle of the room—pink dress, feathers in her hat?"

I eyed the stylish woman with high cheekbones and glowing skin. "She's beautiful," I said, turning back to him. "So, what's the problem?"

He glanced back at the dining room. "I'd rather be alone forever than have a dull companion."

I watched regret, or perhaps nostalgia, sweep across his face. "For all of its stuffiness, this really is a grand old place, isn't it?" He leaned in closer. "Just last month, Princess Margaret sat at that table." He pointed through the windows. "Perhaps you saw her."

I nodded, grateful he didn't press me for details.

"I was eight years old when we moved to London from the countryside," he continued. "Our family was invited to a welcome lunch. Mother insisted I wear a suit, and I pitched a fit of royal proportions. As for tonight, my sister found out that I'd be meeting a group of American businessmen here, and she hoodwinked me into staying for dinner." He smiled, and I immediately thought of Frank. "American men, they all sound like—"

"Cowboys," we said in unison, then laughed.

Our eyes locked for a long moment, and I stifled another

shiver as he extinguished the remains of his smoldering cigar on the balcony's ledge.

"Care for a cigarette?" he asked, pulling a pack from his shirt pocket.

I'd never taken up the habit, but for some reason, I nodded anyway and a moment later we were both sending out puffs of smoke and watching them collide in the cold air.

"So, what about your date?" I asked, feeling a tinge of empathy for the woman inside.

"She'll be fine," he said with a shrug. "She's been making eyes at a gentleman at the bar all evening."

"Well, where do we go from here?" I asked, looking up at him. "It seems there's no exit from this balcony. I guess we're—"

"Stuck," we both said. I quickly deflected my eyes from his gaze.

"I'm afraid so." He pressed his cigarette between his lips again. "January's brutal."

I nodded. "My mum used to get the winter blues, but every day she'd watch for the promise of spring, when the first green shoots burst through the ground. She'd always say, 'Hold on, the daffodils are coming.'" I smiled. "I loved hearing that. I still do." I had no idea why I was telling him this, but the words felt natural, as if I were talking to an old friend.

"That's beautiful," he said.

"Yes, everything about her was beautiful." My eyes met his again. "She passed a few years ago."

"I'm sorry," he replied, touching my shoulder lightly. The warmth of his hand spread down my arm.

"She's at peace now." I paused, searching the snow-dusted

garden below, unsuccessfully, for any sign of daffodils. "January isn't just the coldest month of the year. It comes with a . . . feeling—like the whole world is in a slump because Christmas won't come again for—"

We spoke at the same time: "Another year."

His eyes searched mine with a contemplative smile. "You know, if we keep finishing each other's sentences like this, I may have to . . ." His voice trailed off as he turned his attention to the night sky. "Look at the stars up there, fighting to be seen through all these city lights. It's like a battle between two opposing forces: eternity versus modernity."

I smiled up at him curiously. "Eternity for the win?"

"Eternity always wins," he continued. "And that is the greatest comfort, isn't it?"

I wasn't entirely sure of his meaning, but I liked it, nonetheless.

He gestured toward the city while I listened, enraptured. "Man built all that, invented it, created it. And as remarkable as it all is, the stars were here first." He took a deep breath. "They're wiser."

I stared at him with amazement, as if he were voicing ideas that had always stirred inside of me though I'd never put a name to them.

"Nature, God, whatever you want to call it—it's bigger than us. Bigger and more powerful than anything we can do or dream."

I nodded. "So you're saying what will be, will be, not because we willed it, but because it was a part of a plan?"

"Yes, or a really good novel."

I felt his gaze on my cheek, but I continued to stare at the night sky. "Then you believe this was all meant to happen? Everything in there, and us meeting like this tonight?"

He nodded. "I do."

"And then what?"

"Well," he replied, eyes fixed on mine. "Who knows. Maybe I'll end up becoming your best friend or even . . . the love of your life."

"Well, aren't you presumptuous," I said teasingly, while simultaneously noting the undeniable shift in my heart.

"Who knows," he continued. "Maybe we'll never see each other again, and this will be a pleasant memory."

"Béarnaise sauce on my sleeve and all," I added with a laugh.

He grinned at me. "I like a woman who can laugh at herself. It's a rare trait."

"Oh, is it?"

He nodded. "We English are much too serious. That's why I decided to get a tattoo. But if you ever meet my mother, you must deny everything."

"A tattoo?"

He paused and unbuttoned the top two buttons of his dress shirt until his strong shoulder emerged, revealing what looked like the outline of a . . . violin.

I shook my head, astonished. "Do you play?"

"Never even picked up a bow, but I always wanted to have music in my ear." He smiled. "Get it?"

I nodded. *I'll be the music in your ear.* Even though he couldn't hear my thoughts, my cheeks burned hot despite the cold air on my skin. When the wind picked up, I cinched his jacket around me a bit tighter.

He noticed, taking my discomfort as a cue to change the subject.

"So, how long do you plan to hide out here, exactly? A week? A month?"

I grinned. "As long as it takes."

"If you're waiting for the room to clear out, it won't. I'm sure you're aware that many of them have suites here and stay up late drinking and playing cards." He registered my disappointment, then eyed the garden beneath the balcony. "Fortunately, I have a plan. I don't know why I didn't think of it sooner."

My eyes widened as he led me to the left side of the railing.

"See that," he exclaimed. "A ladder. The building is being reroofed this week. All you have to do is climb down, then you can sneak out the back. Voilà."

"Voilà, except that I'm terrified of ladders. What if I slip?"

"My dear, what's worse? This ladder or the wolves in there?"

I weighed my options, then nodded decisively. "I'll take the ladder."

"Good," he said with a smile. "I'll go first so I can help steady you from the ground."

I watched as he hoisted his strong frame over the railing and climbed down, his muscles flexing under his freshly pressed shirt. "Now," he called up to me from below. "Your turn."

My heart beat fast as I followed his lead and hurled my body over the railing, just as he had done, but the result was entirely less coordinated. I set my foot on the first step, ankle wobbling a bit, but managed to steady myself.

"You're doing great," he said. "Take it slow and steady."

I was suddenly struck by the absurdity of the moment—my grand escape from a disastrous date—and I began to laugh, which was when I lost my footing and slipped.

"I've got you," he said as I tumbled back and downward, landing in his arms.

Out of breath and embarrassed, I looked up at his kind face and into his warm, wise brown eyes. "I . . . told you I don't do well with ladders."

He glanced up at the balcony. "But look, you might have just learned to fly."

I grinned as he set me down on my feet.

"A successful escape."

"Yes," I said, smoothing my dress. "Thank you . . ." I paused. "You know, I don't think I got your name."

He held out his hand. "Edward," he said. "Edward Sinclair."

"Well," I replied, slipping off his jacket. "It was . . . lovely to meet you, Mr. Sinclair. I'd . . . better be going."

He shook his head, slipping the jacket back onto my shoulders. "We were in the middle of a conversation," he said. "One that I hope will continue. If you leave now, how will I find you again?"

I listened, hardly believing what I was hearing.

"Meet me here, tomorrow night. Seven o'clock. I know a quiet spot where the drinks are divine and no one unsavory will be lurking about."

"All right," I said with a smile.

Together we walked to a back door on the lower level and followed the dimly lit staircase to a hallway that deposited us near the foyer.

"Well," he said. "I should probably be going."

I smiled. "I'll see myself home."

"Until tomorrow," he said, bowing deeply.

I watched him walk ahead, disappearing to the right, presumably to the dining room to conclude his awkward date—like a gentleman. I couldn't help but wish I were the woman he was returning to.

"Will you be needing a car, ma'am?" the doorman asked, tipping his cap at me, at the base of the staircase.

I looked out the window and up at the clear night sky. I wasn't ready to go home, not yet. I wanted to linger in this dreamy part of London a little longer. "No, thanks," I said, shifting my gaze to the sidewalk, when suddenly someone collided into me from behind.

"Please forgive me," a man said in a familiar American accent.

I smiled to myself—*the cowboy*.

He placed his large hand on my forearm, his tan face awash with concern, and sudden recognition. "Eloise?"

"Frank?"

"What are you doing here?"

"I . . . was meeting a . . . friend," I stammered, choosing my words carefully and rubbing my side, where his tall frame had plowed into mine. I forced a smile. "What are *you* doing here?"

"I had a meeting with some investors, you know, the ones I told you about the other night," he continued, eyeing my face for any sign of recollection, though the memory of our conversation was hazy.

"Oh yes," I said quickly. "How did it go?"

"Great. I think we sealed the deal. It's a huge contract."

Though he'd explained his work to me on more than one occasion, I still understood very little, just that he was employed by a large manufacturing corporation in Los Angeles. His ill-fitting suits detracted from the truth: Frank was wealthy, very wealthy. Maybe even a millionaire. "That's . . . wonderful," I said, distractedly glancing back to the entrance to the club, Edward's face still fresh in my eyes.

"Whose jacket is this?" For a moment, his boyish smile shifted, and I detected a tinge of jealousy, distrust, even.

"I . . . left my coat on the tube," I said, covering my tracks. "A kind older gentleman lent me his."

Frank's smile returned in an instant, as he slipped out of his own rumpled suit jacket. "Please wear mine. I insist."

I shook my head. "No, no, it's okay. It's cold. You should keep yours on. I'll . . . return it to the club . . . on my way to work tomorrow."

He nodded, momentarily satisfied as a dark car pulled up and idled beside us. "That's mine," he said. "May I . . . take you out?"

"Thank you, but . . . I really should—"

"Just one drink," he said, grinning, the glow of the streetlights reflecting his pale green eyes and revealing his receding hairline. True, he didn't have Roger Williams's swagger or Edward Sinclair's refined way, but Frank did look at me—the real me—as if I were a goddess and that felt . . . nice.

"I know a little place not too far from here. They serve a mean cocktail, and if we're lucky"—he paused to glance at his gold wristwatch—"we might be able to catch the comedy act. What do you say?"

I wanted to say no. I *should have* said no, but Frank's eager smile was infectious, and without my permission, the corners of my mouth crept upward.

"So, it's a yes, then?"

I glanced over my shoulder self-consciously, as if the very walls of the Royal Automobile Club might be keeping tabs on me.

"Okay," I finally said. "But just *one* drink."

"Just one drink," he said, helping me into the car. I held my dress in place as I inched across the seat before he slid in beside me.

"You'd love California," Frank began as the driver started the engine and signaled into traffic.

Maybe I would, I thought, half-listening as he rambled on about his beloved state—the palm trees, the ocean, the sun. All I knew of America was from television, but it all sounded lovely, in a far-off, postcard sort of way.

When we stepped out of the car a few minutes later, saxophone music billowed out of a nearby club. Inside, we found a table, and Frank ordered a round of martinis. I busied myself with the olives in my glass as he recounted his successful business deal and explained that he'd be returning to California soon. "Maybe you could . . . come with me," he said nervously. "To visit."

"Oh, Frank," I replied. "That's very . . . kind of you, but we've only just met."

"I know," he conceded. "But I can't imagine leaving London . . . without you."

I realized, for the first time, that Millie was right about more than one thing tonight. "You're . . . very sweet," I continued, backpedaling. "And I have enjoyed your company, to be sure. But you must understand that this is . . . a little too soon for me to be making such big decisions."

"Of course," he said quickly, reaching for my hand. "I don't mean to rush you, it's just that I . . . I've never met a woman like you, and it pains me to think that we'll be separated by an ocean."

Unable to find my words, I took a long sip of my martini.

"But listen, there is another option," he continued. "I can stay for a few more months. My boss would be fine with it. There's certainly more work to be done here. We could . . . take our time, get to know each other more. How would you like that?"

"I, well . . ." I gulped, unsure of what to say. "Frank, please don't change your plans on account of me."

"But don't you want me to stay?"

"Well, sure, yes, I want you to stay. I mean, I'm not saying that I want you to leave." My words sounded disjointed and ambiguous. But to Frank, they were a siren's song.

"Then it's settled," he replied confidently. "I'll extend my stay, and we'll spend more time together."

I wasn't sure what I'd just agreed to, but suddenly Frank ordered another martini for each of us, and we were toasting our future.

"Let me take you to dinner tomorrow night," he said, beaming. "Anywhere you like. The Ritz, even."

I couldn't help but feel flattered by Frank's interest in me. He looked at me like I was a titled heiress, not a Harrods salesclerk who grew up in the rowdy East End. But tomorrow night was off the table. I was having dinner with Edward.

I shook my head, but he persisted.

"Then how about the following night?"

"All right," I said, unable to think of an excuse.

I ordered two takeout coffees before we left, and when we walked out of the club to the street, Frank eyed me curiously. "I don't drink coffee."

"I know," I said. "This is for the—"

"Let me take you home," he said, leaning in closer to me as his driver pulled up to the curb.

I shook my head. "Thank you, but I'm fine. I'll just . . . hail a cab."

"Please, it's no trouble."

When I declined a second time, he handed me a few pounds to cover the cab fare. I felt equal parts guilty and relieved. Payday wasn't until next Friday, and my pocketbook was growing thin.

"I can't wait to see you again," Frank said, helping me into the cab. I waved to him as we drove off.

"Here," I said, handing a coffee to the driver.

"For me, really?"

I nodded.

He took a sip. "Miss, how did you know that I needed this? I'm working the late shift for the first time since my wife had a baby."

"Congratulations," I said.

"She's a perfect little girl," he said. "I just hope she'll have the life, the opportunities, of a lady such as yourself." He paused. "I want to give her the world, and yet, I'm a humble cabbie."

I smiled. "I can tell how much you love her, and that in itself is enough."

"Aye, I do," he said. "Listen to me gabbing on and on. Where to, miss?"

I recited my address and watched as his eyes widened in the rearview mirror.

"You see," I began. "A woman can't help where she comes from, but she is in full possession of who she becomes. Be sure to tell that to your little girl."

The driver smiled. "I will, miss."

I sipped my coffee and pondered my peculiar evening that began in disgrace and ended in the most unexpected of ways. I smiled, thinking of Frank and his earnest affection, and Edward . . . mysterious Edward.

In front of my block of flats, I paid the fare and thanked the driver, who tipped his coffee cup to me with gratitude as I stepped out onto the street. The temperature had dropped below freezing again, and I was grateful for Edward's coat as I rounded the building and followed the path to the staircase that led up to our second-floor flat. I passed our little garden plot in the alley, where Millie grew herbs and tomatoes in terra-cotta pots during the summer months. Come spring, this miserable canvas of dirty snow and mounds of hardened earth would erupt into a symphony of life—mint, oregano, thyme, and flowers, too. Oh, how I missed the flowers.

As I reached for the key in my pocketbook, my eye caught a patch of lithe green daffodil shoots, bursting up through the sleepy soil with the determination of a thousand springs. Before long, they'd bloom triumphantly.

"*Hold on,*" I heard my mother's voice, whispering. "*The daffodils are coming.*"

Valentina

"YOU HAD QUITE A NAP," THE DRIVER SAYS, SMILING through the rearview mirror. "But look, you woke up just in time." He points ahead. "See it?"

I rub my eyes and peer out the window. Late-morning sunbeams pierce through dark clouds and shine onto a burst of color.

"A Sunday in Primrose Hill," the driver says. "There's nothing finer."

I look out at tall, narrow townhouses and storefronts standing together in a row of pastel Easter-egg hues.

"See the high windows?" the driver says. "That's Regency architecture, right there, though they were likely built in the Victorian era. These are miniature versions of the grand villas surrounding Regent's Park."

High windows, I think. *That means high ceilings.* A lofty room filled with sunshine sounds like just the balm my soul needs right now.

"And you'd never expect it so close to central London," the driver says, "but Primrose Hill is at elevation. Sixty-three meters above sea level."

I smile, grateful to have such a knowledgeable cabbie.

A few minutes later, he stops the car in front of a pale pink three-story building. A sign that reads THE BOOK GARDEN hangs above the street-level door. When a pigeon stops to peck its edge then flies off, I follow its ascent, noticing that the curtains are closed on the upper two floors. Shriveled flowers droop from the window boxes. It hardly looks real, any of it. The scene is something that might have been torn from the pages of a beloved old novel, as opposed to the reality of my own disconnected life.

"This must be it," I say, paying the fare as the driver unloads my suitcases onto the curb.

"Welcome home," he says.

"But I never said this was—"

"I think you're going to like it here," he interjects. "You'll see."

I turn around to take in this unfamiliar place, the setting of my mother's life, the one she led without me. A long-haired cat is sunning himself in the window seat. Through the glass, I can almost hear his purr, as if to beckon me inside. But when I reach for the door handle, it's locked. My inner clock is off, and I'd momentarily forgotten that it's quite early on Sunday morning—much too early for a neighborhood bookstore to be open for business.

I walk around the building to a narrow pathway that leads to another entrance and fumble inside my bag until I find the building keys Bevins and Associates mailed me. As I unlock the door, the hinges screech open as if stretching after a long nap. I wrangle my suitcases inside the little foyer. No sense lugging them upstairs when I've already booked a room at a nearby hotel.

The stairs creak and groan beneath my feet as I make my

way up to the first-floor flat, where I knock on the door to introduce myself to the tenant.

A woman about my age, in her mid-to-late thirties, answers with a cellphone pressed to her right ear; her striking dark curls frame her face like a halo as she fans away a plume of smoke in the air, then motions me inside. "For Christ's sake," she whispers. "Give me a hand, will you?"

She hands me two oven mitts and points to the oven, where I quickly pull out a pan and its unrecognizable culinary remains. Clearly, Sunday brunch has been ruined.

I cough, fanning a billow of smoke from my face as she mouths the words, "Thank you." I look around the eclectic flat with bohemian furniture and colorful pillows scattered about. Vibrant framed artwork lines the walls and dozens of houseplants burst out of their pots as if they were in a rain forest and not a borough of London. By the window a yellow parakeet chirps from a bamboo cage.

"Yes, sir, absolutely, sir," she says into the phone. "Right. I'll make it happen. Consider it done. Goodbye, sir." She ends the call and groans, tossing her phone onto the sofa as if it were a guilty accomplice in the unfortunate chain of events leading up to this moment.

"That was my boss," she says. "He's a certified asshole." She throws her arms into the air. "He'll be here in an hour," she cries. "Now what am I going to do about brunch?"

"Your boss?"

"No," she says, looking at me as if I were born yesterday. *"Jeremy."*

I nod, feeling another wave of jet lag settle in. "Jeremy."

"My *date!*"

"Right," I say.

"He thinks he's getting a five-star brunch," she says. *"He thinks I'm a gourmet chef!"*

I glance at the charred pan. "And I take it that you might have fibbed a little?"

She sighs. "I mean, who would publish a frittata recipe on a food blog and not say *how long* to bake it?"

I try very hard not to laugh. *Rest in peace, dear frittata.*

"Well, so much for that. Now what am I going to do?"

I like her immediately. "There's always . . . takeout?"

She shakes her head. "No, no, no! This is the third date. You never do takeout on a third date!"

"Oh," I say, noticing even more potted plants in the kitchen, all of them a healthy green. "You can't cook, but you're definitely a plant whisperer."

"It does seem that way," she says with a sigh.

I extend my hand. "I'm Valentina Baker."

The corners of her mouth turn upward as she connects the dots. *"Oh!* You're *Eloise's daughter!"*

"Yes, well . . . yes."

"Why didn't you say so in the first place?"

"I . . . was getting to that. And you were on the phone."

"Right," she says, brushing a stray curl from her forehead. "I'm so sorry about your mum. I really loved her." She studies me for a long moment. "You know, I don't see the resemblance. You must take after your dad?"

"Yeah, I . . . guess so."

"I do, too," she says wistfully. "My dad has his good traits, though." She places her right hand on her hip. "I mean, I did inherit his legs."

I smile to myself as she kicks one in the air, Rockettes style.

"Wait," she says, cocking her head to the right. "I see it now. Your *eyes*—there's something about the shape of them. They're just like—"

"Listen," I say, clearing my throat. "I don't want to keep you. I was just . . . hoping we could speak about . . . your flat."

She nods. "Oh, don't worry. I'm not the type to bail on rent or anything. Besides, I really love it here. I mean, it's not Buckingham Palace, and it's drafty as hell in the winter, but you know what?" She pauses to glance around her eclectic space. "I've never lived anywhere I loved this much. In fact, I may never leave!"

"Okay, right," I say, a bit crestfallen. If I had any hope of selling the building, it would be harder than I anticipated.

"I'm Liza," she continues, extending her hand. "Hey, if you're free tomorrow afternoon, I'd be happy to show you around the neighborhood."

"Oh, wow," I say. "Thank you. That would be . . . nice."

Her momentary calm disappears in a flash. "Good Lord, I have to get ready. What the hell am I going to wear?" She runs to the bedroom and returns holding two dresses on hangers—one pink with bright orange flowers, the other solid blue with a tie waist. "What do you think? Is the pink one too much?"

I shake my head, smiling. "No, definitely go with the pink. It's very you."

"Really?" she says, immediately slipping out of her sweats and T-shirt and stepping into the dress. When she struggles with the zipper, I offer to help.

She shrugs, eyeing herself in the full-length mirror against the wall. "My New Year's resolution was to lose ten pounds, but I gained twelve."

I grin. "You look great, I promise."

"Okay," she says with a sigh. "Now if I can just order take-away in time to dish it up and hide the evidence!"

"Good luck," I say, letting myself out.

As I close the door behind me, I hear a dish break, and Liza screaming, "Bloody hell!"

I smile to myself as I walk up to the second floor, where my mother apparently lived for so many years—without me. I pause when I reach the door—her door—remembering how I once longed for this very moment—to be near to her again.

Why did she leave? Why didn't she ever write or respond to my letters? I press the key into the lock, feeling a pang of emotion. All these years later, the pain of my childhood feels just as raw, just as real.

As a girl, I fantasized about running away to London, where I'd show up on her doorstep and everything would be okay. But as time passed, that familiar yearning morphed into something else—resentment, anger, and by the time I left for college, I was no longer interested in reuniting with the woman who'd abandoned me. She became dead to me.

And now she was.

I take a deep breath as I open the door, feeling like a fire-fighter arriving at a house after it has already burned to the ground. Too little, too late.

I step over the threshold. The air is stagnant and foreign. But as I part the drapes and open one of the old windows, I can't help but notice a faint but familiar scent. It takes a few moments to register, but then it hits me. *Her perfume. Her rose perfume.* A part of me quivers, deep down, as memories begin to bubble up. At once, I am a child in that big, sunny bathroom in Santa Monica. She's in her long, pink satin robe, seated in front of the mirror.

"Mummy, can I wear your lipstick?"

"When you're older, sweet one."

I watch her meticulously layer on three coats of mascara before she offers me a spritz of perfume on the inside of my wrist. I hold it up to my nose and breathe in the thick, velvety scent of roses.

Down on the street, a red double-decker tourist bus lumbers by, pulling me back to the present. I run my hand along the soft, pink velvet sofa. A low table is lined with framed photos of unfamiliar people and places.

Suddenly, my heart seizes. Apart from the rest, in a gilded frame, stands a photo of . . . me.

It was Christmas morning, the year I got the dollhouse, when I was seven, maybe eight. My mother spent all morning setting up the rooms with me. The memory is distant, and yet, I can still smell the spicy musk of the cedar walls and the new plastic of my dolls' shiny hair. I can feel the chalkiness of the little porcelain bathtub, with its four claw feet. I'd placed the miniature sofa on the second floor, but Mummy moved it to the first, near a side window "with a better view of the garden."

She was right. She was always right.

I sigh, directing my attention to the small but well-appointed kitchen. A cream-colored vintage refrigerator is fastened with a brass latch and the old gas stove looks as if it should be named Marceline, or maybe Babette.

I admire the Russel Wright seafoam-blue ceramic dinnerware on the open, wooden shelves. It was one of the original colors when the line began in 1939. She knew from her time working at Harrods, and she told me all about it. I imagine her selecting one of the handled lug bowls and eating her favorite foods, poached eggs, fresh berries drizzled with heavy cream.

I walk to the window seat, where a light gray cashmere throw rests on the cushion. I press the soft fabric to my face, breathing in the scent of my childhood, of her. It's as if she were here only a moment ago, instead of gone forever.

I feel a wave of fatigue as I peer into the bedroom, but then I see her jewelry case resting on the dresser. I open it, and memories come flooding back. My mother was a collector of beautiful objects, including costume jewelry. Her favorite brand was Trifari, especially the 1930s Art Deco geometric designs.

"Designer Alfred Philippe learned his craft at Cartier and Van Cleef & Arpels," she said. "Look for the invisible stone settings. He perfected that technique."

She taught me to recognize marks of authenticity. There was the *KTF* stamp, or the Crown Trifari—a crown symbol over the *T*. She'd take me with her to estate sales, and if I spotted one of the markers, I was to hand her the piece quietly, so that no one would know that we'd found a treasure.

"Trifari made pieces for First Ladies and Hollywood stars," she said, "but tastes change."

Hers never did. I pick up an antique Deco bracelet of glass and silver. It's as elegant as she was.

I look over at the bed. The smooth coverlet and fluffy pillows look fresh and inviting. Though my eyelids are heavy, I can't help but notice the book on her bedside table. Its emerald cloth spine is impeccably preserved, as are its gilded-edged pages. I know it in an instant, of course. I'd long hoped to encounter a first edition of Virginia Woolf's *A Room of*

One's Own, but had never had the opportunity. And now it's in my very hands. I carefully fan the novel's pages, wondering if this had been my mother's final read before she passed, or if it had merely been a symbol to her, a mantra for the life she chose. Before I set the book down, a small envelope slips out from the pages' clutches. I reach to pick it up, and see my name written in my mother's elegant handwriting. Valentina, with the *a* at the end curling up into a perfect crescendo. As hard as I tried, I could never sign my name that way. My hands tremble as I tear the edge and pry out the card inside.

My dearest Valentina,

Welcome to London. I have so many surprises for you. Just wait. But first, I'm sending you on a little scavenger hunt. Remember how much you loved those? I did, too, and I learned from the very best.

I have so much to say, so much to show you. But first, I implore you to delve deep—to our last springs, summers, and autumns, but above all, our last winter.

Come find me. I'll be waiting.

With love,
Mummy

I blink back tears, my heart racing with emotion—and questions. *She knew.* She knew I'd come here, to this *room of her own.* She knew I'd be drawn like a magnet to this book. I swallow hard, setting the card on the table, staring at it as if it had its very own pulse.

What on earth does she mean about delving deep—to

past summers, springs, and winters? I'm too tired to make sense of any of it, too tired to think. I should gather my suitcases and find my way to the hotel, but I'm feeling increasingly weary, and I decide to lie down instead, just until this wave of jet lag passes. I pull back the covers, and slide into bed, my body pressed into the very place my mother had rested night after night—all the nights without me. I close my eyes. *Just for a few minutes,* I tell myself. *Only a few minutes.*

I'm dreaming.

I've just come home from school; Daddy is in his chair in the living room puffing a cigar and reading the newspaper, dated June 12, 1990. It's both weird that he's home so early, and even weirder that he's smoking in the house. My mother would be furious. I look around the room, then out at the pool, but she's not there, or anywhere. She's probably just upstairs, I tell myself—though I know instinctively that she's not. I can *feel* it. The house has that vacant, lonely way about it, like when she's out to lunch or gone for the evening. But where is she? She promised we'd go to the mall to get my ears pierced when I got home from school.

I run to the kitchen, where I find Bonnie hunched over at the breakfast table, crying. Bonnie is our housekeeper. I've never seen her cry, and it frightens me. She looks up at me, startled. Neither of us knows what to say.

"What's wrong?" I finally ask. "What happened? Where's Mummy?" From the time I began to speak, that's what I called her, and what she called her own mother. It was the British way.

Bonnie opens her mouth, but no words come out. Then she lowers her head again, continuing to weep.

"Daddy!" I run back to the living room. "Why is Bonnie crying? Where's Mummy? What's going on?"

He continues to puff his cigar, rocking back and forth methodically, even though the chair doesn't rock.

"Daddy?" I start to cry, stomping my foot to get his attention. "Are you listening to me?"

"Valentina, that's enough," he says suddenly. The edges of his mouth quiver. "You're too old to carry on like that. It's time to get control of yourself now." He extinguishes his cigar in an ashtray, turning to me again. "She's gone. Your mother is gone. And she's not coming back."

I swallow hard, taking in what he's just said. It can't be true. They've only had a fight. He's upset. He's saying things he doesn't mean. Mummy's probably out shopping. She'll be home soon, and it'll all be fine. Everything will be fine.

Daddy walks over to me and sets his hands on my shoulders. "I'm sorry, my sweet Valentine," he says. "I'm so sorry. There's no way for me to make this any easier for you." He sighs, reaching for his car keys. "I have to go out for a bit, but Bonnie is here. She'll be moving into the spare bedroom."

I run to the kitchen again, throwing myself into Bonnie's arms. I look up into her red, tear-filled eyes, eyes I've known my whole life, searching them for proof that what Daddy said isn't true.

But it is, and it shakes me to my very core. It's all true, terrifyingly true. Mummy is *gone*.

Bonnie reaches out to embrace me, but I bolt ahead, racing to Mummy's bedroom, where I lock the door behind me and run to her closet—empty. When I open the cabinets in the bathroom, they're completely bare. The drawers are, too, except for one. I reach inside and find a bottle of her trademark rose-scented perfume, which I spritz on my wrist, then breathe in. Did she merely forget to pack it, or, rather, *leave it for me?*

I want her to make me a bath and tell me, as she always does, "Cheer up, Charlie."

"Mummy," I whisper, my voice shaking. "Where are you?"

Eloise

LONDON

January 12, 1968

———

AS I DRESSED, I PICTURED EDWARD'S TALL, HANDSOME form. I remembered his curious mind—and the warmth of his touch.

He's a romantic, I thought. *Sophisticated.*

The midnight-blue lace dress would be perfect. I'd only worn it once before—older, something I'd found on a sale rack at Harrods, but still stylish enough for dinner at the Royal Automobile Club.

In the hall closet, I smiled to myself when I noticed Edward's jacket hanging on the rack, where I'd placed it last night. My own remained at the club, where I'd forgotten to retrieve it. I borrowed Millie's coat instead, deciding to leave Edward's on its hanger as ransom—an excuse to see him again after tonight.

Before departing, I poked my head into Millie's bedroom, where I found her hunched over a thick law textbook. I said I was going out but didn't dare say where. What would she think of me, returning to the Royal Automobile Club after last night's disaster? I'd only told her about Roger and the women on his arms—oh, and the béarnaise sauce—but not a word about Edward.

Until I could believe he might be real, that *we* might be real, he'd be my secret.

IT WAS ALREADY DARK when I arrived at the club. I checked my coat with a woman in a pressed white shirt and black vest. She was about my age and looked a lot like the girls I went to school with, and perhaps she was, because she knew I didn't belong here. I could see it in her eyes.

At the reception counter, I gave Edward's name.

The greeter smiled warmly. "Miss Wilkins, hello. Mr. Sinclair is expecting you." He handed me an envelope sealed with red wax imprinted with his initials: *ES.* When I touched my fingertips to the fine linen paper, my heart tremored a little, but even more so when I pulled out the note, and hand-drawn map inside.

Eloise,

Step into the garden. You'll find the way. X marks the spot. I'll be waiting for you.

> xx, *Edward*

I could barely contain my excitement as I made my way up the stairs, passing a group of well-dressed couples heading into dinner, both of the women wearing this season's Chanel. Covertly eyeing my map, I proceeded down a dim corridor, then to the staircase that led to the garden, where I'd fallen into Edward's arms just last night. I smiled at the memory. But where was he? I studied the map again, continuing along the garden path, past the evergreen topiaries that lined the club's limestone façade. Just ahead, warm light glowed from a window, beside a large wooden door. I knew I'd found the right place.

I turned the knob and stepped into a room lit only by the flames of a roaring fire. A fully stocked bar ran along one wall. Floor-to-ceiling bookshelves covered all the others.

"How delightful," I whispered to myself, stepping onto the wheeled ladder connected to a steel track that encircled the room's perimeter.

"I thought you were frightened of ladders," I heard a voice say.

Edward stepped into the firelight. He was dressed as finely as he had been the night before, in a sharply tailored dark suit.

I didn't greet him. I didn't need to. It felt completely natural to answer as if we were picking up our conversation exactly where we'd left off the night before.

"Oh, but not library ladders," I said, pushing my foot against the floor to make the wheels move.

He grins. "You're a reader, I take it?"

"A ravenous one," I replied.

"I had a suspicion. I am too."

I gazed up at the high ceiling. "Thank you for the map," I said. "It's the only chance I would've ever found my way here. How did you . . . ?"

"Know about this place?" He shrugged. "A boy gets bored when his parents drag him to the club for dinner every Thursday night. I'd sneak down here and pass the time reading."

He spoke so vividly of the memory that I could picture

young Edward right here in this room, running his fingers across the books the way I was doing now.

He leaped behind the bar and took a visual inventory. "It's how I became interested in literature. By accident, really." He set a bottle of gin on the counter. "How about you?"

I continued tracing the spines of the books long enough to make a decision. I decided to take him into confidence about my and Millie's dream, the one we'd had since we were thirteen. "My best friend and I have always had a dream to open a bookstore of our own."

Edward listened intently as I told him about the literary haven I'd created in my mind. "Maybe someday," I said wistfully.

He smiled as he placed ice in a cocktail shaker, mixed me a martini, and handed me a glass, a layer of ice on the rim. "Not maybe," he said. "If it's your heart's calling, it will be."

Somehow, his confidence was enough to boost my own. If Edward believed my dream would come true, I could, too.

"Cheers," he continued, clinking his glass against mine. "To dreams and books—and new friendships."

I took a sip—the gin was strong and botanical, like the first whiff of a fresh-cut Christmas tree.

"Your dress, it's . . ." he said, pausing for a long moment. "Eloise, I'm afraid you've rendered me speechless. What I'm attempting to say is that you look *stunning*. Blue is definitely your color."

"Thank you," I said a bit nervously as we settled into two overstuffed chairs upholstered in emerald-green velvet.

"Tell me, what books will you sell at this bookstore of yours?" he asked.

"Some will be new," I said. "But most will be well-loved

favorites. Did you know that most books—particularly, the very best ones—are likely to pass to an average of seven readers in their life, sometimes more?"

"Fascinating," he replied, absently touching the edge of his shoulder where he'd showed me his tattoo the night before.

"You'll always hear music," I said, smiling, "and I'll always hear stories."

"Or maybe we'll each hear both," he said, his eyes fixed on mine.

I looked away—I had to. It felt as if his gaze was piercing into the very depths of my soul. Maybe he felt it, too—that moment of *knowing*. In any case, he navigated our conversation to new and divergent places—his favorite curry houses in London, the trip to Africa as a child where he learned to whistle, a friend from college who died last year under mysterious circumstances. With each revelation, I felt as if I knew him more deeply, but even more peculiar was the lingering feeling that I'd *always* known him.

He told me about his two younger sisters, both married with young children, and that after getting a joint graduate degree in business and law, he was employed by one of London's biggest real estate development firms, but that he mostly found the work ("making rich people richer") entirely unfulfilling.

"Then what sort of work might you find fulfilling?" I asked him.

He was quick to reply. "The simple life," he explained. "It might sound crazy, but I've always craved a Beatrix Potter sort of existence—away from the city. You know, an old cottage in the country, with a big garden and ample front porch where you can sit at night and have conversations with the stars."

I smiled. "Charming. But what would you *do*?"

"Why, tend to my tomatoes, of course," he said with a grin. "Naturally."

"Let's dream together for a moment, shall we?" he said, leaning in closer as my heart beat faster.

Yes, let's dream together.

"Picture the two of us," he began, "in our front porch rocking chairs. I've just shooed away a flock of menacing rabbits, while narrowly managing to secure a bushel of tomatoes for canning, and while you recount your day at the bookstore."

I smiled at his fictional vision, wanting to linger in it longer. "I'd tell you about the village children who insisted upon waking up the store's cat, who much prefers sunning himself in the window to childish attention, and the window boxes that I just replenished with geraniums, oh, and also Mrs. Maltby, the preacher's wife, who comes in often under the guise of looking for books for her grandchildren, but instead, secretly lingers in the romance section."

Edward grinned at me for a long moment until my cheeks flushed. "The farmer and the bookseller. We're quite the pair, aren't we?"

I merely nodded, though I wanted to reply with an emphatic *yes*. Yes, to this beautiful little storybook life that we could make our own. Did Edward want that, too, or were his words merely flirtatious ramblings that, perhaps, he'd uttered to his date last night, even? I decided to play coy. What did I know of love or the intentions of men?

We talked for hours, and another round of drinks. Time passed, but not really. I merely beamed from one topic to the next. At some point, Edward glanced at his watch and suggested we head upstairs for dinner. "I secured a coveted corner table," he said. "You don't have to worry."

I wanted to tell him that on his arm, I would never worry. I could go anywhere, be anything. It's true, I hadn't been honest with him about my formative years, but I'd tell him in time, and somehow, I knew he'd not only forgive me, but accept me.

But then, our private moment was invaded by a pounding on the door. "Mr. Sinclair!" A uniformed man burst through the doorway, wiping a bead of sweat from his brow. "We've been looking for you everywhere." He paused to catch his breath. "There's a telephone call for you on the third floor. It's urgent. It's about your—"

"Yes, yes, of course," Edward said quickly, his brow furrowed.

I felt like a fictional character, torn from the pages of a suspenseful chapter before reaching its conclusion. Would my ending be happy or tragic? I didn't know.

"Miss Wilkins," Edward said, his spark turned somber. "It has been an absolute pleasure, but I'm afraid I . . . must go. I'd hate to leave you waiting as I'm not sure how long this matter might take. Why don't we plan on seeing each other again, and hopefully soon?" He paused, smiling for a brief moment. "Maybe we—"

"Mr. Sinclair," the man in the doorway interrupted. "Your caller is waiting."

"Yes," Edward said, turning to the door. "Please forgive me, *Eloise*." My heart seized when he said my name. "I'll call you."

I hadn't given him my telephone number, and I dreaded

the thought of him looking me up only to learn that I was not the daughter of a wealthy socialite as I professed to be, but rather, a struggling salesclerk, residing in a ramshackle apartment in the East End.

"Yes," I muttered. "Goodbye, Edward." But he was already gone.

I sighed, taking a final glance at the quaint little library bar before I walked back to the reception desk to retrieve my coat and the one I'd borrowed from Millie. The night, it seemed, was over before it began.

"Excuse me," I said to the woman behind the counter— the one whom I'd encountered earlier. "I need to leave . . . a message for a member . . . Mr. Edward Sinclair."

She raised an eyebrow, then pointed to a nearby tray with a box of note cards and envelopes. I grabbed a pen and wrote:

Edward,

Please don't think me a thief, but I still have your jacket from last night. I've decided to hold it hostage until I see you again. At the risk of sounding too forward, meet me at Jack's Bistro in Mayfair at 7:00 tomorrow night? X marks the spot.

I'll be waiting,
Eloise XX

"Will you please make sure Mr. Sinclair gets this?"
The woman nodded without emotion, silently slipping the

note into an unmarked drawer before answering an incoming telephone call.

I walked outside to the street and looked up at the night sky, where the city lights of London forged their familiar battle with the stars sparkling overhead. I smiled to myself, knowing which side would win, and always would.

Valentina

The Next Day

——

BIRDS CHIRP FROM THE OLD WILLOW TREE OUTSIDE the window as I sit up in bed, gasping when I glance at the time on my phone: 6:23 A.M. I rub my eyes, squinting as a bright stream of sunlight hits me. I've somehow managed to sleep through an entire day—and night.

I stand and yawn, taking a moment to find my bearings. It's Sunday, no, Monday. I'm in my mother's flat. What's-her-name from downstairs—Liza, yes, Liza—had offered to show me around town today (or was that yesterday?). I wonder how her brunch date turned out as I take the stairs to the bottom floor and retrieve the cosmetic case from one of my suitcases. It's going to take some deep moisturizing to revive my tired complexion.

Downstairs in the foyer, I find the things I need, then zip up my suitcases when Liza calls down. "Valentina, is that you?"

"Yes," I say as she appears on the stairs.

"Let me help you with these bags," she says, reaching for one of the suitcases.

"Oh, I'm not staying," I say quickly.

She looks confused. "Not staying?"

"I . . . I mean, I'm checking in to a hotel. I only needed to grab my toiletries and a change of clothes."

"That's silly," Liza says, her hand firmly planted on the handle of the suitcase. "You have your mum's flat right upstairs. Why in the world would you go to a hotel?"

"I . . . I don't know. I guess I . . ."

"Americans are funny," she says, regarding me curiously. "You guess you want to get price-gouged for a tiny room and a bathroom the size of a broom closet when you can have an entire flat for free?" She pauses. "I mean, you own the place, don't you?"

She's right, I guess. But staying in my mother's flat was never part of the plan. It felt too, well, intimate. But when Liza begins lugging one of my suitcases up the stairs, I'm too tired to protest. Besides, she makes a good point.

"How'd your date go?" I ask, following behind. "With, Jeremy, right?

"Terrible," she says, her mouth tensing. "First, he was late—forty minutes late—and then, after I'd gone to the trouble of making him eggs royale, he *claimed* to be allergic to crumpets. I ask you, have you ever heard of someone who has an allergy to *crumpets*?" She shakes her head. "He just sat there. Didn't even take a single bite. And then he had the *audacity* to try to make out with me." She shrugs. "I'm sorry, but if a man isn't going to eat my food, then it's off. Anyway, I told him to leave."

"So, no more Jeremy, then?"

"Jeremy is kaput," she replies.

I laugh, liking her more by the minute.

"It's probably my fault," she continues with a sigh. "I have a thing for bad boys, always have. They're fun, even though it never ends well. After all these years, you'd think I would have learned my lesson, but no." She shrugs. "How about you? Married?" She glances at my bare ring finger.

"No," I say. "I mean, I was, but I actually just . . . well, I'm going through a divorce."

"Oh dear," she says with a gasp. "You poor thing. First your mum, and then . . ." She covers her mouth, deeply concerned. "Have you ever heard that thing about bad luck coming in threes?"

"Yes," I say. "I guess I'm the lucky one who has one more terrible thing to look forward to."

"Maybe it'll be something small, like a . . ." she says, pausing for a few beats, "like a crack in your cellphone screen or something."

I reach into my pocket and pull out my phone, revealing the screen's myriad jagged lines.

"Oh," she says, discouraged as we reach the second floor. "Well, whatever it is, I'm sure it'll be okay. Just, maybe look both ways when crossing the street for the time being."

I nod, unzipping one of the suitcases to look for something to wear.

"Did he break your heart?" She pauses. "Your husband?"

"*Ex*-husband," I say, correcting her. "And, yes, I guess you could say he did." From my suitcase, I pull out a pair of black leggings and a gray, oversized sweater. "Anyway, he left me."

Liza frowns. "I'm so sorry, I—"

"Listen, about that tour you promised me," I say, quickly steering the conversation away from Nick. "Still up for it? Also, I could seriously use some coffee right now."

"Sure," Liza says. "We'll stop at Café Flora first. I saw Jude Law in there the other day."

"The actor?"

"Yes, otherwise known as Mr. Hot Stuff. He lives in the neighborhood. A lot of celebrity types do. He made eye contact with me when I was in line. I'm pretty sure he wants me. But, sadly, he's really not my type." She brushes a smudge off her glittery Doc Martens. "Though, if you're interested, rumor has it that he's presently single."

I smile, stepping into the bedroom to change clothes. "Thanks, but dating is the last thing on my mind right now," I say through the doorway.

"That's what you say now, but just you wait." She smiles as we make our way out to the street. "I know you're probably anxious to see the store, but take it from me, Millie and mornings don't mix well."

"Millie?" The name sounds familiar, but I can't quite place it.

"You don't know her?"

I shake my head.

"She was your mum's best friend," Liza says, looking at me curiously. "She's been running the store since ... Eloise got sick. I mean, they started it together, but Millie was already working as a barrister. She turned things over to Eloise years ago, from what I understand."

I nod.

"Anyway, you said you needed coffee. Let's start there first. We can circle back to the bookstore after I show you around the neighborhood. Millie will be in better spirits by then."

Café Flora is only a few blocks down the street, with its blue awning and bistro tables in front. As we walk inside, a blast of warm, delicious-smelling air hits my face. I order a cinnamon roll and double espressos for both of us while Liza flirts with the heavily inked guy behind the counter, admiring the snake tattoo twisting around his forearm.

"So, what do you do—for work?" I ask as we sit down at a table by the window, remembering yesterday's tense phone call with her boss.

"I'm a personal assistant," she says moodily, "to a dictator."

I raise an eyebrow. "As in the Kim Jong-un variety?"

"Might as well be," she says, taking a sip of her espresso. "He invented some obscure tech widget ten years ago that made him richer than God himself, and he pays me a pittance to run his life—you know, get him theater tickets, pick up his dry cleaning, trim the toenails of his boyfriend's poodle, act as his personal punching bag when he's had a bad day."

"I'm sorry," I say.

She waves at a woman she recognizes, then turns back to me. "Anyway, the job was only supposed to be temporary. Seven years later, and look who's still fetching laundry.

"How about you? What do you do in . . . ?"

"Seattle," I add. "I was a librarian and bookstagrammer, and now I guess I'm a . . . bookseller."

Liza beams. "With your experience, you'll be a godsend to the store! That is, if you can talk Millie into making some changes."

"Tell me more about her."

"Millie," Liza says, pausing, "is wonderful, but she can be a tough mountain to climb. She loves those she loves, and the rest? Well, Lord help them."

I swallow hard. "You said she and my mother were good

friends? It's been so long, but I think I remember hearing about her when I was little."

Liza nods. "Childhood friends, yes. She and Millie opened the bookstore together, though she had her own law career to manage. But when your mum got sick, she'd recently retired, and was able to step in to help."

"That's kind of her," I say. "But now that I'm here, I can . . . manage things."

"Easier said than done," Liza says. "It might take a certified Parliament inquisition to get her to leave." She pauses, looking at me quizzically. "The Book Garden is all she has left of your mum, and she's fiercely protective of it."

I can't tell if Liza is merely filling me in, or giving me a thinly veiled warning.

"It's a shame you never came to visit," she says. "Before she . . . passed."

"Listen," I say a bit defensively. "My relationship with my mother was . . . complicated. If it's all right with you, I'd rather not go into it."

"Right," she says quickly. "I get it. I'm sorry. I didn't mean to bring up a sore subject."

I nod, forcing a smile. "Shall we continue the tour?"

Her expression softens again as we walk outside and continue on. "Besides Café Flora, there's a lovely little Italian spot that's open for lunch and dinner—Bottega—and Chutney's, the curry house around the corner. They actually have the most amazing salads." She pats her rear end. "Which I should eat more of if I ever want to rid myself of these twelve pounds." I grin as we pass a food market, which she tells me is the closest grocer to the flat. "Get your bread at Le Petit Bakery, that is, if you Americans eat that sort of thing anymore. Didn't the entire country declare war on carbs, or something?"

"Not me," I say. "I surrendered."

"It's the practical English blood in you," she says, pointing out the local hardware store, followed by a hair salon and an ice cream shop, where she tells me I must sample their caramel custard flavor.

When a couple approaches us on the sidewalk ahead, she waves. He wears a black leather jacket and combat boots; she has short bleached blond hair and a nose ring. "This is Valentina," she tells them, introducing George and his girlfriend, Lilly. George is in a band, I learn, which will be playing tomorrow night at a nearby pub. Liza assures them she'll be there.

"You should come with me!" she says after they've gone.

"I don't know," I say. "I'm not sure it'll be quite . . . my scene."

"Nonsense. You're coming. Besides, I need some backup. Lilly stole him from me, and she knows it. I want to make her squirm a little."

I listen to the details of that story as we continue down a street lined with pastel-colored townhouses, boutiques, galleries, and cafés. "And don't forget Regent's Park is just up the way," she adds. "It's a great place to have a picnic—or fly a kite, not that I'm trying to get all Mary Poppins on you."

"Noted," I say, smiling, as I reach for my phone ringing in the bottom of my bag. I dig it out, see that it's James Whitaker from Bevins and Associates, and send it to voicemail. I'm in no mood to deal with the dreary details of my mother's estate, at least not now. I'd much rather go to the park, and maybe fly a kite.

WE ARRIVE AT THE bookstore shortly after noon. It's cozy and effortlessly charming, like a page torn from a beloved anthology of nursery rhymes, with no shortage of floor pillows, ottomans, tufted chairs, and sofas where you can sit down with a book and stay awhile. I imagine my mother walking into this empty space for the first time, a blank canvas for her imagination, before settling on the blue velvet drapes (she'd always loved sapphires), the crystal chandelier dangling above the entryway, the vibrant Turkish rugs that soften the wide-plank wood floors, even the bells on the handle of the door—it is all *her*.

"Isn't it like the bookstore of your dreams?" Liza says, watching me take it all in.

"Yes," I say quietly, feeling increasingly overwhelmed.

"Wait here," she says. "I'll go find Millie. She's probably in the back room."

I notice that the floor-to-ceiling walnut shelves are fitted with steel tracks for wheeling ladders. I step onto one and ride it along the expanse of a nearby wall.

I'm still sliding when Liza returns with an older woman who's quite tall, well above six feet. Her graying hair is twisted into a bun atop her head, adding even more height to her imposing stature.

"Millie," Liza says, clearing her throat, "I'd like to introduce Valentina, Eloise's daughter. She recently arrived."

Millie fumbles with the dark-rimmed glasses dangling from the chain around her neck as if she can't believe what she's seeing. But she gets the confirmation she needs when she finally slips them on, giving me a long look.

I step off the ladder a bit nervously. "It's so nice to finally meet you," I say, extending my hand.

But she doesn't say a word. I can't tell if she's disappointed, shocked, surprised, or maybe some combination of all three. Millie and my mother were the same age, Liza shared, so she's about seventy, and yet, her face is quite youthful, even if she is frowning at me.

She walks to the checkout counter and reaches for a box. When she sets it on the floor, her elbow knocks over a jar of pens. "Drat," she says with an annoyed sigh before bending down to sort out the mess. She moves in big, exaggerated gestures, the bookseller's equivalent to Julia Child bounding around her kitchen with a thud here, a clang there.

"Look who came over to say hi," Liza says, breaking the awkward silence.

The cat I'd seen in the window yesterday purrs softly at my feet, then rubs himself against the side of my leg.

"What's his name?" I ask, kneeling to pet him.

"Percival," Liza says. "But everyone calls him Percy." She smiles. "He definitely likes you."

"Percival is a very agreeable cat," Millie says, looking at me. "He likes *everyone*."

"Don't take it personally," Liza whispers to me as Millie dips behind the counter. "She just needs some time to get used to you being here."

I nod. "Should we go?"

"No," she whispers. "She'll come around."

I follow her to the counter, where Millie is looking through a precariously high stack of books that's leaning ever so slightly to the right. "Aha," she says, pointing to a blue hardback in the center. Somehow, she inches it out while keeping the pile intact. It's like the Olympic Games version of Jenga. "Finally," she says, smiling to herself. "I've been looking for this copy of *Rebecca* all day. Evelyn Johnson will be happy."

The bells on the door jingle as a few customers amble inside. A middle-aged man makes a beeline to Millie and asks for help finding one of the Harry Potter books for his son. She nods and leads him to a shelf across the room.

"Boys and Harry Potter," she says, returning with a shrug. "I do wish that children would expand their appetite for literature beyond Hogwarts." She lets out an elongated sigh. "At least it wasn't another request for one of those dreadful Diary of a Wimpy Kid books."

My librarian instincts kick in. "Well, the fact that his son is reading at all says something," I say.

Millie looks up from the counter, seemingly startled by my comment.

"What I mean is"—I pause, searching for the right words—"reading only leads to more reading. As a child, I read the gamut—from the classics to the Baby-Sitters Club. If a kid can find a book that she gets excited about, it will only make her more open to experience that feeling again—in all sorts of other stories."

Millie lowers her glasses on the rim of her nose, looking down at me curiously. "A fine theory," she quips, turning again to the stack of books, "which is just what it sounds like—conjecture."

"With respect," I say. "Many literacy studies over the years have proven this 'theory' to be true, and I've seen it firsthand in my work." I smile. "I'm a librarian."

"Well then," she says, a little startled. "As the expert that you are, I expect you'll be displeased with the way I've been running this bookstore since your mother's health declined. Go ahead and tell me what you have in mind. Don't beat around the bush. What is it? A new computer system?" She presses the back of her hand to her forehead dramatically. "Online ordering? Some social media nonsense? *Booksta-gramming*? Lord help us all."

Clearly, she's never seen my account, @booksbyval. I grin, deciding to take the humorous approach. "Ever considered book deliveries by drone?"

I only meant to lighten the mood, but Liza looks as if she's either about ready to burst into a fit of laughter—or break out in hives.

"I'm only kidding," I say. "About the drones." Millie doesn't laugh.

Sensing the rising tension, Liza steps in. "Now, Millie. You have nothing to worry about. Valentina is here to *help*. She's Eloise's daughter, after all."

"Well, your mother was the bravest woman I've ever known," Millie says wistfully. "She risked everything to follow her heart."

My cheeks burn as I take in Millie's words; before I can stop myself, I open my mouth to speak. "That's quite an interesting definition of 'brave.'"

Millie's eyes are laser-focused on mine. "Valentina," she begins. "I don't know what you were told, or what you *believe*, but I want you to understand that . . . what happened . . . you must know that it wasn't at all what she wanted or planned for."

Her words have only stoked the fire simmering within me. "Then what *was* the plan?" I say, the tone of my voice sharp and piercing but, above all, sad. "Tell me, please. Because all these years I've been dying to know why a mother—my mother—could leave so suddenly, never to be heard from again. You'd think she might have, oh, maybe found a spare moment to call me on my birthday, or, I don't know, perhaps visit one Christmas? *Anything!*" So many long-held emotions push their way to the surface, and I know it's too late to suppress them. "Why? Why didn't she just come home? To me. To her family."

Millie shakes her head gravely, the wrinkles around her eyes accentuated by the overhead lighting. "You really don't understand, do you? You really have no idea."

Before I can make sense of what she means, much less venture a response, the bells on the door jingle and a frazzled-looking woman in her mid-fifties bursts inside, setting a large box on the counter. "You do take *used* books, don't you?"

"Indeed," Millie says, peering into the box. "What do we have here?"

"Oh, I don't know—they're my husband's. I cleaned out his office while he's away on a business trip. Stacks of books everywhere. Really, I'm saving him from himself. He's one step away from becoming a . . ." She pauses. "You know, one of those crazy people on the telly who live in heaps of junk."

"A hoarder?" Liza suggests.

"Yes!" the woman says, loosening the scarf around her neck. "That's exactly it. He has far too many books."

Millie and I exchange knowing looks and, for the first time, find ourselves in a moment of . . . agreement. However repugnant this woman finds her husband's "bad habit," we both know the same truth: There's *nothing* wrong with having too many books.

Still, Millie plays along. "So, he has a bit of a problem, does he?"

The woman nods, exasperated. "The other day, he actually suggested that we turn the guest bedroom into a library. A library!"

"Wow," Millie says, shaking her head in false sympathy. "That's ... terrible." She reaches into the box and selects a leather-bound book from the top and opens the cover. "An American first edition of *Wuthering Heights* by Emily Brontë." She shows us the title page. "Authorship is misattributed to Emily's sister Charlotte. The credit line, 'By the author of *Jane Eyre.*' That's a famous literary mistake." She selects another and raises an eyebrow. "These are quite special. Are you sure your husband doesn't mind you selling them?"

She shrugs. "He's a professor of English literature. If we kept every book that comes into our home, I wouldn't be able to walk into my kitchen."

"Well, then, if you're certain you want to part with them—"

"I'm certain," the woman says immediately. "And I have at least ten more boxes at home."

"All right, then," Millie continues. "It might take me a bit of time to sort through."

The woman turns to the street, where an SUV with hazard lights flashing is parked out front. "Listen, I'm in a bit of a hurry. Maybe just give me twenty quid and we'll call it good?"

Millie's eyes widen. "I have to be honest with you," she says. "These books are worth more than twenty quid."

"All right, I'll take fifty, then. I was supposed to pick my daughter up from a playdate a half hour ago, and at this rate, I'll be late to my Pilates class—*again*."

"Right," Millie says, entering the transaction into the register before handing the woman a sales slip to sign. "Fifty it is, then."

"Well," Millie says after the woman darts out. "At the end of the day, not everyone is a book lover."

"Her loss, your gain," Liza says with a shrug.

Together, we have a look. Millie reaches for one of the books and examines its copyright page as I pick up one of C. S. Lewis's early works. "Can you even imagine your spouse doing something like this behind your back?" I say, my mind suddenly turning to Nick. "Well, I guess I actually can."

Liza nods. "I'd like to be a fly on the wall in that house when her husband comes home and all hell breaks loose. Can't you just see the headline? Breaking news: Man kills wife for selling his rare book collection."

Mille is in her own world, sorting through the treasures in the box. "One of my favorite literary thrillers," she says, holding up a novel I don't recognize. Liza and I follow her as she walks to a nearby bookcase where she tucks it onto a middle shelf. I eye the array of books carefully, and though the obvious disorganization pains my librarian's soul, I know better than to say anything just yet. Instead, I direct my attention to the books and one, in particular, catches my eye.

"Wait," I say, extracting a familiar spine from the shelf. I know it in an instant, of course. *The Last Winter*. Not long after my mother left, a librarian suggested I read it. I always wondered if she had a sixth sense. How else would she have thought to pluck that dusty old copy from the highest shelf? A forgotten novel for a forgotten girl. Well, I read it and read it and read it. It became the soundtrack to my heavy heart, the drumbeat to my beleaguered journey through my teen years and beyond. I must have read it a dozen times—at least.

Millie peers over my shoulder. "One of your favorites?"

"Yes," I say without explanation as I run my hand along the edge of its cover. In the frenzy of the divorce and subsequent house sale, I'd misplaced my beloved copy, and the loss had been a blow.

But Millie merely shrugs. "Go ahead, take it."

"Thank you," I say, searching her eyes once again for even the faintest sign of a peace offering.

"Let's not be silly," Millie says with an air of indifference. "It's your store now, isn't it?"

She's right, of course. What's-his-name from Bevins and Associates explained that Millie had signed over her ownership stake years prior. She'd merely uttered a statement of fact, and yet her words make the hair on the back of my neck stand on end.

"DON'T LET HER GET to you," Liza says later as we walk up the next block to the market. "Under that tough exterior, Millie's really just an old softie. You'll see."

I nod reluctantly, thanking her for today's tour of Primrose Hill before we part ways. Alone with my thoughts, I grab a cart and roam the aisles of the market aimlessly. I used to love grocery shopping, especially with Nick. When we were first married, I looked forward to our after-work trips to Whole Foods. He'd push the cart, and I'd load it up. We were a team, until we weren't.

I sigh, eyeing the foreign-looking labels on the cans and boxes. The yogurt looks different. Everything is different. After thirty minutes, I place my selections on the checkout counter belt—a loaf of bread, a box of granola, a carton of what I think is cream, strawberries, three bottles of cheap French burgundy, a wedge of brie, and one lonely apple. It's a random, mismatched, and empty combination, which feels like a metaphor for my life right now. I am all of these things.

I carry the bag back to the flat, then slump into the sofa, where I finally listen to the voicemail from Bevins and Associates left earlier today. The news isn't good. A hefty inheritance tax (far more than I can afford to pay) is due within six months, or rather, just before Christmas.

Merry Christmas.

Sure, I now own the bookstore and the building, but am cash poor from the divorce proceedings, I don't have the liquid assets to cover the taxes. If only Nick hadn't been hellbent on selling the house so quickly—and at a loss. But Bevins and Associates has a quick fix. *"Fortunately for you, we've been approached by a potential buyer—a developer who is willing to pay a fair price."*

I set the phone down and lean my head against the back of the sofa, trying to face the situation logically: I can't afford the inheritance tax and there isn't any other reasonable solution on the table. I could sell, as the attorneys suggest, and be left with, at best, a small profit, or possibly just break even. It would be a sad end to the store's twenty-year run, but why should I be concerned with a venture my mother took up after leaving her child—me?

I think about the whimsical little shop with Percy purring in the window, even with Millie in all of her cantankerousness behind the counter—despite my best efforts, I am already falling for it, all of it.

"It's your store now," Millie had said so shrewdly. How right she was—down to the very last bill to be paid.

I look around my mother's flat at the relics of her life, from the pillows on the sofa to her favorite books lined up on the shelf. Every little thing she carted home from a flea market or used-book store is infused with her essence, and as I take it all in, I'm unable to stop the emotions rising up inside of me. Like a surge of water pummeling a weary dam, I'm on the verge of caving, and I do. The tears start slowly, then build to a crescendo.

It feels good to cry, but I also feel a need to connect. Since the divorce, I'd posted less and less on Instagram. I'd blamed it on the house sale, the details of preparing for London. But it's time I called my own bluff. I've been hiding—from my followers, the world, everyone. Though I'd rarely talk about my personal life in my posts, there was an authenticity to my happiness. Because I was. At least, I thought I was. Would the forty thousand followers who looked forward to my book tips and literary musings feel the same if they knew the truth? That those I've loved left me, and I am on the brink of financial ruin?

All the books in the world can't change that.

I exhale deeply and reach for my phone, where I quickly scroll through my feed and read the new comments and direct messages. "Everything okay?" one commenter writes. "You didn't post your usual #FridayReads. Going on vacay next week and need to know what to pack in my bag!"

It's insignificant, really, that Leah from New Jersey misses my posts, or Valerie from Oklahoma, or Mei from Toronto. And yet, it feels good to be missed. It's enough to give me the energy to share something a little more personal.

I snap a photo of *The Last Winter*, adjust the brightness a bit and select my favorite filter, then start typing:

Life is like a novel, and to be honest, friends, mine feels like a really tragic one these days. Don't worry, I'm alright, but the plot has thrown a few twists and turns. Thank God for books, right? If you need me, I'll be over here, diving back into an old favorite (always balm for the soul). For me, that's *The Last Winter*, a novel I've read so many times, but need more than ever right now, because books are old friends. Published in 1934 by little-known author Elle Graves, the story takes place in 1920s New York and details the forbidden love affair between Charles, a married physician and aspiring politician, and nineteen-year-old French émigré Cezanne, a ballet dancer who has spent her life fiercely trying to hide her mixed-race identity from the world—even from Charles.

The tragic and emotional story of The Last Winter *has stuck with me, though the book has been out of print for years (fear not, your intrepid local librarian will surely be able to track you down a copy!). My own copy went missing after my recent divorce and move* . . . I pause, contemplating whether to delete that last line, but it feels good to be open, so I leave it on the screen . . . *and my extensive online search for a replacement has been distressingly unsuccessful. Until today!*

I HEAD TO BED with *The Last Winter*, eager to reunite with the familiar story, but especially its characters—old friends. I check my account one last time. Likes and emojis are pouring in. Readers are sharing their own stories of long-lost books, of their own heartbreak. I join the conversation, adding a new post.

What makes books more special than, say, a movie, is that you can hold them. When your own world feels bleak, a book is a portal to anywhere. You can hide within the pages, linger there for comfort or protection. The best part? Whether you're seven or sixty-seven, a favorite book is like an old friend, waiting for you with open arms, and right now, that's what *The Last Winter* is for me.

I sink my head into the pillows, eager to return to Cezanne's world. But when I turn to the first page, I'm a little surprised to find a handwritten note near the top corner. *This has to be one of the most beautiful opening paragraphs in all of literature.*

I reread the words curiously, my arms erupting in goosebumps. I wholeheartedly agree, though I know plenty of other librarians who would eschew any such writing in the margins, and yet, I'll admit, I've been prone to scribbling in pages myself (in the pages of my own books, that is). But, literary controversy aside, this commenter makes an excellent point. The book hadn't been a bestseller or won a Pulitzer, but it's filled with lines that literally sing. I read the words again, letting them marinate in my mind.

"Cezanne wills her lithe body into position as she gazes out at the theatre. In the turbulent sea of human faces, she sees only one: his."

I press my hand to my chest, the line hitting my heart, just as it had the very first time I'd read it. On the next page, I find another note beside an underlined passage. *The description of her lacing her ballet slippers is reminiscent of being tied with chains, bound by society's rules.*

How funny. I'd thought the very same thing.

And then, on page eight, another note appears: *Snow is a metaphor for change, the forces of life that we can't control. Note how Cezanne behaves in the 1922 blizzard.*

Yes, exactly! I nod, recalling how she'd been selected to dance the lead in the most prestigious ballet of the year. It would be the greatest opportunity of her career and provide the funds to support her impoverished family. But then a blizzard strikes the city on the same night a new choreographer dismisses Cezanne from the production. Even though her world looks bleak, she runs out to the street and dances— immersing herself in the falling snow, finding beauty amid the darkness.

Who is this mystery commentator, I wonder. Unable to contain my curiosity, I flip to the inside cover for any clue, which is where I find the name Daniel Davenport, written beside a telephone number.

A quick fan of the pages and it's evident that the book is filled with more intriguing notes sprinkled throughout the prose. I want to study them all. Another one, on page sixty-eight, reads, *If only it were possible to visit Cezanne's New York.* The wish feels eerily familiar, as if plucked from the depths of my brain.

Overcome with curiosity, I delve further, which is when a small envelope slips out into my lap. Just like the one I'd found yesterday, from my mother, this one also has my name on it. I wasn't able to make any sense of the clue in her last note (*I implore you to delve deep—to our last springs, summers, and autumns, but above all, our last winter*) but now I understand.

My darling Val,

You've discovered one of my favorites, just as I knew you would. As I've always said, books have a way of finding you when you need them most, and now you've found The Last Winter. *I promised that I had some surprises in store for you, and this book is only the beginning. Keep it close to your heart, and please, my darling girl, keep that beautiful heart open and curious as you read between the lines. There's so much more in store, my little birdie.*

　　Your next stop is culinary, and close—where flowers grow. Find me on the fourth shelf. I'll be waiting.

Love,

Mummy

My eyes sting with tears as I read the note over and over again, trying to make sense of it. *Keep your heart open?* What on earth could she mean? And what is my next stop, a culinary place where *flowers grow?* Mummy loved scavenger hunts; she'd organized dozens of them for me as a child. And now she'd planned this final one after remaining silent for the latter half of my life. Why? Why now?

I flip back to the inside cover and study the name written in blue ink, and can't help but wonder if this mystery man is somehow the key to it all.

Daniel Davenport, who are you?

Eloise

I STOOD FRANK UP FOR LUNCH AT THE RITZ—TWICE, in fact—but he was undeterred. He sent two bouquets of flowers and called a half-dozen times.

I should have been happy for the interest and attention, but all I could think about was Edward, that magnificent library bar, and the night that had glimmered with promise and ended in mystery. He didn't meet me at Jack's Bistro the next day, nor did he call. But Frank did.

Poor Millie, by the fifth time he rang, I begged her to let him down softly for me. "El," she said later. "You're going to break this poor man's heart."

Even Millie—straight-shooting Millie—was no match for Frank's tenacity. He showed up at our flat the following Saturday night with two tickets to the Sammy Davis, Jr., concert and not a stitch of judgment about our modest living situation. In his eyes, I was a duchess, a princess, even. And who could say no to Sammy Davis, Jr.? Certainly not Millie. She whispered in my ear that night, "If you don't go, I might have to!"

And so, I went out with Frank that night. And maybe it was the music, or the cocktails, but I let him kiss me under a lamppost in Trafalgar Square.

After that, I began to grow *accustomed* to Frank. While we had little in common—after all, to him, numbers told stories, not words—and butterflies might not have swirled inside of me in his presence, I did enjoy his company, or rather: I enjoyed *being enjoyed*.

"Look at you," Millie said as I got ready for another Friday night date with Frank. "You have the glow of a woman in love." It wasn't so much a statement but a smartly phrased question—a barrister-in-training, and a good one, prying the truth out of her unsuspecting witness.

Millie could read me like no one else, and yet my evasiveness about Frank had even her guessing. This was her way of taking my temperature. I smoothed the hem of my dress and wondered if she knew I wasn't thinking of Frank, but rather, the jacket hanging in the front closet that belonged to another man, and the disappointing fact that after that perfect night in the little library, Edward had . . . disappeared.

I'd gone to Jack's the day I'd asked him to meet me, waited an hour for him, swirling in my corner stool at the bar every time someone entered, but it was no use. None were Edward.

I thought about looking him up, stopping in to the club, even, to see if I might find him, but it all felt too forward. If he were interested, truly interested, he would have been there, materialized on the barstool next to mine so we could pick up where we left off in the library. But he didn't, and that was that.

"Well?" Millie asked again.

I don't love Frank, I thought, *but I love the way he adores me. Could his love be enough for both of us?*

I ignored her question, and instead propped open my bedroom window, breathing in the fresh spring air. It was the middle of April, cherry blossoms burst from the mews and twine-wrapped bunches of peonies the size of dinner plates enticed shoppers at the market. Yet this particular spring felt . . . different, down to the lilt of the birds chirping in the tree just outside. *Even they knew.*

"What's wrong, El?" Millie asked, trying to catch my eye, but the ring of the telephone gave me the excuse I needed to change the subject. It was probably Frank, and it was. It always was.

"Hello, darling," he said. Frank had spring fever, too. His voice conveyed an urgent longing. "Would you like to go to Rhett's Supper Club tonight?"

"Really?" I said, cheering at the thought of dining at such a swanky establishment. I'd just recently seen a tabloid photograph of Elizabeth Taylor there. "Wait, how in the world did you get a table? I heard that it's booked out for months!"

"I pulled some strings," he said nonchalantly. "Only the best for my girl. Pick you up at seven?"

I paused for a beat, heart racing. *In time, soon perhaps, Frank will want more of me. And then what?*

"Eloise? We might have a bad connection. Can you be ready by seven?"

"Yes," I replied in haste.

RHETT'S SUPPER CLUB WAS just as glamorous as I'd imagined, and I was glad I chose my black dress and remembered to clean my gloves (a gift from Frank). My shoes might not have been Chanel, but the leather handbag I'd purchased at a steep discount at Harrods was fine enough to pass in the dim light. Besides, Frank seemed to care little of such details.

"Good evening," the host said to us. We checked our coats and were ushered by flashlight to a booth along the side wall. I spotted a man walking by who looked a little like Richard Chamberlain, and he very well might have been. After all, this was *the* place to see and be seen.

"What do you think?" Frank asked, reaching for my hand under the table, his fingers gently grazing my thigh.

I smiled nervously. "I . . . I . . . think it's, well, marvelous!"

He selected a bottle from the wine list, and I couldn't help but notice the price—almost a half-month's rent. When the sommelier filled our glasses, I felt guilty about leaving Millie to spend another Friday night alone. Guilty for . . .

"I propose a toast," Frank said, raising his glass, "to London and to my beautiful Eloise. May we celebrate like this often and . . . forever."

Forever. Did he say forever? I held the glass before me, my arm frozen.

"Darling," Frank said, urging me to drink. "It's bad luck if you don't take a sip."

I nodded, dutifully bringing the glass to my lips, while spilling a drop of red on the pristine white tablecloth.

"What's troubling you, dear?" he asked, leaning in closer. "Are you worried about me leaving next month? You are, aren't you?"

My eyes burned, but I wasn't sure if it was his cologne or the salty burst of imminent tears.

"Yes," I stammered. "That, of course, and . . . I'm . . . worried about Millie. Now that she's in law school, we're having trouble making rent. And . . . well, I guess I just feel guilty that I'm here . . . with you . . . drinking this fabulous, but expensive, wine. I'm sorry. I know I'm probably not making much sense right now."

His face twisted into a smile and then he laughed. "Is that all?"

Is that all? No, it wasn't all. It was merely the tip of the iceberg, but I couldn't tell him that.

"Darling, how much money do you need?"

I could hardly believe my ears. Frank was generous, but this was beyond. "I couldn't possibly . . ." I said. "I'm sure we can figure things out. And, Frank, I wasn't asking for money when I said what I said. I was only—"

"Nonsense," he said, pulling out his checkbook. "Will a thousand pounds get you through for a bit?"

"Frank, I—I don't know what to say. . . ."

"Don't say anything," he said, "just let me take care of you. It's what I *want*." He smiled, and I tried hard to return the warmth he shared. "Just promise me that you'll think about *us*, and when we might make things more . . . *permanent*."

I swallowed hard.

"I don't want to rush you," he continued, placing his hand on my thigh again. "But, darling, you know my business in London will be ending soon." He cleared his throat and narrowed his gaze the way I imagine he did when analyzing the columns of numbers in an actuarial table. "Eloise, it's no secret that I'm in love with you," he continued. "I'm only asking you to consider what the future might look like. *Our* future." He cleared his throat. "I'm hoping that you'll come to California with me—as my . . . wife."

My mouth fell open. I heard his words, and yet, I didn't. They swirled in the air above the table like fragments of a strange dream. Wife. California. Permanent.

"Say, did you read in the newspaper about the London Bridge?" His cadence sounded easy and breezy, as if he'd forgotten the gravity of what he'd just said.

"No," I muttered.

"An American businessman just bought the old thing and plans to move it to the States, maybe even to California." He smiled. "You know, honey, it does seem like a sign, doesn't it?"

His eyes searched mine, but I didn't dare return his gaze, knowing my uncertainty would instantly betray me—and him.

Frank kept talking. "Just think, if the London Bridge can move to America, so can you, right? I know you hate the winter. There's plenty of sunshine in California. And flowers bloom all year round."

I never told him I hate the winter. Why would he say I hate the winter?

As he continued to talk, my eyes wandered the room. I noticed a neon sign hanging over the bar. MARTINIS was missing the letter *n* so it now read MARTI IS. If Millie were here, we'd have a proper laugh about this. She'd talk about all the places "Marti" might be. "Marti is sleeping. Marti is dancing. Marti is ... *not moving to America.*"

"What are you thinking about?" Frank said, attempting to lure my attention back to him.

I pointed to the sign above the bar and explained my humorous take, but Frank only stared back at me blankly, changing the subject a few moments later. He obviously didn't find it funny.

The waiter appeared and Frank began asking him questions about the menu when I noticed a glamorous couple in evening wear being seated at a nearby table. The woman, beautiful with her platinum-blond hair done up in a smart chignon, was carrying a chic and, if I knew anything from working at Harrods, *rare* Bonnie Cashin for Coach handbag. The man was ...

My God. *Edward.*

Our eyes met, only for a moment, but a force surged through me, like lightning. Even in the dim light, I could tell that he felt something, too.

Has he thought of me these past months? Why didn't he come to Jack's? Why didn't he call?

My heart raced as I released his gaze, but the pull to look again was magnetic, and I watched as Edward bantered with his dinner date. When she threw her head back and laughed, then reached her hand out, touching his arm, it actually hurt. *Has he shown her his violin tattoo?* I wondered. *Does she know that he always wishes for music in his ear?*

I felt Frank's hand on the small of my back and I turned to face him.

"You know how I feel about you, *El.* But you haven't told me *your* feelings."

El. Millie was the only one who called me *El,* and I immediately recoiled when I heard the name on his lips.

Suddenly, the room felt like a cyclone, and I was caught up in it—spinning out of control like a kite in Regent's Park on a windy day. I knew I had to will myself back down to earth, and I did. But the landing was a harsh one. *Here I sit in a fancy steakhouse beside a man who is besotted with me—the wrong* man. *The right one is close enough to hear the sound of my voice like music in his ear.*

I wanted to run to him. I wanted to *run away with him.* It was the storybook moment I'd waited for all my life, the moment of *knowing.* But I knew then that my story wouldn't have a happy ending.

"El," Frank continued. "What do you say?"

I stared mutely at Edward, as he stood and removed the jacket of his dark suit, tucking it on the back of his chair, acknowledging me briefly with a curt nod. The room was far too dim to make out any emotion in his eyes, but there was plenty in mine.

I turned to Frank, and refocused my blurry eyes. "I'm sorry, what was your question?"

He smiled. "Darling, the wine must have kicked in." He touched my arm, but I barely felt his fingers on my skin. "My love, I am asking for your hand . . . in marriage." He swallowed hard, and I could see the rise and fall of his Adam's apple. "I'm asking you to . . . spend the rest of your life with me."

How foolish I'd been. To Edward, I was clearly no more than a fleeting memory. But I'd built up our connection in my mind, which I realized was only a work of fiction. It was all a silly fairy tale.

I turned to Frank, finally giving him the attention he deserved. "Yes," I said, this time without hesitation. It was a reflex. It was the only answer. "Yes, Frank Baker. I will marry you. I will come to California."

Valentina

The Next Day

———

MILLIE WAVES FROM THE CHILDREN'S BOOK AREA, WHERE she's helping a mother and her two young boys.

I stand over to the side and watch her pull a copy of *20,000 Leagues Under the Sea* from the shelf, listening as she tells them all about Captain Nemo and his adventures chasing after a giant monster roaming the high seas.

The boys stand in rapt attention. They are hooked.

"Excuse me," I say, kneeling on the rug beside one of the children. "I couldn't help but notice that you like adventure stories." I scan a nearby shelf, then reach for a copy of *Beyond the Bright Sea*, my mind still fresh with the memory of reading the book when I'd covered for the children's librarian during her maternity leave several months ago. As I describe the story, I can feel salty air on my cheeks, and my young client's interest rising.

After she rings up the purchase for both books, Millie waves goodbye to them, then approaches me as I look through a stack of new books. "I'm sorry for my . . . tone yesterday," she says. "Your mother poured her heart into this place, and"—she looks around the store, a thousand memories evident in her eyes—"I guess my fears got the better of me. Clearly, you are here to help." She swallows hard. "Forgive me?"

I have a lump in my throat, too, but am quick to navigate our conversation to friendlier seas. I tell her about the copy of *The Last Winter* I'd taken with me yesterday, and the mysterious commentary inside. "Sounds fascinating," she says, raising an eyebrow.

"And even more, I found a letter from my mother inside."

Millie nods. "That sounds like the work of Eloise."

"Yes," I say. "She loved scavenger hunts. When I was ten, she planted fifteen clues in the house that led me to a chest hidden in the garden."

"And what was inside?"

"The new release from my favorite author, and a note that said the freezer was stocked with my favorite ice cream."

"That sounds about right."

I smile. "But I might need a little help with this one."

"Oh?"

"She mentioned something about a culinary place where flowers grow. Something about finding a clue on a shelf. The fourth shelf, I think."

Millie nods. "Down the street—Café Flora—the owner was one of her dearest friends."

Before I can thank her, or ask for more, a couple enters the store—the man and woman make a beeline to Millie.

"Excuse me, ma'am," the woman says, frowning. She's about my age, and her tone is pressing, urgent. "I need your help." She's very pretty, but has the air of someone who knows it, with her coifed blond locks and razor-sharp features. Her black leggings and cropped hoodie accentuate her svelte figure.

Millie smiles placidly, like a retail veteran who has survived many a battle with the public, though I know the bulk of her thick skin was built in the courtroom, not on the bookstore floor. "Yes, of course, what can I do for you?"

The woman sighs—clearly, this has been a *very hard day*. "I need to find a book for my niece—a particular copy she wants. Today's her birthday and if I can't find it, I . . . well, it wouldn't be a good thing, if you know what I mean." She forms her hand into the letter *L* and holds it to her forehead. "You know, total *auntie fail*."

Her husband, or boyfriend—a tall, dark-haired man in a gray sweater—nods at Millie as if they've met before, then shrinks into the historical fiction section. They're attractive—each of them—and yet, somehow, they seem like an odd couple together.

"I tried to order it online," the woman continues, "but I got an email last night saying the delivery would be delayed until next Tuesday. I mean, seriously? I paid for overnight shipping, and now I actually have to get in my car and drive to a *bookstore*? At first, I was like, do bookstores even exist anymore? Didn't the Internet put them all out of business?"

Millie and I exchange knowing looks.

"But what do I know? My boyfriend, Eric, is a bookworm, and he knew about this shop." She smiles sweetly. "He said you could help."

"Yes," Millie says calmly, although I can tell she's boiling over inside. The woman's comments were infuriating. Ignorant, even. But to Millie and me, these were also fighting words—and our common ground. *How dare she.* I glance at the boyfriend nearby, and he's either oblivious to her ramblings or he's trying his best to ignore them—judging by his uncomfortable expression, I'd put money on the latter.

Somehow, Millie is as cool as a cucumber. "I assure you, Miss . . . ?"

"Easton. Fiona Easton."

"Miss Easton, yes. You see, my dear, you're quite mistaken. Bookstores are far from dead."

"Well," Fiona says, "I didn't mean that, I only meant—"

"Now, now," Millie says. "Let's not waste our time on nonsensical things. What's the name of this book you're in search of?"

Fiona sighs. "You probably don't have it in stock."

Millie is undeterred and, clearly, up for the challenge. "Try me," she says.

"It's called *The War That Saved My Life,* or something like that . . . maybe *The War That Saved Me?*"

"Kimberly Brubaker Bradley, yes," Millie says immediately, pointing to a nearby bookcase. "We have it right here." She lifts a paperback from the shelf and hands it to her dubious client. "You see, Miss Easton, we booksellers are neither extinct nor incapable."

"Right, of course," Fiona says, stunned. "Thank you."

"I told you they'd have it, babe," her boyfriend says, leaning against a nearby bookshelf. He runs his hand through his dark, wavy hair. "Millie can find you anything."

"Hello, Eric," Millie says warmly as if they've had many previous literary chats. "How *nice* to finally meet your girlfriend."

"Yes," he says. "I've been trying to get Fiona up here for ages, but now that she's doing some design work for a new boutique down the road, I was finally able to twist her arm."

Fiona forces a grin. "I'm an interior designer," she says, reaching into her purse and placing a card on the counter. "Just in case you ever need any help"—she pauses, looking around the store—"sprucing things up."

Millie smiles politely, then covertly tosses the card beneath the counter—directly into the recycle bin. "How nice. An *interior designer*. You know, Eric's been coming here since he was in grade school. If I'm not mistaken, you were one of our first customers, weren't you?"

He nods. "My mum would bring me to Eloise's read-alouds. I must have been twelve at the time, but something about the way she read was just . . . magical."

My heart seizes when I hear the mention of my mother's name, and it hurts to think of her spending time with other children when I was the one who needed her most.

"This is Eloise's daughter, Valentina."

Eric's eyes widen. "You're kidding. Really?"

"Nice to meet you," I say.

"I'm so sorry about your mum."

I nod.

"She was really incredible. And this store . . ." He pauses, looking around. "I spent so many hours of my childhood in here. We lived just up the street. When my mum couldn't find me, I was always here. Your mum would let me stay long after closing time."

"Wow," I say, unsure of how to respond.

"I heard that she had a daughter, in America. She always talked about you. It's really cool to finally meet you. Did you ever—"

"Eric, honey, we need to go," Fiona interjects. "I promised

my sister we'd pick up the cake, and you know how much she hates it when we're not punctual." She smiles at me. "It was so nice to meet you. What did you say your name was again?"

"Valentina."

She scrunches her nose. "Valentina. How quaint."

Eric scratches his head. "Well, we better be off. Millie, thank you. And, Valentina, it was a pleasure. I'll be by soon—this visit wasn't nearly long enough."

Millie smiles. "We have some new fiction coming in next week that you might enjoy."

"Until then," he says, nodding at me before following the interior designer out the door.

When they're gone, Millie lets out a sigh.

"I'm sorry," I say, "but what in the world does he see in that woman?"

"I know. She's dreadful, isn't she? They've been dating for at least four years, or so I hear. They might even get married. A shame. He's such a kind young man, and she's, well . . ." Millie's voice trails off as she shakes her head.

I shrug. "Well, you sure called her bluff."

"It doesn't matter if I did," Millie continues. "There are people like Fiona around every corner, the ones who don't believe in the importance of a neighborhood bookstore. But we'll prove them wrong, won't we?"

I nod reflexively, but doubt churns inside of me as she hands me a copy of the store's ledger sheet. "I'm afraid the numbers aren't great," Millie says. "Eloise cared more about her community than the bottom line. Alas, I wish I'd looked into the books sooner." She sighs. "Surely, there must be a solution."

If there is, it's foreign to me. The only options I see are sell and settle the estate debt, along with the looming tax bill, or defy the rules of logic and carry on.

Two impossible choices.

CAFÉ FLORA IS JUST AHEAD, and as I approach, I notice the climbing rose clinging to the building's façade—bare vines now, soon ready to burst into bloom. An assortment of large, terra-cotta containers bear evidence of last year's dahlias, lavender, and roses. This is the location of my mother's next strategically placed clue: *Your next stop is culinary and close—where flowers grow.*

As I walk inside the café, a middle-aged woman behind the counter looks up, brushing a wisp of auburn hair from her temple. I hadn't noticed her when Liza and I stopped in. "Oh, I'm sorry," she says. "We're not open for lunch until eleven."

"It's okay," I say, walking closer. The air smells of freshly baked bread and simmering garlic, and I suddenly feel hungry. "I'm here about . . . something else." I introduce myself, and explain my mother's mysterious notes.

"So, you're the one and only Valentina," she says, looking me over with a wide smile. "Your mother said you'd be coming."

"She did?"

The woman nods. "I'm Jan. I own this place. This was one of your mum's favorites. She loved our watercress grilled cheese." Jan sighs, looking out into the empty dining room as if she can see my mother sitting by the window, daintily dipping her sandwich in a cup of tomato soup. I can picture it, too, somehow. "We all miss her. Very much." She smiles, cinching the string of her apron. "But now we have you!"

"Uh, yes," I say, swallowing hard.

"I can't tell you how much I admire you for stepping into your mother's shoes and keeping the Book Garden afloat. I don't know what Primrose Hill would do without it. In some ways, it's the heart and soul of our little neighborhood."

My hands feel a little clammy, and I tuck them into the pockets of my jeans. I don't tell her that the store's future is in a precarious state. Instead, I smile, and show her the clue my mother left.

"Aha," Jan says with a coy smile. "Your mum always had a bit of game in her, didn't she?" She points to the bookshelf on the far wall. "It's sort of like our little free library—where customers can leave or borrow books as they please. You have those in the States, right?"

"Oh yes," I say, remembering the miniature house on the post I had installed by the curb in front of our home in Seattle. Nick had thought it was embarrassing, a "librarian" thing to do. But I loved it—so much. I'd search used-book stores for copies of my favorite titles—children's books, too— and tuck them into the little library, then perch in the chair by our living room window, and watch people stop and select a title, or leave one of their own to share.

I dart ahead, to the Primrose Hill equivalent, where a sign reads TAKE ONE, LEAVE ONE. HAPPY READING.

"It was all your mum's doing," Jan says, looking on as I survey the fourth shelf from the bottom, just as the note had instructed. But after a thorough inspection of each title, my search comes up empty, and I turn around. "Maybe I'm missing something? There's nothing here."

"Ah yes," Jan says. "Check the far right corner of that shelf a little closer."

I follow her instructions, and immediately notice a small hinge that practically blends into the shelf's wooden back-drop. I give it a little push, and a tiny door opens, revealing a hidden compartment behind the shelf—just large enough to hold a single book—in this case, a well-loved (and by that, I mean, sufficiently tattered) copy of *Little Women*. I hurriedly flip through the book's pages until I find the card inside and eagerly tear the envelope open.

Valentina,

Congratulations on reaching your third clue, my darling girl. Please hug Jan for me. (And if you're ever feeling under the weather, have her make you her famous chicken soup. It is THE antidote.) I hope you're falling in love with Primrose Hill as much as I did when I first laid eyes on it. Isn't it magnificent?

Now, for your next clue, and please, listen carefully: While I may not be there to dry your tears, there are bighearted people in this neighborhood who are. Think of them as your family, because they were to me. When you need comfort, turn to them, and curl up in the nursery and listen as the old lady whispers, "Hush." I'll be wait-ing.

Love, always and forever,
Mummy

"I take it you found your clue?"
I nod, swallowing hard.

"It'll get easier in time," she says.

"No, really," I reply. "I'm . . . fine."

"Honey, you're not fine, and that's okay. I lost my mother, too—five years ago. Grief comes in fits and spurts. One day you're on the top of the world; the next you're drowning in a puddle of tears."

"I don't think you understand," I say, steadying myself. "My mother left when I was twelve years old. I . . . never saw her again before she . . . passed."

"I know," she says. "It'll all be okay in time. You'll see."

"Well," I say with a sigh. "I should go. You have the lunch crowd to prepare for."

"Listen," Jan says before I turn to the door. "I don't doubt that you've been through a lot—more than I can possibly imagine—but I do know that your mum loved you ever so much."

"Thanks," I say, reaching out to embrace her, remembering my mother's note.

Please hug Jan for me.

"That's from . . . my mum."

SHORTLY AFTER SIX P.M., Liza pokes her head in the door of my flat. "Just checking to make sure you're still with the living," she says. "Jet lag is tough."

"Alive and kicking," I reply, telling her about my visit to Café Flora and the headway I'd made with Millie as I open the bottle of red I'd purchased at the market. I pour us each a glass.

"Millie conquered? Check. Third clue? In progress. Next up: finding you a love interest."

"Well, I'm pretty sure that Millie is *unconquerable*. And I do appreciate your sentiment, but men are the last thing on my priority list at the moment."

"I know," Liza concedes. "I'm just trying to think of creative ways to get you to feel at home here. Can you blame me for wanting to have a fun new friend upstairs—who also happens to be my landlord?"

I don't have the heart to tell her that I may not be her landlord for long. "You're sweet," I say instead. "And I do really like it here, but if anything could anchor me to London, it wouldn't be a man. Honestly, I think the only men who stand a chance of capturing my attention are the fictional variety."

She laughs. "Given my dating track record these days, I'm inclined to agree with you. There is no better man than one found in a novel."

"Right? Why is that?"

Liza shrugs. "Because they don't exist in real life."

"Or maybe they do?" I counter. "And you've just been looking in the wrong places?"

"You mean, I should give up on bad boys and go out with a sensible accountant or something?"

"Yeah!"

She shakes her head. "No thanks. I'd die of pure and utter boredom."

"Well, speaking of men in books," I say, taking a sip of my wine. "When I met my husband—my *ex*-husband—I actually believed that he was a modern-day Mr. Darcy." I shudder at the words, embarrassed at my naivete. "I mean, I did. I really did. I thought he was this aloof romantic hero, rough around the edges, yes, but with a solid heart—a gentleman's heart. And then, well . . . how wrong could I have been?"

Liza places a hand on my arm. "Don't feel bad, honey. I once fell for a man who had a pet monkey. He actually had a whole act, with a banana bit, that he did on Oxford Street on Saturday afternoons."

I burst into laughter. "Dear Lord."

"He told me that it was just a side gig to pay the rent while he finished his master's degree," she says. "But I later found out that he lied about that, oh, and also, he lived on his mate's couch. Can you believe I fell for that?"

"No," I say, laughing. "I can't."

She cringes. "The monkey was lovely, though—a total sweetheart. His name was Charles."

Liza's eccentric monkey-trainer boyfriend reminds me of my own dating disasters in college, before I met Nick, who, ahem, also turned out to be a disaster. I try to remember what Joan Rivers wrote in her memoir. It was something like "Don't take life too seriously. No matter what, just laugh because at the end of the day, it's all funny." I can't recall the exact quote, and if I tried to recite it, I'd butcher it, for sure. But the sentiment rings true. If only it were that easy—to just laugh at all the absurdity, from my failed marriage to my mother's dual exit from my life.

"It's good to see you laughing," Liza says.

"I'm trying, but . . . I'm not all there yet."

She squeezes my hand. "I know."

"I mean, one moment I'm laughing, and the next"— I pause, feeling the familiar lump in my throat—"I'm on the verge of tears." I take a deep breath. "Maybe I'm going crazy?"

"Val, you're *not* going crazy. You're just going through a lot. It's normal to feel all the feelings."

I nod. "You want to hear something that's a bit crazy?" I reach for the marked-up copy of *The Last Winter* on the coffee table and point out the notes in the margins on one of the pages. "His name is Daniel, and . . . I don't know . . . he has the most insightful things to say about the story. It's like we're the same mind, or something."

She flips through the book, reading a few of the entries, before placing her hand to her heart. "Val, this is . . . so romantic," she gushes. "You have a crush on a *man you've discovered in a book*!"

"Now, let's not get carried away," I say with a laugh. "I do not have a *crush* on him."

"Well, what would you call it, then?"

I look up at the ceiling, collecting my thoughts. "I'd call it a common interest. Or maybe a kinship."

"A kinship," Liza says, completely straight-faced before cracking up. "I thought you said this was a mystery, not an origin story."

"Kinship, kindred spirits, whatever," I say, laughing at myself, though I have L. M. Montgomery to blame for my preference for old-fashioned word choices. I was obsessed with *Anne of Green Gables* as a girl. Fact: I even begged my parents to let me dye my hair red.

"So, this kindred spirit of yours," she continues. "Stay with me here . . . what if he's actually your *soulmate*?"

I think of Nick and all his broken promises. "I really don't believe in soulmates—at least, not anymore."

"Girl!" Liza continues. "That's like saying you don't believe in Santa, or . . . fairies!"

"Liza, you do realize what will happen if you tell people you believe in fairies. Or, good Lord, Santa."

She brushes off my comments as she flips through the book another time. "What did you say this guy's name was again?"

"Daniel," I reply, my heart beating a little faster. "His name is Daniel."

She nods, simultaneously finding his name on the inside cover of the book. "Daniel Davenport. Ooh la la! And look, his number is written right here. I insist that you call him!"

I grimace. "No way. Besides, he's probably married. Or deceased. Or maybe he's not even the one who wrote those notes?"

Liza nods. "True. If I've learned anything from living above a bookstore all these years, it's that the life of a book can be the craziest journey."

I pour us each more wine, spilling a drop on the coffee table, which I wipe up with the edge of my napkin. "What do you mean?"

"Well, your mother called it a journey, but Millie prefers the term 'life span,'" she continues, sitting up. "Which is actually a pretty brilliant example of their different personalities, but that's for another conversation. Anyway, Eloise used to say that a book—particularly, a very good one—is likely to pass to an average of seven readers in its life, sometimes more."

"Yes!" I say, remembering my mother recounting those very same sentiments. "When I was a child, she used to frequent estate sales in our neighborhood and try to imagine the people who had once owned the vintage jewelry or rare books she'd find. Their joys and sorrows. The stories of their lives."

"Tell me more about your mum when she was in California," Liza asks cautiously.

But instead of closing up again, I remember my mother's reminder to keep my heart open, so I try. My memories are random and disconnected, but they spill out in a cadence all their own. I tell Liza how she'd only get her hair cut on a full moon (one of her superstitions), how she'd taken up the habit of pressing flowers between the pages of her favorite novels (little surprises to find later).

Liza nods. "She really did live life with a flair all her own, didn't she? She had a gift for finding beauty tucked away in the most unexpected places." She picks up *The Last Winter* again, and grins. "And maybe you'll find Daniel in the same sort of way."

"I don't think so," I say. "He could be anyone. I mean, what if he's like nineteen years old? I may be a divorcee, but I assure you, I am *not* a cougar."

She laughs. "Suit yourself. I rather like younger men."

"Well, I *don't*. And even if he is ... age-appropriate ... he could also be ... really ... *old*! What if those notes in the book were written in, like, oh my gosh, *1953*?"

"What's wrong with older men?"

"Okay, point taken: You like *all* men."

She laughs. "That's probably true."

I shake my head. "Wait, he could be a ..."

"Serial killer!" Liza says, stealing the words from my mouth, then shaking her head. "But think about it, would Jack the Ripper really write such thoughtful things inside a book?"

"I guess not ..."

"That's right. Your Daniel is *not* a serial killer." She pauses, as if hit with a sudden stroke of genius.

"My Daniel. I love how you're really going for this."

"You have to call him. Tonight. Right now."

I wince.

"You know who would have loved this so much?" She smiles. "Your mum. And she would have taken my side."

Her comment is like a slingshot to my heart. She's right, of course, my mother would have loved every second of this literary mystery. And even though it will probably—no, definitely—lead nowhere, for some reason, I feel the sudden urge to pick up the phone. For Cezanne, the book's heroine, for Liza, but, really, for me. It's a silly, girlish thing to do, of course, but the mere idea of *Daniel* makes me feel—momentarily—light, when my heart has felt so heavy for so long.

I take a deep breath and punch the numbers into my phone.

"Here goes nothing," I whisper.

Eloise

THE DAFFODILS CAME, AND THEN THEY WENT.

Frank petitioned right here in London to sponsor my immigration visa. We'd marry in California, and I'd become a lawful permanent resident of the United States. All that was left was to say goodbye to my homeland—and my best friend.

"Millie," I said, knocking on her bedroom door. She appeared a moment later with a half-smile on her face. It was clear she'd been crying. "Frank's driver will be here in a few hours. I still haven't sorted through my closet. Can I talk you into lending me a hand?" It was less about needing her help, and more about needing her.

She nodded, looking into my eyes. "Oh, El, do you have any idea how much I'm going to miss you?"

"Millie," I cried. "I'm going to miss you that much and more."

She inhaled deeply. "It's time I make peace with your decision, even if this is all so . . . hard for me." She forced a smile. "Why can't that thickheaded bloke of yours agree to settle down here?"

"I wish," I said, blinking back tears. Millie already knew how hard I'd tried to convince Frank to relocate to London, but he was resolved that Santa Monica was his home, and that it would also be *ours*.

"California has no idea how lucky it is to be getting you," Millie said, hugging me.

"It breaks my heart to leave."

She shook her head. "No, I think this will be good for you. You've outgrown this old place, El. It's time for a bigger pond, bigger stories."

I wanted to tell her that she was wrong, that I belonged right here, with her, and I couldn't shake the feeling that I was failing her.

Since we were barely thirteen, all we'd talked about was the bookstore—our bookstore—the one we'd open someday, together, in a delectable, pastel-colored storefront in Primrose Hill. There'd be comfy chairs, reading nooks, and a fluffy, overfed cat who we'd pre-named Percival (Percy for short). Our customers would regard us as literary practitioners. Just like doctors prescribed medicine for physical ailments, we'd prescribe books for the soul. We had it all planned out and it would be . . . so perfect. Then I'd gone and ruined everything.

"Maybe someday," I said to Millie, "we'll still get that bookstore."

She forced a smile, but her eyes were filled with regret, disappointment. "It was just a silly childhood dream. They don't always come true."

"No, Millie. It was *our* dream. It still can be." I needed Millie to believe, for me.

She opened her mouth to speak again, but stopped when we heard a knock at the door. "That can't be Frank," I said.

"He's not supposed to be here until two." I unhinged the lock, and the older, distinguished-looking man standing in the hallway outside our flat was, indeed, not Frank.

"Miss Wilkins?"

"Yes," I said as he handed me an envelope with a wax seal on the back engraved with the letters *E.S.* And then he was gone.

Millie looked over my shoulder as I tore open the envelope and pulled out the card inside.

> *Eloise,*
>
> *You disappeared, and now I must find you. But you'll have to find me first.*
> *Roses are red, violets are blue, imagine what you might discover inside a nearby shop filled with shoes.*
> *I'll be waiting.*
>
> *With love,*
> *Edward*

"What is this?" Millie asked impatiently.

I didn't have time to fill her in. "I'll tell you later," I said, my heart racing as I reached for my sweater on the hook by the door. "I have to go!"

"Eloise, wait!" But I didn't stay a moment longer. I bolted down the stairs and out to the street. The local cobbler was just around the corner, and when I burst inside, the clerk at the counter's smile confirmed that I'd found the right place. He handed me another envelope, sealed just like the last one, and I opened it immediately.

Eloise,

One step closer, congratulations. Do you remember the night we met? I do. I think about it every day. The memory, I believe, will be forever stitched on my heart, that is, unless you know of a good tailor.

> *Come find me,*
> *Edward*

Mr. Watson, the local tailor! I ran with pink cheeks to his storefront, but the door was . . . locked. "No, no, no," I muttered, pounding on the door, then peering into the dark window, where a CLOSED sign hung against the glass.

"Edward!" I called out into the foggy street. Could he be here right now, watching me from the edge of a street corner? A moment later, a man approached—Mr. Watson, with a pastry in his hands. "Sorry, miss, I just stepped out for a quick bite. How can I help . . ." He paused, his eyes big. "Wait, are you the one—"

"Yes!" I said, reading his mind.

He unlocked the door quickly, and handed me the next envelope.

Eloise,

Checkmate. Now it's time for something sweet—as sweet as you. You know where to find me.

> *Love,*
> *Edward*

Sweet? It had to be the bakery, which grumpy old Mrs. Burbank ran. Her scones were legendary, as was her perennially foul mood. When the church bells chimed, my heart beat faster. Frank would be arriving soon. I didn't have much time, but the bakery wasn't far, and I picked up my pace.

When I arrived, there was a line out the door, but I elbowed my way inside to the front and waved at Mrs. Burbank. "It's Eloise," I said as she eyed me with indifference. "I'm here to receive my message!" The irritated man behind me mumbled something incoherent.

"Look, lady," the disgruntled baker barked. "I don't know what on God's green earth you're talking about, but if you want something to eat, *get in line.*"

"Oh yes, right," I said, deflated, slowly turning to the door, which is when I saw *him.* He stood outside, in front of the window, like a strong ship in rough waters, his eyes wild and an enormous smile across his face.

I pushed myself through the crowd to the street outside.

"Hi," he said, his eyes big and longing.

"Hi."

"And so, you've found me."

All I could do was smile, and take in the sight of him. He looked dapper in a pair of slacks and a light green sweater. I wondered how I must have looked, with my hair askew and beads of sweat on my forehead.

"Scone?" he said, handing me a paper bag.

I nodded, even though I was too wound up to eat. My stomach—and heart—were in knots. I searched his face. "How did you . . . find me? How did you know I lived . . . here?"

He grinned conspiratorially. "I have my ways."

"But . . . I left you a note—at the club. Why didn't you come to Jack's that day?"

He shook his head, obviously confused. "Jack's?"

My heart sank when I realized. "You didn't get it, did you?"

"No, I didn't." He took a step closer, so close I could feel the warmth of his skin in the air. The people outside the bakery were watching, but I didn't care.

"Oh, Eloise. I don't know what to say. I . . . thought you'd . . . vanished into thin air. It took a bit of detective work, but I found your telephone number, and I called, a few times."

"You did?"

"Yes, I . . . never did get through." He swallowed hard. "Listen, can we go someplace to talk?"

"Okay," I said, still stunned.

We set out down the street, at first in silence, glancing over at each other every few moments. He slipped his strong hand in mine, and our aimless path led us to Edgemore Park, where we sat together on a bench. A group of rowdy schoolchildren was embroiled in a pine cone fight in the distance.

"I guess the cat's out of the bag," I said as a belligerent man ambled by. "I'm clearly not the daughter of a wealthy businessman."

Edward grinned, lifting my hand to his lips, kissing my wrist the way he'd done on the night we met. "And you think I didn't know that from the very start?"

"Was it that obvious?"

"You can never be anyone other than your true self, and I, for one, think you're perfect."

I frowned. "I'd hardly call my formative years perfect."

He shook his head. "We aren't defined by where we come from, but rather, who we are"—he paused to touch his heart—"inside."

I smile. "Will you forgive me for my reprehensible fib?"

"I already have." He exhaled deeply. "Listen, I'm sorry that things got off to a rocky start. I'd like to start over again, but properly this time."

My mind raced, thinking of one roadblock after the next—the wedding plans, all of the meticulous preparations Frank had made. I rubbed the engagement ring on my finger nervously. I had to face the facts. "Edward, I'm . . . getting married, and . . . moving to America."

He smiled as if this were a challenge he was willing to accept. "Well then, I'd like to implore you to stay, if I may be so presumptuous."

I was on the verge of tears, though I couldn't help but smile at his bravado. "But I saw you that night at Rhett's Supper Club. I thought you were—"

"On a date? I was. With another dull debutante. She wasn't you, Eloise. No one ever could be."

I swallowed hard. "Oh, Edward, how I wish you would have found me sooner. How I wish . . ."

"But I'm here now," he said, inching closer to take me into his arms. I felt as if I'd melted in his embrace. I'd dreamt of a moment like this since the day I first set eyes on him, and when his lips met mine, it was just as magical as I'd imagined it would be, and more. I'd found my hero, my love—every ounce of my being told me so. And yet . . . it was too late.

I pulled back from his kiss, forcing myself to look away. "Oh, Edward, I want this so much—more than anything."

"And you can have it," he said, offering me his hand, a symbol of now and, I knew, the future.

I shook my head as I wiped a falling tear from my cheek, then lightly placed my hand on my abdomen. Frank didn't know yet, not even Millie. No one detected the tiny new life growing inside of me. It was my secret, and mine alone, but now it was Edward's, too—our burden to bear.

"I see," he said, releasing his gaze from mine and looking ahead into the distance.

I pressed my head against his shoulder, soaking his starched shirt with my tears. He wept, too, quietly, and I could feel him willing away his heart's grip on mine. Time passed quickly in those final moments, but I tried to memorize every second. The angle of his nose. The faint shadow of stubble on his face. The way his hand caressed mine. And when it was time to go—Frank would be here in minutes, even—he kissed me once more.

I walked home alone, and found Millie crying on the sofa. I nestled in beside her. There were no words for a moment like this, so we bathed ourselves in silence—savoring our last minutes—before I walked numbly to my bedroom to finish packing. I'd already sorted through the books I'd be bringing to California, and those were neatly organized in my trunk. But I hadn't gotten to my wardrobe yet, not that it mattered. Nothing mattered. There was no rhyme or reason to my selections. I merely emptied my drawers and threw in this dress or that. It was all a tangled, jumbled mess.

When I heard Frank's driver honk on the street below, announcing his arrival, I heaved my luggage out to the entryway, then looked around the little flat a final time. Millie wrapped her arms around me, squeezing me so hard, it almost hurt.

"I'll write you," she cried. There was a strange tone to her voice, which I chalked up to grief. I was grieving, too.

My nod was merely mechanic. "Millie, I need you to promise me something."

"Anything," she said, wiping away a tear.

I opened the door to the hall closet and pointed to Edward's jacket inside. "Keep this safe for me."

"El, I don't understand."

I closed my eyes tightly, then opened them again, glancing at the door over my shoulder. "I can't take it with me to California, but I don't want to lose it either—ever."

"What do you mean?"

"I know I'm not making any sense, but I don't have time to explain."

Millie nodded. "What's his name?"

"Edward," I said. The word flew out of my mouth. "Edward Sinclair."

"You love him, don't you?"

Tears stung my eyes. "I do, Mill. Oh, I do."

She shook her head in confusion. "Then why—"

"It's too late." I bit my lip as Frank appeared on the stairs to help with my bags.

"Hello, darling," he said, before waving to Millie, oblivious to the conversation that had just been cut short. "My driver says we might run into traffic getting to Heathrow, so we should hustle. We don't want to lose those first-class seats."

When Frank's back was turned, Millie nodded to me. It was all I needed.

"Ready, my love?"

"Yes," I said, feigning cheerfulness.

I took one last look at Millie before turning to follow Frank down the stairs. My legs felt leaden, and each step oozed of irony. I'd spent my whole life dreaming about the day I'd finally leave the East End, kissing my past goodbye, and now that it was happening . . . all I wanted was to stay.

CHAPTER

9

Valentina

"IT'S RINGING," I WHISPER TO LIZA, MY PULSE RACING
after I dial Daniel Davenport's number.

"Hello?" a youngish-sounding woman says. Her voice is
urgent and perhaps even a bit annoyed, but it's hard to tell
over the commotion in the background—dishes rattling,
water rushing from a faucet.

"Oh, um, hi," I mutter. "I'm so sorry, uh, I was calling
for . . . Daniel."

"Daniel? Daniel who?"

I clear my throat. "Daniel Davenport."

"Daniel Davenport, huh?" She laughs. "That's a good one."

"I'm sorry, I don't understand."

"You're calling for my ex, obviously," she says. "Tell me,
what kind of man gives out his home phone number when
attempting to cheat on his girlfriend?" She sniffs. "Yeah, no
cellphone—he missed too many payments. First it was Clyde
Humphrey, then Ben Calloway, and now . . . What was it
again? Oh yeah, Daniel Daven-whatever." She laughs. "It's
not your fault, sweetie. I feel sorry for you, and all of the poor
women he's duped—including me. But now the joke's on
him." I shake my head at Liza, who's hanging on my every

word. "He was arrested last week for mail fraud. They finally got him. Good riddance."

"Oh," I say. "I'm . . . sorry. I . . ."

"Don't be," the woman replies. "Just learn your lesson like I did and don't fall for a sociopath."

"Yes, right," I mutter. "Thank you." I end the call quickly and set the phone down on the sofa, staring at it like it's a stick of dynamite.

"So?" Liza asks, wide-eyed. "Tell me everything!"

"Wrong number." I sigh. "Either that, or our Daniel Davenport is a cheating sociopath who is currently in prison."

"Let's go with the first scenario."

I shrug.

"Don't lose heart," Liza says.

"I think I already have," I say, yawning. "But for now, I need to get some sleep."

Liza reaches for her sweater and casts me a cheeky smile from the doorway. "Good night, honey. May you have the most romantic dream about the handsome and mysterious Daniel."

THE NEXT MORNING, WHILE I don't wake with fond memories of any particularly romantic dream, I do feel unusually steeped in a newfound sense of clarity—about the Book Garden. My mother's life might remain a painful mystery to me, but she did create something beautiful, and worthwhile. I think of the customers who came into the shop the other day—Eric, in particular, even if his girlfriend is somewhat questionable. He practically came of age in the store! I'd witnessed how Jan at Café Flora was practically lit from within when she recounted the Book Garden's important place in the community. If my career as a librarian had any meaning, this could have just as much—or more. How could I live with myself if I didn't at least *try* to breathe some new life into the bookstore? As I fill the teakettle and set it on the back burner of the old stove, I reach for my phone and make some changes to my bio at @booksbyval. I delete "librarian" and "Seattle." I can't straddle two worlds; I must choose one, and I've made my choice. I should be sad, *maybe*? Instead, I feel a rush of pride when I type the new entry. Bookseller. The Book Garden. Primrose Hill, London.

This is the life that my long-lost mother has gifted to me. I have six months to make it mine.

THE DOOR BELLS JINGLE as I walk into the store. "Millie?" I call, out of breath, waking Percy, who stretches his legs in a sunny spot near the front window.

"Just a minute," she replies from the back room.

A moment later, she appears, a bit disheveled, with a broom in her hand. "Wouldn't you think bees would have better sense than to build their hive in a bookstore?" She shakes her head. "They got in through that blasted window again. It happens every year about this time. I've been meaning to get it fixed, and this is the price one pays for procrastinating." She sets the broom against the back wall, but it stubbornly falls to the floor with a smack. "Next there'll be hornets in the Hemingway section!"

"Sorry," I say, stifling a laugh, as I detect a scratching sound coming from the back of the store. "Wait, what is that, certainly not bees?"

Millie rolls her eyes. "Percy! He thinks the corner book-case in the history section is his personal scratching post." She shoos him back to the window, then pauses for an elon-gated moment, studying my face before raising an eyebrow. "Your expression," she says with a nod of certainty. "Your mother used to make the very same one when she was on the verge of something."

I open my mouth to speak, but Millie holds up her hand to silence me. "Something's brewing. I know it. Let's just cut to the chase. You're putting us out of business. You're closing the store, selling the building. Go ahead. Just say it."

I shake my head. "On the contrary, Millie, you could not be more wrong. I'm not *selling* the store. Quite the opposite, actually."

She narrows her gaze, still unconvinced.

"Listen," I continue. "When I first learned that my mother had left me her estate, I didn't know what to think. I mean, I hadn't seen or heard from her since I was twelve years old. That's *a long time*." The familiar ache pulses inside, but I con-tinue, pushing past the emotions. "I've carried a lot of hurt with me ever since. So yes, when I stepped off the plane, I didn't feel all that nostalgic or warm."

Millie listens as I continue. "But then I came here, to Primrose Hill, and saw the store with my own eyes. I met you and Liza, Jan, that quirky guy at the market with the—"

"Beret," Millie adds, smiling as she finishes my sentence.

"And a fake French accent, if I might add."

She nods. "It's unequivocally fake."

I smile. "But it fits, doesn't it? It all fits. All of you. All of"—I pause, glancing around the store—"*this*. I guess what I'm saying is that . . . I'm not going anywhere. I can't." I catch her eyes, harnessing her gaze to mine. "I may never under-stand my mother's past, but I'm going to fight for the Book Garden."

Millie throws her arms around me. "I knew it!" she cries. "I knew you weren't a bad apple!"

I hand her a tissue from the box on the counter and take one for myself.

"But it's the estate tax, Millie," I continue. "I only have six months to pay it, and I don't have the cash. Now, if you're willing to work with me, maybe get a little creative—"

I stop myself from where the conversation is heading. Yes, Millie is retired from her law career and might have the capi-tal to help, but that would be a huge burden to put on my mother's best friend. I decide to set the thought aside and help her shelve the new shipment of books, which is when I tell her about the intriguing comments in the copy of *The Last Winter*, and the wine-fueled evening with Liza where I mus-tered the courage (albeit, *liquid* courage) to dial the phone number written inside the cover.

"This is intriguing," Millie says, eating up my words with rapt attention.

"Yes, but attempting to meet a man you've 'found' in a *book* does seem a little, well, insane, doesn't it?"

"Maybe, but only in the best of ways." She grins, tucking a fresh paperback onto the shelf. "Valentina, did your mother ever tell you about the life span of a book?"

I smile. "The journey? Yes."

Mille nods. "It's vast. That book might have traveled through countless hands before and after this Daniel had possession of it. Finding him might take some work, but I don't think it's impossible."

We'd been so immersed in our discussion that neither of us had noticed the FedEx deliveryman waiting patiently in the doorway. When he clears his throat, Millie startles, apologizing as she quickly smooths her tousled hair, then signs for the packages.

"It's no trouble," the man says, as Millie's cheeks flush.

"Thank you, Fernando," she says, setting the packages on the counter before introducing me.

"Pleased to meet you," he says before turning to Millie again. "And . . . it's always nice to see you, Ms. Wilson." His jet-black hair is graying at the temples, though it's clear he's at least fifteen years her junior. As they stand beside each other, the top of his head barely reaches her collarbone.

"Please, you've been making deliveries here for years. We're basically . . . old friends. You must call me Millie."

"Millie," he says, holding her gaze for a beat before turning to the door. "Afternoon."

"Goodbye, Fernando," she replies with a limp wave, as if her right arm had suddenly lost seventy-five percent of its muscle capacity.

"Well, well, well," I say teasingly as the delivery truck sets off down the street. "Someone has a crush on the FedEx guy!"

"I most certainly do not," Millie insists, snapping out of whatever spell she's just been under.

I smile, helping her finish stocking the new inventory, when I remember my mother's latest clue. I retrieve my purse and pull out the card to read the last lines to Millie: *While I may not be there to dry your tears, there are bighearted people in this neighborhood who are. Think of them as your family, because they were to me. When you need comfort, turn to them, and curl up in the nursery and listen as the old lady whispers, "Hush."*

I look up at her curiously. "Do you have any idea what this means?"

Her eyes sparkle. "Yes, and I know you do, too."

"But I don't! I've been reading it over and over again, and . . . I just can't place it."

Millie sinks into the old upholstered chair by the window. The arms are threadbare, and likely made what's-her-name— the interior designer—break out in hives. "When you were born, I sent your mother a box of children's books—all classics, the ones that have stood the test of time. One, she told me, was an early favorite of yours."

I bite my lip, trying to extract any memory that might shed light on Mummy's latest clue. "Peter . . . Rabbit?" I finally say.

Millie smiles. "Shall I give you a hint?"

"Yes, please."

"Five words. Are you ready?"

I nod.

"'In the great, green room.'"

I gasp, as my early years flash before my eyes. "'There was a telephone, and a red balloon, and' . . . oh my gosh . . . *Millie!* The old lady, whispering hush!" I shake my head, remembering that old beloved book. *"Goodnight Moon!"*

"Yes. By Margaret Wise Brown."

The lines were veritably cemented into my subconscious, and yet, in my grief I'd somehow struggled to access them until now. At once, I'm three years old, sitting on my mother's lap as we linger in the old storybook's pages, with the mouse, the bowl of mush, the dollhouse, and the old lady whispering hush—a mismatched combination of words and imagery that formed the perfect crescendo, at least to me.

I race to the children's literature section, scanning the shelves until I see a single copy of *Goodnight Moon*. But when I flip through its pages, I find . . . nothing.

"Any luck?" Millie asks, peering around the corner.

"No," I say, sinking into the threadbare chair to my right.

"You know, Valentina," she begins. "One of your mother's dear friends is a woman named May Weatherby. She lives three blocks from here, in the top corner flat of the pastel-blue building."

I nod, recalling passing the building on my walk with Liza the other day. The flowers in the upper-floor window box had caught my eye.

"It might interest you to know that May's late husband authored a biography on Margaret Wise Brown. He knew her very well, in fact." She smiles. "I have a feeling she might point you in the right direction."

The bells on the door jingle before I can say anything else, and in walks Eric, but this time he's alone.

"Afternoon, Millie," he says, adjusting the leather messenger bag on his shoulder. I notice his bike parked on the sidewalk outside.

"Eric!" she says, walking over to greet him. I wave blankly from my chair. "I think you'll get a kick out of our latest arrivals. There's something just for you."

"I'm sure I will," he replies. "But first, I wondered if you could give me some advice."

"Try me," Millie says.

He runs his hand through his hair, then looks back in my direction with a furrowed brow. I wonder if his girlfriend's niece didn't like the book. I wonder if—

"It's Fiona," he begins. "The problem is . . . she . . . isn't really a reader. And . . . I just keep thinking that if I could get the right book in her hands, maybe it could open the flood-gates, you know?" He looks at me. "Like when your mum gave me a copy of *The Adventures of Tom Sawyer*. There I was, a surly preteen from London, and suddenly, I was—in my mind, at least—hunting for treasure and sidestepping the scene of a murder on the banks of the Mississippi. It was . . . remarkable, really. The thing is, once you get lost in a story, you want to get lost in another. It's a self-fulfilling prophesy."

Millie smiles at me. "Isn't that your theory, Valentina, that reading leads to more reading?"

I nod, walking over to the counter, where Millie and Eric are talking.

"That's just it," he continues. "And it's what I hope for Fiona. I want to find *the book* that turns her on to the world of books."

When Millie has sufficiently absorbed Eric's plight, she turns to me. "Valentina, why don't you help our friend Eric find just the book for his dilemma?"

"Sure," I say, reaching into my deep, professional librarian reserves. Millie has just tossed a bomb into my lap, which is about to ignite—and she knows it.

Eric follows me as I wind through a maze of bookshelves, waiting patiently for my clairvoyant literary pick, and yet, I am altogether baffled. *What on earth am I supposed to suggest that his vapid girlfriend read?* There's no way she'd manage ten pages of Nora Ephron's *Heartburn,* or care a thing about Maeve Binchy's *Tara Road*. Forget the classics, forget the usual suspects. This assignment was a *challenge*—a big one.

I search high and low, hoping that something—anything—

will jump out at me, and then it does. "Have you read *The Time Traveler's Wife?*" I ask, turning to Eric, who nods quickly.

"Oh my gosh, yes. I couldn't put it down. If I recall, I think I read it in a day."

"Me too," I say, cracking a smile. "My gut tells me Fiona might like this one. Maybe she'll even be impressed that it was made into a movie?"

He shrugs. "Maybe, though—"

"Movies never compare to books," we both say in unison.

"Ever," I add, grinning.

He nods. "I'll get it for her, then," he says, pausing to glance back at Millie. "I'll let you know if she takes the bait."

"Good luck," I say.

He pauses, scratching his head. "Fiona's childhood was far from idyllic. Her dad left when she was young, and her mom lived off government assistance. She grew up with absolutely nothing." The Gucci crossbody bag I recall her wearing the other day is a reminder that exteriors can be deceiving, and I instantly regret typecasting her. "She'd be mortified if she knew I told you that. I guess what I'm trying to say is that she didn't have the opportunities you and I might have had, and there certainly wasn't anyone who shared the love of reading with her." He pauses for a long moment, then smiles. "Your mum was that person for me."

"That's . . . wonderful," I say casually, shrouding the wave of emotion rising up inside of me. While I was motherless in California, she was here, doting on the neighborhood children. How could they possibly have needed her more than I did? Fiona and I obviously have one thing in common: hiding the pain of our pasts. "Well," I continue, collecting myself. "I hope it goes well with . . . the book. Good luck. I . . . have to be going."

"Of course," Eric says. "I'm . . . sorry to keep you."

"No trouble. I do love matching people to books."

He smiles. "Like mother, like daughter, I guess."

"Yeah. I guess."

IT'S RAINING OUTSIDE—LARGE RAINDROPS pelt my head from above—but I don't turn around to grab an umbrella. May Weatherby's house isn't far, so I hasten my steps, walking two blocks ahead before turning the corner, where I see the light blue building in the distance. The rain blurs the scene, as if I've stepped into an Impressionist painting, which somehow puts me at ease.

I climb the steps to the stoop, where I find a placard that reads WEATHERBY beside a call button, which I press. A moment later, an old woman's voice quietly comes through the little speaker beside me. "Hello?" She sounds frail, and a little taken aback, and I regret not calling first. Surely Millie had her phone number.

"Hello, yes, is this May Weatherby?"

"Yes."

"This is . . . Valentina Baker—Eloise's daughter."

"Oh, what a nice surprise on this gloomy day," the woman says. "You know, dear, I've been expecting you. Come up immediately and get out of this rain! I'm on the second floor."

I hear the automatic click of the door unlatching, and I step inside, shaking off the rain from my sweater as I climb the stairs. On the second floor, I approach the open door, peering inside cautiously. "Hello, Mrs. Weatherby? It's Valentina."

"Yes, yes," May calls to me from inside. "Come in, dear. I'm just putting on some tea for us. Make yourself at home."

I proceed inside, to the royal-blue settee by the window, and sit down. The tidy flat feels like a time capsule from the 1950s. I eye the collection of antique ceramic figurines on the nearby shelf. Above it is a black-and-white framed photo of a young man with an older woman, both smiling gleefully.

A few minutes later, May appears carrying a tray with a teapot and two china cups. Her arms teeter a little as she sets it down on the table, then she takes a seat in a blue-and-white, toile-covered Louis XV chair facing me. She's at least eighty, perhaps older, but she holds herself with the air of a woman who was once very beautiful. In fact, she still is. Her wispy gray hair is swept up into a bun, showcasing her high cheekbones and pale blue eyes. "I'm afraid you caught me in my robe," she says, smiling. "I don't get a lot of visitors these days, but you are a very special one."

"I, uh, thank you so much for having me in," I begin. "I'm sorry I didn't call ahead."

"It's fine, dear." She narrows her gaze. "Now, tell me, how can I help you?"

Unsure of how much she might already know, I start from the beginning—recounting my mother's scavenger hunt and the previous clues that led me here. I pull out the most recent note from my bag and show it to her. "Millie thought it might have something to do with Margaret Wise Brown's *Goodnight Moon*. My mother read it to me as a child."

"Ah, yes," May says, setting her reading glasses back onto the coffee table. "I have it right here." She stands up and walks to an old scroll-top desk across the room, then returns with a copy of *Goodnight Moon*. "I think this is what you're seeking. Your mother asked me to give it to you. When you came."

I smile, taking the book into my hands, where I find the next envelope tucked inside. I set it aside—for now—while May eyes me curiously.

"You're troubled, aren't you, dear."

I shake my head, displaying a saccharine smile. "No, no. I'm just fine."

She nods. "Your mother was, too, when I first met her. Life hadn't gone her way—far from it—and I suspect that you might feel the same." She continues before I can protest. "The fact of the matter is bad things happen to good people. They do. All the time. But it's our choice whether we wallow in them for the rest of our lives, or whether we accept the invitation."

I furrow my brow, confused. "The *invitation*?"

"Yes, to begin life's grand second act. You see, that's what your mother learned. Once she stopped looking back, she could finally move forward."

I clear my throat. "Listen, I don't mean to be rude, but I don't think you understand. My mother left me when she came to London. She never returned. I don't know if that's what you'd call a 'second act'?"

She smiles, undeterred. "I had my own second act," she continues, glancing up at the black-and-white photo on the wall. "See that handsome young man in the picture?"

I nod, my eyes returning to the photo I'd noticed when I'd arrived.

"That was my husband, Charles Weatherby. My, was he a dreamboat. There he is with Margaret." I reflexively glance at the copy of *Goodnight Moon* in my lap. "She owned a cabin in

Vermont near his childhood home, and sort of took him under her wing when he was a child. But anyway, when I met him the day after my twenty-first birthday, it was love at first sight. The only problem was that I was engaged to another man." She smiles to herself, letting the memories comfort her like old friends. "I married Charles, of course. How could I not? As you can imagine, it was a terribly painful time leading up to that. I broke someone's heart and angered my entire family in the process. My mother didn't speak to me for two years. But that was it for me—my second act." She watches me for a long moment, and the silence is heavy and uncomfortable. "Eloise didn't have the same good fortune, dear."

"So, you're saying that she didn't love my father, that she loved . . . *someone else?*"

"What I want you to understand is that the human heart can only be pushed so far, and then it takes on a mind of its own. Whatever reasons your mother had for leaving California were big ones, brave ones even. It was her second act."

I nod blankly. Her words linger in the late afternoon air. They try to penetrate my heart, but I won't let them.

"Well, enough of me rambling on. Aren't you going to open the card?"

I hesitate for a moment but finally lift the edge of the envelope as she watches in anticipation.

Dear Valentina,

You've arrived at your next clue! I do hope this one wasn't too hard to track down. I knew it might take some digging, but I wanted you to meet May. When I returned to London, the world felt like such a dark place. May was one of those magical people here in Primrose Hill who lit a lamp for me and helped me find my way. And I did, in time. I can't tell you how I know, but let's just say a little birdie told me your world is feeling a bit dark right now. I wish I was there to make it better, and that I'd been there for you in the years you needed me most. But there is no going backward, only forward. So, I'll leave you with a little cheer: daffodils. Ask Matilda, and she'll offer you her velvet green blanket, but do keep an eye out for the foxes wearing gloves: They'll show you the way to the little house.

I'll be waiting,
Mummy

Eloise

LOS ANGELES, CALIFORNIA

May 17, 1968

"WELCOME HOME," FRANK SAID, SQUEEZING MY HAND as the plane touched down on the runway. I'd never been on an airplane before, so I didn't know whether the sudden thud was normal or if the aircraft was about to spontaneously combust. Besides, I'd spent the entire flight fighting tears and was now merely going through the motions.

Home. How could a foreign land ever take the title? I blinked back tears as bright sunlight streamed through the window, steadying myself as best I could. I would not let Frank see me cry.

I spotted palm trees in the distance as passengers descended from another plane, clutching their bags and hats. A fashionable woman with hair much blonder than mine cinched a silk scarf around her neck and handed her bag to a handsome man with dark hair and smart-looking glasses. Of course, I thought of Edward, but immediately scolded myself for it.

"You're going to love it here, darling," Frank said. "The city is changing every day. Take LAX. It's an airport for the jet age. The terminal area opened only seven years ago. And in the Theme Building there's a restaurant in the observation deck with a view of the entire airfield. We'll have to try it some night."

I nodded despondently, following him down the plane's exit ramp as the sun beat down on my pale skin. Squinting, I caught a glance at the city shimmering in the distance. *So, this is America. Home of the new.*

But my heart belonged to the past.

Even the sound of Frank's voice made me think of Edward and the chapter I'd left unfinished in London.

Suddenly, I was back at the Royal Automobile Club.

"American men, they all sound like—"

"Cowboys," we said in unison, then laughed.

Frank turned to me, beaming. "Darling, are you feeling all right?"

"Yes," I said quickly. "I was just a little . . . air sick. I'm better now."

He reached for his wallet, then handed me a few strange-looking bills. "Why don't you grab yourself a snack while I get our bags?"

"Thanks," I said, walking ahead. I found my way to a café inside, and ordered two black coffees—to go—lingering beside a magazine stand before I reunited with Frank outside, where he already had a cab waiting.

"Darling, you know I don't drink coffee," he said.

I glanced down at the two Styrofoam cups in my hands. "No, no—this one's for the driver," I said, reminding him of my quirky habit of buying an extra coffee for cabbies in London.

"Do you want to know what's great about living on the

west side of Los Angeles?" he asked, turning to me. It was obvious that he wanted my attention *here* and not back in London. "It's really the perfect location. Of course, we have everything—the best restaurants, beaches. But you can't beat the proximity to the airport. We'll be home in a few minutes."

Home. That word again. I gazed out the window at the city skyline. It looked nothing like home but rather a distant planet, populated by . . . who knew what.

"There are no true skyscrapers here," Frank said. "Since 1926, the tallest building has been city hall, at four hundred and fifty-four feet. Leading architects planned it that way. Their vision was to keep the development spreading horizontally, to maximize the benefits of city living over the largest possible area."

The buildings that whizzed past were commercial and low to the ground, and there were few pedestrians, nothing at all like the neighborhood feel of Whitechapel Road in the East End, teeming with people who worked and shopped and ate and drank right where they lived.

Twenty minutes later, the driver turned onto a palm-lined residential street. The car climbed a hill, and from its peak I could see the blue ocean. We passed dozens of white-stucco homes with roofs made of terra-cotta tile, or something like it. Everywhere were carefully tended lawns, fruit-bearing citrus trees, and clipped hedges with not a single leaf askew.

Frank pointed to a large, modern-looking home just ahead that seemed like it belonged in a design magazine. "There she is," he said, smiling. "Welcome home, Mrs. Baker, or rather, soon-to-be Mrs. Baker."

I gasped, genuinely astounded. "Really, Frank? It's . . . beautiful." And it was, shockingly so. Beyond the manicured lawn and garden with two tall palm trees framing the entry-way, the two-story home sat perched on a large corner lot, with giant picture windows facing the ocean. It was the sort of house you'd imagine movie stars living in, not regular people like . . . me.

As the driver unloaded our bags, Frank took my hand and proudly led me through the front door.

A stocky woman in a black dress and white apron, with dark hair pinned back into a tight bun, smiled at me from the first step of the staircase. Her kindness warmed me, and I liked her instantly.

"Eloise," she said with an accent I couldn't place. "Welcome."

"My dear," Frank said to me, "this is Bonnie, our wonderful housekeeper."

"Very nice to meet you," I said, returning her smile.

"You must be tired," she added, beginning to fuss over me. "May I take your purse? Can I get you any—"

Frank cleared his throat. "Bonnie, I take it you've made all the preparations I wrote you about?"

"Yes, Mr. Baker," she said quickly, beaming with pride. "The house is ready for your bride, just as you asked." I wondered what she must think of me, this stranger Frank had carted home from London . . . like a souvenir.

"Darling, let me show you around," he said, taking my hand. He told me about the very important architect he'd hired to design the home and how he'd spared no expense in the construction process, attending to every detail. And, oh, the details. I'd never seen a refrigerator this big, or a sofa so plush, or a . . . I paused, looking out at the terrace equipped with a swimming pool . . . to think that I had a pool *of my very own.*

Upstairs, Frank pointed out the bedroom that would be converted into a nursery, and then two additional bedrooms. When we reached the master suite, he stood back and marveled, then looked at me. "Right after I met you, I had this room redone, hoping you'd share it with me. What do you think?"

The truth was plain and simple, a girl from the East End, like me, might spend her whole life trying to disguise her accent, like I had, but she'd never imagine sleeping in a bed this big, or in a room so grand—and larger than my entire London flat! Did I like the burnt-yellow coverlet and pillows? he asked. I didn't dare tell him the truth, that I would have chosen blue, the color of the sea, or maybe pink—I've always loved pink. But none of it mattered. It should have been enough to drown out my heartache. If *only* it were enough.

Frank tucked his arm around my waist. "You love it, don't you?"

"Yes, dear, I do," I said quickly, running my hand along the duvet, my thoughts pulsing like an aberrant heartbeat. *This is the bed where I will sleep with Frank. This is where Frank will undress and make love to me night after night. These are the pillows that will absorb my secret tears, for London, for Millie, and . . . the path not taken.*

IT ALL HAPPENED SO fast. In the week after my arrival, we obtained our marriage license, booked the church, and by that Friday, we were man and wife.

Frank paid for Millie to fly in, and she was the only witness on my side, though Frank invited a handful of his colleagues and their wives, who looked at me curiously, like the new pet he'd carted home from a foreign land. I remember catching Millie's eye as we recited our vows, and the look on her face startled me. It wasn't worry or apprehension, nor was it pity. For the first time, she looked at me as if she didn't know me. I'd become a stranger to her, and perhaps even to myself.

On the morning of our wedding, I told Frank about the baby. I'd been waiting for the right moment, and it seemed to be the one. He was ecstatic, of course, though I never doubted he would be. His joy gave me joy, but so did this new life inside of me. It made me feel . . . less alone. In London, Frank had always been available. But in California, he was scarce. And even with Bonnie, our housekeeper, bustling in and out, I felt constant pangs of loneliness. But when my mind lingered too long in the past, or I found myself missing Millie, I looked down at my round belly and remembered that I was not one, but *two*.

Never in my life had I suffered insomnia, but in this new place, I found myself tossing and turning for hours, long after Frank began snoring beside me. I read books to pass the time and wrote letters to Millie. When sleeplessness bled into the early morning hours, I'd walk to the bedroom window and count the stars, before the sun peered up over the horizon and Frank got up for work. Later, Bonnie would bring breakfast up on a tray, then sit in the chair by the window, encouraging me to eat a bite of this or that. Food didn't interest me, but her stories did, particularly of the family she left behind in her native Russia. She reminded me that I wasn't the only one experiencing homesickness.

Permanent dark circles formed under my eyes. In those months, I was so nauseous from the pregnancy that I often stayed in bed until noon, and sometimes later. But while the morning sickness eventually passed, the loneliness didn't. California was supposed to be the fun capital of the world, but it had the opposite effect on me, somehow. In fact, it made me feel like a vegetative version of myself.

"Come out to the patio and sit by the pool," Bonnie said one afternoon, doing her best to extricate me from the gloom of the bedroom. "A little sunshine will do you good." I acquiesced, but only because I didn't want to disappoint her.

"Here," she said, handing me an oversized black straw hat as I settled into a chaise longue by the pool. I imagined it was one of many things Frank must have had Bonnie purchase before my arrival, including the myriad of luxury toiletries in the bathroom's medicine cabinet. I smiled to myself, thinking back to my first day in Los Angeles. He'd been so excited to bring me home and show me all of the preparations he'd made—for me. No one else had shown me such generosity, and I was at once overcome by a surge of gratitude.

I fitted the hat on my head, eyeing my reflection in the window. Frayed at the edges—purposefully—and floppy in all the right places, it oozed glamour, and I loved it immediately.

"It suits you," Bonnie said, smiling approvingly as my baby kicked against the edges of my belly. She brought out a pitcher of iced tea and poured me a tall glass, squeezing a fresh lemon wedge on top.

"Thank you," I said, reaching for the book I'd begun reading last night, *The Last Winter*. I'd purchased it in London, at the recommendation of a friend at Harrods—Gemma, whom

I hadn't pegged as a reader, but when she went on and on about her favorite books, I remembered that it's never a good idea to judge a book, or a person, by her cover.

I found a copy at the bookstore I used to frequent on my lunch breaks while tending the ladies' accessories counter at Harrods. I couldn't believe it'd taken me this long to pick it up again. Funny to be reading a book with "winter" in the title while in the peak of summer—in California, home of the endless summer. And yet as I immersed myself in the story, it felt . . . perfect. The main character, a prima ballerina named Cezanne, lived a life that felt achingly familiar, perhaps only to me.

I read chapter after chapter before my eyelids grew heavy—not from the story, but rather, from my weariness. Yes, Cezanne and I were kindred spirits, but our lives took divergent paths. As I closed my eyes, I thought about that. While I had security and comfort that she did not, Cezanne wasn't willing to give up on the love she knew to be true, or herself.

WHEN I WOKE, the sun had shifted in the sky. It now hid behind the row of palm trees in the side yard. I heard voices inside the house followed by a slamming door. Then I saw Frank standing over me.

"Oh, hello," I said groggily, sitting up to greet him with every last bit of cheerfulness I could muster. "It's a beautiful day," I said, reaching my hand out to him, but he didn't take it.

"That hat," he said pacing beside me. "Where did you get it?"

I reflexively touched its wide brim, confused and a little

worried. Had I displeased him somehow? His mouth was tense—his lips pressed together tightly—and there wasn't a hint of kindness in his eyes.

"Bonnie . . . gave it to me." I paused. "Is something the matter? I assumed that you . . . bought it for me?"

He shook his head, neither answering my question nor confirming the source of his frustration. "She shouldn't have given this to you."

"Oh," I said. I lifted the hat from my head and set it on the chaise longue, feeling like a child who'd been caught wearing her mother's prized necklace without permission.

Frank sighed, then retrieved the hat and walked inside, closing the sliding door with a forceful shove.

It must have been a gift he'd purchased for me. I wasn't supposed to find it yet. Of course. He'd only been upset because I'd ruined the surprise. That, and maybe he had a bad day at the office.

But as the sun dipped below the horizon, taking its warmth along with it, my skepticism grew. I shivered as the wind picked up, rustling the palm trees overhead, as if they were whispering a secret—a secret I wasn't privy to.

IN THE FOLLOWING WEEKS, Frank was mostly absent. There were several business trips I knew about, of course, but also the late nights at the office that took me by surprise. One evening, I'd even planned a special dinner for him and made my mum's meatball recipe, but his plate sat on the dining room table for three hours and got cold.

"He's such a good man," Bonnie mused one morning as she fixed me a plate of raspberries with heavy cream for breakfast—my favorite. "He works very hard, so he can spoil you, Mrs. Baker!"

I reminded myself that American men were more devoted to their careers. I thought of Roger Williams, the playboy. He spent his days meeting women, and his nights forgetting them. I grimaced at the memory, and yet, if not for Roger, I wouldn't have met Edward, which, in some ways, made me wish I hadn't met Roger.

"Bonnie?" I asked, picking at my bowl of berries.

"Yes, dear?"

"You know Frank quite well, don't you?"

She smiled from the sink, where she was loading the dishwasher. "Well, he's been my employer for fourteen years now, so yes, I suppose so."

"It's just that," I begin, "he got so *upset* with me the other day, over the silliest thing—that straw hat."

Her eyes widened.

"Do you have any idea why?" I took a deep breath. "The way he looked at me, the way he spoke . . . I've been playing it over and over again in my mind. There was resentment in his eyes."

"No, no," Bonnie replied. "Mr. Baker does not resent you! He loves you!"

I shook my head. "But . . ."

"Please don't worry, Mrs. Baker," she said, returning to the sink. "He's just been working too hard, that's all." She smiled. "It takes its toll on a man."

I sighed, trying to resign myself to the matter. "You're right. It was probably just a bad day." I scooped the final raspberry into my mouth, then brought my dish to the sink.

"That's the spirit," Bonnie said, turning back to the dishes.

I decided to put the matter out of my mind—and my wor-ries along with it. That morning I went on a walk around the neighborhood, eventually finding a nearby café, where I sat at a corner table, drank coffee, and wrote to Millie. *The croissants aren't nearly as good as they are in London, but I like some of the other items in the case, like bagels, which are these unusual, doughy things that look like the second cousin of a doughnut, except that they're not fried. Americans can't get enough of them! I also tried an avocado for the first time yesterday. It was soft and strange, and I wasn't quite sure how I felt about it.*

I set my pen down before I could write what I really wanted to: *Did you return Edward's jacket? Did you . . . see him?*

I sighed, tucking my pen and paper back into my bag. I'd left my book at home, so I picked up the newspaper and checked the neighborhood listings, happy to see a nearby es-tate sale planned for the afternoon.

The address led me to a grand Craftsman home a few blocks away. The door was open, so I let myself in to find table after table of meticulously sorted items that the late owner must have collected over a lifetime. From fur stoles and vin-tage jewelry to home décor and art—every piece appeared to be of high quality, and my heart fluttered as I took it all in. *This is better than Harrods.*

I spent hours combing through the tables, letting my eye guide me, weighing each selection in my hand.

The indecision that had burdened me since arriving in California instantly vanished. I saw a box of earthenware the color of the ocean and claimed it as mine. I looked through every book and selected the first editions. An iridescent vase stamped FENTON's enchanted me, as did the Art Deco jewelry. I tried on geometric brooches and bangles, imagining myself in the Golden Age of Hollywood. And there she was, my new American tradition—or maybe alter ego—hunting for treasure from the past.

Frank had given me his checkbook, but I had never once used it. That day, I pulled it out and paid for it all.

Valentina

The Next Day

———

"MORNING," I SAY TO MILLIE, WHO'S STARING INTENTLY at the store's computer screen. I hand her a cup of coffee that I picked up at Café Flora.

"Wow, thank you," she says, taking a sip. "Did you know that your mum used to hand out cups of coffee to whoever needed them? It was her thing."

I nod, recalling my mother at the little café near the beach, balancing a drink tray with a lemonade for me, and two cups of coffee—one of which she'd share with anyone from a local homeless man to the postman on the corner of Park and Ocean. Somewhere along the way, I'd taken up the habit, too—a part of her in me, I guess.

"How's it going?" she asks as Liza walks in and waves at us.

"Good," I say, waving to Liza. "I found my mother's latest note."

"You did?" Liza squeals. She and Millie both hover over my shoulder as I pull it out of my bag. I can smell Liza's trademark vanilla perfume. As she told me the other day:

"I've tried a million fragrances, and this is the one. Men like women to smell like warm, fresh-baked cookies."

"'Foxes wearing gloves'?" Millie says, rereading the note I'd found tucked into May Weatherby's copy of *Goodnight Moon*. "What on earth does that mean?"

Liza sets her bag down and smiles. "She means foxgloves, obviously."

I shake my head, still lost.

"You know," Liza continues. "The flowers!"

"Oh," I say, scratching my head. "But . . . where are they?"

The wheels in Liza's brain are turning quickly. "Foxgloves and daffodils." She pauses for a long moment. "*Matilda!* Val, she's left your next clue in the garden down at Regent's Park!"

I'm still lost. "Wait, who is Matilda?"

It seems that Millie is connecting the dots, too. "The Matilda Fountain," she explains, nodding. "Of course. Eloise loved that old statue of the milkmaid shielding her eyes from the sun. She was fascinated by it, though I never did understand why. But that was her way. Eloise could find a story in anything."

I reread my mother's note again. "What do you think she means by the 'little house'?"

Liza shakes her head. "Well, she's stumped me there."

"Me too," Millie adds.

"Listen," Liza says, turning to the door. "I have to run some errands for my boss today—it's a long list, I'm afraid—but why don't we head down to Regent's Park tomorrow morning and see what we can find?"

"Okay," I say, thinking of Mummy's sign-off. *I'll be waiting.* If only she were. If only . . . I wave goodbye to Liza and join Millie behind the counter. Since our new website went live yesterday, she tells me, we've received eleven orders.

"That's wonderful," I exclaim, eyeing the stacks of books waiting to be packaged and picked up for shipment.

"Well, yes, it's encouraging," Millie replies with a sigh. "But it's going to take a lot more than eleven orders to keep afloat." She squints at the screen. "I keep looking at these numbers every which way, trying to figure out if there's any expense we can shave and put toward that inheritance tax."

Percy purrs at my feet, and I scoop him up in my arms. His fluff tickles my nose. "I had some savings," I say. "But after the divorce expenses, my account is pretty much drained." I frown. "Did you know that my attorney charged two hundred and fifty dollars an hour? It's criminal."

"It is," Millie replies.

I nod. "And that's coming from a lawyer herself."

"We have our own problems in the U.K., but the family law system is sorely broken in America. It's all about righteousness and winning—manipulation, even—versus doing what's right for children and families." She frowns, turning back to the computer screen.

"I take it you ran your law practice differently, then?"

"Well, I wasn't in family law," she says. "It's just toxic. But yes, I ran my practice differently. I was the rare bird who took on clients who needed my help most, regardless of their ability to pay. I loved my work, and it kept a roof over my head, but it was hardly a lucrative enterprise. Like you, I'm afraid I don't have any extra funds to contribute, as much as I wish I did."

"Millie," I say quickly. "I would never ask you for financial help. The way you stepped in when my mother . . . the way you took over like you did, and completely pro bono at that, well, it was an amazing gesture of friendship. And all the legal work you did to benefit others"—I pause, smiling—"not many people would do that. It's ... pretty wonderful, actually."

"Well," she says, eschewing my compliments in her very practical manner, "if I were as wonderful as you profess, I'd be able to figure out a way to get us out of this ordeal, but I fear that the cards may be stacked against us."

"We have to keep trying," I say, swallowing hard. "She'd want us to."

Her expression softens. "She would, and we will."

"I might have been able to fix this all immediately if I had the money my dad had set aside for me in his will, but after the medical bills were paid, along with the funeral expenses, there was nothing left. The lawyers told me he'd made an investment that went sideways the year before he died. Nick was furious that we had to call off the kitchen remodel we'd planned, but I didn't care about the money. My father was such a hard worker, and he gave me a beautiful life. It killed me knowing that he carried the burden of that financial loss into his death."

"I heard that he passed," Millie says. "I'm sorry."

"Six years ago," I say. "Complications from a heart attack."

"I was at their wedding," she says.

"You were?"

Millie looks as if she wants to tell me a story, but doesn't quite know where to start—or whether she should.

"Were they in love once, all those years ago?"

She pauses, the corners of her mouth turning upward into

a half-smile. "Your father was a generous man, and . . . he did love your mother, very much."

I picture both my parents at our dinner table in Santa Monica, each of them with their own secrets. "Before my dad died, he told me that he wished things had turned out differently—that she'd stayed." A rush of emotion swirls inside me as I recall the pain and regret in his eyes in his final days, the lonely void I'd spent my teen years trying so hard to fill for him, while simultaneously ignoring my own pain. By then, he was so very weak and his voice was just a whisper. I'll never forget the last time we spoke. He told me he was sorry, and it broke my heart. The only person who owed us both an apology wasn't there.

"I'm sorry," Millie says.

I nod, looking away. "It's just that, all these years, I haven't been able to make sense of it. How could a wife—a mother—just up and leave her family?"

"Valentina, it was all very . . . complicated," she replies.

"Well, you knew them. What happened?"

"I only knew your father for a short time, before they moved to California. I suppose it seemed like a fairy tale from the outside looking in—a dashing, successful American sweeping her off her feet and whisking her off to glamorous California, but over the years, your mother confided in me that there was more to the story."

"Like what?"

Millie's expression remains guarded. "Like any other troubled relationship, theirs was . . . complicated."

I sigh. There was that word again. "Right, I get that people get divorced, obviously. But what I don't understand is how she could run off to London, leaving her daughter behind, and when she gets here, everyone thinks she's a saint. How is that okay?"

"Let me make something clear," Millie retorts. "For your mother, being separated from the child she loved was never *okay*. In fact, she carried that sadness with her until her very last day." She reaches for my hand, giving it a squeeze. "Let her reveal herself to you in her own way. I'm confident that in time, you'll come to understand, and maybe even forgive her."

I nod reluctantly.

"But look—she turned her pain into this beautiful place," she continues, gazing around the store. "Sure, it's your mother's life's work, and even if you don't choose to forgive her, this place is about more than just her. The Book Garden has found its way into the community's collective heart—and that's worth fighting for, don't you think?"

"It is," I say, straightening my shoulders. "And I want you to know that I plan to fight, for as long as it takes."

Millie smiles. "That's my girl."

"I just wish our financial outlook wasn't so grim."

"As you've said, we're going to need to get creative."

I glance out the window and eye the sign hanging beneath the awning above as it sways gently in the breeze. Outside on the sidewalk, a middle-aged woman walks by with an enormous bouquet of flowers in her arms—a compilation of blossoms in varying pink hues—which is when an idea hits me.

"The Book Garden!" I exclaim, turning back to Millie. "That's it! What if we riff on that a bit? Maybe use the extra space up front to sell plants, even flowers? I mean, you've heard of bookstores selling gifts and toys, right?"

"Sure," she says. "But—"

"We could sell houseplants, bunches of daffodils, maybe find someone to help us part-time, so you and I can focus on the business of books. It would be an added expense in the beginning, I know, but it might just pay off." I smile to myself. "Books and green things. They can grow together."

"I loathe houseplants," Millie says before cracking a smile. "But your idea is actually . . . rather brilliant."

"Do you really think so?"

She nods, looking at me for a long moment. "I was wrong about you," she finally says.

I shake my head. "What do you mean?"

"She loved this place so much," Millie begins. "But when she told me her plans to leave the store to you, I . . . worried . . . that you wouldn't love it as much as she did—that you'd unload it as quickly as possible. But, no, Eloise knew what she was doing. She left the Book Garden to you because she knew she was placing it in the most capable, protective hands." She smiles. "Will you forgive me for doubting you?"

"I already have," I say.

"Well," Mille says, glancing at her watch. "I better go unlock the door. It's almost nine." She flips the CLOSED sign in the window over, just as a FedEx truck pulls up outside.

"Oh no," she says, suddenly panicked as she tucks her hair behind her ears and takes a deep breath. "Drat! He's early today."

I watch with amusement as Millie races to the counter where she pulls out a tube of lipstick from her purse, then hurriedly swipes some on. She pretends to busy herself with paperwork as I unlock the door.

A moment later, she looks up, crestfallen to see a tall man

with light blond hair pulled back into a scraggly ponytail. Not Fernando.

"Sign here, please, ma'am," he says.

"Where's . . . Fernando?"

"No clue," he says. "Out sick? Or maybe they put him on a new route. Corporate's always changing things around."

Millie sighs. "Oh."

"I think it's high time you admit it," I say as the truck barrels off. "You have an honest-to-goodness crush on that deliveryman."

"*I do not.*"

"Oh yes, you do. And you know what? I think he has a crush on you, too."

She turns to me, astonished. "You *do*? Really?"

I nod, somehow comforted by the realization that no matter our age, love can apparently find us and turn us into schoolgirls again. "I saw the way he looked at you the other day. I'll bet he's trying to work up the courage to ask you out."

"You're only flattering me," she says, quick to dismiss my romantic notion. "We both know he would never be interested in a woman of *my age*."

"Nonsense," I say, curiously studying her blue eyes, which glimmer in the light. "Were you . . . ever married?" I finally ask.

"No," she says. "But there was someone once, a very long time ago. Someone I deeply admired." Her eyes cloud with memories. "But, alas, he wasn't for me. His heart . . . belonged to someone else."

I instantly regret the question when I see her mouth pinch inward and her presence close up, like a tulip in the cool of night.

"Look at the time," Millie says, collecting herself. "I have so much new inventory to catalogue." And just like that, the glimmer in her eyes is gone.

UPSTAIRS IN MY FLAT, I sign on to @booksbyval and reply to dozens of messages inspired by my last post on collecting as many books as the heart desires. My followers are fully on team #booksmakepeoplehappy.

I start a new post.

> What's your big life dream? My mother's was to have a bookstore, all her own, and she did, and it was, and is, magnificent. But the funny thing I didn't realize about dreams is they can be shared. While I'd never imagined myself running a bookstore in London, and while my relationship with my mother was ... complicated ... she gave me a gift far greater than simply property be- queathed in a will. In fact, she handed me her dream with the hope that I could make it mine. And guess what? I've decided to try.
>
> What's your big dream? I look forward to reading your comments.... #bookishmusings #bookdreams #abookstoreofonesown

LATER THAT EVENING, I knock on Liza's door to tell her all about the idea Millie and I discussed. I've caught her fresh from the shower, but she doesn't seem to mind.

"Okay, it's no secret that the Book Garden needs to up its income in order to pay the estate tax. Millie and I put our heads together, and we came up with some ideas. First, I'm going to link my @booksbyval account to the store's website, where we'll announce plans for a community fundraiser."

"Oh!" Liza squeals. "I love it!"

"But I also had another brainstorm, and this is where you come in."

I explain the plan to convert the front of the store into a plant and flower shop, of sorts. "You could . . . run it for us!" I finally say.

Liza throws her arms around me, squeezing me so tight I can hardly take a breath. "Really?"

I nod. "Yes! I mean, we can't pay much, at least not at first, but we could sure use your green thumb, and you might get a kick out of it. What do you say?"

"I'm a hundred percent in," she says, smiling, her skin still dewy from the shower. "And you don't have to pay me. It'll be a labor of love, and it's the least I can do, especially after those months when I couldn't pay my rent, and your mum wiped my debt clean. She was special like that."

She *was* special. But she also left me. The duality of those two facts makes my heart ache.

"When do you want me to start? I can juggle my job with this, I'm sure."

"How about . . . tomorrow? I mean, whenever you can find time. I have no idea where to begin with plants, let alone flowers. I'll leave all of that to you."

"I've been a personal assistant for most of my adult life, and if I'm good at anything, it's figuring things out." She untwists her towel from her head, revealing her newly colored head of *bright blue* hair.

"My goodness, what . . . happened?"

"Oh," she says. "I thought I'd try something new." She turns to the mirror and fluffs her cerulean curls. "I had to use a god-awful amount of bleach to make sure the color would stick, so I'm afraid my hair might be fried, but I have to say, I rather like how it turned out. What do you think?"

"I think it's very . . . *Liza,*" I say, grinning.

"Yeah, I think so, too," she continues. "I was going for more of a turquoise hue, but, you know, I think this suits me. Would you call it sapphire?"

"Definitely," I say, heading to the door.

"Wait, how's the search for your literary lover going?"

I pull out my copy of *The Last Winter* from inside my bag and eye the cover. "I don't think I'd call it a search, more like a dead end."

"Hold on," Liza says, suddenly snatching the book from my hands. "I don't know why I didn't notice it before."

"What?"

"This stamp on the back cover." She points to it, and together we see the emblem of Queen Mary University.

I shake my head. "What about it?"

"It means that maybe—just maybe—this book was used in a college course. If you could figure out which one, maybe you'll find your guy."

"Well," I say as she hands it back to me, "I admire your tenacity, but don't you think that sounds a *bit* far-fetched?"

"You never know what you might find. Come on, do a little more digging—for me?"

I roll my eyes. "Fine. For *you.*"

Eloise

August 1968

———

ONE NIGHT OVER DINNER, FRANK TOLD ME THAT LABOR Day weekend was coming up. It was a particularly American holiday that was best celebrated with work colleagues. We'd be hosting a dinner party for some of them and their wives.

"Take the checkbook and go shopping at Fred Segal for some new clothes—dresses and some swimsuits," he said.

I went to look through my closet to take inventory, pulling out four dresses, then setting each back on the rod. None would do. I had zero appetite for a shopping trip, but Frank was probably right. My wardrobe was definitely more London than L.A., not that I could fit into any of them given the size of my growing belly. And why on earth had I thought it was a good idea to bring my heavy coats to a climate that only knew sunshine? I made a mental note to ask Bonnie to take them to storage.

As Frank suggested, I took a cab to Fred Segal where I purchased a number of new items that fit my expanding figure, but more important, made me feel as if I could *fit in*. On the night of our first dinner party as a married couple, Frank

was in the living room when I made my way downstairs wearing one of the new dresses. Blue, with a subtle floral print and
an empire waist—I'd loved it the moment I laid eyes on it,
and I hoped he would, too.

"Hello, darling," he said cheerfully. "Is that one of your
new dresses?"

I nodded, searching his eyes for approval. "Do you like it?"

He paused, then stood up, walking closer to inspect the
garment. "It's lovely, really it is, but it's just that my colleagues'
wives tend to dress to the nines. Do have something a bit
more formal, and maybe a different shade? You know I love
you in pink."

I turned back to the stairs, momentarily deflated, but then
I remembered how important the party was to Frank; he
merely wanted every detail to be flawless, so I selected a pink
crepe dress and a pair of vintage earrings I'd purchased at an
estate sale recently. The pale pink gemstones matched the
dress's fabric almost perfectly.

"How's this?" I asked Frank in the living room again,
happy to see the pleased look on his face.

"You are a vision," he said, kissing my cheek.

I hoped my smile concealed the nagging pain I felt in my
lower abdomen. Probably just indigestion—Bonnie's cooking
was divine, but in acquiescing to Frank's preference for heavily spiced dishes, sometimes meals didn't sit well with me. In
any case, I vowed not to let an upset stomach ruin the evening, or worry Frank, who was prone to fuss about anything
these days. When I had a prolonged case of the hiccups the
week prior, he called the obstetrician for reassurance.

"Look at the artful detailing on those earrings," he said.

I grazed my hand against the edge of one of the pink

stones dangling from my ears, grateful to hear the doorbell chime, and that Frank hadn't asked how much I'd paid for them. They were expensive. Quite.

"Ah, our first guests have arrived," he said, taking my hand. "Let's go greet them, shall we?"

AT HALF-PAST TEN, when the last couple had finally departed, I sank into the sofa and kicked off my heels. The party was a success—at least in Frank's eyes. There had been eight couples in attendance, all from his firm, including his superior, Jim, and Gabrielle, his prickly wife, who sat beside me during dinner. I tried my best to make conversation with her, but it was like talking to a brick wall—with frosted pink lipstick.

The other women weren't much warmer, though I did strike up a conversation with one named Connie, who was about my age and nice enough, but all she seemed to want to talk about was her suspicion that her husband was having an affair with a particularly buxom secretary in the office. In an attempt to steer the subject to calmer waters, I told her about the big idea that had been keeping me up at night, and in the very best of ways: opening a bookstore in Santa Monica. Unfortunately, though, Gabrielle took an interest in our conversation and poked her head in.

"Oh, how *adorable*," she said, "A bookstore. So quaint. So London. But, darling, you do realize that nobody reads in L.A., don't you? We watch movies."

The memory was still fresh as Frank slid onto the couch beside me.

"Did you have fun?"

"Yes," I lied.

"They're really wonderful people."

"They are," I said, lying again as I felt my belly tighten and a surge of pain radiate in my lower back. I instantly regretted eating dessert.

"You love California, don't you?" Frank asked, his question more a statement of fact.

I paused for a moment, forcing a smile. "I do like the palm trees, and . . . the sunshine . . . but, Frank, there's something I want to talk to you about." I steadied myself. "I've been thinking that . . . after . . . the baby comes, I'd like to spend time doing what I've always dreamed of."

He set his drink down on the coffee table, a bit distracted. "And what is this dream of yours?"

"Frank, you know—the *bookstore*. I told you about it—in London. I've always wanted to open one, and there's a lovely storefront for rent on Main Street—I walked by it recently— and it would be the perfect location." As his interest waned, my persistence grew, as did the pace of my speech. "I'd sell used books, mostly, but new titles, too. It'll take a bit of fixing up, but I can do most of the work, and . . . oh, Frank . . . can't you just picture it—shelves of books, comfy chairs in every corner!"

I waited for his reply, but he just sat there on the sofa staring at me as if I'd said the most ridiculous—or amusing— thing he'd ever heard. "Darling," he finally said, "let me get this straight. You want to sell *used* books?"

I nodded. "Yes, and I—"

"Eloise, there's no money in used books. It would be a losing proposition from the start." He patted my leg. "If you're looking for something to do, why don't I make a few calls. I'm sure there's a charity board we can get you on. In fact, Jim's wife, Gabrielle, heads the Children's Hospital Society. You could help them out with a fundraiser, after the baby is older, of course."

I didn't tell him that Gabrielle was my least favorite person at the party, nor did I reveal what I overheard her say to one of the other wives beside me—it couldn't be true. In any case, she was the last person I'd want to work with, even if her charity was an admirable one. I merely stared ahead as Frank yawned and retired for the night.

There goes my California dream.

I had too much on my mind to sleep, so I wandered into the kitchen to make a cup of tea, where I found Bonnie finishing the dishes. Her smile vanished when she saw my face. "What's wrong, dear?" While we hadn't known each other long, her kind eyes were a sponge for my pain. "Did you have a nice time at the party?"

"Yes," I said with a sigh. "I guess."

"Tell me what's on your mind."

The emotions I'd kept bottled up since that last day in London were pressing on my heart with such force, I felt like I might explode if I didn't confide in Bonnie. I told her how lonely I'd felt since arriving in America, how Frank had all but dismissed my entrepreneurial ideas.

"Give him time, dear," she said. "Mr. Baker can be set in his ways at times, but he's a generous man, and he loves you. He'll come around."

I *wanted* to believe Bonnie, desperately so, but I struggled to understand. If he professed to love me, as he did, wouldn't he choose to support my dreams instead of disregarding them? But no, I feared that I knew something about

Frank that Bonnie didn't: When he made a decision, it was final.

"Anyway," I said with a sigh as she handed me a cup of chamomile tea, "it's okay."

"It's late, dear," she replied. "Being a hostess is hard work. You need rest. The sun will shine tomorrow."

It reminded me of something my mother—the ultimate optimist—would have said, even in spite of her own troubled life. Yes, the sun would shine tomorrow, and the next day and the next, and I'd continue on the hamster wheel, pretending to be happy, pretending that everything was fine . . . pretending.

"Yes," I said with a yawn. "I should probably turn in." But I couldn't shake what I'd overheard Gabrielle whispering at the table. I didn't dare bring it up with Frank, but I wondered if Bonnie could provide some reassurance.

I stood up, turning to the kitchen door before glancing back to her. "There's just one more thing," I said. "During dinner, one of the women said something that was . . . rather strange."

"Oh?"

"I probably misheard, and perhaps they were referring to another person entirely, but Gabrielle and Connie were talking about another woman, and it sounded like . . . Frank's *first wife*."

Bonnie's eyes widened.

"Which is ridiculous, right? Frank wasn't married before. Surely he would have told me if he was." I searched Bonnie's eyes for validation, but didn't find any. "Wait, is it true?" I paused, my pulse quickening, as Bonnie turned to the kitchen sink, her back to me.

"Bonnie, please, I have to know."

"And you deserve to," she said, shifting to face me, her eyes filled with regret. "But . . . it isn't my place."

"But if not you, then who?"

She nodded hesitantly, her expression troubled and pensive. "All right," she finally said with a sigh. "Please, dear, sit." I slid back into the chair as the muscles in my stomach tensed and the pain I'd felt earlier returned, but this time, more intensely. Still I kept my eyes focused on Bonnie's, not wanting to miss what she was about to say.

"Mr. Baker was married once, a long time ago," she began. "Shame on those women. They were cruel to *her*, too."

I shook my head as the tears welled up. Suddenly Frank's moods, the unexplained distance—it all started to make sense. In London, I was a fantasy, but in California, only a square peg that, try as he might, didn't fit into the round hole—the gaping hole—left by the woman in his past. I was not her, and would never be. Nothing I could do or say would be good enough. "But, Bonnie, why didn't he tell me?"

"Dear one," Bonnie said, pulling me to her ample chest. "He would have, when he was ready."

I tried to picture her, this woman I knew nothing about, other than the fact that she once occupied the bed I shared with Frank. Was she beautiful? Accomplished? Did she break Frank's heart? I wanted to ask Bonnie a thousand questions, but I chose only one.

"Does he still love her?" I closed my eyes tightly, as if instinctively protecting myself from what Bonnie might say. I'd gone from being casual about Frank's love to desperately needing it. And I needed it more than ever when the pain in my stomach radiated to my lower back, releasing a slow trickle of warm liquid that ran down my legs.

"Eloise," she continued as I noticed a patch of bright crimson soak through the edge of my dress. Blood. "Diane died five years ago in a car accident. She was pregnant." She paused, swallowing hard as I clutched my belly. "Frank was at the wheel."

Valentina

———

"YOU READY?" I SAY, POKING MY HEAD INTO LIZA'S FLAT the next morning. We'd agreed to set out for Regent's Park at nine, and I wait in her doorway as she laces up her sneakers.

It's a sunny day, and the park is only a ten-minute walk, so we set out on foot. "I packed a blanket and picked up some treats from Café Flora this morning. We can have a picnic."

"Great," Liza says. "I'm starving."

As we walk, she points out various places, including her ex-boyfriend's flat (his name is Earl and she despises him), along with her favorite pubs, and an old church with a pointy steeple that she tells me she'll get married in someday—when she finds the man of her dreams, of course. I smile to myself as she chatters on about this and that, until we find the entrance to the park. A gravel, tree-lined pathway deposits us on the edge of a large lawn, buzzing with activity, mostly children playing and a handful of people flying kites. The scene reminds me of Mary Poppins's mythical chalk-art excursion.

"Look at the photographers over there," Liza says, pointing ahead. "It might be a celebrity."

I eye the photoshoot in progress, where a blond woman

sits on a stool in a pink sequined evening gown, which looks jarringly out of place against the backdrop of the park, but maybe that's the idea? Her hair is swept up in a loose bun, and when she turns in our direction to adjust her necklace, I recognize her immediately—but not because she's the celebrity Liza had hoped. "Wait, I think I know that person."

"You do?"

I nod. "It's . . . Fiona. She's the girlfriend of this guy who came into the store recently—Eric."

Liza shakes her head. "I don't think I've met him."

I watch as a stylist smooths a flyaway from Fiona's temple. "He grew up coming to the bookstore. He knew my mother. Anyway, his girlfriend, Fiona, isn't really a reader, and he is, so he asked me to help him find something to entice her."

"That's adorable," Liza says. "I'm telling you, a man who thinks of special things like that is rare in this world."

"Well, I hope she found the book as special as his gesture." We continue on, but when Fiona waves at me, I pause and walk over to her.

"Valentina, right?"

"Yes," I say. "And this is my friend Liza."

"Hi," she says, her expression feigning embarrassment, though it's obvious that she's someone who likes the attention. "How funny do I look in this gown in the middle of the park?"

"It's . . . gorgeous," I say.

"Well, when *D Magazine* asked to feature me in a cover shoot, I had no idea it would entail freezing my ass off in a ballgown." She smiles at the photographer.

"*D Magazine?*"

"*Design Magazine,*" she says. "It's the *most important* interior design publication. Everyone reads it. Oh but, right, you're not in the design world—duh!"

"Right," I say, smiling mechanically. "Well, congratulations, on the cover. That's a . . . a huge accomplishment."

"Thank you," she says as the stylist dusts her nose with a makeup brush.

"Oh, Eric came in the other day looking for a book for you. Did you—"

"Eric and his mission to have us be a couple of old bookworms together," she says with a sentimental eye roll. "I mean, is he adorable, or what?"

"It was sweet of him, yes. I hope you liked *The Time Traveler's Wife*? It's a favorite of mine. The way the author weaves the past and present is—"

"Wait," she says, interrupting me with a little laugh. "You actually think I've already read it? With a schedule like mine?"

"Oh, I . . . I just thought that—"

"Eric *thinks* I read it, and that's all that matters. But, just between us girls, he has no idea that I saw the movie years ago."

"Fiona, sorry to interrupt," the male photographer interjects. "We need to set up a bit farther down. The light isn't quite right here."

"We won't keep you," I say quickly. I wave politely, but our interaction has left me conflicted. Who would lie to their significant other about anything, much less whether they've read a book or not?

"She's a piece of work," Liza says when we're a good distance away.

I shrug. "I'll admit, she's not my favorite."

"What, you don't know *D Magazine*? The most important publication of the modern era!"

I laugh as we make our way to the other side of the park. "Enough of that. Let's go find Matilda!"

The fountain isn't far, just around the bend, and when I see the iconic statue, I instantly understand my mother's infatuation with it.

"She's . . . beautiful," I say, eyeing the woman made of bronze. Her dress is delicate and feminine, and her face is so lifelike—even if it's cast in metal and not flesh. She holds her hand to her forehead, perhaps to block the sun, but I can't help but wonder if she's searching for something—or someone—just like me.

Liza senses my curiosity and follows the trajectory of the statue's eyes, which seem to gaze out at a patch of grass ahead.

Ask Matilda, and she'll offer you her velvet green blanket.

I follow Liza and spread the blanket out on the grass, smiling at the thought of my mother sitting on this very same patch of grass, looking out at the park toward Matilda—each of them with their secrets, and me with mine.

It was too soon for daffodils to bloom, so I looked around for other clues.

. . . but do keep an eye out for the foxes wearing gloves: They'll show you the way to the little house. I'll be waiting . . .

I hand Liza a croissant and help myself to one, too. "I don't see a little house, or have any idea what foxgloves look like."

"They're purple," she says. "But you won't find them this time of year."

"Oh," I say, crestfallen.

"Wait," she says, leaping to her feet and walking ahead. I

follow close behind, watching as she kneels beside a thyme-carpeted garden bed and lifts up a pale brown twig. "Look, a foxglove seed pod."

We found the foxgloves, but where's the *little house*? I survey the soil around the garden beds, but there are only pine cones and shriveled leaves.

"Have you lost something, miss?"

I look up to see an older man in coveralls holding a rake, presumably a park gardener.

"No," I say, quickly standing up and walking closer. "But I am trying to *find* something. Before my mother died, she left a sort of scavenger hunt for me, with one clue leading to the next. The most recent one led me here, to Matilda, and the flowers." I pull the note card from my pocket, and when I show it to him, his eyes get big.

"Why, you must be her daughter," he says, astonished.

"Eloise's daughter, yes."

His smile is warm. "She said you'd be coming. Your mother was a regular here. She loved this corner of the park." He points to the blanket on the lawn where Liza is. "She'd sit there for hours, just like that, reading." He extends his hand. "I'm Louis."

"Valentina," I say with a smile, before turning back to my mother's note. "She wrote something about a 'little house,' see?" I point to the line. "Do you have any idea what she might have meant?"

"Ah yes," he says. "Let me show you."

I follow as he walks ahead, our collective footsteps producing a symphony of gravel crunching beneath our feet. He stops in front of an old oak tree, its trunk thick and knotted.

"Here we are," he says. "The Little House."

I shake my head, confused. "But *what is it?*"

"If your mum were here, I suspect she'd tell you to use your imagination," he says with a wink.

And she would. I think back to my childhood, when we'd collected colorful rocks together on the beach in Santa Monica. I'd ask her where each one came from, and she'd encourage me to make up a story for every one of them, and together, we did. *"This is Sam, the gray stone. He's a very serious rock, who doesn't like it when people pick him up. And this is Ethel, the beige rock. She has four children, and nine baby grand-rocks."* I can almost hear the waves crashing onto the shore as the wind rustles the branches of the oak tree, and it makes my heart ache.

I banished her voice from my heart for so long, but now I can *hear* it: *"Use your imagination."*

Steadying myself, I survey the base of the trunk, where the tree's roots bulge out of the soil, like octopus's appendages. My childhood voice echoes in the breeze: *"Mummy, do trees have eight roots like octopuses have eight arms?"* I place my hand on the trunk, imagining a well-worn face in the jagged edges of its bark, before reaching higher up, where I press my finger against a large, rounded knot just above my head. To my surprise, it releases, as if held in place by a hinge.

When Louis clears his throat, I startle, expecting an owl to fly out, but then I remember the old oak tree in the yard of our home in Santa Monica—with a prominent knot, just like this one. My mother named it the "Little Fairy House," where she left little treats, notes, and toys inside for me to find.

"You've found it," he says. "The Little House."

I reach my hand into the hollow of the tree and pull out the envelope inside. The paper is yellowed and weathered by the elements, but my name is written clearly on the front—in her handwriting. I tear the edge and pull out the note card.

My darling girl,

You've found me, and I'm so glad. Did you say hello to Matilda? She's an old friend. When I was little, your grandmother took me to this very park, and I would sit and watch her for hours. I used to think that if I stared at her long enough, she might come to life and tell me her secrets. Alas, she never did. But maybe she'll tell them to you. Look after her, please? Oh, Val, I have so much to say. And it gives me so much comfort knowing you're reading this right now. As I'm writing you at this moment, my health is failing. It isn't fair. In fact, it's cruel. We have so much more life to share together, and I hoped we'd have all of those moments. But I'll have to find another way to make you know how much you are loved. I'll always be here, loving you, but I want to leave you with two more surprises. The first, you'll find by paying attention to these words from Cicero (though, I'll admit, I'm partial to libraries):

"If you have a garden and a library, you have everything you need."

My sweet daughter, do you agree?
Come find me. I'll be waiting.

Love,
Mummy

Eloise

July 12, 1977
————

I HELD THE VINTAGE STRING OF PEARLS TO THE NAPE of my neck, eyeing my reflection in the window. Nine years had passed since I moved to L.A., and, in some ways, little had changed since I stepped off that airplane. California still felt as strange as it did then. I'd thought about that earlier this morning as I took a cab to the ritzy Pacific Palisades neighborhood for an estate sale that had gotten a lot of buzz in the newspaper—and judging by the assortment of treasures I'd found, for good reason. In fact, it took all my self-restraint to stifle my excitement when I'd discovered a beautifully preserved copy of Hemingway's *A Moveable Feast* that even bore the faint mark of the author's signature on the title page.

"That necklace looks stunning on you," a fellow bargain-hunter said, catching my eye. "Definitely, get it. Your husband will think you're a goddess."

I smiled at the kind stranger, but she had no idea how wrong she was. There was no necklace on earth, I feared, that would make Frank think I was a goddess.

I'd come to Los Angeles as a young bride, hopeful that I'd made the right choice, even if it was my only one. The pregnancy bound us together, replacing my hesitation with duty, which remained even after the miscarriage and its onslaught of pain. Frank and I grew increasingly distant, and yet, somehow, the chains that bound us together were tighter still. It made no difference if I'd left my heart in London. We'd created a life together, and lost it. For that, our lives would be forever entwined

Frank was appalled when I suggested the baby—a boy—be cremated. At the time, things were so bad between us that I considered filing for divorce and imagined taking his ashes home with me—to London. But Frank insisted that *his son* be buried in a plot beside his parents—and first wife—in a local cemetery, and that was that. I was too heartbroken and weak to argue, and I was still bleeding at the burial. A part of him—Frank, Jr.—was still leaving my body as the tiny casket was lowered into the earth.

After that, we didn't argue much, nor did we really speak at all. We merely floated—passing each other in the house like ghosts in the night, each so haunted by the past that we were unable to remain in the present.

I paid for my estate sale purchases—including the pearl necklace—then caught a cab back home thinking about something Bonnie had said to me years ago. "Grief is a treacherous journey, but it doesn't last forever."

What if she's wrong? I asked myself, lying by the pool later that day. *What if it does last forever?*

I looked up from the chaise longue when I heard the front door open and close. "Bonnie?" I said, squinting at the sliding door, confused because it was Tuesday—her day off.

Instead, it was Frank, and his appearance on the patio startled me. "I thought you'd already left for Hong Kong," I said, sitting up. The two-week trip had been on the calendar for months, and, as I understood, with an imminent business merger, it was a very important one.

"Darling," he said softly, sitting down beside me. "I . . . canceled the trip."

I adjusted the right shoulder strap of my new blue bikini. "Why?"

"Eloise," he continued. "We need to talk."

This is it. He's going to suggest we divorce.

I imagined myself packing. It wouldn't take long—I'd only bring the essentials. It would sting, of course, like the final opus of a tragic opera, but at least I'd have an ending. And I could finally go *home*. Of course, I'd have to make a new life for myself. I had nothing waiting for me there, except for Millie. She had a flat and a successful career as a barrister. I could stay with her until I got back on my feet. It would be like old times, as if I'd never even been to California. As if . . . none of it ever happened. All these years, I'd felt unable to break from the confines of our union, but what if Frank could . . . set me free?

The wheels in my mind were turning so fast that when Frank began caressing my shoulder, at first, I barely noticed his touch. But then our eyes met, and I saw the longing in his gaze. It was clear, then, that he wasn't about to say goodbye.

"Eloise . . ." Frank continued. "These years have been hard, for both of us. I haven't been there for you. I only pray that you can . . . forgive me. If you're willing, I . . . want to try to mend things."

My book fell to the ground. I'd been rereading my favorite, *The Last Winter*, about the lonely ballerina Cezanne, who found herself caught up in a complicated love affair. But in some ways, mine was even more so. There was Frank, finally opening his heart to me, but I didn't know if I could open mine to him.

I felt caught between Cezanne's fictitious world and my own, but then I reminded myself: *The ending to Cezanne's story will never change, but mine can—if I try.*

"Darling," Frank said. "I work and travel and leave you here alone far too much. You're lonely, and it's my fault. I'm so sorry about . . . us. I'm deeply sorry about what our marriage has become."

I slowly nodded, taking in his words, but struggling to process them. *I've never felt that Frank understands me, but is he finally trying?*

"Let me take you out tonight. Let's get dressed up and have fun like we used to . . . in London."

I thought of our weekly dates when he was courting me. It felt like a lifetime ago. I did appreciate the care he took, the way he surprised me with reservations to all the best establishments. The way he adored me. How I missed being adored, being noticed. In California, I felt veritably invisible, wandering in and out of the pages of novels, one endlessly sunny day blurring into the next.

But in that moment, I was suddenly back at Rhett's Supper Club. Frank's adoring eyes were fixed on me. It was also the night I saw Edward with another woman. The night I accepted Frank's proposal of marriage and took a bold step forward—to a new life.

Then I remembered what Bonnie told me shortly after I'd arrived in California. "Frank needs you."

Edward never needed me.

I began to wonder if I needed him, too. Needed him in

more ways than I'd ever imagined, my American cowboy. We'd had better days, but maybe we could have them still?

"A night out sounds . . . nice," I said, my face softening into a smile.

He smiled back at me, his pale green eyes matching the hue of the pool. As he reached for my hand, I wondered what had sparked Frank's change of heart, what had melted all those years of ice. But whatever it was, it didn't matter. We were at a fork in the road. I could explore the next leg of our journey, or I could turn back—alone.

"So, what do you say?" he asked, searching my eyes. "Will you let me take you out?"

I felt pulled in both directions—the road forward, and the road back. True, I wanted to go home, desperately so. But Frank's eyes beckoned. His expression was filled with anticipation, but also something I hadn't seen in so long: love.

"Yes," I finally said.

WE DROVE TO A QUIET Italian restaurant in Venice Beach. Frank did most of the talking, content to remain on a surface level—work, his plans to install a sauna in the backyard— which was fine. It was as if we were two wartime friends getting reacquainted after knowing each other on the battlefield. Some subjects were better left untouched.

Instead, I told him about my walks around the neighborhood, my favorite café—small details that two strangers might share upon meeting, not two people who'd been married almost a decade. But if we were to start over again, we'd have some catching up to do. I shared how I took joy in finding objects from estate sales and shells from the beach. I didn't dare bring up *Diane,* especially after broaching the subject a few weeks after the miscarriage, when I was still on pain medication and highly emotional. *Do you still love her? Am I merely a replacement? Why did you keep this from me?* Frank's response was far from reassuring. In fact, he shut down entirely. I realized then that the subject was, and would always be, off-limits—a vault that had long been locked, even if he still held the key. If we were going to reconcile, I would have to abide by those rules.

When our dinner conversation waned, I decided to talk about flowers.

"In London, daffodils were my favorite," I told him. "Here in Los Angeles, I'm partial to roses, oh, and fuchsias. Did you know they're the only native plant that flowers at the height of summer?" I smiled, my singsong voice sounding foreign in my ears, but at least I was *trying.* If Frank could take a step forward, I could, too. "They'll be in bloom soon."

"I wish I had a bouquet to give you now," he said, cautiously reaching across the table for my hand. "My California rose."

I couldn't help but wonder if Frank showered his first wife with the same sort of compliments, at this very restaurant, even. The thought threatened to poison our evening, and so were the lingering memories in my heart—but I decided not to let them. Instead, I smiled back at him warmly.

"You look absolutely stunning tonight," he continued. "Just as lovely as the day I first met you. Remember that?"

I squeezed his hand as I took a sip of the wine he'd ordered, a crisp Nebbiolo that immediately warmed my cheeks, or maybe it was just Frank's gaze.

"You were standing in line at that bistro, and I bumped

into you like an idiot." He paused, smiling at me the way he used to all those years ago, the earnest American who wore his heart on his sleeve. Where had he been hiding all these years?

"And you spilled my tea," I added.

He laughed, before his eyes filled with emotion. "It was ... the best thing I ever did, and I mean that, Eloise."

A burst of emotion bubbled up inside of me, too, and I blinked back tears. The California sun may have been warm, but until tonight, I'd mostly felt cold in Frank's world. I wanted to believe that I could change, that *we* could change.

I felt tipsy as we left the restaurant and clutched Frank's arm on the walk to the car. Out on the street, we passed a group of hippies, one of them strumming a guitar with a smoldering cigarette dangling from his lips. Frank tossed a few bills into his open guitar case.

He unlocked the car door and helped me inside, but I reached for his hand before he could step away. I pulled him closer, pressing my lips to his.

"Wow," he said. "What was that for?"

"For nothing," I said. "And everything."

FRANK UNLOCKED THE DOOR and set his keys on the entryway table. The tick of the clock in the living room pierced the still air, lit only by moonlight streaming through the windows. Frank and I stood together at the base of the stairs. I knew he was about to tell me good night, to follow the wellworn path to his own bedroom and leave me to head to mine—alone—which was the routine we'd kept all these years after the miscarriage. At first it was a necessity—Frank had to get up early for work, and my sleep schedule was all turned around, so I stayed up late reading in bed. Books gave me comfort when I needed it most, but the light bothered him, so he took up in the guest bedroom. In the beginning it was an excuse, but it quickly morphed into the status quo.

I wondered if we had the strength to break down those walls, and when I searched Frank's eyes, I found my answer, and a memory of my mother. She used to tell me the story of the night I came to be—the night she felt a shift in her heart. It began from a place deep inside her, she said, like an untapped well bubbling up from the depths of a parched, sand-swept desert. She knew the moment I was conceived. It was love, she said, but not for my father—love for the child she was meant to carry. Me.

As Frank kissed my cheek good night and turned to the stairs, I thought of my mother, her essence coursing through my veins as my husband's eyes searched my face.

"Don't go," I whispered, letting my lips find his as he turned back to me.

I felt him hesitating and sensed his internal struggle. Losing one child was horrific, but Frank had lost two and his fear was palpable. But the sadness between us had festered for far too long; we were both on the verge of drowning in it. And I knew something he didn't. I felt it.

When I kissed him again, he yielded to me, pressing his body against mine with a force I'd never felt from him before, a thirst that had to be quenched.

Upstairs, moonlight filtered into my bedroom window, illuminating Frank's face as his body rose and fell against mine. I looked into his eyes, laser-focused on mine, and studied the way the muscles in his cheeks tensed and released, like a tug-of-war between pleasure and pain. "Tell me you love me," he said, cupping my face in his hands.

"Darling, you know I do," I said.

He shook his head. "But you . . . never say it."

I realized, for the first time, that I'd underestimated the fragility of Frank's heart. As much as he'd feared any more trauma and pain, he also doubted my love for him.

"Say the words," he pleaded, his body hovering above mine. "Please. I . . . need to hear them."

I parted my lips to speak, but nothing came out. My mouth felt as if it had been cast in cement. "I . . ."

Frank's gaze was glued to mine, his heart hanging on every passing second.

"I . . ." I bit my lip, hating myself for my hesitation, for marrying a man I could never give all of my heart to. I might not have been able to force myself to love him in the way he wanted me to, but I could make myself say the words he deserved to hear. For Frank, I could pretend.

"I love you."

His breath quickened as he kissed my neck, my collarbone, my breasts. I counted the stars twinkling outside the window, as the energy from Frank's body surged through mine.

A moment later, he lay beside me, drifting off into the most peaceful sleep. He was unaware, of course, that the tiniest new life was forming inside of me. But I knew.

I was meant to be *her* mother.

Valentina

———

THE FOLLOWING WEEK BROUGHT MORE OF THE SAME
for the Book Garden. While the uptick in online orders was
encouraging, it wasn't nearly enough to pay the enormous
tax bill. Instead of losing heart, we worked to get the front-
end flower enterprise going, while also planning the details
of the community fundraiser. We picked a date, and Jan offered to host the event at Café Flora, which was a godsend.
My task this week is ticket sales. We'd need to bring in at
least one hundred and fifty attendees to reach our funding
goal, and even with that, the store's future still looked grim.
But Millie and I agreed that we wouldn't close our doors
without a proper fight, and both of us were prepared to enter
the ring.

I'd get to the work of the fundraiser soon, but first, I show
her my mother's latest clue that I'd found in Regent's Park.
She nods, taking me to a nearby shelf, where I find two copies
of Cicero's work. Alas, neither contains another envelope.

"Now what?" I say, turning to Millie with a sigh.

"I don't know. But don't lose heart. You'll find it."

I reshelve the books as the store's bells jingle. It's Eric, the
long-suffering boyfriend. Millie heads to the counter to greet

him, and I wave, joining Liza at the front of the store, where she's working on our new botanical endeavors.

"Is that the guy who's dating Miss Prim from the park?" she whispers.

I nod.

"Is it just me or are they an odd match?"

"Definitely," I say. But what do I know? I thought Nick and I were a great match, but he left me for a woman who posts Instagram photos of herself in pink bikinis.

"Valentina," Eric says, smiling, "I just wanted to stop by to tell you that Fiona loved the book. She raved about it, in fact!" He pauses, beaming with gratitude that's palpable. "I just wanted to say thanks."

I don't have the heart to tell him about our recent interaction at the park, where she'd recounted a slightly different story. "Well, that's . . . wonderful," I say, returning his smile. "A new reader is born."

He nods. "Fingers crossed."

I glance at the clock. "Wow, it's already noon. I should probably get going. I have an . . . appointment." I told no one about my mission, to visit a professor at Queen Mary University who I hoped would have more information about my copy of *The Last Winter*. At first, Liza's suggestion had seemed far-fetched, but when I finally decided to call the university, a woman in the English literature department offered some interesting background. While the book wasn't being used in any courses at present, a quick computer search revealed that it once was—seventeen years ago, in fact. She gave me the professor's name, and today I planned to meet him to see if he remembered anything about his former pupil Daniel Davenport.

"I have to run, as well," Eric says. "Perhaps we could walk together?"

"Oh," I say, reaching for my bag behind the counter. I feel Liza's gaze on me, but I don't make eye contact. "Sure."

"Nice day," Eric says outside.

"Yeah," I say, smiling. "It sort of reminds me of Seattle on one of our rare sunny days."

"Your hometown?"

"Well, I was born in Los Angles, but Seattle's where I ended up. I left recently, after my husband and I split."

"Oh, I'm sorry."

"It's okay," I say, momentarily surprised by my own confession, and that it hasn't insinuated the usual wave of pain and self-loathing. Eric is easy to talk to, and although I barely know him, I somehow feel comfortable pulling back a few layers. "We were poorly matched from the beginning, but I was too stubborn to see it."

It's hard to tell from his expression if he feels sorry for me, or if my words have resonated on a deeper level.

"Anyway," I continue, "some things are just not meant to be, and I'm learning to make peace with that, but it's not easy."

He smiles. "Well, when you do crack the code, will you please share it with me?"

"Sure," I say with a laugh.

"What's Seattle like?"

"It's not all that different from London," I continue. "When the sun comes out, people get manic."

Eric laughs as I continue.

"When I first moved there, the stretch of dark days seemed endless—I mean, compared to California. But when the sun finally comes out, you can literally feel the city's collective mood swing." I recall the way my usually reclusive neighbors would venture outdoors on a rare sunny day, triumphantly greeting one another, tending their barbecues, stampeding the local plant nurseries to buy pansies by the truckload. London has a similar vibe today. The sidewalks brim with smiling faces and every corner pub is packed to capacity.

"Where are you heading today?" Eric asks.

"Oh, I just have a few things to . . . take care of," I reply vaguely. "And you?"

He glances at his wristwatch. "I'm meeting a contractor at my flat this afternoon, but I have a little time. If you're not in too much of a rush, maybe we could . . . grab lunch somewhere? I'm starving."

"Sure," I reply, my stomach growling at that very moment. "I actually haven't eaten anything today." Café Flora is just ahead, so I suggest we stop there, and he agrees. When we arrive, Jan greets us, and I'm surprised to find that she and Eric know each other.

"Hey, doll," she says, giving him a hug. "How's your father doing? I heard he had heart surgery."

"Yeah, last month," he replies. "He's better, but not out of the woods quite yet. It'll be a long recovery."

Jan nods. "Well, he's lucky to have you looking out for him after your mum passed."

"Thanks," he says. "I do my best."

She smiles, glancing toward the kitchen. "Well, I should get back. It's good to see you, sweetie. You, too, Val." She winks at me before weaving through the dining room.

I eye the menu and decide on the Cobb salad, which I order when a young waiter stops by our table. Eric selects the same, but with chicken.

"I'm sorry about your mother," I say a moment later.

"Thanks," he says. "Something else we have in common, I guess."

"So you grew up here, in Primrose Hill?"

"Yes," he replies. "Just around the corner."

"Wow," I say, a bit envious of Eric's seemingly idyllic childhood. "You must have wonderful memories."

"All of my memories are with Mum," he says, "which makes it so hard. My dad worked a lot. He was always busy. I think it took Mum's death to really make him pause and realize what he missed along the way, you know?"

I nod.

"But I suppose that's the unlikely gift of experiencing a loss, it makes you see things more clearly."

I don't tell him that my own mother's passing seems to have had the opposite effect.

"Well, I'm very sorry for your loss."

He smiles. "She's been gone for twelve years now, but it never gets easier, especially here in Primrose Hill, where every single corner brings back a memory. She used to drop me off at your mum's bookstore before her hair appointments down the block—for read-alouds with Eloise."

I feel a lump in my throat, but quickly collect myself as he continues.

"Mum was my whole world. She gave me a magical childhood."

"Mine did, too," I say, surprised by my admission. "At least, for the time we were together."

He nods. "I just wish I could have known her better in my adult life, and that she could know me in mine." He sits up straighter in his chair and runs his hand through his hair with a sigh. "Sorry, I'm rambling."

"No, not at all," I say quickly. "In fact, you bring up an excellent point. What you just said—about knowing someone, but not *knowing* them . . . it's so true—especially when it comes to our parents. They lived entire lives before we were born, weathered their own private storms, but as children, we don't know them that way."

He nods in agreement.

"Like you, my mother was also my whole world, and when she moved to London, I was never quite able to fill the hole she left. I spent a long time feeling confused by her sudden departure, and later angry. But now that I'm here"—I pause, exhaling deeply—"I'm beginning to realize that there's more to her story than I knew. I still feel the pain of her absence, but I'm . . . trying to understand it, if that makes any sense."

Eric's eyes burst with compassion, and it warms me. "It absolutely makes sense, and I can't begin to imagine what you must have been through. But if it's any consolation at all, you should know that Eloise talked about her daughter—the amazing Valentina—so often that it was almost as if you were a fixture in the bookstore."

I smile. "Really?"

He nods as the waiter sets our salads on the table. We both forgo the fresh-ground pepper.

"Were your parents ever happy together?" he asks.

I shrug. "I mean, yes, in an outside-looking-in sort of way. But even as a child, I suppose I always knew that something was off. They led separate lives."

"Mine too," he says. "I was the one thing that—"

"Kept them together," we both say, then laugh.

Eric smiles, but there's hesitation in his eyes. "I guess not everyone gets a fairy tale."

I adjust my napkin in my lap. "And you don't think you're one of the lucky ones?"

"No, I mean, I do—I mean, I hope so." He pauses. "Fiona and I *are* lucky, and happy—I guess. But watching my parents all those years made me extra cautious about forever, if that makes any sense."

I nod.

"She wants to get married, have a family, and I do as well, but . . ." He rubs his forehead. "I just want to be certain, you know?"

"Oh, I know."

"Sorry," Eric says, setting his fork down. "I'm oversharing."

"No, your honesty is refreshing."

"Well, I'm glad we're becoming friends, Valentina."

"Me too," I say, smiling.

I decide to tell him about the scavenger hunt my mother left for me, and he's immediately fascinated.

"That's brilliant," he says.

I fill him in on her latest clue, left in Regent's Park— omitting the bit about running into Fiona—and his eyes widen.

"Of course, she'd bring up Cicero," he says, beaming. "But it's not a book she wants you to find."

"Then what is it?"

He scratches his head and looks off into the distance as if sorting through a flurry of memories. "When my mum used to take me to Eloise's read-aloud hours, all the children would sit around her on the carpet and before she began, she'd pass around this little wooden box and we'd each pick a lollipop from inside. It was magic." He smiles. "That's it, Valentina."

"I don't understand."

"The box—I can still picture it, like it was yesterday. It was made of mahogany, with a shiny varnish. But here's the thing: On the top, there was an engraving that read: 'Cicero's Sentiments.' I had no idea what it meant at the time, and as a kid, I read it phonetically, at least in my mind, as 'kick-er-o.'" He laughs. "But looking back, I think it was very telling of your mum's literary humor. I mean, Cicero was one of the greatest thinkers of the Roman era, right? And she kept candy inside. It was brilliant."

She *was* brilliant.

"Anyway, if you can find the box, I bet you'll get your next clue."

"Wow," I say, astonished. "Thank you. I'll ask Millie about it."

Our conversation shifts to other topics as we finish our meals. I ask him about his work, and he tells me he's a journalist, which piques my curiosity, but Jan returns to the table before I can ask him more.

Eric reaches for his wallet, but she insists on treating us, and waves us off before we can stage a protest.

"That was fun," he says on the street outside. "Maybe we can get together again sometime?"

"I'd like that," I say, and then we part ways—he in his cab, and me in mine.

I tell the driver to take me to Queen Mary University, then lean back against the seat smiling to myself as I think about the last hour at Café Flora. If I ever do meet Daniel Davenport, I wonder if—and if I'm being completely honest with myself, *hope*—he'd be a little, or a lot, like Eric.

WHEN I SEE TOWER Bridge approaching, I ask the driver to drop me off so I can take in its iconic structure up close. I think of my mother's stories of her beloved London, which most often included references to this very bridge—a stalwart of her formative years. She told of riding her old bike, with an attached basket and a bell on the handlebar, pedaling gleefully, wind in her hair, across the River Thames. I knew her childhood in one of London's poorer neighborhoods hadn't been easy, but to me, her stories still seemed like the very best fairy tales, and I longed to live in them.

I follow the path that leads to the bridge's pedestrian walkway, dodging an oncoming jogger and brushing off a stray droplet of his sweat when it hits my arm before zigzagging past a group of tourists ambling along slowly behind their guide. When I reach the other side, I check the navigation on my phone and realize I'd miscalculated the walking distance to the university, which is still forty-five minutes away. I could hail a cab, of course, but the sunshine beckons, and I decide to keep going. These are my mother's old streets, after all. And even though we're separated by so many years, I cautiously let myself imagine her walking beside me now, our strides in step, as she shows me her homeland. It's almost as if she were whispering in my ear. "Do you see that corner over there. It's where I skinned my knee walking home from school when I was eleven. The pain wasn't nearly as bad as my embarrassment that Johnny Easton saw the whole thing. And,

Val, look, the old Cornish Café. On the last Sunday of each month, if my mum had any spare change, she'd take me there for breakfast."

I think of what Eric and I spoke about at lunch, about knowing our parents as adults. Would we be friends, my mother and me, if she were here right now, if I could . . . forgive her?

After I cross the bridge, I walk on, lost in my thoughts, while checking the navigation on my phone from time to time. Eventually, Queen Mary University's sprawling campus appears in the distance. I round the next corner, then follow a brick walkway, where a regal-looking white stone structure stands in the distance. It looks like a palace, which is fitting, given the sign at the entrance that reads QUEEN'S BUILDING. A clock tower in matching pale stone juts out above the trees, presiding over students as they scurry in and out of the entrance.

I ask one of them for directions to the English department. She shifts her headphones to the side as I repeat the question, then points to a building just ahead, on the left. I thank her and continue on until I find the entrance and follow two backpack-clad students into the lobby.

"I'm here to see Mr. Harvey Ellison," I say to the front-desk receptionist, who has the look of someone who isn't interested in doing any favors.

"Do you have an appointment?" she asks, smacking her gum.

I immediately regret not calling ahead. I mean, I intended to, but then I had lunch with Eric and . . .

"No, I'm afraid I don't," I say. "But I only need to speak to him briefly. It won't take more than a few minutes."

"Are you a student?" she asks, her suspicion growing.

"No, I—"

"Then I'm afraid you'll have to do things in the proper fashion and make an appointment in advance. Mr. Ellison is quite a busy man, and I'm afraid we have a no-drop-in policy."

I sigh, taking a step back as a nearby classroom door opens and students begin flooding out. A male student waits outside as I decide what to do. "Excuse me, Professor Ellison," he says a moment later when a man in a tweed suit appears in the hallway. "I have a question about today's assignment."

Encouraged by my good fortune, I linger until their brief exchange ends, then seize the opportunity to approach. Fortunately, the watchdog receptionist has stepped away from her desk.

"Professor Ellison," I say, catching his eye. "I'm sure you must be very busy, but may I have a word?"

He looks at me quizzically, then nods. "Sure, but I only have a minute. The last class ran over, and I'm sorely behind."

"Of course," I say, following him down the hall to his office.

"Now," he says, running his hand through his salt-and-pepper hair, and for a moment, I remember how much I used to love the kiss of gray at Nick's temples. "Is this about your semester's-end paper?"

"No, no," I say, momentarily flattered that I'd passed as one of his twentysomething pupils. "I'm . . . not a student. I actually came here about something else." I reach into my bag and pull out my copy of *The Last Winter*.

He grins, eyeing the book in my hands. "Ah, such an overlooked gem. It's been years since I've dipped into that one. If I didn't have so many bloody papers to grade, I'd—"

"I couldn't agree more," I say, quickly getting to the subject at hand. "And that's why I'm here. It might sound crazy, but I'm sort of . . . on a *mission* to find the person who once owned this book."

He cocks his head to the right, then turns to look at the expansive bookshelf spanning the wall behind his desk. "I have my own copy somewhere in here, so I can assure you, the book isn't mine."

"Yes, I know," I continue. "I just hoped you might recall something"—I take a step closer—"about this particular one." I hand him the book. "Look inside. There's a name."

He scratches his head. "I've had so many students over the years, I'm afraid it's impossible to remember them all."

"Right, of course," I say defeatedly, reaching for the book, but he doesn't hand it back. Instead, he pulls out the reading glasses in his shirt pocket and slips them on before examining the writing on the inside cover. "Daniel Davenport," he says, looking up at me with a glimmer of recollection in his eyes.

"I know it's been so many years, but . . . I couldn't help but wonder if you might remember him."

He flips through the pages, stopping to read some of the notes, before looking up at me with wide eyes. "I *do* know this book."

I press my hand on his desk, eager to hear whatever he might say next.

"Yes," he continues. "These notes in the margins . . . I'd almost forgotten."

"Forgotten what?"

"One of my students gave it to me at the end of that semester."

I search his face for understanding. "Gave it to you?"

"Yes," he says. "I made an announcement about donating used books for future classes. At the time, we were experiencing shortages at the campus bookstore due to order issues with our book supplier. Several students offered, but I distinctly remember this one." He opens the book again to examine its pages. "He said it was marked up, and he didn't know if it would be acceptable to pass along. I remember reading a page or two and thinking just the opposite. The notes were quite insightful." He hands the book back to me, then turns to his computer, where he begins typing. "Let me just have a look at our alumni database." More typing. "I'm probably breaking the university's privacy rules right now, but a literary mystery is a worthy cause," he adds with a wink.

I smile, waiting in rapt attention as he shifts his screen for me to see. "It seems that the fellow you're looking for is right here in London, at the Snow Goose."

"The Snow Goose?"

"A pub down in Mayfair." He smiles. "According to our records, he owns the place. A rather curious use of an English literature degree, if you ask me, but to each his own."

My eyes brighten. *The Snow Goose.*

A BLAST OF COLD AIR hits my cheeks as I step off the tube. So much for the sunshine. Dark clouds have moved in, and as I check Google Maps, I feel a raindrop hit my cheek. I quicken my pace as the rain intensifies, but it's no use; within a minute, I'm soaked. I look right, then left, and just ahead, I see it—the glow of lamplight, a quaint blue awning, and a sign hanging over the entrance with an artistic rendition of a coat of arms. The Snow Goose.

It's noisy and packed inside, as if everyone within a five-block radius has chosen this pub to wait out the rainstorm. Fortunately, I notice an open seat at the bar, and I make a beeline to snag it before hanging my soggy jacket on a hook under the counter and smoothing my wet hair.

"What can I get you, miss?" the bartender asks.

"A dirty gin martini, please."

I watch as he scoops ice into the cocktail shaker, remembering how Nick would ask for cheese-stuffed olives—even at dive bars, which always read as tone deaf to me.

"Here you are," the bartender says a moment later, sliding the drink my way. A bit sloshes out on the napkin.

"Is your owner—Daniel—here, by chance?" I ask, before taking a slow sip.

He shakes his head, pointing to his right ear. "Sorry, sweetie, you'll have to say that again." There's a loud group of men to my right, and one releases a boisterous chortle every few seconds.

I lean in closer. "Your owner. Is he here?"

"Ah, yes. Sorry. You must be his date."

"No, no," I say quickly, then pause, nervously tugging at the edge of my sleeve. "No, I'm *not* his date. But I . . . would like to speak to him . . . if he's available."

"Yeah, sure." He looks toward the kitchen. "Give me a moment, all right? I'll go see if I can round him up for you."

Daniel might appear any minute, and then what? Salt stings my lips as I take another sip, and my mind, once again, turns to Nick. At first, I push the memory aside, annoyed with myself for letting rogue thoughts creep in. After all, I'd cried my tears, and there were no more left. So why am I thinking about him now? I recall one of the many self-help

I'd turned to after Nick left, and a particular passage comes to mind. "Trauma isn't a single event, but rather an ongoing process. The brain wants to move on quickly, to stomp out any memories associated with the trauma. But the heart wants to *understand*."

Maybe that's the explanation for my flurry of memories today, and why I find myself thinking about our first date—a setup by a mutual college friend who, ironically, we both ended up losing contact with. We met at a pub not much different from this one. I was ten minutes early, Nick ten minutes late. It was the sort of small detail that seemed inconsequential at the time, easily forgotten, even. But if I'd been wise, I might have seen it for what it was: a warning sign.

A few minutes later, I feel a tap on my shoulder. I turn around to find a tall man with an athletic build smiling at me.

"I was told that a beautiful American asked for me," he says with a grin that reveals a small gap between his two front teeth. He's about my age and attractive, with dark hair, pale blue eyes, and a light dusting of freckles on his nose.

My hair is still damp, and I nervously run my hand through the ends in a last-ditch attempt to pull myself together. "Yes, hi," I say. "I'm Valentina."

He waves at the bartender, who quickly fixes him a whiskey on the rocks as he slides onto the empty stool beside me. "Now," he says. "Please satisfy my curiosity and tell me why such a beautiful creature has materialized out of nowhere and asked to meet me."

"Well," I fumble. "I . . . found something of yours, from a long time ago, and I wanted to meet you in real life, to return it."

"Found something? What?" He pauses. "Wait, did you

find my wallet? I left it at Wembley Stadium last week. You're an angel."

I shake my head. "No, no. I'm sorry about your wallet. But I came to see you about . . . something else." I reach into my bag and hand him the book, then watch as he flips through the pages.

"You see, Daniel, this book is—"

"Wait, did you just say Daniel?"

"Isn't that your name? Daniel Davenport?"

He shakes his head. "I hate to say this, but I think you've got the wrong guy. I'm *David* Davenport."

"Oh," I say, disheartened. The professor must have keyed the wrong name into the alumni database.

He nods at someone in the kitchen, then turns to me and grins. "Listen, I've got to run. But—if you don't find this Daniel of yours, why don't you let me take you out sometime?" He grins. "Daniel, David, Donald—I can be whoever you want me to be, love."

I force a smile as he disappears into the kitchen, leaving the barstool beside me . . . empty.

Well, that's that.

When I step outside, I'm happy to discover that the rain has stopped. The air is bone-chillingly cold, and I cinch my jacket tighter as I round the next block and wave down a cab. "Primrose Hill," I tell the driver as I climb into the car and sink into the backseat.

When I realize that it's not quite five, I decide to call Queen Mary University and ask to be transferred to Professor Ellison, who, I'm happy to discover is still at his desk. I tell him about the Daniel-David mix-up, and he's immediately apologetic. "Let me do another search," he says, pausing for a moment. "Ah, yes, there is a Daniel Davenport on file, and he was a literature major. Class of ninety-eight. But, I'm very sorry, that's all I have on him. I do know that the alumni database is in the process of a major upgrade at the moment. But you know how long things take at universities." He sighs. "It's death by committee. You might try back in a few months or so."

"No," I say. "It's okay. And thank you so much for your time."

I sigh as my phone buzzes in my pocket. A quick glance, and I see that it's a text notification from . . . Nick. My heart freezes as I read it: "Val, I don't even know where to begin. But I can only say that I've made the biggest mistake of my life. Can we talk? I miss you. I'm so sorry."

Eloise

Nine Months Later

————

VALENTINA ELIZABETH BAKER WAS BORN ON A SUNNY Thursday morning. My water broke shortly after three A.M., and Frank had been as panicked as a schoolboy in an air-raid drill. On the drive to the hospital, he ran three red lights. By then the contractions were coming fast—one after the next. Two hours later, the pains of labor were a distant memory when I laid eyes on her perfect face.

Frank was in love, too. When the nurses whisked her away to the nursery, he became distraught with the pain of missing her.

"Would you look at this sweet baby!" Bonnie gushed the day we brought her home. She lifted her out of my arms, cooing and whispering phrases in her native language.

"Is everything prepared?" Frank asked, carrying our bags upstairs.

"Yes, Mr. Baker," Bonnie replied. "Just as you specified." She smiled at me.

Frank pointed to the mahogany crib with yellow gingham bedding nestled against the side wall. I ran my hand along its slats, eyeing the mobile hanging overhead with its cluster of plush pastel-colored stars and a windup music box.

"See, it plays 'London Bridge,'" he said, smiling proudly.

"Soon to be her favorite song," I said, sinking into the rocking chair upholstered in beige linen speckled with yellow-and-gold stars. "It's . . . perfect," I said, indulging his need for approval.

Bonnie appeared, holding the baby. "Excuse me, Mr. and Mrs. Baker," she said. "But Valentina is beginning to fuss. I think she might be hungry."

"Ah, yes," I said, glancing at the clock on the bedside table. "It's been a few hours." I took her tiny, swaddled body into my arms and Valentina latched on to my breast as Frank and Bonnie tiptoed out of the room.

"Val," I said when her belly was full and her eyes sleepy. "You have a favorite song. Now you need a favorite book. One day I'll show you the pictures, but for now I'll just say the words out loud."

She cooed softly, as if in agreement.

"'In the great green room,'" I began, then stopped.

"I forgot to tell you the title of the best story of all. *Goodnight Moon.*"

Val shifts in my arms, as if to hear me better. "'There was a telephone / And a red balloon / And a picture of . . .'"

I knew all the words by heart, and soon Val would, too.

She was too young to know that the author who so beautifully chose the words for her story didn't have the most beautiful life. I knew from reading her biography that she was unlucky in love, with a broken engagement, a disastrous affair, and a longer romance that ended at the time of her sudden and early death.

Hers was a tragic tale. I held Val tighter, determined to set my daughter on a path toward happiness, one that mirrored the very best stories. Hers would have a happy ending.

Valentina

The Next Day

———

"HOW DO YOU FEEL ABOUT CARNATIONS?" LIZA ASKS, tapping a pen against her chin.

"Well," I say, looking up from the computer screen at the bookstore. "I guess I've always thought that they're kind of . . . sad?"

Liza nods. "Exactly. They have a bad reputation. But what if we changed that? What if we gave them a *rebrand*?"

"That might be a slightly ambitious goal for carnations, let alone our fledgling flower shop," I say with a laugh. "But if you're up for the task, then why not?"

Liza shrugs, turning back to her laptop screen where she's perched in the window seat at the front of the store. She arrived early this morning to take an inventory of the space and make a list of the various items we'd need for our new botanical endeavors: potted plants and succulents (which are all the rage right now, she says), large containers to hold cut flowers, a greeting card rack (smart idea), and a few small tables for novelty gifts and sundries.

"Look," she says, shifting her screen so I can see. "With the empty shelves in the storeroom and those tables we aren't using, we should only have to buy a few things before we're ready to roll."

I smile. "That makes me happy."

I tell her about Nick's text, and that I still haven't replied. She shakes her head. "I've heard that line before. Don't take the bait."

"I didn't." Though I admit I did scroll through our wedding photos on my phone. Damn, did he look good in a tux.

"But you're thinking about it. I can see the look in your eyes."

Millie pokes her head in on our conversation before I have a chance to respond. "See *what look* in your eyes?"

"Val's ex texted her," Liza explains. "He wants her back."

Millie frowns. "And you'll have none of that! Tell that rotten man to piss off."

"Don't worry," I say with a laugh. "I have no intention of rekindling anything with him."

"I would think not," Millie adds.

The bells on the door jingle again as the FedEx man arrives with two boxes. It's Fernando this time, and by the look on Millie's face, she's obviously elated—and tongue-tied.

"Hello," she says.

"Hello," he replies.

They're like a pair of love-struck teenagers, and Liza and I are their peanut gallery.

"I thought you were . . . gone," Millie says. "I mean, assigned to another route."

"I was," Fernando says, taking a step closer. "But I asked to be put back on this one. I really missed . . . my customers."

"Oh," Millie says, beaming. She's obviously trying to keep her cool, but it's clear that her heart is doing a backflip.

Fernando sets the boxes on the counter beside Millie. She really is substantially taller, and he really is substantially *younger*, but somehow neither detail matters. I smile to myself. They might be the most awkward couple of all time, but perhaps also the most adorable.

"It's always so nice to see you, Millie," he says, smiling as he turns to the door.

"You too, Fernando," she replies, her cheeks flushed.

When the door closes Liza gasps. "Millie, I'm telling you, he is *smitten*."

"I agree," I say. "Next time he comes in, you should slip him your phone number."

"You girls are very sweet, but clearly out of your minds. For heaven's sake, I'm old enough to be his mother!"

"Love is ageless," Liza argues as Millie rolls her eyes.

"And also confusing," I say after I glance at my phone and see a new text from Nick: "Val, can we talk? I love you. I miss you so much."

I don't respond. Instead, I ask Millie about my mother's Cicero box, which Eric had told me about yesterday. "Ah, yes," she says, peering underneath the counter. "The famous candy box. I don't know why I didn't think of it. She kept it right here, under the—"

I watch her fumble through the lower shelf, then another. She looks through two drawers and then a third. "Where in the world would it have gone?"

"Did you possibly put it away when we were cleaning recently?"

"Maybe," she says, disappearing to the back room, but she returns a few minutes later empty-handed. "I'm afraid it's not there, either."

I sink into a chair beside the nonfiction section.

"I'm sure it's here somewhere. We'll find it."

"But will we?" I say with a sigh. What I'd initially approached with amusement, curiosity even, has turned into so much more. My mother was trying to tell me something. She was trying to help me *understand*. But would I?

"Valentina, good things take time," Millie says. "Don't lose hope."

She's right, of course. I read somewhere that it took Tolkien sixteen years to write a follow-up to *The Hobbit*. I'd find Mummy's message, and I'd find my way in life—eventually.

"You've been working so hard," she continues. "Why don't you go for a walk—to clear your head. Liza's here; we've got things covered."

I decide she's right, so I set out on Prince Albert Road toward Primrose Hill park. What once was royal land, and the private hunting ground for Henry VIII, is now a small public park. Liza told me it was a favorite among locals and tourists alike for its panoramic views of London, and I'm somewhat of both.

Primrose Hill is already above sea level, but Primrose Hill park rises even higher. Just as my driver had noted on my first ride into town, the elevation is sixty-three meters above sea level, which the sign at its entrance declares. In the distance, architecture enthusiasts cluster, pointing their cameras at BT Tower and the London Eye. But I'm here for the literary landmarks. On the slope, there's an oak known as Shakespeare's Tree, planted to commemorate the three hundredth anniversary of the playwright's birth; goosebumps erupt up and down my arms when I see it.

Turning in a slow circle, I take in my surroundings. The

grass is green, and the trees are low so as to show off the view of all of London. I spot the Shard and the towers of Mammon, landmarks I'd only ever heard about or seen photos of, but now they're right before me—in my own backyard.

I continue climbing until I reach the summit and my ultimate prize—a stone engraved with the words of William Blake. I post a photo to @booksbyval with this caption:

> "I have conversed with the spiritual sun. I saw him on Primrose Hill," said William Blake. He saw the light, and so have I. I'm finally and utterly at home.

Within mere moments, my Instagram notifications flood in, and one in particular catches my eye—from Nick: "Your heart is my home. I love you."

I feel a pang of emotion, which quickly morphs into anger. While his previous texts had, admittedly, stirred my heart, this note does the very opposite. In fact, it gives me greater clarity and *understanding*. How dare Nick post something so personal on my Instagram? He hadn't commented on any posts on @booksbyval in our entire marriage, and now he jumps into the ring looking like a wounded husband who misses his wife? I'd done my best to keep our private matters, well, private, and now he has the gall to use my platform to get my attention, or worse, elicit pity from my followers? My cheeks burn red, and I consider deleting his message, or even blocking him entirely. Instead, I tuck my phone into my bag and try to remain in the present. Nick left *me,* and I've made a new life for myself—or at least, I'm *making* one. Nothing he can say or do will change those facts. Just like my mother's life in London, with her secrets I wasn't privy to, this is *my time,* and mine alone.

I walk home with a new sense of strength, and purpose. My life is no longer the tragic novel I'd assumed it was, but something entirely different—a great adventure, a thriller, even, and maybe, just maybe, a brilliant love story.

Once home, I sink into the sofa, and reach for a new thriller that came into the store recently. I don't know the author, and I've rarely dipped into the genre, but a quote on the cover caught my eye: "Heart-stopping and unforgettable, this story will make you question everything—from the roads not taken to the person lying beside you in bed."

And it does, indeed. I read for two solid hours, then snap a photo of the book and share it in an Instagram post:

> Whether trying out a new author or genre, or making a big life change, I'm the first to admit that stepping out of our comfort zones can be a little scary. But what if we could see our lives in reverse and confirm that those risks, hard decisions, even impulsive leaps of faith, were the key ingredients for a fully maximized life? That's what I'm thinking about, anyway, even if I have no idea what might lie on the road ahead. But I have this book to keep me company, and it's quite the unusual pick for me. But I'm open to what I'll find in its pages and in my own life. Tell me, what big risks have you taken—literary or otherwise? xoxo, Val #takingachanceonbooks #newgenre #oneday-atatime

I crave tea, so I put the kettle on the stove in my mother's kitchen that is now my own, then search her record collection until I find just the right album: Art Tatum. I release the vinyl from its sleeve and carefully set it on the turntable, listening for the familiar crackle, the melodic piano. "Tea for Two."

I close my eyes, and there we are, *Mummy* and me. We're far away and many years from here, twirling in our Santa Monica living room. It's as if nothing has changed, even though everything has. For now, maybe that's the secret. I could pretend the pain away, and so I do.

Tea for two and two for tea. Me for you, and you for me.

Eloise

———

AFTER DINNER, I SCANNED THE ESTATE SALE FINDS I'D carted home—a large crystal vase and a stack of rare books. But my favorite purchase of all was obtained by pure happenstance. I decided to take a rare jaunt out of our neighborhood and cab to Beverly Hills, the site of a particularly interesting newspaper listing. Though the sale had been, at first, a disappointment, I found my way into the grand home's library, while the other bargain-shoppers scoured through bins of the previous owner's stash of vintage Chanel. And, oh, what a discovery. Not only did I procure a bagful of first editions, but I also found the unlikeliest of treasures, if only to me.

On a coffee table in the home's library lay a varnished wooden box engraved with the words "Cicero's Sentiments." The green sticker on its lid signaled its price: one dollar. When I saw it, I smiled with curiosity, wondering if it had once held sentimental value for its owner. Noticing the hinges, I kneeled down and lifted the edge. I laughed when I saw what was inside: candy—in particular, individually wrapped lemon drops.

Of course, I knew that Cicero was a revered philosopher and writer dating back to Roman times, but I couldn't help but admire the juxtaposition—candy inside a box labeled as the sentiments of a literary great. I loved it instantly, especially when thinking of my long-held dream of opening a bookstore. Even if I knew it was a near impossibility in California, still, I let my imagination think otherwise. In my mind's eye, there I was, the proprietor of a lovely corner bookshop, where I opened the little box to pass out treats to youngsters who came in for story time.

A long time ago, Frank had squashed my hope of making that dream a reality. But ten years had passed since then, and I wondered if this time, I could convince him. True, the brief spark we'd rekindled before Valentina's birth had dimmed and we'd settled into a stale domestic routine, but we weren't adversarial. He just lived his life, and I lived mine. And, over the years, as Frank recoiled deeper into himself, and away from me, I stopped trying, too, and instead, accepted our marriage for what it was—two completely different people held together by the mutual love of their child.

Valentina was the glue, and being her mother was the greatest joy of my life, and yet, the older she grew, the less she needed me, which is when the bouts of loneliness returned. One day, when she was at a playdate at a friend's house, I decided to speak to Frank.

I found him in his favorite chair in the living room, barricaded behind an open newspaper.

"Can we talk for a second?" I asked.

"Sure," he replied. His eyes remained fixed on the article that held his attention.

"Frank," I said taking a deep breath. "I've been thinking . . .

Valentina is growing up. She doesn't need me as much as she used to. She's so mature and independent, and well . . . I have more free time to pursue other things and I think—I think I should."

He nodded blankly, which I took as a cue to proceed.

"I . . . mentioned this a long time ago . . . you may not remember, but, Frank . . . I want to open a bookstore."

He finally set his newspaper down, then looked up at me—his expression a mix of amused and annoyed. "Eloise, you were a salesclerk at a department store when I met you. What on earth makes you think you can operate a small business?"

His response cut deep. I steadied myself and ignored the lump in my throat. "Frank, this has always been my *dream*— the one I've had for as long as I can remember." I took a deep breath, inching forward. "Listen, there's a storefront on Ocean Drive that's available the first of the month. It's lovely, with a sunny little window seat." I felt silly, and nervous, like a little girl convincing her father that she wants a pony, but I pressed on. "We'll source mostly used books, all kinds of hard-to-find treasures. It'll be a place where people can find homes for their old books and discover new ones, too."

He chuckled. "Darling, I'm afraid to say it, but that doesn't sound like the most profitable enterprise. Especially since you only seem to read one book, over and over again."

I frowned at his dismissive reference to *The Last Winter*. It was true that I lingered in Cezanne's world often, but Frank's comment discredited the stacks of books on my bedside table. But he didn't know that because he was never in my bedroom. He had his own.

"Listen," Frank continued, cutting into my thoughts.

"Clearly you have spare time on your hands that you're looking to fill. Why don't I make some calls and see if I can get you a job on the sales floor at Fred Segal? Your work at Harrods might just get your foot in the door. How would you like that?"

"*How would I like that?* Frank, you're missing the point entirely. I don't want to keep *busy;* and I certainly don't want a job at Fred Segal. I want to follow my heart and do what I'm passionate about. I *need* this, Frank. I need a reason to get up in the morning—a purpose. Can't you understand that?"

"And our daughter isn't *purpose* enough for you?"

"Don't bring Valentina into this," I snapped. "It's perfectly normal for a woman to need more than motherhood to fulfill her." I thought of a handful of people we knew socially. "Do you think Barbara Matthews loves her sons any less because she works at the hospital? Or Claire Greenspan. Does her architectural career make her less of a mother?" I shook my head. "Frank, I know we have plenty of money. You bought a new Porsche last month. The start-up costs for my business would be a fraction of that."

"Don't get cute with me, Eloise," he said, the corners of his mouth twisting. "And don't, for a moment, tell me how to spend *my money*."

My eyes narrowed. "You really have no respect for me, do you?" Suddenly, everything was clear—frighteningly clear. For the first time, I realized that—

"Mummy?" Valentina said, standing in the doorway, her pigtails still wet from swimming. I heard a car pull out of the driveway and realized I'd forgotten that her friend's mother had agreed to bring her home.

"Why are you and Daddy fighting?"

I ran to her and kissed her honey-scented hair. "We're not fighting, love. We're only having a discussion. About... grown-up things. Everything's fine."

She paused, looking up at me with her big brown eyes as Frank watched us from his chair. "Are you and Daddy going to get a divorce? Janie's parents are getting one."

My heart felt as if it had just been plucked out of my chest and hurled off a skyscraper.

"Of course not, dear," Frank said, swooping in before I could venture a response.

He patted her head, then I kissed her cheek. "Cheer up, Charlie."

"Okay, Mummy," she said sweetly, smiling up at her father and me before skipping up the stairs. I turned to follow, leaving a void of silence as big as the Grand Canyon in my wake.

"Wait, Eloise," he called out to me. "I'm sorry if I... seemed..."

"It doesn't matter," I said without turning around. But it did matter. My God, it mattered so much.

Valentina

The Next Day

————

I OPEN MY EYES AND GLANCE AT THE CLOCK, SHOCKED
to see that it's nearly eleven A.M. Granted, I stayed up late
listening to Mummy's old records, but still, I haven't slept this
late since ... college. I dress quickly before heading downstairs to the store, where I find Liza arranging a vase of flowers.

"Wow," I say. "The window display looks incredible."

"Do you like it?" she asks, surveying her work skeptically.
"I can't decide if we ought to move this table a bit to the left,
or maybe add in another row of shelves?" She tilts her head to
the right and frowns. "I don't know, is it working?"

"Um, Liza," I say, "you're a miracle worker. "It's *perfect!*"

I ask her if she's seen the elusive Cicero box, but as expected, she hasn't. "Sorry," she says, snipping the thorns and
excess leaves off a few dozen long-stem roses. "I'll keep my
eye out."

"Thanks," I say with a sigh.

"You know what you need?" Liza continues, looking up at
me. "Some girl time. Let's cut out of here and go to my friend
Debbie's salon."

"I'd love to," I tell her, "but I have so much work to do before the fundraiser. I don't know if I can—"

"Nonsense," she replies, plucking a few fallen rose petals from the floor. "You need a blowout more than I need a boyfriend."

"Uh, Liza, what exactly does that mean?"

She smiles. "That we're going to the salon."

After Millie arrives, we head out. The salon is less than four blocks away, and Debbie greets us at the door. She's tall, with shoulder-length light brown hair and blunt bangs that form a perfect line across her forehead.

"Think you can fix her up?" Liza asks as I slide into Debbie's chair.

"Without a doubt," she says. "I hear you're the new owner of the Book Garden. I've been following your Instagram! That post on William Blake helping you see the light really inspired me."

"Oh," I say, flattered. "Thank you for saying that. I do have a decent following, but sometimes I get the feeling that the only person who's really reading my posts these days is my ex-husband."

Debbie grins. "Those menacing exes. We all have them." She and Liza exchange a knowing look. "But I assure you, sweetie, a lot of us are reading. And what is this I hear about a fundraising event for the bookstore? You should definitely post about it. You never know who might show up!"

"You're right, Deb," Liza adds. "We might even get Prince Harry." She nostalgically catches her reflection in the salon's mirrored wall. "I've always had a thing for him."

I laugh. "Well, I highly doubt we'll get Prince Harry over to Primrose Hill, but you do have a point. The event is in three and a half weeks, and I should probably start promoting it on my feed."

Deb leads me to a chair by the window and takes a long look at me. "You need a haircut—and highlights."

"I don't know," I say reluctantly.

"I'll just pop in a few foils, and it'll brighten you right up. You'll love it, I promise."

"Okay," I agree, sliding my head back as she runs her brush through my long-neglected hair.

"Val, you have to tell Deb about Daniel!"

"Daniel?" she asks, intrigued.

I share the story of the book with the notes inside, which resulted in my rather hapless search and present dead end.

"Well, that stinks," she says before clipping my hair into sections and getting to work on my highlights. "So, let me get this straight: The Daniel at the Snow Goose wasn't the Daniel from the book?"

I nod. "No, his name was actually David Davenport not *Daniel* Davenport."

"Stop it," Debbie says, taking a step back. "You're joking."

I shake my head, confused.

"Daniel *Davenport*?" She turns to Liza. "I've known a fellow by that name since I was a wee thing. We used to run around in nappies together. Our mums were best friends, still are. They had an elaborate plan for us to grow up and get married, and I'll admit, I used to wish that would happen. He's quite a catch. Devilishly handsome and kind in the way that most good-looking men aren't, you know? Oh, and he's smart, too."

I sit up in the swivel chair. "Hold on. What?"

She nods. "He's a movie producer, or a screenwriter, or something." She shakes her head. "In any case, he works in film—in some capacity. My mum mentioned something about documentaries."

It's a crazy coincidence, I admit, but there's no way Debbie's Daniel could be *the* Daniel. Liza and I had already googled the name—there were more than a hundred results in London alone.

"Wait," I say. "What do you know about his education? Did he happen to attend Queen Mary University, by chance?"

Debbie's eyes widen. "As a matter of fact, he did."

"Val," Liza says with a big smile. "I think we just found your guy."

"Why don't I call him?" Debbie says, reaching for her phone. "I talked to my mum the other day, and he's definitely single. I could set you two up for a lunch date or coffee."

I shake my head. "No, no, it's okay. And besides, aren't you sort of smitten with him yourself?"

"Please," she says, holding out her left hand to display a diamond ring. "I'm engaged. Besides, our window of romantic possibility expired the year we both turned nine. Kissing him would be like . . . kissing my brother. *Eww.*"

I laugh.

"So," she continues, taking another section of my hair, "will you please let me set you two up?"

"I can't believe this," I say, turning to Liza for validation. "I don't know. Shouldn't it happen . . . I don't know, more *organically?*"

Liza nods. "Maybe you could go to his favorite café and *accidentally* bump into him, spilling coffee on his shirt or something?"

"Yeah, that," I say, "but minus the bit about me spilling coffee on his shirt."

Liza holds up her index finger. "Wait, you could steal his briefcase on the train, and then follow him and return it!"

I shake my head. "Definitely no."

Debbie nods. "In grade five, I did something like that. I was completely besotted with this boy named Craig. I concocted an elaborate plan to get his attention by accidentally poking the edge of his arm with a plastic fork at lunch. I fantasized about how he'd think it was funny, and that we'd laugh about it for years to come. I imagined that after we got married, he'd tell people how hilarious it was that I'd stabbed him with a fork on the day we met. The thing is, somehow the fork missed him, but the ketchup on my tray didn't. It splattered all over his polo shirt." She shakes her head.

"Tragic," Liza says.

Debbie nods. "It was." She turns back to me, her gaze meeting my reflection in the mirror. "Let me call him later and work on setting you two up."

"All right," I finally say.

She smiles and hands me a pad of paper and a pen. "Here, leave me your phone number so I can pass it along to him."

I scrawl my number onto the page and laugh to myself. "Will somebody please tell me why I feel like I'm fifteen years old all over again."

Liza smiles. "And with that, Val, you may have just uncovered the best-kept secret about adulthood—that there's no such thing."

"YOUR HAIR LOOKS NICE," Millie says later when I stop into the store at the end of the day.

"Thanks," I say happily. Debbie had indeed brightened me up, and it felt like a nice change in the wake of . . . everything.

"It was quite a banner day," she says, flipping off the lights. "The best sales we've had in weeks."

"Really?"

She nods.

"Why don't I walk you home? You can tell me all about it."

"Sure," she says, locking up the store. "Come along if you like, but not because you think I need protection. I've been walking far darker streets of London longer than you've been alive, my dear."

"I know," I say with a laugh. "I just thought you might like a little company, that's all."

I tell Millie about my latest call from James Whitaker of Bevins and Associates. He's encouraging me to consider two new offers that would easily settle the estate taxes. Of course, both involve closing the bookstore and demolishing the building to make way for a modern block of flats, but the longer this drags out, the deeper in hot water I find myself.

"Lawyers never give up," Millie says.

"I don't want to make any decisions until after the fund-raiser," I say. "We still have time."

"Exactly. Be vague. Tell him you're considering your options. He'll get his answer in time, and hopefully for us, it'll be a big fat *no*."

I nod as I feel my phone buzz in my back pocket. When I glance at the screen, I don't recognize the number, but I decide to pick up, just in case.

"Hello, is this Valentina?" It's a man with a deep, resonant voice.

"Yes," I reply.

"This is Daniel. Daniel Davenport."

"Daniel," I say, a fluttery feeling creeping up inside of me. "Hi."

"Hi," he replies.

Millie grins, then mouths "good night," before disappearing around the next corner.

"I'm sorry, am I interrupting you?" Daniel asks.

"No, no," I say quickly, perhaps too quickly. I take a deep breath as I lean against a lamppost on the sidewalk. "Not at all."

"Good," he says. I can picture him right now, smiling out the window of his loft flat in the city, with dark, wavy hair, a coy smile, dinner simmering on the stove beside a freshly uncorked bottle of wine—a book on his nightstand. "I spoke to our mutual friend Debbie today, and she tells me that we have a lot to talk about."

Eloise

March 1990

———

A STREAM OF LIGHT SPILLED OUT TO THE HALLWAY FROM Frank's bedroom door. I normally knocked, but I had a water glass in one hand and his shirts on hangers in the other. Besides, he'd left his door ajar, so I didn't worry about disturbing him.

"Hi," I said, pressing the door open with my elbow.

He was lying on his side, in the striped pajamas I'd bought him for Christmas two years ago. When he heard my footsteps, he sat up quickly. "Eloise," he said, startled. "I've told you to please knock."

"Oh," I said, taken aback. "I'm sorry. I picked up the dry cleaning this morning and just wanted to put your shirts in the—" I paused, suddenly noticing dozens of photographs laid out on his bed, some black-and-white, some color. "What are you doing, Frank? What are these photos?"

"Nothing," he said, gathering them into a pile as quickly as he could, but one escaped him, falling to the floor, where it lay, faceup, in front of me. The clump of hangers fell from my hand as I kneeled down to pick it up.

I noticed her eyes first—big, enchanting orbs—and then

her other features: high cheekbones, perfect, plump lips, a tiny waist. Her blond hair cascaded in soft waves that hit her shoulders. She was laughing, beaming, as if the person behind the camera was everything to her. I swallowed hard, looking up at Frank. I knew the answer to the question I was about to ask, but I asked it anyway. "This is her, isn't it? This is *Diane*."

Frank took the photo from my limp hand and set it on top of the others, before tucking the stack into a manila envelope and placing it inside the drawer of his bedside table. He didn't say anything, and neither did I, both of us cloaked in an icy silence.

A few moments passed before he turned to me, his eyes filled with regret, tenderness even. "Eloise, I'm . . . so sorry."

"Don't, Frank," I said, shaking my head. "All these years. I could never reach you. I used to think it was me, that I wasn't good enough, pretty enough, interesting enough. But I see now that it wasn't any failure on my part. Frank, I couldn't reach you because you were unreachable—because your heart is still with *her*."

WE DIDN'T SPEAK OF that night again, but Frank behaved differently thereafter. He came home in time for dinner more often and even offered to take me to the new seafood restaurant on Main Street one night, though I politely declined.

I behaved differently, too. Sometimes I didn't come down for breakfast or opted out of a black-tie event I didn't feel like attending, even if I knew it would ignite gossip in our social circle. I even got my driver's license, which felt like the boldest move of all.

Valentina was my first passenger.

She came out to the patio, where I was reading, and sat beside me on the lounge chair by the pool. "Can you take me to the beach?"

"All right," I finally said, glancing at my watch. "Let me get dressed and get you a snack and then I'll drive you."

Valentina leaped to her feet, beaming. "You're the best mummy in the whole wide world!"

"And you're the best daughter in the whole wide world." I smiled.

"IS IT FUN TO DRIVE?" Valentina asked as I backed the Volvo station wagon out of the driveway. I gripped the steering wheel anxiously. While practicing for my driving test, I'd run into the mailbox. Frank wasn't happy about it, naturally, but Valentina thought the episode of "Mummy Demolishes the Mailbox" was the funniest thing she'd ever seen.

"I don't know that I'd call driving *fun*," I said, putting the car into drive as we set off down the street. "But it is *freeing*." And it had been—so much so, that I'd wondered why it had taken me so long to take the plunge.

"I bet," Val said, gazing through the open window, the warm air flirting with her sun-kissed hair. She stuck her arm out as she'd done since she was little, letting her hand skim the breeze as if it were surfing on air.

"Hey," I said suddenly. "Let's stop and grab an ice cream and then walk to the beach? Orange sherbet?"

She smiled. "No, bubblegum!"

"Bubblegum it is, then," I said, taking a sharp left turn

down a side street that led to the boardwalk, where I kept an eye out for a parking space on Ocean Drive, but after ten minutes and three loops around the block, no luck.

Then Valentina pointed ahead. "There's one, Mummy! See it? Right up there."

I shook my head. "I'm afraid I'm hopeless at parallel parking. In fact, I almost failed my driver's test on account of that."

She smiled. "How are you going to get better at it if you don't practice?"

"Aren't you my very wise daughter," I replied, grinning as I sized up the challenge before me. "Now, you better not laugh at me when I botch this up."

I pulled forward, then shifted into reverse, inching backward at an angle as I'd been taught, but I quickly realized I'd overshot the angle and would have to start over. After eight more tries, I was beyond frustrated.

"Maybe you could just drop me off," Valentina suggested sweetly, "and wait while I get our ice cream?"

"But then we wouldn't get to go to the beach," I said with a sigh.

"Excuse me," a man said, catching my attention through the car's open window. "I couldn't help but notice that you were having some . . . difficulty getting into this spot. Would you like some help?"

I peered out the window and looked up at him—tall, with brown, wavy hair and a kind smile. I never talked to strange men, but there was something in his expression that disarmed me.

"Yeah," I said with a laugh. "I guess I must look pretty pathetic."

"Nah," he said. "I assure you that you're not the only person in Santa Monica who struggles with parallel parking." He pointed to a condo building behind him. "I live right up there, and I see it all the time. Men are the worst. The egos. You should see how their tempers flare when they can't fit into a spot. It's pretty funny to watch."

I smiled as he stepped back to assess the parking space. "It's a bit tight, but I think we can nail this one. I'll guide you."

"All right, coach," I said as Valentina giggled beside me.

"Bring it up a bit," he said, motioning me forward. "Okay, now stop and slowly crank the steering wheel to the left." I did as he said, and he nodded approvingly. "Yes, just like that. A little more. A little more. There. Now straighten her out. There, perfect!"

I turned the engine off, marveling at our parking feat, then rolled up the windows and stepped out of the car and onto the sidewalk with Valentina. "Who are you, the Patron Saint of Parking?"

He smiled. "I'm Peter," he said, extending his hand.

"Eloise," I said, my cheeks flushing a little. "And this is my daughter, Valentina."

"Pleased to meet you both," he said, catching my eye again. "Hey, if the two of you are interested, I—"

"I'm sorry," I said suddenly. "We really ought to be going. I promised her ice cream. But thank you . . . Peter, for your kindness. It was . . . very sweet."

"The pleasure was all mine," he said. "And maybe I'll catch you another time, that is, if you're ever in need of more parking assistance."

I smiled, then took Valentina's hand, feeling his eyes on my back as we walked away.

That's when I saw it, the empty storefront on Ocean Drive where I had imagined my bookstore.

"Let's go window-shopping," I said, stopping at the vacant shop.

"Mummy," Valentina said with a laugh, "that store is empty. There's nothing in the window."

"Oh, but, darling, you're so wrong," I said. "You have to use your imagination."

She looked up at me curiously. "What do you see?"

I smiled. "Books. So many books."

"DO THEY HAVE ICE CREAM in London?" Val asked, licking a drip of pink ice cream from the side of her waffle cone as we sat on the beach together, watching the waves crash onto the shore.

"Well of course they do," I said, "though I didn't grow up eating a lot of it. It's more of an American thing."

"What treats did you like when you were a little girl?"

"Candy, of course," I said. "I would do anything for a lemon drop."

"What else?"

"I used to love my mother's scones with clotted cream," I said, remembering how she always served the cream in individual ramekins. "*It's the proper way,*" she'd tell me, even if it unnecessarily dirtied more dishes. Mummy was always focused on being proper, both because her upbringing hadn't been, and also, it's what she wanted for me. I wondered what she'd think of me now, living in California, married to a wealthy man, able to dirty as many dishes as I liked. It was the sort of life she'd always hoped for me, and yet, I knew she'd be able to read me like a book, seeing the emptiness I tried so hard to keep hidden away.

"Can you take me to London?" Val asked, slurping up the final bit of melted ice cream in her cone.

I wipe a bit from her chin. "I would love to, honey."

"When?" she asked. "Can we go next month, during my school break?"

"You know," I said. "That's not a bad idea."

I missed London so much it hurt—Millie, too. Our letters had become infrequent over the years, but I knew that whenever we finally reunited, we wouldn't miss a beat.

"I'll speak to your father about it tonight," I said. "Now go run and dip your toes in the ocean!" I smiled, watching her gallop off to the water's edge, flirting with the tide and shrieking as the water crept closer, the way she'd done since she was tiny. Unlike me, Valentina was fearless; then again, life had yet to disappoint her.

I let her play for a few more minutes before we headed back to the car.

"That man was nice," she said suddenly, brushing a dusting of sand from her cheek and watching me with an air of wisdom far greater than her years.

"He was," I said, unlocking the car. I turned on the engine then lowered the windows to let out the hot air.

Val pointed to the windshield. "Mummy, what's that paper under the windshield wiper?"

"Great," I said with a sigh. "After all that, I got a parking ticket." I stretched my arm out to retrieve the slip of paper, but upon further inspection, I realized it wasn't a parking ticket.

"What is it?" Valentina asked curiously.

"It's . . . nothing," I said quickly, tucking the scrap of paper into the pocket of my jeans. I didn't tell her that it was actually a note—from Peter—and that he'd left his phone number. Of course, it all meant nothing. I would never call him, nor would I ever let myself think of what might happen if I did. I gazed up at the condo building facing the beach and smiled, feeling girlish and effervescent, like that fluttery sensation that comes only after the third sip of champagne.

AS I SORTED THE MAIL, I noticed a letter from Millie by the familiar curve of her handwriting and opened it immediately.

Dear Eloise,

How are you, my old friend? It's been ages, and I miss you—so much. London will never be the same without you. I suppose your life in California is way more exciting, though. I have a bet going with a friend at the pub that one of these days I'll see you on television. "That's my best friend," I'll tell everyone, but of course, no one will believe me. Remember Susan Whitehall? She asked me when you're going to divorce Frank and marry someone like Tom Cruise. If anyone could pull off something like that, it would be you, El. Bloody hell, I really hope Frank isn't reading this letter. I should probably mention how handsome, smart, and wise I remember Frank being. Okay, okay, I'll just stop this subject there.

In your last letter, you asked if I ever think about our old bookstore dream, and yes, I still do—a lot, actually. I'm sorry that it didn't work out for you to open a store in

*Santa Monica, but selfishly, it made me hope that our
little venture may one day have a chance! Can you
imagine how lovely it would be, and how much fun we'd
have? Well, dreams never die, do they? That's what I tell
myself, anyway.*

*How is Valentina? I think of you both so often. Send
photos!*

*With love always,
Millie*

Tears stung my eyes as I tucked the letter away. I missed
home, and Millie, more than ever. I decided to have a word
with Frank about taking Valentina to London.

I smiled, thinking of all the sights I'd show her. The crown
jewels! Buckingham Palace! That little bakery I used to love
in Notting Hill. Would it all still be there, waiting for me, just
as I remembered it?

The phone rang in the living room, and I hoped it was
Frank, so I could propose the idea straightaway. He could
probably have his secretary help us with airline tickets, hotel
reservations, and the like.

"Hello?"

"Hello, darling," Frank said. "I just made it to Chicago
and I—"

"I'm so glad you called," I said. "I . . . I wanted to ask you
something."

"What is it?"

"Frank, I . . . want to take Valentina to London."

There was silence on the other end of the line.

"Frank? Are you still there?"

"Yes, yes. Here."

"I said, I'd like to take Valentina on a trip to see London."

"I heard you." His voice sounded sharp, businesslike.

"Oh, okay. So, may I, please?"

"Darling, I'm afraid I just can't support that. There are far too many terrorist attacks in Europe these days. I couldn't live with myself if—"

"And I couldn't live with myself if I don't get the chance to show my daughter my home."

Frank raised his voice to get the last word.

"*Your* home is in California, and *our* daughter will be fine waiting until she's of age to travel abroad."

I'D GIVEN BONNIE THE night off, and with Frank gone and Valentina at a sleepover, the house felt emptier than ever. Normally, I'd drown out the silence with a book, but instead, I went to my closet and selected a lightweight blue sweater and jeans. I added a belt and a pair of nude heels, then tucked my wallet and a tube of lipstick into the quilted Chanel bag Frank bought me for Christmas the year Valentina was born. I reached for a silk scarf in the top drawer of my dresser and paused when the jewelry box in the far corner caught my eye. My mother had given it to me on my eleventh birthday. She could never afford to buy something so expensive; it had been passed down from her own mother, who had been given it when she worked as a seamstress for one of London's wealthier families. But it wasn't the jewelry box that pinged my heart—it was what I'd placed inside.

I lifted the lid and pulled out the note that I'd found on my windshield, from the man at the beach. Peter. I should have thrown it away immediately, but for some reason, I sim-

ply couldn't. And there it was, and here I was, in heels on a
Friday night. I tucked the scrap of paper into my purse and
reached for my car keys.

LATER THAT EVENING I slid onto a barstool at Vino Vol-
letta, a newly opened wine bar in the neighborhood. It felt
strange to be out at night alone, but also strangely *wonderful*.

The bartender smiled at me, sliding a water glass and
menu across the marble counter. "Anyone joining you tonight?" he asked, hesitating as if to reach for another menu.

"No," I said quickly. "It's just me."

He nodded, pointing to the top of the menu. "Our appe-
tizers are right here. Below that are salads and starters, then
mains. The chicken is really nice tonight. And on the other
side, you'll find our wines. The flights of three are at the bottom."

"Oh yes," I said, liking the sound of a flight. "I'll have one
of those. Which of the reds do you recommend?"

"Well," he said, "considering your accent, I take it you
might have an affinity for European varietals?"

I smiled. "I do miss home."

"Then I'll bring out a flight of French reds," he said decisively. "You won't be disappointed."

I certainly wasn't, and when I finished the three pours, I
decided to order a glass. The bartender immediately reached
for a bottle he described as "special," and it was. A few minutes later, I was feeling light and happy and, perhaps, a bit
emboldened. I reached into my pocket.

I remembered how Frank had spoken to me on the phone,
how he'd dismissed me. I'd been so lonely for so long. He'd

admitted as much himself. What would be the harm in merely ... talking to someone who wanted to talk to *me*? I took another sip of wine, then waved to the bartender. "Excuse me, sir, but do you mind if I borrow your phone?"

"Sure," he said, pointing to the end of the bar.

I walked over and dialed the number. It rang two times before he picked up.

"Hello?"

"Yes, hello ... Peter?" I clutched the edge of the bar to hold myself steady.

"Yes, this is."

My heart beat so fast, I felt as if I might faint. *What am I doing?*

"Hello?" he said again, before I panicked and set the phone back into its cradle.

Valentina

LONDON

About Three Weeks Later

———

IT'S NEAR CLOSING TIME ON A FRIDAY NIGHT, AND THE Book Garden staff is feeling the tension rising. The fundraiser we'd organized is planned for tomorrow night, and Millie, Liza, and I knew in the very marrow of our bones that this would be make or break for us, hopefully the former. As such, we'd spent the last week embroiled in preparation—folding and tying ribbons on programs, printing raffle tickets, and making tags for silent auction items.

"I don't know how on earth we're going to raise all the money we need," Millie says, fretting as she turns away from the computer screen, then sinks into one of the store's several sofas.

"The event is sold out," I remind her. "If nothing else, the Primrose Hill community is showing their support."

Before Millie can respond, a young woman with a pixie haircut comes in requesting Kerouac. Millie, of course, leaps to her feet, leads the customer to the right shelf, and puts a book in her hand. She leaves with her purchase in a bag emblazoned with the store's new logo, the shoots of a daffodil sprouting from the pages of an open book.

"The book business may be changing," Millie says, "but as long as there are readers, there will always be sixteen-year-old girls in search of Kerouac." She shakes her head. "But for God's sake why Kerouac when there's Sylvia Plath? I'll never understand."

Millie turns her attention to the rows of gift bags adorned with the same new logo. Thanks to the generosity of local merchants, from the bakery to the grocer around the corner, we'll fill each of them to the brim.

Liza sighs, examining the ribbon she's just tied on one of the gift bags, and I can tell that Millie's worries are contagious. "Do you think any of this is going to make a difference? I mean, can one fundraiser really get us where we need to be to pay the estate tax and stay in business?"

"That's the goal," I say. "Primrose Hill needs its bookstore. The ticket sales alone are proof!" I don't state the obvious, that the gratis dinner at Café Flora might also be a draw.

Nevertheless, we stay the course, and the three of us have quite the assembly line going. Millie stocks each bag, then passes it to Liza, who ties a pink tulle bow on each handle before passing it to me to tag and place in the boxes that correspond to the various table numbers.

Liza looks up suddenly. "Val, isn't your date with Daniel tonight?"

"Yeah," I say, unable to stop smiling at the mention of him. When he'd first called, he was preparing for a business trip, and would be gone for about ten days, but now he's back and he asked me to have dinner with him at a little Italian restaurant in Notting Hill, where he says they serve some sort of eggplant dish that has gotten rave reviews from food critics. I didn't have the heart to tell him that I despise eggplant. Anyway, I hope he'll be as wonderful in real life as he seems on the phone. Debbie, the hairstylist, at least thinks so.

"Are you nervous?" Liza asks expectantly.

"It's been more than fifteen years since I've been on a first date," I say with a sigh. "So yeah, a little."

"Don't forget a flirty blouse and a spritz of perfume." She points to the back of her ears, her collarbone, and each of her wrists. "Placement is key, and may I suggest vanilla?"

Before I can reply, the FedEx truck pulls up, a bit earlier than usual. Given that Millie plans her day so that she has time to powder her nose and swipe on a little lipstick before her daily dose of Fernando, any minor schedule change catches her off guard. Today, he finds her sitting on the floor, surrounded by gift bags, with a shiny nose and pale lips. Judging by the look on his face, he doesn't seem to mind.

"Hi, Millie," he says, setting a few packages on the table beside her.

"Oh, Fernando," she replies, as tongue-tied as she always is when he comes in.

"What are you working on?"

"We're . . . getting ready for the store's fundraiser tomorrow night," she says quickly.

He smiles. "I'll be there. I bought a ticket last week."

Millie beams. "You . . . *did*?"

He nods. "I wouldn't miss it for the world. Hey, I was . . . thinking . . . that maybe . . . I mean, if you wanted to, I could, or I mean, *we* could, well, go . . . together."

Millie's mouth falls open. She's stunned silent, so Liza answers for her. "She'd love that, Fernando!"

He exhales, smiling big as if Liza's response—any response—is more than acceptable.

"Why don't you come by and get her here at five-thirty tomorrow night and you two can walk over together," the dating pro continues.

"Yes," Fernando says, grinning at Liza, then Millie. "That sounds perfect."

"That sounds perfect," Millie echoes, a bit dumbfounded as he heads to the door.

When he's gone, Liza squeals, and I join in the fun. "Millie! Are you breathing? Fernando asked you out on a *date*!"

I can't tell if she's about to laugh or cry or both, but then she turns to us and lets out a squeal of her own. "Did that really just happen?" she asks, wide-eyed.

"Yes, it did," Liza says as Millie returns to the counter, unable to stop smiling. It's so good to see her happy.

"I THINK WE'RE GETTING close to the restaurant," I say to the cab driver over the scrape of the windshield wipers. It's raining so hard that the driver has set them to maximum. Visibility is as low as a foggy night in Seattle.

"You said Bella Norma's, right?"

"Yes."

The driver nods. "It's just over there, across the street."

I wipe the fog from the window, and there it is—a charming little corner spot that's dimly lit, with candles flickering in the windows. *Perfect.*

I pay the fare, then dash through the crosswalk. Ducking for cover under the restaurant's awning, I pat the water droplets off my cheeks, praying that my waterproof mascara will hold.

"I'm Valentina Baker," I say to the hostess stationed at the entrance, "here to meet Daniel Davenport." *I like the sound of that.*

"Ah, yes. I have your table ready." She selects two menus and leads me through the small dining room, stopping at a cozy table for two near the window. I'm five minutes early, as usual. Would Daniel run late, the way Nick always had? I'm too nervous to look at the menu. Instead, I gaze out the window at the rain-drenched street, eagerly anticipating his arrival, which is impressively cinematic, as seems appropriate for a filmmaker.

At the top of the hour, precisely as the clock strikes six, the man who must be Daniel Davenport walks inside the restaurant—not early, not late, but right on time. He hands his coat to the hostess, and I can see that he's tall and handsome, even beyond what Debbie had described. As he begins walking toward the table, my heart beats faster with each of his steps. I'm suddenly plagued with anxiety and have the urge to cover my face, or maybe bolt to the restroom, but somehow Daniel's gaze tethers me to my seat.

"Well, hello there," he says, his tall frame looming over the table.

"Hello," I say in a squeak. I don't know what to do with my hands and I feel as if my legs have quite possibly become paralyzed, or maybe it's that they've melted into pools of gelatinous liquid beneath the table. I can't feel them. I can't feel anything, and I'm positive that my cheeks are at least fourteen shades of crimson. Possibly even sixteen.

"I hope I haven't kept you waiting long," he says, sliding into his chair.

A man who apologizes for being on time? Who is this guy? Is he even real?

"Oh no," I begin. "The thing is . . . my ex was always late. And I'm always early. So, I guess I'm just used to men being late." I cover my mouth. "Oh my gosh, I must be nervous. I'm rambling. And talking about my ex. Sorry." I rub my forehead. "I'll shut up now."

"Don't apologize," Daniel says. *Look how white his teeth are.* "I'll confess that I'm a little nervous, too. First dates are awkward, but I have to say, you're even prettier than I imagined. And, don't get me wrong, from the way Deb described you, I imagined you'd be quite pretty."

"Well, thank you, I guess," I say, straightening my fork on the table so it's parallel to the knife. "You're quite handsome yourself."

"Deb also tells me that you're trying to solve a mystery," he adds. "As a documentary filmmaker, I must admit that piqued my curiosity."

"Yeah," I reply. "It's about an old book, filled with annotations—"

He nods, then picks up the menu in front of him. "There'll be plenty of time to delve into all that over dinner. What sounds good to you?"

I glance at the list of entrées, though they fail to hold my attention. My eyes drift up to his face again and study his deep-set brown eyes. When a waiter comes to check on us, Daniel orders a bottle of wine.

"I'm afraid it all looks good," I say, setting my menu down. "Perhaps you should order for us?"

"Well, there's always the eggplant ceviche," he says, raising an eyebrow. "It was written up in *The Times* recently."

"Oh," I say. "About that. Um, I have a confession to make." He leans in.

I crinkle my nose. "I've . . . never liked eggplant. Um, or ceviche." I smile. "And you're probably seriously doubting my investigative abilities right about now, given that I can't even parse a menu."

He bursts into laughter. "No, I trust your instincts even more. I actually hate *eggplant*."

"But you suggested it!"

"I know," he continues with an air of self-deprecation. "I was trying to sound posh. But . . . I got caught."

"You know," I say, laughing, "that's one of the funniest confessions I've heard in a long time. You're an eggplant fake."

"Guilty."

"We both are," I add.

He cocks his head to the right, looking at me with an amused and rather boyish smile. "You know, I have a feeling that we have more in common than our aversion to eggplant, Ms. Valentina Baker."

"Oh really, Mr. Daniel Davenport?"

"WOULD YOU LIKE TO walk for a bit?" Daniel asks after the waiter has cleared the table. He takes care of the bill before I can even offer to contribute. "Indulge a documentarian," he says. "I have questions, and I'd like to get to know you better."

I laugh as we walk outside, grateful to see that the rain has subsided. "Yes, sir," I say. "But only as long as you let me turn the camera on you. Debbie says you have quite the interesting career in film."

"Right. I see she told you about my twenty-nine Academy Awards, did she?"

I glance over at him, grinning. "Well, she did sing your praises."

"The problem with working in film is that everyone thinks it's very glamorous, when, in fact, you might even find it a bit dull. At the end of the day, I'm just a humble storyteller—with no Academy Awards." He smiles. "Do you still like me?"

"I'd hardly call that dull," I say. "It sounds fascinating. And yes, I still like you. Tell me, what subjects most interest you?"

"Oh, it runs the gamut. We put out a film last year about what life is like for children in one of the poorest regions of the Philippines, specifically Apayao. It garnered some humanitarian interest that seems to be making a difference, at least a bit." He smiles. "That's really all that matters to me."

"I love change-making projects," I say, blowing some warmth onto my cold hands "That's sort of what I'm doing here in London, at the Book Garden."

"And what drew you to books?" he asks.

"In a nutshell? My mother. She read aloud to me from the time I was a baby. She loved books and taught me to love them, too."

"So how did you end up in London again?"

I tell him about my mother's abrupt departure from my life, when she'd left for London to start a new life—or maybe the same one, all over again.

"Ah," Daniel says. "Just as I suspected. We're getting to the source of your deepest unknowns."

I smile nervously. "The documentarian takes note."

"So, after your mother left, how did you stay connected to her?"

"I didn't, really. She went from being my whole world to being . . . gone. For a long while, time seemed to stand still. Or perhaps it was just me who remained frozen in place. But books saved me. I spent a lot of time at the library, reading books I thought she might have enjoyed. I studied library science and worked as a librarian for many years."

"Like mother, like daughter," Daniel continues. "And then what happened?"

"Well, after my marriage ended—and that's the subject of *another* inquiry—I came here to London and took over her bookstore, which has been like a treasure trove for me. She even left a scavenger hunt, with clues all over Primrose Hill that I'm still finding."

"She loved you very much," he says. "That's abundantly clear."

I nod. "I know that, and also I . . . don't."

He nods, pausing in front of a closed café as he looks up to the sky. "The stars do, though."

I look up, too, taking in the sky over London. "My mum used to tell us that the stars have this thing with the city lights—a battle, so to speak. Eternity versus modernity, or something like that. It always gave her comfort that no matter how much technology advanced or how sophisticated we think we are, the stars still shine brighter. They always will."

"Wow," he says. "That's . . . really beautiful, and thought-provoking stuff. When did your parents split up?"

"When I was twelve. Divorce is awful, and apparently, history repeats itself. Mine will be finalized soon."

He stops suddenly, turning to me with a grave expression.

"I'm sorry, Valentina. It's been a . . . really fun night, and it's been lovely meeting you, but I don't think I can be with some-one who's divorced."

"Oh," I say, taking a step back. "I . . ."

He laughs. "I'm only kidding. Obviously, I don't care at all that you're divorced, or rather, almost-divorced."

I exhale, giving his shoulder a playful punch. "You know, I actually believed you for a second."

"Sorry, I couldn't help it. I'm actually divorced, too."

"You are?"

"Indeed. Her name was April and we were both twenty-one. Turns out, she had a thing for my best man."

"No!"

"Yes," he continues. "Of course, I was devastated at the time. I felt as if she'd taken a bulldozer to my heart." He presses his hand to his chest and shakes his head solemnly. "I never thought I'd get over it, but you know what's funny? The other day, I realized that I'd completely forgotten her eye color."

I laugh.

"Were they green? Blue?" He shakes his head. "Maybe brown? I'm absolutely serious. I have no idea, and nor, of course, do I care. But it reminded me that the human heart has an incredible capacity to heal." He slowly reaches down for my hand, and when he does, I feel a tingle that creeps up my arm. "And to love again."

"I like that," I say, smiling. "Hey, you know what's funny? We haven't talked at all about *The Last Winter*."

He stops in front of a lamppost and looks at me for a long moment, the light's reflection adding a bit of glimmer to his gaze. "We'll have all the time in the world to talk about the past. All our lives even, if we're so lucky. What do you say we stay in the present for now?"

"Deal," I say, but I can't help but wonder if Daniel's literary foray ended with that college course. What if he isn't the voracious reader that, say, Eric is? Would we be compatible?

"I'd love to see you again, Valentina," he says, his eyes fixed on mine as my hesitations slip away. "What are you doing tomorrow night?"

I tell him about the fundraiser for the bookstore. "Wait, why don't you come?"

"I'd love to," he says quickly.

And just like that, Daniel Davenport jumped out of a book's pages and into my life.

Eloise

June 1990

———

AFTER DINNER, I WENT UPSTAIRS TO DRESS, THEN STOPPED into Val's room, where I found her reading, of course.

"Mummy, why are you all dressed up?" she asked, her eyes awash with concern when she saw me. "Are you going somewhere?"

"Just into town for a little while, honey. I'll be home soon."

She smiled and turned back to her book as I kissed her head.

Frank was in the living room when I reached for my keys. "I'm heading out for a bit," I told him as he looked up.

"What on earth are you doing dressed to the nines on a Thursday night, may I ask?"

"I thought I'd check out the art walk, down on Abbot Kinney," I reply casually. If he could have his private world, I could have mine.

He eyed me curiously. "An *art walk*?"

As long as we'd been married, he'd never remarked on my comings and goings, but lately, he seemed interested. Perhaps, *too interested*.

"There'll be rows of galleries, all kinds of emerging artists.

You mentioned wanting to replace that Impressionist oil in the living room with a more modern work. I thought I'd have a look."

"That's right," he said. "I know you love the nineteenth century, but this house needs something more modern. Why don't you pick something out to my taste this time?"

Val appeared on the stairs before I could reply that I'd pick out what I wanted to, thank you very much.

"Mummy and Daddy, what do we think of a pink-and-white striped birthday cake next year?" she asks. I couldn't help but smile—my daughter, with her effervescent zest for life. Barely two months had passed since she turned twelve and blew out the candles on her cake (adorned with candied violets—her idea), but that didn't stop her from dreaming about next year's party.

"I think that sounds perfect," I tell her.

Frank sat in silence as Val and I discussed the merits of fondant frosting, finally agreeing that buttercream was a better option. I gave her a kiss before she ran back to her room. She had homework to do, but I knew she'd spend at least as much time thinking about next year's guest list, as well as the cake.

In the entryway, I slipped on a sweater, applied a bit of pink lipstick before checking my reflection in the mirror by the door.

"You look awfully beautiful tonight," Frank said, startling me from behind.

"Thank you," I said, catching my breath. His comment felt less like a compliment and more like an accusation.

"Is everything all right?" he continued. "You don't seem like yourself tonight."

"That's funny," I said, reaching for the keys to the Volvo, "because I've never felt *more* like myself."

AT THE ART WALK that night, I perused vendor booths, stopping when something caught my eye. I was alone, of course, as I so often was in California, but for the first time in so long, I didn't feel *lonely*.

I paused to take in a landscape painting, which reminded me of the English countryside where my mother took me once as a child, but my mind was still on Frank—his troubles, his need to control the narrative and *me*. I sighed, walking ahead, stopping to look at a modern painting on a table to my right. The scene immediately resonated—oil on canvas, depicting a little girl jumping into a pool, with a mid-century modern home in the background. It was small, but I knew Frank would love it, and surprisingly, *so did I*.

The intersection of two worlds, two hearts, I thought as I reached into my purse, pulling out the money I'd made from selling a few of my old dresses from Harrods at a consignment store recently. I paid the artist and tucked the painting—a gift to Frank—into my bag. A peace offering.

I started walking back to my car when I heard my name echoing in the night.

"Eloise?"

I turned around to find a man standing a few feet behind me. It was dark, so it took me a moment recognize him and connect the dots, but I did.

"It's Peter," he said, smiling. "We met down by the beach. You were having parking issues. Do you remember?"

I remembered.

"Yes, of course. Hi . . . Peter."

"How are you?"

"Fine, thank you," I said, walking ahead, sideswiping a man with a heavy camera strapped to his shoulder as Peter followed.

"The paparazzi are out in full force tonight," he said. "Rumor has it that Goldie Hawn and her daughter are here."

"I may have my own problems," I said with a smile, "but I'm grateful that lack of privacy isn't one."

"I know," he added, catching up to me. "I wouldn't trade my freedom for anything."

Freedom. I thought about what Peter just said, though I could only partly agree. While he might live the life he chose, I would never have my American dream. Land of the free, home of the brave, they say, but I felt neither free nor brave— just . . . invisible.

"Hey, what are you doing tonight? Maybe we could . . . grab a late dinner, or a drink?"

But now, I felt . . . *seen.*

I paused, immediately flattered, as I adjusted the tote bag in my hand, with Frank's painting inside, while considering Peter's invitation. At first, it seemed harmless, fun even— a quick drink, a little conversation, maybe we'd even walk to the beach and kick off our shoes. It would be crossing the line, of course, but oh how I longed to know what was on the other side of that line that kept me in my safe, comfortable, but lonely place for far too long.

I could feel Peter's gaze imploring me to take the first step, to join him in this new world of freedom. But as appealing as it was, I knew he wasn't my ticket out. No man would ever be.

"I'm sorry," I said. "I'd love to, I really would, but you see, I'm married. And I just . . . can't."

"Oh," he replied, his face equal parts understanding and disappointed. "Well, if anything changes, look me up, okay?"

"Sure," I said waving goodbye.

But I wouldn't. I'd walk to my car and drive home, kiss Valentina's sleepy head, and wander into my bedroom alone.

Valentina

The Next Day

———

THE EVENING OF THE FUNDRAISER ARRIVES WITH AS much excitement as it does nerves. Millie and I meet in Liza's flat to start the evening with a celebratory toast.

"How do I look?" Millie asks, nervously surveying her reflection in the mirror.

"Gorgeous," I say, admiring her long, black-sequined evening gown. "Fernando will be starstruck. Speaking of, when will he be here?"

She glances at her watch. "I'm meeting him in front of the store in ten minutes. Goodness, we have to hurry!"

"Now, hold still," Liza scolds, attempting to dab Millie's eyelids with a dusting of taupe eye shadow. "You don't want to look like a racoon, do you?"

After a few moments, she steps back to admire her masterpiece, nodding with satisfaction before applying a mist of setting spray.

I'm glad to see she's chosen a classic, muted palette for Millie, and not one more suited to, say, the members of an all-girl punk rock band.

"There," she says. "Perfection."

I pop the champagne as Liza slips into her dress—a short blue number with a flouncy waist and a spray of peacock feathers on the shoulder. If anyone can pull off such a zany fashion statement, it's Liza. Besides, it matches her hair. I smile to myself, pouring us each a glass of bubbly as she dabs her eyelids with a swath of blue shimmer.

"To the Book Garden," I say, raising my glass. "May it live on."

"To the best of friends," Millie says.

"And to new romances," Liza adds, winking at us both as we clink our glasses and gather our handbags.

I give myself one last sideways glance in the mirror. While I'd packed for an indefinite stay in London, I hadn't antici-pated dressing up, much less going on a second date with a man I'd discovered in a book. Thankfully, Liza's initial tour of Primrose Hill had included the little boutique down the street. Just as I'm hoping my fellow local business owners will support the Book Garden, I'm doing my part for them. I found a few options, eventually settling on a simple but flat-tering black cocktail dress with a tie at the waist.

"You need a necklace," Liza says.

I shrug. "I'm afraid I'm out of options on that front."

"Your mother had quite a jewelry collection," Millie says. "Come with me."

I follow her upstairs, and it's clear she knows Mummy's flat like the back of her hand. "In here," she says, pointing to an enormous jewelry box in the bedroom. I'd noticed it the day I arrived, and yet, somehow, I couldn't bring myself to inspect its contents.

But Millie does it for me. I watch as she opens each drawer, carefully examining every piece until she finds just the one. "Here," she says, clasping a chunky crystal necklace around my throat. "It's a gorgeous dress, but you need a statement piece to jazz it up."

I touch my collarbone as I glance at my reflection. I'd never, in a million years, think to wear something like this, but just like a bit of lemon zest heightens the flavor in a dish, she's right—a splash of color amplifies the cut of my dress.

"Naturally, it suits you," Liza adds, standing in the doorway.

"This one was special to your mum," Millie explains. "One of the 1930s Trifari pieces she collected at estate sales in California."

I place my fingers on the necklace again, then reach for my champagne.

As I do, Millie clears her throat. "Val, Liza," she says. "Come close."

She raises her glass. "One more toast is due—the most important of them all. To Eloise."

"To Mummy," I say under my breath, the words filled with years of pent-up emotion.

"Isn't it just like her to make everyone she loves more beautiful simply by having known her?"

I smile, letting her words sink in. Millie is right, beauty followed my mother—but so did pain. Tonight, however, I will myself not to focus on the latter.

"Listen, you two," I say to Liza and Millie. "No matter what happens tonight, if our efforts are successful or not, let's take comfort in knowing that we did our best."

Millie smiles, raising her champagne glass again. "To Valentina," she says. "Our fearless leader."

I prayed she didn't see the fear in my eyes as we set out for the event, and this great unknown.

LIZA AND I FOLLOW behind Millie and Fernando as we walk the three blocks to Café Flora together. He'd arrived at the bookstore precisely when he said he would in a freshly pressed suit and holding a bouquet of pastel-colored roses for Millie, who was so stunned, Liza had to coax her to take them from his outstretched arms. All she could do was smile, and oh what a smile as they walked ahead together—Millie adorably towering above him.

We arrive at Café Flora to find that, not surprisingly, Jan and her husband have truly outdone themselves. Not only does each table feature gorgeous cut flowers and linens, but there are also clever literary touches everywhere, like classic book covers for table tags and cocktail menus that double as bookmarks. All around the perimeter are the donated items for the silent auction.

"It's just perfect," I say to Jan as the jazz trio in the corner begins warming up. "Thank you ever so much."

Before long, guests begin filtering in, and I wave at a few of our regular customers as Millie greets them.

"When's Daniel coming?" Liza asks, reaching for a drink from a passing waiter's tray.

"He should be here soon," I say, glancing at the clock on the wall, a little disappointed to notice that he's already fifteen minutes late.

Another twenty minutes pass, however, and as everyone takes to their tables for dinner, the chair beside me remains empty.

"He's probably just stuck in traffic," Liza says, appeasing me.

I nod, checking my phone to find a text from Daniel. "Val, I'm so very sorry. We've had a production crisis, and I'm stuck here working tonight. I feel terrible and pray that you can forgive me. I'll make it up to you, I promise."

"He's not coming," I say to Liza with a sigh, tucking my phone into my purse.

"Not coming?" Liza asks, clearly infuriated on my behalf.

"Some work crisis, I guess."

"Ugh," she says, motioning to a waiter, who hands me another glass of champagne. "I don't like that at all. Does he have any idea how important this night is to you? It's like he's—"

"Excuse me, ladies, is this seat taken?"

We both look up to see Eric standing tall behind us, and I smile.

"No, it's all yours," Liza says. "You can be Val's date. Hers stood her up."

"Oh," Eric says, settling into the seat beside me, his eyes filled with concern. "I'm sorry to hear that."

"He didn't *stand me up*," I say, correcting Liza. "He just . . . had a work thing."

Eric nods, reaching for a glass of champagne from a nearby waiter. "Well, that's no fun. But his loss, and my gain, I guess." He smiles.

"Thanks for coming," I reply. "Your support means a lot to us."

"I wouldn't have missed it for the world. I'm just sorry Fiona couldn't be here. She has a big deadline looming for a client in Chelsea. I guess that leaves us both orphans with workaholic dates."

I laugh. "It seems we do have that in common."

"Look at all of this," he says, glancing around the room. I notice Millie watching us from a nearby table, but I don't make eye contact with her. "Your mum would be so proud."

Would she? I watch as our guests mill about the room, making bids on auction items on the tables along the perimeter, hoping it will be enough.

"It's funny," I say, turning back to Eric. "When I arrived in London, I didn't expect to fall in love with Primrose Hill the way I have." I wave at the local butcher, Tom, who walks by with his wife, Greta.

"It's an easy thing to do," he replies, setting his salad fork down. "Just as this community has fallen in love with *you*."

A burst of color rushes to my cheeks, and for some reason, Daniel's absence isn't weighing on me anymore. I feel light and free, happy even, like the effervescent bubbles in my glass of champagne.

After dinner, Eric suggests we have a look at the silent auction, where he places a generous—winning—bid on a basket of wine, and another on a card beside a box of some of my mother's vintage first-edition books. They'd been difficult to part with, but I knew their value would bring a considerable amount for the Book Garden's benefit, and it made me happy that they'd find a new home on Eric's bookshelf. He'd look out for them.

"Hello, you two," Millie says, walking up to us. "I have a good feeling about this night."

"Me too," I say as Jan takes to the microphone to make a few remarks before the waiters begin passing dessert—individual ramekins of vanilla custard with raspberries on top.

Eric and I mingle with other guests, and at one point, I reflexively reach up to adjust his tie, which is a bit askew. "Sorry," I say. "I couldn't resist. It was a little crooked."

He grins. "You've let me walk around with a crooked tie all evening? What sort of friend are you?"

"Obviously a very bad one," I say, laughing.

"I'm only kidding," he says, his smile turning serious. "You're actually the . . . very best sort of friend." Before I can reply, he glances at his watch, as the party winds down. "I should be going. I need to let the hostess say her goodbyes."

The evening passed in a mere blink of an eye, it seems, and I wave to Eric as he sets out to the street with his basket of wine.

"Val," Jan says, approaching, "we just received a very generous phone-in donation. The caller wanted to pass along a message to you."

"A message? For me?"

"Yes," she says, smiling. "One thousand pounds, from a gentleman named Daniel, who asked me to tell you how sorry he is that he couldn't be here tonight."

"Really?" I say, grinning. "That's . . . amazing." The grand gesture was enough to make me forgive him immediately.

Millie, Liza, Fernando, and I stayed for the next hour helping Jan's staff clean up, which is when I noticed the box of vintage books Eric had bid on earlier, left behind on the table. "Oh shoot," I say to Liza. "He forgot these."

She smiles. "No, he didn't."

"What do you mean?" I glance at the auction card beside the box. "See, he placed the winning bid."

"He bought them for you, silly," she continues, which is when I notice a note taped to the edge with my name on it.

Val,

If anyone deserves to have these treasures, it's you. Happy reading.

Your friend,
Eric

I BEND DOWN TO collect a few programs from the floor as Millie approaches.

"Well, what do you think?"

"I think we did it," I say, smiling. "Did Fernando have a nice time?"

Millie nods wistfully. "He just left."

"And how did it go with *him*?"

Her expression erupts in a smile that appears impossible to hide. "Good. No, it was *perfect*."

"Oh, Millie. I'm so happy for you."

"But are *you* happy, dear?" she asks, her wise eyes cutting right to my heart.

I swallow hard. "Yes," I say. "It was just a . . . big night. I guess I'm feeling a lot of different emotions right now."

"I know," she says. "Come, I'll walk you home."

As we walk, our conversation naturally turns to my mother, and I find myself recounting the weeks and months after she left for London. "I wrote her every day for an entire year. An entire year, Millie. After that, I continued writing, less frequently, but often." I pause, shaking my head, tears welling up in my eyes. "She never wrote me back—not once. I used to tell myself that I'd been sending the letters to the wrong address. Or that Mummy was busy, and that when I finally got a letter from her, it would be as long as a book." I search Millie's eyes, like a treasure map, for any clue. "But I never did."

She shakes her head, mouth agape.

"What?"

"Val, she did write you," Millie says, *"every day."* Her words sting. *"Every single day.* She'd stop by the post office each morning—it was her daily routine. Valentina, your mother was *always* writing to you. *Always.*"

"But, Millie, I . . ." I say, my voice shaking. "I . . . never received any of them."

Eloise

Later That Same Night

———

I PULLED THE CAR INTO THE DRIVEWAY, AND GATHERED my bags before walking along the familiar path that led to our front door. Crickets chirped in the warm night, singing their lullabies for my sleeping family inside.

I rushed upstairs, then tiptoed into Val's bedroom. The floppy-eared bunny rabbit she'd slept with since birth had fallen from her grasp. I bent down to pick it up, then tucked it in beside her, kissing her cheek gently. She still looked like a baby when she slept, even if she was well on her way to womanhood.

I decided it was time to tell her a love story. My love story.

Val stirred in her bed. "Mummy? Is that you?"

"Yes, my darling. Mummy's here. Don't wake up. I'll sit with you, while you sleep."

"Tell me a story," she murmured softly, "about London."

I closed my eyes. "Yes, let's travel back in time, to the year 1968."

"Let's go," Val said, only half awake.

"That was the year I met my love." I pause. "The year I met your father."

Val curled tighter into her blankets, comforted.

I was emboldened to continue.

"There once was a fine place in London," I said. "Someone like me would never have been invited. Until I was."

I skipped over the part about my lifelong, crippling insecurity, my feeling of never belonging anywhere, except in the pages of books.

"Everyone there was dressed in fine clothing. The tables were set with real silver and china. Only the tastiest dishes were on the menu."

"Is that a real place, Mummy?" Val asked. "It sounds too pretty to be real."

"It did feel like a dream," I said. "A dream come true."

I retreated into myself then, my thoughts spiraling until I could no longer separate the stories of the two men on that fateful night. Frank and . . . Edward.

The night I met him . . .

He understood me at once.

He finished my sentences.

He was kind.

He looked at me like I was the one he'd been waiting for.

And then he was gone.

And then he took me away.

"That's where the story ends, Val. And where you begin. He changed my life forever. He brought me to you."

Valentina

Two Days Later

———

AT THE BOOK GARDEN, MILLIE, LIZA, AND I ARE HARD at work—and also trying to take our minds off the results of the fundraiser, which haven't come in yet.

"Have you heard from Daniel?" Liza asks me.

While his absence at the event had been a disappointment, to be sure, he'd made up for it with his generous and unexpected donation. And yet, two days had passed and my thank-you text to him went unanswered, which I tell Liza.

"He's probably just busy," Millie chimes in.

Liza shakes her head. "No, I think it's more likely that he's playing the game."

"The game?"

She nods. "Yeah, he doesn't want to seem overly eager. Everyone knows that after the first date, you wait three days to call or text. After the second, you wait two, and after the third, you wait one. Those are the rules."

I shake my head. "The . . . *rules*? So, what happens after the fourth date?"

"Oh, that's when you can call or text freely, but not too freely until after the *third month*."

I bury my face in my hands. "This is *way* too complicated for me. I quit."

"Now, now," Millie says. "It will all work itself out."

I smirk. "That's easy for you to say. You and Fernando call each other every five minutes! And you're not playing by any rules."

"Well," counters Liza, our resident relationship expert—who, I might add, is presently single. "If you count all the flirting that led up to their first date, you could argue that the rules don't apply to them. They've already surpassed all that. You, on the other hand, still have work to do."

"This is too much for me," I say, placing my hand on my forehead for dramatic effect as Millie answers her phone. Naturally, it's Fernando.

"Those two," Liza says with a sigh, "are getting a bit nauseating. But bloody hell, are they cute together."

"They are," I say, glancing at my phone with a sigh.

"Any word from Jan?" Liza asks.

"Still waiting." She'd promised to call today or tomorrow with news about the total amount raised, as some credit card transactions and checks required a few days to clear. We'd need at least £250,000 to pull us through. I know the goal is staggering and the likelihood of succeeding small, but we made a pact to remain optimistic—it's all we can do.

When my phone rings, I startle, but it's neither Daniel nor Jan, just an unknown number. I decide to answer.

"Val? Oh my gosh, I'm so glad you picked up."

It's Nick, and I instantly regret answering. His voice

sounds different—familiar but far-off, too—like someone I knew in high school—or a former life. "I'm calling from a friend's phone, because . . . you haven't been picking up. I've been trying to get ahold of you, and—"

"Look, Nick," I say, with a sigh, "I'm not sure I really want to talk."

"Listen," he says, "I just . . . wanted to tell you how sorry I am. I screwed up in the most terrible way. I have so many regrets."

"So, I take it that you and what's-her-name broke up?"

"Yes, we did," he replies soberly. "Val, I don't know what I was thinking. I had the perfect thing with you and I . . . I threw it all away. And I just . . . I wanted to tell you how sorry I am, for everything."

I don't know what to say, so I remain silent, taking in his words, letting them marinate in my mind, and heart.

"Don't hang up," Nick says.

I hear a commotion in the background.

"Where are you?" I ask.

"In the kitchen. I'm cooking, at least, *attempting*."

"Nick, *you don't cook.*"

"I know," he continues. "I mean, I didn't, but I'm learning out of necessity. I . . . miss your cooking. I miss all your books lying around everywhere. Val, I miss . . . *you.*"

Part of me still longed to hear those words. For a long time, it was all I dreamed about—the fantasy of Nick begging my forgiveness, pleading for another start. But so much had changed since then. I'd changed. Even if he had apologized—and learned to cook—Nick was no longer my sun, moon, and stars. In fact, I'd found a whole new universe.

"Say something, Val," he says nervously. "Talk to me. Tell me you miss me as much as I miss you. Tell me you'll forgive me. I'll come to London. We can have a new start. Please, babe, I'll do anything."

And that's when it hits me. I don't want him to come to London. I don't want him to *set foot* in London.

I take a deep breath, pausing for a long beat before I reply. "Nick," I finally say. "Thank you for calling, for . . . saying what you did. The thing is, I did miss you. For a long time, actually. But I've finally healed. I've found my way."

Liza and Millie are listening with wide eyes.

"I tell you what I do miss, though," I continue. "I miss . . . the dream of us. I miss the girl who wore a white dress and carried a bouquet of pale pink roses and looked ahead to a full life—of family, love, happiness. I miss looking into the eyes of my husband and trusting him. I miss . . . what might have been, but now, never will be." I swallow hard. "But you know what I don't miss? Feeling lonely. Because, Nick, in our marriage, I was so deeply lonely."

"Val, I . . . I'm so sorry. I wish I could say something to—"

"Don't," I say. "It's okay. I want you to know that I forgive you. I'll always wish the best for you. Goodbye, Nick." I end the call before he can say anything more.

"Damn, girl," Liza says, clapping her hands. "That was *impressive*."

"You handled that brilliantly," Millie says.

I wipe away a tear—the last one I'll shed for him. "It's over. It's really over."

The three of us pause when we notice two men speaking loudly to each other outside on the street. One gestures toward the building with large arm movements, as the other pulls a tape measure from his pocket and runs it along the length of the front window.

"Who are *they*?" Liza asks, walking to the window suspiciously.

A moment later, the men walk into the store.

"The lot's an unusual size," one says to the other. "But it'll work."

"Look," the other says, pointing ahead. "It narrows in the back a bit, like the architect said. Can we work with that?"

"It'll take some creative engineering," the other says. "But I don't see why not. The price is right." They both laugh in unison.

"Excuse me, gentlemen," Millie says, stepping forward like a protective mother bear. "May we help you?"

"Good day to you," the taller of the two says to Millie. "And who might you be?"

"The real question is, who might *you* be?"

The shorter man digs into his pocket and pulls out a crinkled business card. "Bayer Construction, general manager. Hate to bring up a sore subject, but after the tax lien's in place, we'll be the new owners." He kicks the edge of a bookcase with a heavy boot. "Look at that. Solid mahogany. They don't make 'em like that anymore." He turns to the other man. "Could we salvage these, maybe? Sell them?"

"That's enough," Millie says. "I don't know who you two think you are or what you are doing, but, gentlemen, if you're not here to buy a book, I'll have to ask you to leave."

The taller man smirks, squaring his shoulders. "My, my, the old librarian is quite a feisty one."

"Indeed, she is," I say, standing my ground. "I'm the owner

of this building, and as of today, I'm unaware of any reason—tax liens or otherwise—that allows you to loiter in our store. I'll remind you that this is private property, and if you refuse to leave immediately, I'll be forced to call the authorities and make a harassment complaint."

The doorbells jingle and Fernando appears, reading the situation. His eyes are laser-focused on the two men.

"Gentlemen," I continue, "I think it's time we show you to the door."

"Perhaps you're hard of hearing," Fernando adds when the men don't budge. "The lady asked you to leave." He walks closer, cracking his knuckles in a loud crescendo, which makes me want to hug him.

We watch in silence as they saunter out, gasping collectively when they're gone.

Millie rushes to Fernando and kisses his cheek as Percy stands guard at the window, meowing loudly.

"Is it true?" Liza whispers. "What they said about . . . *taking possession once there's a tax lien on the building?*"

I shake my head as Millie and Fernando look over. "No," I say with more conviction than ever. "Until our very last moment, we're going to keep selling books."

"HELLO," I SAY, ANSWERING my phone in my most breathy, carefree voice. It's 9:13 P.M.

I've just finished loading the dishwasher, and I'm in my sweats, about to head to bed with a book.

"Val? Hi, it's Daniel."

"Oh, hi, Daniel," I say breezily, though my heart is beating so fast, I fear it might leap out of my chest. I remember

Liza's "rules," and pause. "Um, will you just . . . give me a moment? I had a little party tonight and I . . . I'm just saying goodbye to . . . some friends." I wave to a few imaginary party guests in the doorway, before sinking into the couch.

"How have you been?" he asks.

"Fine, great," I say. "Excellent."

"Fabulous," he says. "Listen, I'm sorry I haven't called. The craziest thing happened."

"Oh? What?"

"The day after your event for the bookstore, I left my phone in a cab. It was a drag, and I was out of touch with everyone until I got it back this evening. I had to track it down from the driver, who had left on a trip to Ireland, but anyway, all is well." He exhales deeply. "Anyway, I want to apologize to you, for the other night—in person."

"It's really okay, Daniel," I say quickly. "Of course, I understand. And I'm sorry about your phone."

"When I said in person, I meant it. I'm here now."

I sit up in a momentary panic. *"You are?"*

"Yeah, I'm standing in front of your bookstore, at least I think I am. It's the Book Garden, right? Didn't you say that your flat is above?"

I cautiously peer over the sofa, look out the window, and there he is, standing on the sidewalk outside, holding a bouquet of flowers. I duck down immediately.

"Uh, yes, yes, it is."

"So, you're having a party?"

"Um," I say. "Well, I was, but everyone . . . just left— through the back alley."

"A shame," he says. "It would have been lovely to meet

them." He pauses. "Hey, it might be too late, but I was thinking . . . maybe I could come up and say hi."

"Oh," I say, my heart racing as I immediately begin tidying up the flat. I shove a pile of laundry into the closet and toss an empty wine bottle into the trash can. "Now?"

"Yeah," he says. "I mean, if it's too late, I can always . . . come back another time. I know it's a bit last-minute."

"No, no," I say quickly, "It's fine. Come up. Use the side entrance. The code is 7893. I'm on the third floor."

What in the world did I just do? Daniel in my flat? I'm wearing sweatpants, for crying out loud. I race to the bedroom and change into a pair of skinny jeans and an off-the-shoulder sweater. My heart lurches when I hear a knock at the door. I take a deep breath and turn the knob, and there he is, standing in my hallway.

"Hey," Daniel says, a look of surprise on his face.

"Hey," I say, leaning into the doorframe casually. He hands me a bouquet of flowers, grinning.

"Thank you," I say, "they're beautiful."

"Tell me," he says, casting an incredulous look my way as I fumble through the kitchen cabinets until I find a vase. "Do you always wear a mud mask when hosting a party?"

I touch my face, then gasp, remembering the black charcoal goo I'd smeared on my face a half hour ago. "Good Lord. I forgot I had this on!"

He grins. "It's rather cute. In a . . . reptilian sort of way."

"Oh my gosh," I say, mortified, sidestepping to the bathroom. "I'll just go and . . . wash this off."

I scrub my face, then swipe on a bit of lipstick before evaluating myself in the mirror. It's not my best look—far from it—but I'm grateful that the living room lights are dim.

"Can I get you something to drink?" I ask.

He glances at my glass of red wine on the coffee table. "I'll have what you're having."

I open a fresh bottle and pour him a glass, then return to the sofa beside him. I shift positions nervously, expecting him to resume the documentary-style interview of our first date, but tonight seems to be different, somehow. Our conversation takes a grand tour—his favorite London neighborhoods, my thoughts on the royal family, an old friend of his mother's who is presently incarcerated, fir trees, life and death, and California.

He seems a bit nervous, too.

And then, suddenly, I feel his hand on my hand.

"Listen," he says. "Can I just kiss you and get this over with?"

I laugh, unsure of how to answer. Do Liza's rules apply to moments like this?

"I don't know if I'm breaking the rules," he says, making me smile, "but, damn, Valentina, do I want to kiss you. Is that"—he pauses, inching closer to me—"all right?"

I want to be kissed, too. "Yes," I whisper.

I close my eyes as Daniel's lips meet mine, and for a moment, I feel as if I'm practically levitating. In fifteen years, I'd only kissed one other man—Nick, obviously—but this is different, and new.

Daniel smiles, cupping my face in his hands, then kissing my forehead softly. "We should do more of that."

"We should?" I say, a bit stunned. "I mean, yes, *we should*."

"What are you doing tomorrow night?"

"Nothing," I say quickly.

"Good," he says. "Then I'd like to take you to dinner at the club."

"The club?"

"The RAC," he says, pausing when I don't connect the dots. "The Royal Automobile Club. My family has been members for ages. It's a stuffy old London curiosity, but it can be pretty fun, if you like that sort of thing. They filmed a scene of *Downton Abbey* there a few years ago. Anyway, I'm supposed to meet a friend of mine and his girlfriend there for dinner tomorrow night at seven, and, well, would you like to join me?"

"A double date."

"Yeah," he says. "So, what do you say?"

"Well, yes—of course. I . . . can't wait."

"Good." He kisses me a final time before heading to the door. "Sweet dreams, Valentina."

Eloise

The Next Day

———

I SAT UP AND YAWNED AS THE MORNING SUNLIGHT FIL-
tered in through my bedroom windows. A moment later, Val
barreled in the door, leaping onto my bed with her pink back-
pack strapped to her shoulders. "Good morning, Mummy!"
she exclaimed, nuzzling in beside me. I glanced at the alarm
clock on the nightstand; Bonnie would be taking her to
school soon.

"Don't forget the flowers," I said, "for your teacher's birthday. I left them on the breakfast table."

"Okay, Mummy," she said, hugging me tightly. Soon, her
childhood would be over and she'd blossom into a young
woman. As much as I looked forward to knowing her in
adulthood, I longed to keep her just like this—my adoring
baby girl. "Hurry now, you'll be late!"

She skipped ahead out the door as I sighed and got up for
the day. I dressed, then pulled my hair back before reaching
for the painting I'd bought the night before—for Frank. I
planned to hang it near the entryway as a surprise for him
when he got home.

"Good morning," he said, startling me when I reached the base of the stairs.

"Frank," I said, taken aback. "I thought you'd already left for the office."

"I'm taking the morning off," he said from the sofa, his arms folded across his chest. "Eloise, I think we should talk."

"Oh, okay," I said cheerfully, eager to show him the painting. "But first, I have a surprise for you." I sat beside him, setting the artwork on the coffee table for him to see, but he barely paid it any attention before his eyes drifted off ahead.

"I consigned a few of my old dresses recently," I continued. "Anyway, I bought it last night, at the art walk—for you. It reminded me of Val, and our house a bit. Do you see the resemblance? Do you like it? I thought we could hang it over there, by the—"

"Eloise," he said, "where were you last night, exactly?"

"Why, Frank, you already know—at the art walk. I told you."

A shadow covered his face; I couldn't make out his expression. "Why don't you tell me what you were *really* doing."

"Frank, what on earth do you mean?"

He handed me a manila folder. "Look inside."

Stunned, I pulled out the stack of photos. On top was a closeup of Peter and me, talking on the sidewalk last night. I looked away, but Frank grabbed my chin, forcing my gaze back.

"Look at them," he demanded.

I obeyed, flipping through the other photographs—some from months prior—of me walking in or out of homes in the areas where I'd visited estate sales. "Frank, this is ridiculous,"

I finally said, my heart pounding in my chest. "You had me followed while I was shopping?"

"I just have one question, Eloise," he said, his eyes filled with disdain. "Did you think you could fool me? Did you *actually* think I wouldn't find out?"

"Frank," I cried. "You've lost your mind."

"I've lost my mind?" He laughed. "I'm not the one traipsing around the city in the night having romantic encounters."

"Romantic encounters?" I shook my head. "I was at an art walk, Frank."

He reached for a photo of Peter in the stack. "Exhibit A."

"You can't be serious," I cried. "I don't even know him!"

He smirked, tossing a scrap of paper in my lap. "Then why did I find this in your purse?"

I gasped, eyeing the note Peter left on my car that day at the beach with Val. *"You went through my purse?"*

"Say what you will, but I have the facts; my private detective confirmed everything. The man in the photos is the same man who wrote you the note you kept in your purse. I have all the evidence."

"Well, the 'evidence' is wrong," I said. "The photos show nothing, because there's nothing to see! Frank, for the love of God, why are you doing this?"

"I'm the one asking the questions, Eloise."

"So you're interrogating me."

"I'm presenting the truth."

"No, you're not," I said. "You're creating your own narrative, as you always have. I did absolutely nothing wrong last night. And the other photos that your brilliant detective took of me were from estate sales. You know it's a hobby of mine!"

I felt cornered, out of options, but Frank was undeterred.

He was in control now, and I couldn't say anything that would change things.

"Look, your chin's quivering," he said. "You're scared, aren't you?"

He was right. I was scared—of where this inquiry was going. Frank had snapped, gone completely off course, and I was struggling to pull him back on the track.

"The newspaper listings will confirm the dates and addresses of every one of those estate sales," I said. "Tell your PI to go match them up. That will prove I'm telling the truth."

"I have a photo of you standing close to a man in the dark," he countered. "That's all the proof I need."

"Frank!" I cried. "Stop this nonsense!"

"Eloise, the only nonsense to speak of is the way you've prioritized your own selfish pursuits above your family."

There he went again, creating his own story—the one he wanted to believe. It made no difference what I said, but I defended myself anyway. "You know that family means everything to me!"

He didn't seem to hear my words. "Eloise, I suggest you start packing. Lord knows what you've amassed in that closet of yours."

I thought of all my carefully curated treasures—from beloved first-edition books to antique vases and jewelry. How could I possibly pack it all, and where did he think I would go?

"I'm not leaving, Frank."

"Let's not make this any harder than it needs to be," he said, his face momentarily softening. "Listen, I know this is very hard, for both of us. We could both use some space." He handed me an envelope thick with cash. "Why don't you take that trip to London you've always talked about—go home and visit your friend Millie for a while. In time, we'll sort all of this out."

I searched his tired face for any shard of the man I'd met in London so many years ago. His youth had long since disappeared, but I failed to remember exactly when he'd changed, really changed. Our fragile connection, it seemed, had withered like daffodils do under the burgeoning late-spring sun.

"Please go pack. When you're ready, I'll call you a cab."

I didn't know what to say or do. But I did know that I had no other choice than to do as Frank said—I knew it in my bones. My husband might have become a stranger, but I still knew him, and well. When he made up his mind, it was final.

I climbed the steps, one at a time, as if my legs were made of bricks. When I finally reached my bedroom, I scanned the closet, unsure of where to begin. It felt ironic, and sad, that I came to Santa Monica with two suitcases, and I'd be leaving with the very same ones.

I pushed past the row of dresses I'd worn to dozens of painfully stuffy cocktail parties and instead surveyed my books, collecting the essentials, which, of course, included *The Last Winter*. I reached for my jewelry case and a small painting of a French country scene I'd fallen in love with, even if Frank hated it. It pained me to leave so many of my other books and treasured finds, but I had no other choice. *I'll be back,* I told myself. It was only a . . . *break.* Frank would come to his senses. He always did, in time.

I ran my hand along my bedspread, and eyed my bathroom cabinets, selecting the necessities, and leaving the rest—including an extra bottle of my perfume. I spritzed my neck a final time, then set it back—for Valentina to find.

My heart practically burst when I thought of her coming

home from school to find her mother gone. I'd call her later and explain that I'd decided to take a quick trip, and that I'd be back before she knew it.

I zipped up my bags and lugged both large suitcases downstairs—each so heavy with the weight of books. Frank called a cab, then we sat in silence for several minutes until I finally found my voice.

"Please, Frank, can we talk rationally for a moment," I pleaded. "This makes no sense. I can't just leave my daughter. Frank, I—"

"Eloise, there's nothing more to say. We both need time."

His cold gaze softened, somehow, but I couldn't make sense of his words. What did he mean by "time"?

"You were my California rose, my everything," he continued. "But I should have known that a flower cannot grow in foreign soil. Your heart is in London, and that's where you belong." He wiped away a tear.

"Frank," I cried. "I belong here—with you and Val!"

He handed me another envelope.

"What is this?"

"A plane ticket to London. Your flight leaves at one o'clock."

I shook my head, in shock. "Frank, what are you doing?"

"Go home. Take your time. We'll figure this out."

The doorbell sent chills up my spine. "The cab's here," he said, walking calmly to the door.

"Frank . . ."

He looked away. "Please, Eloise. Go. It's what you've always wanted. We both know that."

I wanted to scream, to plead with Frank—I wanted anything but to get in that cab, but it was no use. I walked numbly to the street where the driver leaned against the side of a yellow taxi. He extinguished a cigarette on the pavement, smashing it with his foot casually as if this were an everyday occurrence, the obliteration of a family.

Frank watched from the sidewalk as the driver loaded my bags into the trunk, then walked up the path to the house and disappeared inside.

Val couldn't hear me, but I whispered my goodbyes. I told myself that I'd be back. *Of course I will,* and I prayed that she'd understand . . . someday. "I'll write you every day, my darling, until I'm home again."

My head was spinning when the driver started the engine and looked back at me. "Where to, miss?"

Frank had finally offered me freedom, but at what cost? Leaving the love of my life—Val—in California until her father and I sorted out our differences? What if we didn't? What would that mean for her? That was the tragedy of it all, and perhaps even the theme of my life. I could have one thing, but not the other.

As the cab drove on aimlessly, I wiped away a tear, inhaling deeply. I'd left a piece of my heart in London all those years ago, and I'd be leaving another piece here in America. After that, I had little left. It was time to reclaim some part of me. Yes, I'd go as Frank insisted, but I would be back—for Val.

"Miss," the driver asked again, this time more impatiently. "Where are you heading today?"

"Take me to the airport," I finally said, steadying myself. "I'm . . . going home."

Valentina

The Next Day

"MORNING," I SAY TO MILLIE AND LIZA CHEERFULLY, before scooping Percy into my arms and planting a kiss on his fluffy head.

"Somebody's in a good mood," Liza says, looking up from an arrangement of roses she's fussing over for a client who'd placed an order for flowers and Jane Austen for an ailing friend—a perfect pairing.

I smile, studying her bouquet. For an amateur, Liza's actually quite a natural at floral design.

"Daniel came over last night."

She reaches for another rose. *"And?"*

"And, it was . . . nice."

"Aww, I'm happy for you. I really am, Val." She scrunches her nose as she looks over her arrangement. "I won't even tell you about the bloody awful date I had last night."

"I'm sorry, I—"

"Don't be," Liza says with a shrug. "It's sort of the story of my life." She turns back to the vase of roses, then reaches for a sprig of eucalyptus. "True love may exist for other people but not for me."

"If my mother were here, she'd tell you to perk up and stop being a pessimist. Cheer up, Charlie."

Liza sighs.

"She believed in true love, even if she didn't have it with my father. Even as a child, I could sense that her heart longed for someone—or something—whether real or imagined. It was as if she was . . . I don't know . . . sort of lost in a daydream, if that makes any sense. I guess I always wondered if—"

"His name was Edward," Millie says, clearing her throat from behind the counter.

Liza and I turn around, confused.

"The man your mother loved. She was head over heels for him from the very moment she set eyes on him."

Even though I always knew that my parents' marriage wasn't quite the storybook variety, I suppose a part of me had hoped I was wrong, that maybe they did love each other, very much, despite their differences. As weird as it sounds, believing that I came from a union forged by love gave me some sort of comfort, security, even. But now I want the truth more than a fictional sense of comfort, so I listen with a lump in my throat, waiting for Millie to continue.

"They didn't have much time together," she says. "But they were the best days of Eloise's life."

"How . . . did they meet?"

"At the Royal Automobile Club, on Pall Mall in St. James's."

I feel time stop. *I know this place, but why?*

"Wait," I say. "The Royal Automobile Club. That's where Daniel is taking me for dinner . . . tonight!" I pause, considering the fact that I'm about to visit the place where my mother's heart changed forever.

"He gave her his jacket," Millie says, continuing her reverie with such detail, it was as if the memories had been taken from a page in *her* heart. "I'd never seen finer fabric." She pauses. "He was devilishly handsome, and warm—one of those people that has a way of harnessing the attention of an entire room when they walk in." She smiles to herself. "Your mother shared that trait."

"So, what happened? Why didn't it work out?"

"Val, this part of your mother's story might surprise or even shock you."

I nod cautiously as Millie proceeds. "They were victims of the most tragic timing. By the time Edward professed his love to her, it was . . . too late. She was expecting a baby—with your father."

I connect the dots quickly with a heavy heart. This child my mother carried wasn't me, of course, but rather a sibling that must have passed long before I came to be. "So she . . ." I can barely say the words.

"She lost the baby, yes," Millie continues. "And it shattered her already broken heart and put a tremendous strain on your parents—both of them."

There it was, the truth my mother had kept hidden in the deepest layers of her heart all those years. She was unhappy because she married *the wrong man*.

"Why didn't she just go home, then," I ask, "and find the man she really loved?"

"By then, it was too late. He'd married someone else, and even if he hadn't, Eloise could never leave Frank—

not after what they'd been through. Loyalty ran thick through her veins. She did what she thought was best. But it came with a hefty price—her happiness." She sighs. "But then you came along, and, honey, you lit up her whole world."

I turn the thought over in my mind, feeling the earth momentarily shift. If she'd chosen the other man—Edward— she would have been at peace, and I would have been . . .

Millie places her hand on my shoulder. "I'm sorry. I know this must be very hard to hear, but don't you see the beauty in it, too?"

I shake my head. What beauty? I only saw pain.

"You, my dear, were your mother's greatest love of all."

I lean my back against the edge of the counter, taking in the gravity of Millie's words. I want to believe her, but I struggle. "If that's true, tell me this: How do you leave the person you love most?"

Millie opens her mouth to speak but no words come out, because maybe there is no explanation, or maybe there's more to the story that she's simply not telling me.

I shake my head, wishing I could make sense of it all, wishing my mother were here to explain, to tell me something— anything—that might justify her abrupt departure from my life. If she couldn't give me the answers I needed, could this man she loved?

"Millie, is . . . Edward . . . still in London? Did they reconnect when she moved back here?"

"Yes, and no. He is in London, but I'm afraid they never had that chance. By that time, he was married, with a family." Her eyes look distant. "It wasn't an option."

I nod, craving more information about the man who held

my mother's heart. "What was he like, I guess, besides what you already told me?"

"Well," she begins. "I know he was a successful business-man, and a devoted father. Years after Eloise moved to California with your father, I once saw him pushing a pram in Regent's Park." She smiles to herself. "Eloise told me about an . . . interesting tattoo he had on his shoulder."

"A tattoo?"

"Of a violin."

I cock my head to the right. "Did he play?"

Millie shakes her head. "It's quite clever, actually. Your mum said he got the tattoo so he'd 'always have music in his ear.'"

"YOU HANGING IN THERE, doll?" Liza asks as we head up-stairs to my flat together.

"Yeah, I guess. It's just . . . a lot to take in." I sink into the sofa, and she slides in beside me.

"I know," she replies. "I'm sorry. If it makes you feel any better, when I was twenty-three, I found out that my mother had been having a ten-year affair with one of my teachers from primary school. Mr. Hartley. I just couldn't make any sense of it. I mean, the man used to trim his nose hairs at his desk."

I laugh.

"Seriously, he'd use the scissors from the craft box and just get in there. It was so gross. To this day, I don't know what my mum saw in him." She smiles, but her expression turns seri-ous again. "Listen, Val, there's something else about . . . Ed-ward, that Millie didn't say because she doesn't . . . know."

"What do you mean?"

Liza takes a deep breath. "Before Eloise passed, he . . . visited her, on several occasions. Right here."

"Really? How do you know?"

"Because I saw him coming up and down the stairs. He brought her takeaway, flowers—carried her out to the park, even." She searches my face. "One day when I came to check on her, she told me that his name was Edward, and that she'd met him a lifetime ago. She looked so happy."

"Liza, why didn't you tell me?"

"I'm sorry," she says. "I wasn't trying to keep anything from you, I just . . . didn't want to upset you."

I nod. "But why did my mother keep that from Millie? It seems strange. They were best friends."

Liza shrugs. "I can't say. I only know that Eloise asked me to keep her secret, and I did. They didn't have much time together before she passed, but he was here every day. Millie is right in her description of him. He's a wonderful man."

"I need to meet him," I say. "Can you help me?"

"I wish I could," she says. "But I don't know where he lives, or even his last name."

"I'll ask Millie."

"You could," Liza replies. "But if your mother didn't want her to know about their final days together, then maybe that's not the best idea. I mean, why would she keep something so monumental from her closest friend unless it was a pretty big deal?"

"Listen, I won't tell Millie about their reunion, but I would like to see if she can help me find him. Surely she knows his last name."

Liza shrugs. "Maybe she does, maybe she doesn't. Millie is a—"

"Tough mountain to climb," we both say in unison before laughing.

"I'm so glad you're my friend-slash-tenant," I tell her. "I couldn't have hoped for a better one."

She smiles. "So, tell me about this big night of yours."

"I'm meeting Daniel at the Royal Automobile Club at seven. Another couple is joining us—an old friend of his and his girlfriend."

"Ooh la la," Liza says. "A double date! You should definitely wear your best dress tonight—and one of your mum's necklaces."

"What shoes?" I say.

"Take my black Louboutins."

"I don't know," I say. "Stilettos give me anxiety."

"Trust the personal assistant," she assures me. "The Royal Automobile Club is a stiletto sort of place—you'll see."

THE CAB DRIVER POINTS out 10 Downing Street before dropping me at the regal-looking entrance to the Royal Automobile Club, where Daniel is waiting.

"I knew you'd be five minutes early," he says, greeting me with a quick kiss, which, surprisingly, already feels natural. "You look absolutely ravishing tonight."

If I look ravishing, he looks *dashing* in his tailored blue suit and patterned tie. His belt perfectly complements the color of his loafers, and I can't help but wonder about the woman who taught him how to dress this sharply.

He takes my hand, leading me inside to a grand foyer with an enormous crystal chandelier overhead. Liza was right. The women here are impeccably dressed; the stilettos were a good call—even if they're pinching my feet in all the wrong places.

The club is both foreign and familiar—like I'd seen it once in a dream or maybe in one of my mother's bedtime stories.

We check our coats, then proceed up a flight of stairs to the dining room, where the host informs us that our guests have arrived and are waiting at the table. He selects two menus and leads us across the room. All around, chic-looking couples are engaged in important-sounding conversation and eating dinner in the dignified and particular British manner, which consists of precisely held cutlery, dainty bites, and an exorbitant amount of chewing.

As we make our way across the vast dining room, Daniel releases his hand from mine and waves at a couple sitting at a table in the distance. Teetering a bit in borrowed footwear, I suddenly lose my balance when one of my heels catches on the carpet, throwing my equilibrium into a state of chaos.

Frantically, I reach for Daniel's arm, but he's out of my grasp, which is when I begin to topple over. My arms flail to break the inevitable fall, and in the process, I graze the edge of a nearby table, knocking over a domed platter of food and, just my luck, also a freshly uncorked bottle of red wine.

A scream sounds as I land on the carpeted floor, which is now splattered with wine and bits of food. A stray potato rolls under a table where it stops beside someone's foot. When I look up, the room is excruciatingly quiet. Every eye, it seems, is on *me*.

"Val, are you all right?" Daniel asks, kneeling beside me.

He helps me to my feet, and I sway a bit, finding my balance again.

"I'm fine," I say quickly, brushing a splatter of unknown sauce from my dress, grateful that it's black.

The whispering begins, followed by pockets of laughter. I apologize to the table whose dinner I have just annihilated, along with the waitstaff deployed to clean up the mess.

"Well," Daniel says, taking my hand, "you certainly know how to make an entrance."

"Sorry," I whisper. "I'm completely mortified."

"Don't be," he replies. "They'll forget all of this, just as soon as they move on to their next unwitting victim." He gestures to a woman who's just walked into the dining room wearing a very loud, and unfortunate, fluorescent yellow dress. Legions of necks strain to watch the poor soul walk across the room, tongues wagging as she passes.

"See," Daniel whispers with a knowing smile. "They've forgotten about you already."

When we reach our table, I'm astonished when I recognize Daniel's friends, in fact, *I know them already*. "Eric!"

"Val?" Eric turns to Daniel. "I guess I didn't get the memo that your Valentina was *this* Valentina."

Daniel is equally surprised. "I take it you two know each other, then?"

"We do, though I prefer to refer to myself as *the* Valentina," I say, playing along.

"Indeed, yes, I—I mean, *we* know the One and Only Valentina," Eric explains. "From the bookstore."

"Eric was just at our fundraiser the other night," I say, smiling at the memory.

"I wish I could have been there," Daniel adds. "I was—"

"By the way, Eric," I add, "I've been meaning to thank you for your generosity, and how you left me those books. I can't tell you how much it meant to me."

"The pleasure was all mine," Eric says. "It was a wonderful night, wasn't it?"

"It really was."

Daniel and Fiona exchange glances, and I get the feeling we ought to steer the conversation to more communal grounds. But before I can speak, Fiona does.

"I do hope you aren't hurt," she says. "That was quite a nasty fall."

"Nasty and embarrassing," I say, owning my moment of shame. "But really, I'm fine."

Eric smiles as a wayward lock of his wavy hair falls over his left eye. "I'd like to congratulate you," he says, brushing it away, "for staging one of the most epic entrances of all time."

"I don't know if I'd call it epic," I say, grinning.

"I mean, do you think we can get that inducted into the *Guinness World Records* book?" He glances around the room teasingly. "Tell me someone got it on video."

I laugh, while simultaneously wincing. "Please, God, no."

He pours Daniel and me a glass of wine. "In all seriousness," he says with a smile, turning to Daniel. "You know what's so great about *the One and Only* Valentina?"

"Besides the fact that she's smart and gorgeous and an independent business owner, you mean?"

"Stop, I'm already blushing," I say. "You're making it worse."

"It's that she can laugh at herself," Eric continues. "So many people can't."

Fiona, who looks more beautiful than ever in her full-length black gown, appears disinterested in our banter as she adjusts the black-rimmed glasses on her nose to study the menu. Seconds later, she sets it down with a sigh, as if nothing pleases her.

"Darling," she says, turning to Eric. "Can you be a dove and go find our waiter? I need to see if they have any gluten-free options." She makes a pouty face. "I'm afraid there's nothing on this menu I can eat."

He nods dutifully, setting his napkin on the chair before zigzagging through the dining room.

Daniel turns to Fiona. "It's really good to see you two. It's been far too long."

"It has been too long!" she exclaims, squeezing his arm. "And now you have this lovely creature in your life."

"It really is a wonderful coincidence," he says.

"How wonderful that we can go on double dates *again*!"

I'm immediately curious about the most recent woman who'd been on Daniel's arm, though, of course, I don't ask. Instead, I listen as Fiona tells us, in great detail, about her plans to remodel Eric's flat, which she intends to move in to once it's . . . up to her "standards." "Men haven't any idea about the importance of quality bathroom lighting," she says, smiling at Eric as he slides back into his chair. "Valentina, of course, *you* get that."

I nod in agreement, even though I have no idea what she's talking about. Isn't a light a light?

"Eric has these dreadful fixtures with the most unflattering lightbulbs," she says. "Anyway, they just won't do. I'm changing everything."

"That's great," Daniel says. I can't tell if he's entirely oblivious, or if finds her as dreadful as I do, but I hope for the latter. "I'm sure his place can use a woman's touch."

Eric hands a new menu to Fiona—presumably a *special* one. "Thank you, my love," she says, batting her eyelashes.

"So," Daniel continues. "How exactly do you know Val, again?"

"Well, the Book Garden is my favorite bookstore, of course."

Fiona gives Daniel a knowing look. "You know Eric and his bookstores."

He smiles. "My mum brought me to the store as a kid, and Eloise, Valentina's late mother, led the most magical readalouds." He pauses, looking at me. "I presume you call it 'story time' in the States?"

"Correct," I say with a nod.

"I loved it, of course," Eric continues. "But I think my mum's prime objective was an hour to herself."

I laugh. "Well, I'm pretty sure that's every mother's dream, isn't it?" I catch Daniel's eye, and he smiles back at me.

"Indeed," Eric says.

My mind is caught in a time warp—hyper-focused on a part of my mother's life I wasn't privy to but Eric was. What was it like to be a child in her bookstore? What was it like to sit on the carpet and listen to her read? I imagine Eric as a boy, and my mother standing at the store's counter, the way Millie does now.

"Well," he adds, "your mum was a larger-than-life fixture in my formative years. She could—"

"Do the voices," we both say in unison.

I smile. "There was no one who could read a story like she did."

"She was . . . one of the greats."

"She was." I feel a pang of emotion, which subsides when Daniel places his hand on mine under the table.

"Excuse me, sir," Fiona says, waving at a nearby waiter. "Sir!" When she has his attention, she points to her menu. "I do see that these are gluten-free selections, but I'm not finding anything *vegan* on here."

"I'm sorry, ma'am," he says a bit nervously. "I could . . . I could talk to the chef, ma'am."

"No," she says, sighing as if the ordeal has been deeply exhausting. "Just tell the chef to bring me a plate of *steamed* vegetables, will you, please? *Steamed,* not grilled. No butter. Just lightly salted. *Sea* salt. And olive oil on the side." She holds up her finger. *"Extra virgin."*

"Yes, ma'am," he replies, nodding.

"She has a sensitive stomach," Eric says to the waiter apologetically. "We appreciate your extra attentiveness."

After he takes the rest of our orders, Eric tops off our wineglasses. "Tell us how you two met," he says looking at me, then Daniel.

Daniel squeezes my hand under the table, and I give him a sly smile.

"A childhood friend of mine set us up," he says quickly. He notices my confused expression, but his face tells me to play along. "And naturally, Valentina couldn't resist my charm and rugged good looks."

"Yes, that," I say, rising to the occasion. "But you could say we met because of a . . . literary mystery."

Eric raises an eyebrow. "Daniel, you actually have time to read with that filming schedule of yours?"

"As much as I can," he says. "Valentina and I have that in common."

"Wait, is this your second or third date?" Fiona asks, suddenly interested in the conversation.

"Third," Daniel says.

"Look at how cute they are," Fiona says to Eric. The observation feels like less of a compliment than it does a mark on a score card, a commentary on a subject I'm not privy to.

"How's work going?" Daniel asks Eric, changing the subject.

"Still chugging along," he replies.

Daniel turns to me. "Eric's a columnist for *The Times*."

"Oh," I say, a little surprised. When we had lunch at Café Flora, he'd been vague about his work. All I knew was that he worked at a newspaper. "What do you write about?"

"The real question is what does he *not* write about?" Fiona adds, laughing.

Eric nods. "I guess you could say I'm a generalist."

"That piece you did recently," Daniel continues, "about the Dutch. It was fascinating."

"Yeah," he says. "I've always found it interesting that they don't close their curtains—some don't even have any—even in dense urban areas like Amsterdam."

I shake my head. "Really?"

"It's a total cultural phenomenon. The sun goes down and you can take an evening walk and there they all are, sitting in their living rooms, for all to see, watching TV or eating pie or doing whatever they do. It's incredible, really, how willing they are to put themselves on display, how unashamed they are of the private details of their lives." He shrugs. "Anyway, it's quite a contrast to how private and closed off we are here in London."

"Well, *I* couldn't live that way," Fiona says emphatically. "The thought of some voyeur watching me from outside." She shudders. "No, thank you."

"Yeah, I understand why you feel that way," I add, making a mental note to look up Eric's work. "But living so openly, and unafraid . . . I don't know, something about it sounds kind of freeing."

Dinner arrives and so does another bottle of wine. Daniel and Eric rehash stories from their university days, and Fiona fills us in on her interior design work—apparently Kate Middleton inquired recently (albeit via a palace assistant).

At nine-thirty, Daniel takes care of the bill, refusing Eric's offer to pay, before we head downstairs to retrieve our coats.

"Should we get a nightcap?" Daniel asks tentatively.

Eric opens his mouth, but Fiona beats him to the punch. "We'd love to, but I have an early conference call in the morning and I'm impossibly underprepared. Raincheck?"

"Of course," Daniel says.

"We've had so much fun tonight," she continues. "Daniel, I just adore Valentina." Fiona flashes me a quick smile. "Promise me we'll get together again soon."

"Of course," Daniel says on my behalf as they depart.

"She makes me nervous," I whisper when they're out of earshot.

"She'd make a *lion* nervous."

"But Eric is . . . great."

"Wait till you read his columns," he says, nodding in agreement. "He has an incredible voice."

I stare ahead curiously, watching their two figures disappear into the night. "Who does she remind me of?" I say, trying to place her face. It had been gnawing at me all evening. "An actress maybe?"

"Yeah," Daniel says, wracking his brain. "Maybe the girl from *Mad Men*? Draper's wife?"

"*Yes*, exactly! January Jones!"

"It's funny," he says. "I've known Eric since our first year of university, and I never pictured him with someone like her."

I nod, but privately consider the fact that when you look like January Jones, men might find a way to make an exception. "Have you two been close all these years?"

"We actually didn't reconnect until a few years ago. My ex worked at Fiona's design firm."

It's the first mention of his ex, so I pay close attention. "The one who used to go on the double dates with you all?"

He nods, and I wait for him to reveal more. "Fiona takes some getting used to," he adds. "But she's a good person, and she really does love Eric. They balance each other out."

To me, it seemed more like Fiona *drowns him out*, but I decide to keep that sentiment to myself, wondering instead if Daniel's ex balanced *him* out. Was she once the yin to his yang? At one point, Nick had been mine, or at least, I *thought* he was.

"At the end of the day, I guess it just boils down to happiness," he continues as we round the next block—a walk with no destination, my favorite kind.

"Right," I say, catching his eye. "And what makes *you* happy?"

"Ah, I see you've put on the interviewer's hat."

"My turn now," I say with a smile.

"All right then, I'll tell you. What makes me happy . . . well, lazy Sunday mornings, for starters, preferably spent in bed." He grins. "Laughing with someone you're not afraid to share your dreams with." He stops in the middle of the sidewalk and wraps his arms around my waist, gently pulling me toward him. "And something just like *this*."

Eloise

London, England

———

I CALLED MILLIE FROM THE AIRPORT IN LOS ANGELES, crying so hard she could barely make out my words. Somehow, she managed to calm me down.

"Just get on the plane," she said. "We'll figure everything out together."

The first time I flew across the Atlantic I was a young bride-to-be. But this time, I was returning a wife whose marriage was crumbling—without her beloved daughter. Nothing made sense, and I'd not only given in to my hysteria, I was drowning in it.

Like Cezanne in *The Last Winter*, I'd gone out into the snow alone. We were both weary, with unbelievably heavy hearts, but unlike her, I couldn't dance. I could only weep.

And oh, I wept—through most of the flight. My eyes were bloodshot when I spotted Millie, poking her head out of the crowd at Heathrow. I felt as if I'd been crawling through a desert for an endless stretch of days, parched and delirious; the sight of my best friend in the distance was like a mirage.

She waved at me as if nothing at all had changed in the

twenty-plus years since I'd left for California, though we both knew that everything had.

I ran to Millie, letting my bag slide off my shoulder and fall to the ground as I threw my arms around her. Aside from a touch of gray at her temples, she looked exactly the same. "I can't believe I'm finally here with you," I cried, burying my head into her shoulder.

"Now, now," she said, taking a long look at me. "No more tears."

"Oh, Millie, I don't even know where to begin."

She nodded like a wise mother hen. "We'll get it all sorted, don't you worry. But let's get your bags first."

As we walked together to baggage claim, Millie glanced over at me curiously.

"What is it?" I asked, patting a tissue along the corners of my eyes.

"You look . . . different," she replied, studying my high-lighted hair, the geometric Trifari bracelets on my wrist. Her statement was neither a critique nor a compliment, merely an observation. "California's had its way with you."

"Maybe," I said, my eyes meeting hers again. "But I'm still the same girl from the East End. I'll always be."

She helped me lug my suitcases off the conveyor belt. "These can't be filled with clothes," she said. "They're too heavy."

"Mill," I said, "I can't wait to show you what I found."

FROM THE BACK OF the taxi, I peered up at Millie's block of flats as we approached, immediately taken with its pastel blue color. She'd long since moved from the East End to a quiet street in the Primrose Hill neighborhood.

"My flat's on the first floor," she said proudly. "It's not much—just two bedrooms—but it's all mine."

"It's charming," I told her. I couldn't help but envy Millie's autonomy and immediately began thinking about what my life might look like had I not followed Frank to California all those years ago.

We climbed the stairs to her door. The flat might have been small, but its high ceilings and freshly painted plaster made it feel far larger.

"Just leave your suitcases over there, by the window," she said. "Let me make you some tea."

On the drive from the airport, I'd managed to bring Millie up to speed on my situation: namely, Frank's accusations and his insistence that I leave.

She'd listened calmly, eyes growing big now and again. "I'll help you find a lawyer," she said. "I worry that Frank may have something up his sleeve."

"What do you mean?" I thought back to Santa Monica, that look in his eyes. Could Millie be right?

"I'm just saying that you're going to need to be careful. If divorce is what he's after, his plan might have been to get you here."

I shook my head, unsure of what exactly she was getting at, and yet, it frightened me—to my core.

"I'll call a few of my colleagues," she said. "We'll make sure you talk to someone who knows about U.S. family law. From what I understand, it can be riddled with loopholes and technicalities."

"Thanks," I muttered, too exhausted to think about what

technicalities she might be referring to. Instead, I turned my attention out the window to the street below, where a woman on a bicycle glided by, fresh flowers in the basket attached to her handlebars. Primrose Hill. It was almost as if it were daring me to cheer up.

"This is where we always hoped to open our bookstore," she said with a faraway look in her eyes. "Remember?"

"How could I forget?"

Millie smiles. "Maybe we will—someday."

I nodded, feeling fresh tears well up in my eyes. I knew that Frank would never let me move Val to London. He'd fight me at every turn to keep our daughter firmly planted on American soil.

"I can't stop thinking about Valentina," I said, glancing at my watch. "She came home from school and . . . I wasn't there. Millie, I miss her so much."

"I know you do," Millie replied, her eyes aching with concern. "You're in a considerable amount of pain right now. Just take a deep breath. We'll take this one day at a time."

"She's my everything," I said, swallowing hard.

"And you'll fight for her. I'll help you." She smiled. "Now, cheer up, Charlie." It warmed me to hear my favorite saying, even in these circumstances.

Crippled by exhaustion, I fell asleep on Millie's sofa. When I woke up, an hour and a half later, Millie coaxed me to venture out. We ordered sandwiches at a little café around the corner and ate them at a table under the outdoor awning. We walked for a bit afterward. The sun had just emerged from behind a gray cloud and its warmth was a balm to my tired eyes and tearstained cheeks.

Millie waved at various passersby strolling along the

sidewalk as she pointed out the bakery, the market, and a bistro that looked like a comfortable sort of place where I could imagine myself spending hours reading and sipping wine.

We passed a hardware store and then, on the next corner, a clothing boutique—a proper village. I felt more at home than I had in the last two decades in California.

"Show me the local bookstore," I said.

Millie shook her head. "There isn't one. Can you believe that?"

I peered up at a particularly charming pale pink building ahead.

"Really?" I walked closer to the façade, noticing a real estate sign affixed to the front window, my excitement growing. "Millie, look. It's for sale!"

"I know," she said. "It's been on the market for years. It needs significant work, but it has good bones. I can't believe it hasn't been snapped up."

I looked inside the window, then turned back to Millie. "Can you imagine how perfect this place would be for a bookstore?"

"Oh yes," she said with a smile. "I admit, the thought has crossed my mind more than a few times."

Just then, a car pulled up, parking on the street in front of the building. A man with a manila folder tucked under his arm got out and smiled at us. "Sorry I'm late," he said. "The traffic in London," he began with a sigh, "well, I swear, one of these days, it'll be the death of me."

Millie and I looked at each other, confused.

He extended his hand to Millie. "Alastair Fairfield, with Fairfield Real Estate," he said before greeting me next. "I hope I haven't kept you waiting too long. If traffic weren't already enough, my assistant seems to have a penchant for double-booking my calendar. In any case, I'm glad you reached out. This building is really one of the most special gems of Primrose Hill, and the pictures in the offering brochure don't do it justice."

He pulled a key from his jacket pocket and inserted it into the lock on the front door as Millie flashed me a "just play along" look.

He led us inside the ground floor, which was thick with dust and cobwebs, and the remains of the business that had once occupied the space. A black swivel desk chair with a missing arm sat dejectedly in the center of the room.

"As you can see," the agent explained, "it's in need of some elbow grease and ingenuity."

I nodded, admiring the wide-plank hardwood floors and matching dark wooden trim around the perimeter. Millie ran her hand along what looked like an old sales counter, obviously just as intoxicated by its possibilities as I was.

"There's excellent storage in the back," the agent continued. "A large, locked utility closet. Over the years, it's been a restaurant, a hat shop, I think, and most recently an architect's studio." He stretched his arms wide. "It would really be great for . . . just about anything. Do you mind my asking what plans the two of you are considering?"

"A bookstore," we both said in unison, smiling when our eyes met.

"A bookstore, *oh yes*. How charming. It's a curious thing that there isn't one in Primrose Hill. I've often thought that some enterprising person ought to put one in, save local readers the arduous trip to central London."

He led us out a back door and then down a little path to a side entrance. "There are two flats upstairs, so you could live above the shop if you wanted."

Like the ground floor, both living spaces are in need of a thorough update, but they ooze potential, and I'm especially taken by the second-floor flat, with its big windows that look out at the street.

"Remind me of the asking price?" I asked, turning to the agent expectantly, but when he handed me a flyer, my heart sank. It was far out of our reach.

"The seller is quite motivated," the agent added, sensing our apprehension. "In other words, don't be afraid to make an offer—any offer. As you know, the market's been in a bit of a slump this year and he's intent on unloading some of his real estate holdings."

I nodded. "Well, thank you. We'll . . . let you know."

"Why don't I take down your name in case any other listings come up, or, if you have further questions about this one."

I shook my head. "No need, we—"

"Sure," Millie said, interrupting me. She gave him my name and her phone number.

"Eloise Baker," he said, nodding. "All right, I'll be in touch."

"Why did you do that?" I asked later as we began walking back to the flat.

"Do what?"

"Lead him on like that! You know we can't afford to buy the building."

"Oh, my friend," she said. "Where's your sense of adventure?"

I left it behind in London all those years ago, I thought as I turned around to give the pale pink building one last glance. *But maybe I can find it again?*

LATER, I PHONED CALIFORNIA, timing the call to when I was sure Frank would be at work.

Bonnie answered, and I was flooded with relief at the sound of her voice.

"Hello, Bonnie," I said.

"Mrs. Baker!" she cried. "It's you!"

"Yes, Bonnie," I said. "It's me. I'm in London while ... Frank and I sort everything out. Is Valentina there? May I talk to her, please?"

"Uh," Bonnie said, pausing. "I'm sorry, Mrs. Baker, she is ... not here."

"Oh, where is she, then?"

"She is ... out with Mr. Baker." The connection sounded muffled. "He asked me to take down your phone number and address if you called."

I gave Bonnie the information, then asked her to have Valentina call me.

"Mrs. Baker," she said in almost a whisper, "it's not the same without you."

Nothing was the same.

After I hung up the phone, I found a pen and paper, and began a letter to my daughter:

My darling Valentina,

I didn't want to leave you, honey, but I had to. In time, I'll try to explain.

I'm here in London now, visiting my old friend Millie, who I've told you about so often. Oh, Val, I wish you were here with me. I know you'd love London as much as I do. After all, you have English blood running through your veins.

There are things I wish I could tell you to help you understand, but I can't. Because of that, I'm asking you to trust me, please. I know it's hard when I'm not there to look into your eyes, when I can't dry your tears or help you understand. But, I'll be home soon. Until then, I'll be loving you every second of every day, and always.

With love
from London,
Mummy

Valentina

The Next Day

———

I'M STANDING AT THE STORE COUNTER, SORTING THROUGH paperwork I don't have the heart to show Millie or Liza. It's an offer to transfer deed and ownership to Brighton Construction, the company that plans to bulldoze the bookstore. Attached is a tidy architectural plan detailing a new, modern-looking condo development.

The fundraiser results are our last hope. If they don't meet expectations, it won't be long until the Book Garden is encased in caution tape and bracing for the wrecking ball.

The phone rings, and Millie answers.

She speaks little, ending the call with, "Thank you. I understand."

"What is it?" Liza and I walk over to the counter.

She takes a long breath, exhaling slowly. "That was Jan," she says. "The numbers are in. We raised . . . ninety-six thousand pounds."

"Which means," Liza says, pausing to do the math, then frowning, "we're more than one hundred and fifty thousand pounds short."

At first, Millie stands stoically, eyes downcast, but it isn't long before she dissolves into tears. Every book, every shelf holds a memory, and she'll have to say goodbye to them all—we all will.

"Why don't you take a break," I suggest. "Go get some coffee." But like a captain clinging to her sinking ship, Millie refuses to relinquish the wheel and there's no convincing her otherwise.

"There has to be something we can do," she says before bolting to the back room in tears.

"Let her be alone for a bit," Liza says.

I nod.

"But, Val," she whispers, "what *are* we going to do?"

I shake my head. "I don't know. I really don't. We need a miracle."

She nods gravely.

"Look out for Millie today," I say. "Obviously this is hard for all of us, but especially for her."

"I will," Liza promises, pointing to a stack of books. "Where should I put these?"

"Over there," I say vacantly, pointing to the travel shelf on the far wall as I notice today's issue of *The Times* on the counter. I think of Eric and pick it up, thumbing through the newspaper to find his column, which I begin reading:

———

I WOULD LIKE TO ADDRESS a valuable and once-prized trait now rare among Londoners. Call it evolutionary exclusion, or a form of social habit-forming gone bad, but somehow along the way, we as a people, have forgotten how to laugh at ourselves.

———

I smile, hearing his voice in my ears.

————

THIS CAME TO MY attention on a recent evening when an American woman made a frightful entrance at the Royal Automobile Club. Unsure on her feet in a pair of stilettos, she toppled a nearby party's five-course dinner. Was she mortified? Why yes, she was. And so would any of us. But her next act, after pulling herself together, was truly remarkable. Few among us would be capable of what she did with ease. What was her Herculean skill, you ask? Why, it's simple, really: She laughed at herself.

————

My cheeks flush as I read on.

————

AND SHE ACCOMPLISHED THIS in the midst of great personal tragedy: Her mother passed recently, and a tax bill might spell the end to her family business, the Book Garden, the much-loved bookshop in Primrose Hill that has been a community fixture for decades. The results of a recent fundraiser are still pending—but will they be enough?

————

The article is as surprising as it is touching. I don't know whether to be amused, flattered, mildly humiliated, or some combination of all three.

When the phone rings, I set down the newspaper and peel myself off the floor to grab it.

"Hello?" I say.

"Yes, hi. My name is Sharon McCready, and I just read the column in *The Times* about the Book Garden. I'm just horrified to hear that you might be forced to close your doors. I want to help."

I pause, putting the phone on speaker, and motion to Liza to listen in.

"Ten years ago, my sister was sick with cancer," the woman continues. "I moved in to her flat to look after her. It was just a few blocks away from your store, and I often stopped in to find books to cheer her up. Honestly, reading was the only thing that kept her going. The owner . . . I can't remember her name now, I'm afraid . . . but she was beyond lovely. She never failed to find just the right book for my sister. I don't know how, but she just *knew*."

Millie smiles, nodding to herself.

"Her name was Eloise," I say. "And I'm her daughter, Valentina."

"Ah, yes, Eloise. I remember now. She was so kind. I'm so sorry for your loss, Valentina. I read in the article that she'd passed. I lost my sis, too, but because of your mum, she had stories to distract her from her pain. Anyway, is the fundraiser still open? I'd very much like to make a contribution."

Liza sidles up next to me. "Yes indeed, ma'am. I'm Liza, the store's . . . head of finance—and botany."

"Oh?" the woman replies, a little confused.

"It's a long story," Liza continues, grinning. "Although the fundraiser is over, there is another way to contribute." I watch as she opens up a Web browser to a page with our logo on the left. "We've set up a GoFundMe for members of the broader

London community to contribute to. It would be an honor if you'd like to help."

"When did you do this?" I whisper to Liza.

"A few weeks ago, while you were in doomsday mode," she whispers.

I smile as she shares the GoFundMe information with the woman on the phone. In the following few hours, more calls—and emails—come flooding in. So many people want to help, because—just like us—they can't imagine a world without their favorite bookstore.

IT'S BEEN A LONG DAY, and when six o'clock rolls around, Millie looks weary—I'm grateful when she agrees to go home and rest.

"What's the latest with lover boy?" Liza asks after Millie's gone.

"He's in Scotland right now filming part of the documentary he's working on," I tell her. "But he's flying tomorrow morning, and guess what?"

"What, he's whisking you off on a holiday to Bali?" She steps onto the ladder, tucking a book back on the shelf.

I grin. "Not quite. But he did invite me to have dinner at his parents' house—tomorrow night."

"Wait, he asked you to *meet his parents*?"

"He did."

"Well, that's a *development*."

"Do you think they'll like me?"

"Honey, they're going to love you."

The phone rings again, as I tuck the newspaper with Eric's

column in my bag, wishing I had his phone number so I could call and thank him.

LATER THAT EVENING, LIZA convinces me to meet a few of her friends—members of a band (whose name I can't recall, only that it sounded like a synonym for a violent crime). They were all having drinks in city center at a place called Sexy Fish, which also gave me pause.

What I thought sounded like a strip club in Vegas, she described as one-part nightclub and three-parts high-end restaurant—with a sprinkle of circus thrown in for good measure.

She pulls a dress from her closet and hands it to me. "You would look *divine* in this!"

"I don't know," I say, unconvinced as I eye the teeny-tiny minidress dangling precariously from its hanger. "There's no way I'm going out in that."

"Stop being a prude," she says. "It's meant to stretch. Try it on! It'll look amazing on you. Besides, do I need to remind you of the bet you lost last week?"

"Fine," I concede with a hazy memory of our wine-fueled card game. "I'll try it on, but I'm not sure if I have the energy to go out tonight, especially to a place called Sexy . . . Whale?"

"Fish," she corrects me.

I roll my eyes as I pull the dress over my head. "I'm so not wearing this."

"Whoa," Liza says, nodding. "Seriously, Val, you look like a million bucks."

"More like five bucks," I say, tugging at the hemline with a frown. "Or four-fifty."

"Here," Liza says, turning to her overstuffed closet, where she extricates a swath of shimmery, black fabric from its hanger. "You just need a wrap." She hands it to me. "Put this on." She drapes it over my shoulders and shifts me toward the mirror. "See, look how gorgeous you look! Come out with us tonight!"

"Well," I say, shifting to see my reflection from the side. Daniel is in Scotland until tomorrow morning, and . . . it would be fun to meet some new friends. "Okay."

AS WE WALK THROUGH the entrance of Sexy Fish, our steps keep time with the bass thumping from the DJ booth inside, where a glittery strobe light dangles overhead. I think of the chandelier at the Royal Automobile Club and smile at the memory, and also the contrast. Tonight, I feel as if I've been thrust into the taping of a music video, except for the fact that I'm much older than the college-aged girls standing in line. Oh, and also, I can't dance.

I look around nervously as Liza speaks to the hostess. I wonder how she manages to hold a conversation over such loud music, but then I realize that maybe that's the point.

"Our table's ready," she says, waving at a guy in a leather jacket with bleached blond hair. "That's Damian." He waves back and motions us over to his table. "He'll probably try to hit on you, but don't worry, he's harmless."

I nod, attempting to pull my dress down lower over my thighs, but it inches up rebelliously with each step.

I'm grateful when we reach the table, where I slide into one of the empty chairs, my legs under protective cover, as Liza introduces me to her friends: Damian, who holds my hand a few moments too long; Raul, a broody character whose tattoos creep across his collarbone; Cara, a twentysomething with jet-black hair who hangs on Damian's every word; and Trina, with dyed-red hair pulled into a high ponytail, revealing her half-shaved head. She nods only long enough to be polite then turns back to her phone.

Leave it to Liza to assemble this motley crew.

Damian speaks, but the loud music drowns out his words.

"I'm sorry," I mouth, pointing to a nearby speaker. "I CAN'T HEAR YOU." The moment the words leave my lips, I at once feel seventy-five years old.

He leans in closer to me, which is not what I intended, but at least I can finally hear him. "I ordered drinks and some bites," he says.

"OH, THANK YOU."

Liza casts me a look of charity as she chats with Cara. When the drinks arrive, I occupy myself with a novelty fish-shaped stirring stick to avoid making eye contact with Damian. But Liza clearly has other plans. I watch as she tells him something that I can't hear, then shows him her phone.

"The Book Garden!" he exclaims, turning to me. "That was my mum's favorite place. Liza says you're in trouble?" He reaches for his phone. "I'm going to make a donation right now."

"Wow," I say, glancing at Liza. "Thank you so much, but I assure you, I didn't come here to solicit."

"Nonsense," he says. "My mum loved your store—rest her soul. It's the least I can do to atone for what a bloody hell-raiser I was as a teen."

I smile and thank him as Liza flashes me a sneaky thumbs-up. After the second round of drinks, Raul, who at one point, appeared to have dozed off, perks up and suggests we go somewhere else. He says he knows a pub where a band is playing tonight. Everyone agrees that this is a great idea . . . except me.

"Thank you so much for the drinks—and for everything," I say to Damian, who picks up the tab. "I hate to be a party pooper, but I'm exhausted. You guys go ahead without me."

"Ah," Damian says, planting his elbow on the table as his face sinks into his palm. "But we were just getting to know each other."

"Sorry," I say. "Maybe we can . . . *all* do this another time."

"You okay?" Liza whispers as the cab arrives, which, apparently, they're all squeezing into, along with another guy they ran into outside.

"Totally," I say. "It was a fun night. I'm just super tired."

"Gotcha," she says. "Can we drop you off on the way? I'll slide in next to Trina. There's still room!"

"Thanks, but that's okay," I say. "I'm going to walk for a little bit, get some fresh air."

"All right," Liza says. "You be careful in that dress, now."

I smile, waving as she climbs into the cab. When it speeds off, I release a long sigh and pull Liza's wrap snugly around my body as I begin walking ahead, following the streetlights until I see a cab on the next block, which I flag down.

"Where to?" the driver asks.

"Berkeley Square," I say immediately. Millie had mentioned the storied London park while we sorted books the other day. It was home to some of London's oldest living trees, many dating back to the early 1700s, she said, but also one of my mother's old haunts. I want to see it for myself.

A few minutes later, when I step out of the cab, I take in

the trees' enormous trunks, older than the very United States of America, in fact, and then it hits me—the song by Nat King Cole my mother used to play on the record player in our Santa Monica living room: "A Nightingale Sang in Berkeley Square."

My father didn't have the same affinity for the old tune, but I did, and I immediately hear the lyrics in my ears—and my heart: *The moon that lingered over London town ... how could he know we two were so in love, the whole darn world seemed upside down.*

I glance up at a lamppost, as a bird—a nightingale?—takes flight into the dark sky above. I look down at my feet—Liza's high heels are killing me—wondering if my mother had ever stood right here, in this very spot.

When I see a park bench ahead, I stop and sit, staring up at the sky. A hint of a constellation glows overhead, and I can't help but feel like the stars came out tonight just for me.

It's late, but Berkeley Square is abuzz. People meander past me on the pathway—a man and his dog, a hound of some sort, who presses his nose to the pavement as if he's in the middle of a very serious foxhunt; a young couple stealing a few quiet moments while their baby snoozes in a stroller. I can't help but notice that they seem to be arguing as a middle-aged woman immersed in a very intense run powers by, followed by a man with a messenger bag slung over his shoulder. I sit up when the light from the lamppost hits his face, squinting to get a better look.

When his eyes meet mine, he stops and smiles. "Valentina? Is that you?"

"Eric?"

"What are you doing here?"

"I was just out walking," I say.

He grins. "In that dress?"

"It's a long story. And it may involve me losing a bet." I grin. "But hey, at least I can laugh at myself, right?"

He sits beside me, setting his bag on the ground. "I take it you saw the column."

I nod.

"I hope you weren't . . . offended."

"On the contrary," I reply. "I was flattered. What you wrote about the store, well, it meant so much to all of us. People have been calling in all day, making donations. It's been overwhelming in the very best way." I smile. "Thank you."

"You should see the emails I'm getting. One person actually suggested you be knighted for your valiant efforts to restore humility to a city corrupted by overexalted egos." He pauses, pulling out his phone. "And listen to this one." I wait as he scrolls. "This reader describes you as a 'beacon for our times,' a 'suffragette for the cause of literature.'"

"Wow," I say, smiling bigger. "As a humble librarian-turned-bookseller, I'm not sure I deserve those accolades."

He nods. "You do."

I kick off my heels and tuck my bare feet under my legs when he takes off his jacket and drapes it over my shoulders. "Here, please put this on. You must be freezing."

"Thanks," I say, "for the jacket, and for . . . what you did." I pull his jacket around me. It still radiates the warmth from his body. "I wanted to call to thank you, but I didn't have your number."

"Please, no thanks necessary." He reaches into his bag and pulls out a card, which he hands to me. "And next time, you can just ring me up."

"Okay," I say, tucking the card into my purse. So, what are you up to tonight?"

"Oh, just heading home from the office."

"At this hour?"

"Well," he says. "Let's just say I didn't want to be anywhere near my flat today."

"Why?"

"Fiona and I broke up; she came to collect her things today."

"Oh no," I say. "I'm so sorry."

"Don't be. This split has been in the making for two years now, and if I'm being honest, maybe even longer. We were never right for each other. We both knew that. I should have pulled the plug a long time ago, but definitely when she insisted that I replace all my light fixtures."

I laugh cautiously. "Yeah, that did seem a bit strange."

"Trust me," he says. "Strange is an understatement. I haven't even told you about the refrigerator."

"The refrigerator?"

"It would take an hour to explain, and it would be very, very boring." He shakes his head. "And confusing. Did you know that there are sixteen different appliance brands that don't contain ice makers with *filtered* water?"

I laugh. "Oh dear. That bad, huh?"

He nods. "Let's just leave it at that." He looks up at the sky, tracing the faint outline of a constellation overhead with his finger. "It's like I've been living in this weird, hazy dream where I have to tiptoe around in my own flat." He exhales deeply. "I can finally breathe again."

I smile. "Well, then I'm happy for you. But I know it's never easy." I follow his eyes up to the sky, thinking about the papers I'd signed, scanned, and emailed back to my attorney earlier. "My divorce was just finalized today." It feels cathartic to say that, even better to have it all behind me.

"Sorry," he says.

I shake my head. "No, I'm good. Great, even. Like you describe, I can see clearly now."

He looks up at the sky again. "If it were spring, we'd be able to see Virgo, the maiden."

"Who?"

"The constellation," he continues. "She's a rather reclusive old girl, only shows her face when she wants you to see her." He turns to me. "When I was a kid, I found this old book in my granny's attic. And by old, I mean *old*. It was printed in the eighteenth century." My eyes widen as he continues. "Each page described a different constellation. But Miss Virgo is special." He smiles at me. "She brings good luck and calm in a storm. Maybe she's looking out for you right now."

I study his face. "You really believe that stuff?"

Eric shrugs. "I believe in science—and stories."

"I do too," I say, feeling a shiver creep up the back of my neck.

"Where's Daniel?" he asks suddenly.

"In Scotland—working on a film project. But he's coming home in the morning. I'm meeting his parents for dinner tomorrow."

"Wow," he says.

"Should I be worried?"

"I haven't met them, but I'm sure you have nothing to worry about. Daniel's a great guy."

He is, I think.

"I'm happy for you two."

"Thanks."

He glances at his watch. "All right, Miss America. I have to get going, but we should find you a cab." We walk back to the street, where he hails a taxi. The driver flashes his lights and drives to us.

I slip off his jacket and hand it to him. "It was good running into you tonight," I say, climbing into the cab and rolling down the window.

"To think, of all the people in London, our paths happened to cross. Now if you don't call that a bit of stardust luck, I don't know what is."

I grin. "Stardust luck. I like that. Maybe fodder for your next column?"

"Definitely a contender," he says, grinning back as the car starts down the street.

When I feel my phone buzz, I find a text from Daniel. "Hi from Scotland. Missing you."

I turn to look out the back window to wave at Eric once more, but he's already disappeared into the starlit night.

Eloise

Two Months Later

—

"IT WAS THE BEST OF TIMES, IT WAS THE WORST OF TIMES," Charles Dickens wrote in the famous opening of *A Tale of Two Cities.*

He was referring to Paris and London, of course. But in my life, Los Angeles stood in for Paris, and London? Well, that would be Frank's petition for divorce.

It came quickly—far faster than I could have imagined. The vile papers were delivered by a courier to Millie's flat, on an otherwise lovely Tuesday afternoon.

"Eloise Baker?" asked the man standing in the doorway.

"Yes," I said, confused as he handed me a thick envelope.

I was served, Millie explained—and, oh, was I served. Frank seemed to regard me like one of the failing businesses he so expertly targeted then eliminated. But this was a new kind of warpath, and it cut deep. Never mind the fact that he'd petitioned the judge to cut me out of any spousal support or alimony, citing my non-citizen status, it was the pages about Valentina that broke my heart. He'd referenced my "abandonment" as justification for full custody, with no visita-tion rights, in addition to requesting the court restrict Val's travel out of the United States. Frank's legal petition was the ultimate blow, and if he prevailed, I might never see my daughter again.

"Millie!" I screamed, my hands trembling.

She came quickly, taking the bundle from me, then confirming what I already knew. "He's gone nuclear."

The attorney in Mayfair I'd been talking to, a friend of Millie's from law school, had feared this very thing, though I refused to believe Frank could stoop to such levels. But he did, and every weapon in his arsenal, it seemed, was deployed and laser-focused on me.

"What am I going to do?" I cried, slumping over on the couch.

She sat beside me, calmly setting the papers on the table. "You're going to fight this, of course. He's out of his mind."

I nodded.

"But, first, you're going to get on a plane and go back. I'll find you an attorney in California." She looked deep into my eyes. "You're not leaving without Valentina."

THE PLANE'S LANDING AT LAX was so smooth, the wheels nearly kissed the runway—a sharp contrast to the turbulence that lay ahead. I raced to retrieve my bag and catch a taxi to Santa Monica. In the car, I rehearsed the plan in my mind, which Millie and her colleague had helped me with. As hard as it sounded, I'd have to go home as if nothing at all had changed. I'd merely taken a vacation to London, as Frank had suggested. I would return to a home and a daughter who were rightfully mine. If he balked—or worse—I'd call the police.

If Frank could fight, I could, too. And I was ready. He'd

obviously instructed Bonnie that Val was forbidden from speaking to me—I could hear the regret in her voice each time I called. Eventually, my daily calls went unanswered. The phone just rang and rang and rang, becoming the soundtrack to my sorrow.

But I'd see my daughter soon. I'd run to her and take her into my arms, kissing her tears away. *Mummy's almost home,* I whispered as the taxi turned onto our street. I could see the house ahead, the twin palm trees, the manicured lawn. Val was probably in the pool, or maybe reading in her room. I wondered if she'd finished the last book of the series she loved so much. We were both eager to know how it ended, in victory or tragedy—just as I wondered about my own life circumstances.

"Thanks," I said, paying the driver. He handed me my bag from the trunk and motored off, leaving me standing in the empty driveway. But something was wrong. Something was *off.* The house looked different. There were new flowers beside the walkway that I hadn't planted; a strange welcome mat lay on the porch. I reached for the doorknob, but it refused to budge, so I fumbled to find my key, inserting it into the lock only to discover that it didn't work. Frank must have changed the locks. Of course he did.

"Valentina!" I cried, peering into the living room window. What happened to the painting on the wall above the fireplace? The sectional in the living room was gone, too, replaced with a blue sofa that I didn't care for.

"Excuse me, ma'am? Can I help you?"

When I turned around, a young couple and their toddler daughter stood in the driveway looking at me curiously. The little girl's blond hair was in two pigtails.

"No, no," I said quickly. "I'm fine. I'm just . . . having some trouble with my key."

They walked closer. "Ma'am," the man said, shaking his head, "are you all right? Do you need help?"

And then it hit me. I hadn't noticed the FOR SALE sign on the corner, but there it was, with a SOLD placard tacked to its edge. The blue sofa, the flowers, the welcome mat—it began to make sense. *My God, Frank sold the house.*

"Ma'am," the man said again, cautiously approaching.

"I . . . I . . ." I muttered. "I know this might sound crazy, but I used to live here . . . a long time ago. Do you know anything about the family who sold to you?"

This time, the woman spoke. "Yeah, it was a single dad and his daughter. She was so sweet. I think her name was . . ."

"Valentina," I said. "Her name is Valentina."

"Yes, that's it. She was so good with Abigail." She looked down at her own daughter. "It's a shame they moved to Seattle. I would have loved to hire her to babysit. It's so hard to find a good one these days."

Seattle? My heart pounded so loudly, I could barely hear anything else. Their mouths opened and closed, but the only thing audible was the erratic thumping in my chest.

I ran to the street, clutching my bag, looking this way and that. What would I do? Where would I go? The nearest pay phone was in town, so I set out for Main Street, alternately running and walking—out of breath. Using a calling card, I dialed Millie, waking her up in the middle of the night, to bring her up to speed.

She was as shocked as I was and very sympathetic. But her words were sobering. "I'm afraid he's four steps ahead of you, El."

"Millie, but this isn't a game of chess—it's my daughter!"

"I know, honey," she said. "But he has the upper hand. Even if you did go to Seattle, even if you did find them, then what?"

"I'll try to talk some sense into that man," I said. "And if I can't, I'll fight."

"Listen," she continued. "It's no use fighting from there, with nowhere to stay. We can file a response to the court from here. Come home, El."

"But, Millie, you told me not to leave without Valentina!" A woman walking her dog paused on the sidewalk, regarding me curiously. I was hysterical, but I didn't care. "I won't leave without her!"

"But what other choice do you have, Eloise?"

The connection became garbled, and I could barely make out anything else she said. When I hung up the phone, I was alone again—deeply and utterly alone.

IN THE FOLLOWING MONTHS, I merely existed. Millie had to coax me to eat, to shower—everything but to breathe, which, if it hadn't happened automatically, I might have given up on, as well. My world—my heart—had been cunningly ripped from my grasp.

Millie's attorney friend agreed to help me, pro bono, but as grateful as I was for her time and generosity, it wasn't enough. Our petition to the court was denied and Frank was granted full custody of Valentina. All visitation rights were voided due to a child psychologist's assessment. She wrote: "At this juncture, I recommend zero contact between mother and child. Any time spent with a parent after abandonment can result in pain and trauma for the child. Valentina has been through enough; her focus should be on healing under the care of a licensed child psychologist, as well as her custodial parent—in this case, the father. I also am concerned about flight risk in this case. The mother lives in London, and is not a U.S. citizen. The father has valid concerns about the mother taking the child to Europe. In summary, it is my professional opinion that the mother is unstable and a risk to Valentina's safety and development."

I wanted to burn those papers. I wanted to find that damn child psychologist and throttle her. But the decision was final, my only consolation being the address in Seattle where Frank had moved. So I wrote to Val every day. I wanted her to know the truth, but above all, I wanted her to know that I loved her—with every part of my being—praying that someday she'd understand and forgive me for being outsmarted by her father.

In time, I learned to accept this nightmare for what it was, my new reality, though I knew I'd never escape my pain. I had to learn to live with it, and I did so by writing to Val. I was always writing.

That year was a blur, but in all of it, there was a glimmer of joy in the rubble, and it came in the form of an unexpected phone call—from the real estate agent who'd given us a tour of the pink building. He had surprising news: The owner, he explained, needed to unload the property immediately. He would sell it to us for a fraction of the asking price, even provide any financing we might need.

I could hardly believe our good fortune, but Millie was immediately skeptical. Were there dead bodies in the basement? Was the foundation infested with termites? In the end, we ignored our practical instincts and decided to take the plunge. And oh, what a plunge.

By then, I'd returned to Harrods, where I worked part-time on the sales floor. I didn't have enough cash—or credit—to make the purchase on my own, but Millie co-signed the loan, and together, we became the unlikely owners of one of Primrose Hill's most charming buildings.

The night we took ownership, we christened the site of our future bookstore with a bottle of champagne, and I began to understand the important lesson that sustained me in the years to come. I might always carry deep pain, but I didn't have to let it rule me. I learned to set aside what I couldn't control and focus on what I could: finding some semblance of joy in life again, through the bookstore we decided to call the Book Garden.

In the months since I'd returned to London, I'd left one of my suitcases unopened in the closet, but I was finally ready to face my past. Out came the California shells and the drift-wood. Then the Russel Wright seafoam-blue ceramics, which I was relieved to see hadn't cracked on the transatlantic jour-ney. Next, I opened the jewelry case filled with rare Trifari necklaces, bracelets, and brooches.

Millie took it all in, watching me examine the relics from my past. I told her about the estate sales I frequented in L.A., the solitary hours spent roaming the city.

"I had no idea you were so lonely, Eloise," she said sadly. "But not anymore, and never again."

Finally, I brought out the books—dozens of valuable first editions I'd rescued from estate sales. I'd focused on the 1940s, an excellent decade for books. English and Ameri-can authors. Ernest Hemingway's *For Whom the Bell Tolls*.

Richard Wright's *Native Son*. W. Somerset Maugham's *The Razor's Edge*. Evelyn Waugh's *Brideshead Revisited*. William Faulkner. C. S. Lewis. Norman Mailer. George Orwell's *1984*.

"We'll stock our shelves with these, Millie, and so much more."

Tucked in the far corner of the suitcase were two framed photos of Val, and my heart ached when I saw them. I wasn't strong enough to face them until that moment, and even then, seeing her sweet face nearly slayed me. But I remembered what I'd come to learn—that I could be in pain but not be defined by it. I placed one of the photos on Millie's side table, near the front door, where I could see my daughter as I came and went, and the next in the bookstore, where she could be my muse. She was my heart, and she would be the bookstore's soul.

By day, Millie continued working in the city while I rolled up my sleeves, clearing out junk, hammering loose floorboards back into place, and scrubbing each surface until it gleamed.

I wrote to Valentina about all of it in my daily letters. It dulled the ache inside and also gave me hope. One day, she'd find me. One day, I'd see her face again. After all, if daffodils could forge through the frozen earth each spring, I could press through my pain.

With her law career in full force, Millie remained a silent partner. And though I'd moved into the building's top-floor flat, she decided to keep her own flat, where she'd been comfortable and happy for years.

"How are you feeling?" Millie asked me over dinner at her flat. Our second week of business had been a success, and we were celebrating with a nice bottle of burgundy and a roast chicken that she'd just pulled out of the oven.

"Happy and sad," I said.

She nodded in understanding. "Sappy, then."

I laughed. "Yes."

"Mill," I said after a long silence, "you may not remember—it was so long ago—but before Frank, there was someone else. His name was . . . Edward."

"I remember," she said, avoiding eye contact.

"I've been thinking," I continued. "Now that the divorce is final, do you think I should . . . look him up? Or is that . . . ridiculous?"

She rubbed her forehead. "El, it's just that . . . so much time has passed. People change, and . . . I'd hate to see you get hurt. You've already been through so much."

"That's no answer, Millie. There's something you're not telling me. What is it?"

When her eyes finally met mine, I waited patiently, but her words surprised me. "I don't know how to say this, but it must be said." She sat down at the table, folding her hands. "After you left London, I ran into Edward one day in Mayfair." She paused. "Well, to be perfectly honest, I looked him up."

"What do you mean?"

"El, I knew nothing of this man, only his name, the jacket in the closet—and the look in your eyes. I had to find him. I just had to. And when I did, well, I understood. I understood everything. We had lunch that day, and we met again a week later. Eventually, we became good friends, and I . . . got to know him very well."

I shook my head. "Why didn't you tell me?"

"I should have, but . . ." Her voice trailed off. "Listen, I knew that you cared for Edward very much, and I didn't think it would help your situation in California to ramble on about him in my letters. We became dear friends, bound by our unique bond: you. We both missed you so very much."

I smiled, listening in rapt attention.

"There's something else I need to tell you," Millie continued, clearing her throat, her expression suddenly pained. "In time, I began to . . . feel *more* for Edward."

I looked away, my heart filled with pangs of emotion—jealousy, hurt, surprise. This was the last thing I'd ever imagined my best friend telling me, and yet, I knew I had no right to feel betrayed. After all, I married someone else and moved halfway around the world.

"He didn't feel the same way," she finally said. "His heart was inextricably yours."

I didn't know what to say or do, and so we just sat there for a long moment in silence until I finally found my voice.

"Where is he now? Do you know?"

She nodded. "He moved to the countryside . . . with his wife and child."

The revelation hurt as much as it warmed my heart. "Good," I said. "He's tending his tomatoes."

Millie shook her head. "What do you mean?"

"Nothing," I replied. "He's happy. That's all I needed to know."

Millie walked to her bedroom, returning with a man's evening jacket on its hanger, which she handed to me. I knew it in an instant, of course, and the memories of the night we met came rushing back.

"You kept it, all these years?" I asked, astonished.

"Well, I made a promise, didn't I?"

I smiled.

"El, will you forgive me? I never meant to—"

"I've already forgiven you," I said, nodding. I was just as eager to put the subject back on the shelf as she was. "We don't have to talk about it anymore."

"I just want you to know that there was only one woman Edward could ever love. It wasn't me. It wasn't anyone else. Eloise, it was always you."

I pressed my nose to the jacket's collar and breathed in a mix of mothballs, Millie's favorite candles, and . . . memories.

"It was the best of times, it was the worst of times."

Valentina

The Next Day

———

"MORNING," LIZA SAYS, BURSTING THROUGH THE DOOR with an armful of pastel pink flowers—I spy roses and peonies—which she places in a bucket of water beside the windows. "Did you have fun at Sexy Fish?"

Millie looks up from the desk, confused. "Sexy *who?*" She shakes her head. "Whatever are you girls talking about?"

"It's a restaurant in Mayfair, and also a club, well, sort of." I smile at Liza, then turn back to Millie, who is staring at the computer screen, fretting. I know she's stressed. I am, too; I've been constantly refreshing the GoFundMe page on my phone. Eric's newspaper column had been a boost, but, sadly, it appears we're still net short.

"What did you end up doing last night?" Liza asks, ignoring Millie's mood. "Did you head home right away?"

"I just wandered over to Berkeley Square," I tell her, "where I ran into Eric, actually." I feel Millie's eyes on me. "We talked for a little while. He broke up with Fiona."

"Good riddance," Millie says.

"Hold on, Shakespeare is *single?*"

"He's a columnist, not a playwright, my dear."

"Well, either-or, I'm glad to hear that he's rid himself of that awful woman."

"Me, too," I say, thinking back to our conversation last night. "He looked happy."

A black town car pulls up in front of the bookstore—probably the same one I'd noticed driving by the other day, though I hadn't mentioned it to Millie. Probably another real estate developer. They were circling like vultures.

When the car drives off, I sigh, directing my attention to the ringing phone.

"Is this Valentina Baker, by chance?"

"Speaking."

"Ah, good. Ms. Baker, this is Bill Fairchild, your account manager at London Trust Bank."

"Yes?"

"Ms. Baker, this is highly unusual, but we've just received a wire notice for your account."

"I'm sorry," I say, rubbing my eyes. It's only half-past nine, and I'm already exhausted. "I don't understand. Are you saying that a check was canceled?" It occurred to me that Millie might have paid a bill before the proceeds from the fundraiser cleared.

"No, ma'am," he continues. "Actually, it's just the opposite. There's been a deposit *into* your account, and a pretty large one at that."

"Hold on, what?"

"Ms. Baker, three hundred thousand pounds just posted this morning."

"I'm sorry, is this some kind of joke?"

"I assure you; this is not a joke."

"Who would have sent that kind of money?" I ask, my heart beating faster.

"There isn't a name on the transfer slip, just an account number. I could look into it, if you like."

"Yes," I say, the news slowly sinking in. "Sir, do you know what this means for us? Do you know?" Millie and Liza hang on my every word, even if it's only half of the conversation.

"Ma'am," he says. "I do not. I'm merely a banker."

"Well," I continue, "you wonderful, magnificent, brilliant banker. You see, you've just informed me that our little bookstore here in Primrose Hill will be able to carry on. I could kiss you right now!" I lay a smooch on the phone's receiver before hanging up and leaping over the counter. "Guess what?"

Liza grins. "You have the recipe for Café Flora's cinnamon rolls, and they're calorie-free?"

"Even better!" I cry. "Someone just wired three hundred thousand pounds into our account. Three hundred thousand pounds!"

Millie searches my face cautiously. "Is it true? The Book Garden will . . . *survive?*"

"Survive and *thrive!*"

Liza walks to the window, scooping up Percy, which is when the same black town car circles back again—and this time it parks out front. "Why don't you people go piss off," she says through the window.

"The nerve of them," Millie says. But as the driver emerges and opens the passenger door, helping an older gentleman out onto the sidewalk, her eyes get big.

"Millie," I say. "Who is that?"

The doorbells jingle as the distinguished older man walks inside. "Hello, Millie," he says. His thin gray hair is neatly combed and his clothes freshly pressed. He's handsome for an octogenarian, and has the appearance of someone who was probably even more so in his day.

Millie looks as if she's seen a ghost, and perhaps she has. "It's you."

"I stayed away for far too long," he says. "But even so, I was always near."

"I take it you know that Eloise . . . passed."

Liza and I exchange glances.

"Yes," he says solemnly. "I was able to say my goodbyes."

Millie swallows hard. "Oh . . ." Her voice trails off as she takes in his words, and his presence. "I'm . . . glad—for the both of you."

He looks up to the ceiling when a few drops of water hit his shirt, and Millie sighs. "I'll have to call a contractor. It looks like the pipes are leaking again."

"Nothing the dry cleaner can't remedy," he says, unbuttoning his shirt, revealing the faint outline of a . . . tattoo. The edges have blurred on his aging skin, but then it hits me. All of it hits me.

"The violin," I say suddenly, my eyes meeting his. "You got the tattoo, because . . . you always wanted music in your ear, is that right?"

"That's right, young lady," he says with a smile.

"Edward?"

"Yes."

"The man my mother loved."

"Oh, and did I ever love her," Edward says. "Eloise was the brightest star in my sky. She still is.

"You must be Valentina."

I nod.

"You're exactly as your mother described. Beautiful, like her. Kind eyes." He nods. "You have her nose."

"Do I?" I say, compulsively touching the tip of my nose.

"And oh, how she loved you."

Hearing his words feels like the stamp of approval on an official document, one that I can file away and return to for proof, in moments when I need it most.

"It was you, wasn't it? You sent the money. You saved the store."

He takes a deep breath. "Well, there's no way I could stand by and watch London's finest bookstore get transformed into another dull block of flats. I only wish I'd known sooner that you were in trouble. Eloise didn't mention it, but then I saw the article in the newspaper, I'm afraid, a bit late, but hopefully not too late."

Millie merely nods, unable to find her voice.

"I . . . I don't know what to say other than . . . thank you. Thank you so very much."

"Well," he says with a smile, "enough of these dull matters. We have a great deal of catching up to do." He looks at Millie, and then me. "I've come here to ask you both to join me for lunch. It would be my great honor if I could spend a little time with Eloise's two favorite people."

"Yes," I say immediately. "I'd love that."

"And, Millie?" he continues. "Will you join us?"

There's a far-off look in her eyes, as if she's returning to a chapter of an old favorite book that stirred her heart, and still does. "Thank you, but no," she finally says. "You two go ahead. I have . . . so much to do here."

Edward looks disappointed, but Millie's made up her mind. He turns to the window and motions to his driver, who's waiting outside.

"Wait," Millie says. "Before you go. I . . . have something for you." We watch as she walks to the back room, returning a moment later holding a garment bag, which she hands to Edward. He pulls the zipper, revealing a man's jacket. "Do you remember?"

"Like it was yesterday," he says.

"El asked me to keep it, and . . . I always did."

"David," he says, smiling as he turns to his driver. "Will you please call Claridge's and let them know we need a table? Their best one, if it's available. I'm an old man, but a very lucky one. I'm taking one of the loveliest women in London to tea." He winks at me. "And I'll be wearing this dinner jacket I left behind in 1968."

EDWARD IS COMFORTABLE IN the past, and I encourage him down whichever paths his memory leads him, hoping to catch glimpses of my mother.

She's there with him.

First, on the balcony of the Royal Automobile Club, where they met by chance, laughed, and finished each other's sentences, agreeing to meet again the following night.

Edward tells me how he left her a hand-drawn map to the club's secluded library bar that he'd discovered as a boy, and how she'd shared her dream of opening a bookstore before their conversation was interrupted by an urgent message. One that turned out to be false.

"My sister saw me with Eloise that night on the balcony,"

he said. "She planted a seed of worry in my family. You see, as an heir to a sizable fortune, she felt that an East Ender, no matter how bright and magnificent, was an unacceptable match." He takes a sip of his tea, and I notice the way his hand trembles a little as he sets the cup back on the saucer. "Genevieve's prejudice didn't matter to me, but my parents' love did. It took me some time to convince them that if I were to marry, it would be for love—and love alone. Eventually, they came around."

"But it was too late for you and my mother?"

"I hoped it wouldn't be," he continues. "I saw her once, months later—at Rhett's Supper Club. I was with another woman, and she was with . . . your father." He swallows hard. "She looked . . . so beautiful that night. It took all of my strength to will my eyes away." He nods. "I called her several times after that, but I never got through to her. I had to see her again, so as I did the night of our second date, I arranged a scavenger hunt for her, with notes I'd left around her neighborhood."

I smile.

"And we found each other again, and it was . . . magic. She was magic. There was nothing I wanted more than to start a life with her, right then and there; she wanted that, too. The heart wants what the heart wants, after all. But as before, time wasn't on our side."

"What do you mean?"

"She'd already accepted your father's marriage proposal."

"And she was expecting a baby," I add. "Millie told me."

"Yes," he says.

I used to love to look at my parents' wedding photo, with Mummy dressed in white. I had no idea what that dress was hiding, though—a pregnancy that bound her to my father, who whisked her away to California, and the inevitable miscarriage that followed.

Edward blinks hard, fighting back tears. "As you can see, our timing was . . . tragic."

I nod.

"Just like Eloise, I married someone else, too. We had a happy life, two children. From the outside looking in, people might have thought we had it all. But inside, my heart belonged to someone else. When I heard Eloise had moved back to London, it took all my self-restraint not to go see her, and I didn't—out of respect for my wife. But the year after she passed, I finally did. But by then, your mum was quite ill; we didn't have much time. But I treasure the moments we had at the end of her life. I always will."

"Wow," I say, shaking my head, taking it all in.

"I'm sorry that you're hearing all of this from me and not your mum." He glances down at the paper bag on the chair beside him. "But I have something for you—from her."

My eyes widen as he lifts the bag into his lap.

"She asked me to find you and give you this. I'm sorry it's taken me this long." I watch as he pulls out a small wooden box. On the lid are the unmistakable words "Cicero's Sentiments." He places it in my hands, and I lift its lid, retrieving the sealed envelope inside: the clue I'd been looking for.

My dearest Val,

You've now met Edward, and I hope the two of you have gotten acquainted. Just like you, I loved him in my mortal days, and I will also love him in eternity. While my life didn't go exactly to plan, I had what many people don't— true love—even if it came with its own heartache. But nothing makes me happier than knowing that you two are together, perhaps even right now. I dreamed of this moment a thousand times. I only wish I could be there with you both. Val, I wish so many things. . . .

Now this brings you to your final clue: Percy will show you the way, and when he does, Millie holds the key.

I'll be waiting.

Love,
Mummy

Edward doesn't ask what my mother wrote to me, and I don't tell him. We sit together quietly for a while, staring at the little vase of daffodils on the table.

AS I STEP OUT of my taxi, I double-check the address Daniel texted earlier, taking a deep breath as I climb the front steps of the townhouse where he grew up. It's a charming home in the loveliest part of Notting Hill. A wreath made of bay leaves hangs on the door and I lean in to inhale the scent, which reminds me of California.

Before I even lift my hand to knock, the door swings open and a pretty, well-dressed woman in her sixties appears with outstretched arms.

"There you are!" she says, her brown hair in loose curls around her face. "We've been so excited to meet you, Valentina! Please come in! I'm Daniel's mother, Barbara." She's the spitting image of Daniel; they have the same eyes. "Ah, you're as lovely as he said you'd be. Now, let's get you inside. They say it might snow tonight!"

"Hi, babe," Daniel says, greeting me with a quick kiss before leaning in and whispering, "My mum loves you already."

I smile as he takes my hand and leads me into the living room.

"Did you just say something about snow in the forecast?" he asks as Barbara pours us each a glass of wine. "Mum has this uncanny ability to know every detail about the weather."

She nods. "I just heard it on the news. They say a front's moving in, might even be a blizzard."

Daniel frowns. "Seriously? Bloody snow. I hate the stuff."

I turn to him. "Really? You hate snow?"

"I do," he says, shaking his head. "Messes everything up. Two years ago, one of my projects came to a dead halt because of a few flurries."

"Nothing's changed," Barbara continues. "Even as a little boy, he had no interest in it." She shrugs. "Daniel always knew what he liked and what he didn't."

"Well," I say, "I, for one, think snow is . . . pretty magical."

"Says she who grew up in sunny California," he spars back.

I hold firm. "Says *anyone*! Besides, I spent the latter half of my childhood in Seattle, remember?"

He nods, but my argument holds little weight—he's anti-snow. "Dad," he says as I gaze out the window, eager to spot the first snowflake. "Join our debate over here. Are you on Team Snow or not?"

His father, a rather handsome silver-haired man, leaps to his feet and ignores my outstretched hand. Like his wife, he opts to embrace me instead. "Son, I'm on whichever team this charming young lady is on."

"One more for Team Snow," I say as Daniel shakes his head.

I meet Daniel's sister, Evelyn (Evie), who I'm told is six months pregnant with a baby girl. Her husband, Mark, smiles quietly by her side. They both seem great. In fact, they're all great. Every one of them.

Daniel squeezes my leg under the table as his sister and mother bring out the dinner, plate by plate—chicken curry, rice pilaf, salad, and a platter of lightly steamed vegetables.

"Tell us about Scotland, dear," Barbara says, passing the rice to Daniel and beaming with pride.

"It was cold," he says. "Very cold. But we managed to get the shots we needed before the cameras turned into ice cubes."

Evie leans in, dishing the chicken curry onto Mark's plate and then her own. "Daniel, remind me what this one's about."

"A shipwreck," he says, "that dates back to 1908, the cause of which has never been proven."

"Fascinating," his mother says, turning to me. "Daniel always picks the most interesting topics."

I smile.

"Indeed," he continues. "But what makes the story even more interesting is a lesser known detail: A certain British countess with ties to the throne happened to be on board—never to be seen again. Historical accounts have always pegged her death to a horseback riding accident, but my production crew found her name on the ship's manifest."

"No! Really?" Evie exclaims. "So her death was a cover-up?"

"Perhaps," he says with a sly smile. "But you'll have to watch it yourself and see. I refuse to spoil the ending—even for family. Besides, I signed an NDA yesterday . . . with Net-flix!"

"What?" I say, turning to Daniel. *"That's incredible!"*

"My parents already know," he continues. "But I wanted to tell you in person."

I smile. "News worth celebrating, indeed," I say, clinking my wineglass to his.

"It was a huge surprise to me and the crew. I mean, we knew they were considering it, but we had no idea it would get picked up this quickly, and with such enthusiasm."

"I'm so proud of you, my Danny Boy," his mother says, turning to me again. "What are we ever going to do without him when he moves to India?"

I turn to Daniel, my smile fading. *"India?"*

He looks at his mother and then back at me. "Mum . . . spoke too soon," he says, faltering. "Listen, I haven't had a chance to tell you. I promise, I was going to. Tonight." He swallows hard.

"Dear Lord, Daniel," Barbara cries. I can't tell if she's scolding him or, perhaps, about ready to burst into tears. *"You didn't tell her?"*

He reaches for my hand. "Val, it's only for a year, maybe less. It's an incredible opportunity, a chance to work on the most important film of my career—maybe even my lifetime. Netflix is backing it in a huge way. I know we're just . . . getting started, but . . . I hope you can understand that I . . . have to do this."

I look away as he reaches for my hand again.

"You could . . . come with me?" he continues.

"Daniel," I say, as I fumble to find the right words. "It's okay. Really. I'm happy for you."

"WELL, THEY SURE LOVED YOU," Daniel says as we leave his parents' house. The air is bitter cold outside, but so far, no snowflakes.

"They were lovely."

We walk in silence for a few moments—aimlessly—until he finally speaks. "Listen, I want to apologize, for what my mum said. I was going to tell you . . . tonight." He looks as handsome as ever in his dark jeans and overcoat, a shadow of facial hair dusting his chin. "I should have brought it up sooner. I . . . I guess I was scared."

"Scared?"

"Look, I know it's bad timing. Horrible timing. But I've loved every minute we've spent together, and I was afraid that if I told you about India, you'd . . . disappear."

"With all due respect," I say, "you should have told me."

He sighs. "You're right. And I'm sorry."

I notice a cab approaching, and I begin walking ahead. "I should probably go."

"Val, please," Daniel says, gesturing to a bench in front of a closed café. "Can we talk for a little longer?"

I nod, sitting beside him on the bench. "What more is there to say? You're moving to India."

He opens his mouth to protest, but I stop him.

"Daniel, you don't even like snow!"

"That's true," he concedes.

"Exactly!" I say, the channels in my mind beginning to fire. "And I love snow!"

"Well, we both hate eggplant. We have that in common!"

I frown. "Apparently that's the only thing we have in

common—aside from the book we both love." Our eyes meet for a moment, but he looks away quickly, pausing to rub the side of his neck, as if my comment has just elicited a sharp pain. "Val, listen," he finally says. "Oh, bloody hell, I don't know how to say this."

My eyes widen. "You're gay? Married? No—you're impersonating a successful documentarian who is not, in fact, moving to India?"

He laughs. "None of the above. But honestly, all of those options would be . . . easier than what I need to tell you."

"What?"

"Those notes in the pages of your book . . . they . . . weren't mine." He sighs, his eyes filled with regret.

"Why didn't you tell me right away?"

"I should have," he replies. "But, look, when I met you, it was all so . . . surprising. Here was this gorgeous, interesting American woman who just appeared in my life out of nowhere. Yes, I should have set the record straight right away, but then what? Miss out on the opportunity to get to know *you*?"

He tries to catch my eye, but I look away.

"I'm sorry," he says. "That makes two apologies in one night. I'm on a roll."

"I'm sorry, too," I say, standing up when I see a cab approaching. "Listen, I loved meeting your amazing family and . . . you. But *I have to go*. Good luck in India. Good luck with everything."

"But, wait," he says, reaching his hand to me, but I don't take it.

"Goodbye, Daniel."

Eloise

April 13, 1996

MILLIE WALKED THROUGH THE DOOR AND SET A BOU-
quet of peonies in a vase on the counter.

"Good morning," she said, greeting me, but I didn't smile.
"Why the glum face?"

"Today is . . . Valentina's birthday. Her eighteenth."

"Oh, El," Millie whispered, placing her arm over my
shoulder as we both looked at the framed photo of my daughter that had remained on the store's front counter since our
doors opened.

I wiped away a tear, catching it midway down my right
cheek. "It's been six years since I've seen her. What do you
think she's like now?"

"That's easy," Millie replied. "She's vibrant, thoughtful,
and passionate—just like you."

"I hope she's happy." I paused, pulling out the envelope
I'd tucked into the back pocket of my jeans earlier. "I think
this will be my last letter. She's probably headed off to college this fall, and even if Frank hasn't been intercepting her
mail all this time, there'll be no stopping him when Val's

away. My only prayer is that she knows how much I love her."

"Of course she does," Millie said before glancing down at the wicker basket in her hands. "Now, you look as if you could use a little cheering up, and fortunately I have just the thing." She set the basket on the counter, just as a fluffy kitten poked its timid head out.

"A proper bookstore needs a cat," Millie said.

I squealed, scooping the tiny creature into my arms. "Look at you," I said to the kitten. "You're perfect."

"He's a boy, and he needs a name."

"Easy," I said, smiling. "We'll call him the name we chose as girls, remember?"

Millie nods. "Percival—Percy, for short."

"Welcome to the family, Percy."

The bells on the door jingled as a woman and her young daughter walked in.

"Can you help me find a book?" the little girl asked, squealing with delight when she noticed the kitten.

"Of course, I can!" I said, walking around the counter to kneel down beside her. "Now tell me. What sort of story are you looking for?"

"A happy one," she said.

I nodded. "All right, let's find you one that makes you smile." We walked together to the children's section and I began to peruse the shelves. "What's your name, sweetie?"

"Anna Maria," she said.

"Well, Anna Maria, when my daughter was about your age, you know what I told her?"

"What?" Her big blue eyes gazed up at me.

I nodded. "That the best books choose you."

She looked up at her mother, confused, then back at me. "You mean," she said, placing her hand on the edge of a nearby shelf, "books have feelings?"

"Yes," I said with a smile. "And only you can unlock them. It's easy, though. All you have to do is read the pages."

The little girl squealed, running ahead as her elbow knocked an endcap out of place. Dozens of books fell to the floor, but one remained on its perch—hers.

"Mummy, Mummy," she cried, reaching to pick up a copy of *The Little House,* a story of a tiny home in the country thrust into fast-paced city life.

"See," I said, smiling. "That one was meant for you."

Valentina

The Next Day

————

THE BOOK GARDEN IS BUSTLING WITH ITS USUAL ENERGY, but somehow there's a glorious hum to it all—the way an old man might whistle happily as he walks when everything is at peace in his life. Customers meander in and out, deliveries are signed for, plants and flower arrangements brim from carts up front, books make their way into new hands; it's as it always was—without any worries about the store's future in the backs of our minds.

"Look what I found this morning," Millie says, handing me a well-loved copy of *The Little House*. I know that it was first published in 1942 because Mummy told me. In fact, it was one of my favorites as a child. "A customer brought in a box of used books. Look inside. It's a first edition."

"Amazing," I say, fanning the pages. The illustrations bring back a parade of memories, waving their flags and beating their drums as they demand my attention. I'm at once five years old, lingering over its pages as I look up at . . . Mummy. *"Was the little house sad? Did she miss the children?"*

I post a photo of the book in my hand on @booksbyval—

with a lively scene of the store in the background—as I compose an impromptu post.

> I have a memory of my mother reading this book to me as a child. It's the story of a special house. Much like the building I'm standing in right now, the house is a final holdout of urban sprawl. It stood proud on a grassy spot, where children played in the meadow in spring and skated on the iced-over brook each winter. But change crept in like a dark cloud, bringing with it modernization and progress, cars and railroad engines, and more and more people.
>
> At the end of the book, the little house is surrounded by a bustling city, built all around her.
>
> There is no brook, no meadow.
>
> Her roof is covered with soot from the city and there is no longer a blue sky overhead.
>
> But the Little House found her way—back to the country, back to the children, back to the brook. I'm happy to share that the Book Garden will know a similar happy ending. Our fundraising goals were met, and this beloved bookstore will live on. And, as long as I am able to do so, I'll make sure it does.

I set my phone down and reach into my bag to retrieve the Cicero box that Edward gave to me.

"Oh look, you found it!" Millie exclaims. "Where?"

I smile. "It just . . . turned up." As she leans in closer, we both reread my mother's most recent clue, particularly about Percy showing me *the way* and Millie having *the key*.

She nods to herself. "Yes. She said I'd know when you were ready."

"Ready for what?"

She reaches into a drawer beneath the counter, then says, "Come with me."

Percy ambles ahead, to the far corner of the store, stopping to purr beside the history section. The edge of the shelf is littered with claw marks, evidence of his long-favorite scratching post.

Percy will show you the way.

I scan the shelves, looking for something, anything, in the rows of spines—a book on Paris during Nazi occupation catches my eye; so does an Istanbul travel guidebook. But what am I looking for, exactly?

Then, Millie pulls a key from her pocket, before pressing on the edge of a nearby shelf. It hinges open, and behind the false shelf is a padlocked door.

"What is this?" I ask, my heart beating faster.

She smiles. "Your mother's secret library."

I watch with rapt attention as she inserts the key into the lock.

Millie holds the key.

"She thought that every proper bookstore needed one, so when we first opened the Book Garden, she transformed an old utility closet into, well, *this*."

The hinges creak as Millie opens the door, releasing stale air and scents familiar to every book lover, but especially this one—rosewater and leather, must and old paper. There's a little chair in the corner and enough room for two people to fit, if rather snugly.

"She loved being surrounded by her favorite books," Mille says. "I haven't been in here since ... she got sick."

She watches as I run my hand along the edges of one of

the shelves. I recognize some titles as old favorites. Others surprise me, but it's clear that each book was chosen for a special reason.

"She always said you can tell a lot about a person by the books they keep," I say.

Millie nods as I scan the titles on each shelf for clues about my mother's private world. I pause when one spine in particular catches my eye. "I can't believe it," I say, suddenly feeling breathless. *"The Last Winter."*

I first read the novel not long after my mother left, which makes the discovery feel less like a coincidence and more like what she always said—that books find *you,* or in this case, both of us. The fact that she kept it here, in her treasured library, meant that it was as special to her as it is to me.

"That isn't the only surprise," Millie says, smiling. "Look inside the bench for the finale." She points ahead to an upholstered seat along the wall, then slips out, leaving me alone in my mother's most sacred space. I run my hand along the gray fabric. It's a bit threadbare, and its tufts are missing a few buttons, but it reminds me of a similar bench—the one that had been in my Santa Monica bedroom as a child. I kept my most treasured toys inside.

I lift the edge and it opens, revealing two cardboard boxes inside. An envelope with my name on it is taped to the top of one. I reach for it, tearing the edge open hastily:

My darling girl,

Congratulations! You've reached the end of our little scavenger hunt. I hope you've enjoyed it as much as I have enjoyed putting it together for you. I wanted you to get to

*know my little world here in Primrose Hill, to meet the
people I love so dearly, in hope that you could feel at home.*

*I also wanted you to know me. We missed so much
time together, and that will always be my deepest regret.
But I pray that the letters I wrote you over the years—
inside these boxes—will help to make up for that. I've
organized them by date, so you can start from the beginning. As you read, I pray you'll understand.*

*The greatest failure of my life was leaving you. Will
you forgive me, my little birdie?*

*I love you,
Mummy*

I wipe away the tears on my cheeks, then pry open the
edges of the first box and gasp. Just as she wrote, there are
dozens of thick stacks of letters, bundled with rubber bands.
I reach for the first, and pry the letter on top out. It's from
Mummy and addressed to me, but unopened. The postmark
is June 13, 1990. I tearfully open it, pulling out the carefully
folded page inside.

My darling Valentina,

*I didn't want to leave you, honey, but I had to. In time,
I'll try to explain.*

*I'm here in London now, visiting my old friend
Millie, who I've told you about so often. Oh, Val, I wish
you were here with me. I know you'd love London as
much as I do. After all, you have English blood running
through your veins.*

There are things I wish I could tell you to help you

understand, but I can't. Because of that, I'm asking you to trust me, please. I know it's hard when I'm not there to look into your eyes, when I can't dry your tears or help you understand. But, I'll be home soon. Until then, I'll be loving you every second of every day, and always.

> *With love*
> *from London,*
> *Mummy*

With love from London. My heart feels as if it might burst, and it nearly does as I pull out another bundle of letters, and another. All of them are the same—to me from Mummy—all unopened. My father must have kept her letters from me— and yet she kept writing. *Every day.* I think of all the letters I wrote to her, too—how I'd handed them to my father each day to stamp and take to the post office. Did he intercept those, too? Is that why he felt such remorse when he apologized to me at the end of his life?

I feel weak—and angry—as I sink into the chair beside me. But for the first time in so long, I also feel *loved.*

Eloise

A DELIVERYMAN WALKED INTO THE BOOKSTORE HOLDING an enormous bouquet of ivory and pink roses. "Eloise Baker?"

"Yes," I said, a bit confused. "There must be some mistake." *Who would send me flowers?*

He shrugged, handing me an envelope. I tore open the edge and read the card inside:

> *Eloise,*
>
> *If I were a country farmer, and you were a sophisticated bookstore owner, would you marry me anyway, would you be my lady?*
>
> > *Yours, always*
> > *and forever,*
> > *E*

At first, I laughed, then tears stung my eyes. *Edward.* Millie was on the top rung of a ladder taping red and pink paper hearts to the window when she saw the flowers on the front counter. I wondered if she'd noticed the earth shift on its axis as I read the card.

"Who sent *those*?" she asked, climbing down.

"A ... customer," I said. "For Valentine's Day ... I guess." My heart raced as I tucked the card into my pocket. I wanted to keep the moment to myself, at least for now.

Millie watched me curiously, but then turned to the door when a young woman walked in. She was about the age Val would be right now, I guessed.

"Good morning," she said cheerfully. "I'm here about the first-floor flat for rent."

"Yes," I said, coming to my senses. I placed a sign in the window just yesterday after we'd had the oven replaced and refinished the hardwood floors.

"Oh my gosh," she gushed. "Is this the most adorable bookstore of all time, or what?"

She was in her early thirties, I guessed, if that, with a rather eclectic sense of style that matched her personality. I liked her instantly.

"I'm Eloise," I said. "And this is Millie."

The young woman smiled. "Is your formal name Millifred or Millicent? Millesandra?"

"Just Millie."

"Well, it's very nice to meet you, Eloise and Just Millie. I'm Just Liza. And unfortunately, my parents were not the literary types, so there was no inspiration taken from Eliza Doolittle. Dad was a car mechanic, and Mum didn't finish school. I honestly don't know if either of them has ever completed an entire book in their lives." She shrugged. "But I have. A zillion of them. I love books." She spun around to survey the shop. "And maybe if I'm lucky, I'll be the girl who gets to live above all these stories. Hey, I wonder if that means you'd have really sweet dreams living here?"

Millie laughed. "I'm not quite sure about that, but I can take you up to see the flat."

The expression on Millie's face was a carbon copy of mine—somewhere between amusement and curiosity. I decided, right then and there, that even if Liza's name wasn't inspired by classic literature, she was still one of the most interesting characters I'd ever met.

"I'll take it!" she said thirty seconds after stepping foot in the flat.

"She's a lively one," Millie said after she was gone.

"And just what we need around here," I said, agreeing. "Some youthful energy."

Millie looked up at the heart-studded window and frowned.

"I see your vendetta against Valentine's Day is still alive and well."

"It's as strong as ever," she replied, ever the romantic cynic.

"Well, bahumbug all you like, but people expect a whimsical flair from their neighborhood bookstore." I glanced back at the flowers on the counter. "Besides, who knows what Cupid has up his sleeve." Percy waddled over with a red bow affixed to his collar and pressed himself against the side of my leg. "Millie, try as you might, you don't fool me for a second. Underneath all those hardened layers, you're a softie. And one of these days, some man is going to walk through that door and pierce that jaded heart of yours, you'll see."

"We don't sell that kind of romance novel here," she said, cracking the tiniest smile as she climbed down the ladder to have a look at the window decorations. "Is it whimsical enough for you?"

"It's perfect," I said, grinning.

"Good," Millie added. "Because I'm nominating you for the St. Patrick's Day décor."

"Deal." I paused, wincing a little, as a surge of pain radiated from my lower back. I reached my arm around and clutched the side of my hip.

"You okay, El?"

"Yeah," I replied, a bit breathless. "But it's odd. I've been getting these strange back pains lately—probably just digestive issues." I found a bottle of Advil behind the counter and took two.

"When's the last time you had a physical exam?" Millie asked.

"I'm embarrassed to admit, but I really have no idea. Maybe sometime after Valentina was born?"

"Eloise, you can't be serious!"

I shrugged. "You know I never get sick."

"Still," Millie said. "You should go see Dr. Hester. Just to make sure everything's all right."

I knew the local doctor well enough, but not as a patient— only a customer, who brought his twin daughters in on weekends to pick out new books.

"When I went in last month," Millie added, "he ran some labs and it turned out that my vitamin D levels were quite low. I'm taking a supplement now. I bet you're deficient, too. None of us get enough sunshine in this bloody city."

"Okay, I'll make an appointment," I said, glancing out the window. It might have been an impossibly gray day, but after reading Edward's card, all I felt was the warmth of the sun.

A FedEx truck pulled up in front of the store a few minutes later, and the driver carried in a stack of packages, including one very large box. He set them on the counter as I signed for them. "You must be new," I said to the man. "I don't think we've met."

"Yes," he said, smiling. "I'm Fernando. It's my first day on the job."

"I'm Eloise, and this is Millie."

"Pleased to meet you both," he said, glancing at our window display, then turning to Millie, who had decided to tape one more pink heart on the right side of the window. "It looks nice," he added as she began climbing down the ladder. But when she missed the third step, her foot slipped, and Fernando offered his hand to steady her.

"Thank you," she said, blushing. "I'm ... glad you were there. I might have twisted my ankle."

"That would have been a shame," he said, holding her hand for a long moment. Millie towered above his diminutive frame, and yet somehow, they looked ... adorable standing next to each other. I smiled to myself. A pair of funny Valentines.

After he left, I sorted through the deliveries, turning to the large box when the address caught my eye. "Millie," I said. "Look, it's from ... Frank's sister in ... Seattle." I recognized the name immediately—Ellen Reeves—even though I'd only met her a handful of times before Frank and I divorced. What on earth could she have sent me?

Millie stood beside me as I ran the sharp edge of a pair of scissors along the box's taped seam and pulled the edges open. Inside was an enormous assortment of mail—hundreds and hundreds of letters. I reached for one, then another, and another. My knees felt weak. All were from me, addressed to Valentina, and every single one was *unopened*.

"Millie," I cried, my hands trembling. "He . . . kept the letters all those years. He never let Valentina read them. Not one of them."

She placed her hand on my shoulder. "Oh, El, I don't know what to say." She searched my face. "I know you always suspected something like that was happening, but," she said with a sigh, "this is cruelty . . . beyond comprehension."

When I noticed an envelope taped to the inside edge of the box, I opened it and read it aloud:

Dear Eloise,

This may come as a shock to you, and I'm very sorry. After my brother, Frank, passed, I found these letters in his study, and I felt that you deserved to have them. As a mother myself, it seemed inconceivable that he would have kept them from Valentina, but I'm sure Frank had his reasons and I won't question those, especially now. I considered giving them to Val, but I didn't feel it was my place. Instead, I'm sending them back to you. I hope you will one day come to forgive Frank. I can only imagine that he had many regrets at the end of his life. Despite his challenges, he was a good man. And I know he did love you once, very much. Again, I'm very sorry.

Kind regards,
Barbara

Valentina

One Year Later

————

IT'S THE FIRST OF DECEMBER, AND WHEN MILLIE AND I arrive at the store that morning, we find Liza wrangling a strand of white fairy lights. She quit her assistant job a few months ago and came to work for us on a full-time basis, which was a great comfort to me. If I remember correctly, the letter of resignation she sent to her boss consisted of only two words: "Piss off."

"I found these in the back room," she says. "I thought we could decorate today."

I smile, lifting a faux evergreen wreath from the open box beside her, which I hang on the front door. "Here," I say, grabbing the end of the strand. "Let me help."

"Thanks," she says, pointing to the window seat, where dozens of plants with ruby-red leaves stand at attention. "The poinsettias came in today, look."

I smile, remembering my childhood Christmases in Santa Monica. "Mummy loved poinsettias."

Fernando appears in the doorway with his morning deliveries. He waves at Liza and me, then gives Millie a quick kiss. Her engagement ring sparkles from across the room.

"I brought in the mail," he says, depositing a large pile on the counter.

Millie sorts through the stack, then pauses when something catches her eye.

"Look, Val—you got a postcard," she says, handing it to me. "From Daniel."

I smile at the photo of the Taj Mahal, then flip it over to read his note.

"So," Liza says, leaning over my shoulder. "What did he say?"

"He says India has been amazing and his project is almost complete. He plans to come back soon, maybe by Christmas." I set the postcard down. "He says hi to you two."

"That was nice of him . . . to think of you," Millie says.

"It was," I say, though I remained rather unfazed. When he left for India, Daniel and I agreed to go our separate ways, and I hadn't thought about him much at all over the past year.

"Maybe the story isn't over for you two," Liza says, glancing over from her flock of poinsettias.

"I think it is," I say with a shrug. "But that's okay." And it was. For the first time since I could remember, I felt happy. Perfectly happy. I'd just completed a light remodel of the third-floor flat—repainting the kitchen, updating the appliances, and retiling the bathroom. Over the months, I read Mummy's letters, every one of them. They offered the greatest gift of all—healing. I finally understood her, and when I looked up at the stars at night, I prayed she understood me, too. Everything finally felt as if it had found its place, including me.

"Shoot," Millie says, fumbling beneath the desk. "Where's my mind? I was going to ask Fernando to take a box of books over to Mrs. Wilson this afternoon. She's been ill, and her special order came in yesterday."

I reach for the box, eyeing the address. "That's not too far, is it?"

"More or less."

"Don't worry, I can bring it over to her later," I say. "I planned on taking a walk today."

"Thanks, honey. She'll be grateful. But bundle up. I hear there's snow in the forecast."

I glance out the window, smiling at the thick clouds rolling in. "I hope so."

AROUND THREE, I LACE UP my boots and tuck a scarf around my neck, just in case, then reach for a tote bag hanging on the hook by my door. I tuck my wallet and Mrs. Wilson's package inside, then sling it over my shoulder and set out down the street, waving at John in the bakery, and Jan in the window of Café Flora. Life could bring joy or sorrow, and a million twists and turns, but it comforted me knowing that Primrose Hill would remain unchanged, down to its pastel-colored soul.

I greet Mrs. Wilson on her front porch. She looks pale, but her expression warms when I hand her the box of books. It warms me, too.

I walk ahead, the cold air kissing my cheeks. If I take a slightly different return route, I can follow Prince Albert Road to Primrose Hill park. I notice a café on the next block, and I decide to stop in for a coffee and the chance to thaw my chilly fingers.

"You look like someone who could use a warm drink," says an older man behind the counter.

"Yes, please," I say, ordering a cappuccino. As I reach into my bag for my wallet, I notice a stowaway inside—*The Last Winter*—and I realize I'd completely forgotten about it. I sit down in a chair by the window, fanning the pages. It feels good to be reunited with an old friend, even if "Daniel" didn't quite turn out as I'd expected.

I sip my coffee, thinking about the last year, and my mind turns to Eric. I'd seen him a few times, when he'd stopped in to the bookstore on occasion, but it has been months since his last visit. I knew from reading his columns that he was on assignment in France, but it wasn't clear if he'd returned to London yet. Then I remember that he'd given me his card. I have it in my wallet somewhere, so I have a look, and sure enough, there it is, hiding behind the old Amex card Nick and I used to share. I make a mental note to cut it up at home.

Eric Winston, columnist, it reads. His cell is printed on the bottom line, and without giving it a second thought, I spontaneously dial the number. He picks up on the second ring.

"Hi Eric, it's Valentina," I say.

"Valentina, hi! How are you?"

"I'm well, thank you. I don't know why, but you just crossed my mind . . . and I wanted to call to say hi. Are you back from France?"

"I'm so glad you did," he says, "and yes, I've been home for three weeks now. What are you up to?"

I look out the window as people pass on the sidewalk, watching a little girl—no more than three—skipping along in pink rain boots, clutching her mother's hand. *How lucky she is,* I think, *to be able to hold her mother's hand.* "Reminiscing, you could say. I was out walking after dropping off some books for a customer, and I popped in to a little café up on the hill."

"What café?"

I peer at the sign on the wall. "Greenberry Café."

"You're kidding me," he says. "My flat's just around the corner."

"Really?"

"Yeah. I could . . . come by and say hi, if you're not leaving soon?"

"Yes," I say quickly. "I'd love that."

A few minutes later, the café door creaks open, letting in a blast of cold air. I shiver as I glance at the door. Eric sees me immediately and smiles, slowly unwrapping his wool scarf.

"Hi," he says, pausing to order a coffee from the counter before sliding into the chair beside me.

"Hi," I say. His green eyes glisten under the café's lights.

"How've you been?"

I tell him about the bookstore, my mother's letters, then ask him about his time in France, which he describes as equal parts beautiful and lonely. *The Times* put him up in a flat in Montmartre to write an eight-part series about English-French relations. I don't divulge that I've been reading his columns.

"What are you doing tonight?" he asks suddenly.

I smile. "Absolutely nothing."

"I don't know, maybe we could . . . walk—take in the snowstorm?"

"I'd like that," I say, my smile widening.

We bundle back up and head out to the street. It's nearly sunset, and even with the dense swirl of clouds overhead, the air has a pink, ethereal hue to it.

"I hear that Daniel's coming home soon," he says. "I bet you're looking forward to seeing him."

I nod vacantly.

"Maybe you guys will pick things up where you left off?"

I shake my head. "I don't think so."

"Why?"

"No reason in particular," I say. "I mean, he's great, but we just—"

"Didn't work," we both say at the same time.

I nod, with a laugh. "I guess that's the beauty of getting older. We learn to listen to our instincts."

He grins. "I wish I'd done that years ago."

"Me too."

We walk in companionable silence, glancing over at each other every few moments as if waiting for the other to say something. Eric finally does. "Have you ever been to Feng Shang Princess?"

I shake my head.

"It's a Chinese restaurant on a floating, three-tiered pagoda houseboat," he explains. "There's nothing like it anywhere in London."

"A houseboat and a princess?" I ask. "That sounds like a combination I need to experience as soon as possible."

"It's along Prince Albert Road in the Cumberland Basin of Regent's Park. We can walk there from here. Are you free for dinner?"

I give him a coy smile. "Are you asking me out?"

"Why, yes . . . yes, I am." He grins. "I mean, it's not the Royal Automobile Club, but—"

"I'd love it."

Fifteen minutes later, we're seated in black leather chairs at one of the circular tables inside the floating restaurant. Festive red lanterns dangle from the ceiling.

Eric orders dim sum, and when the waiter recommends duck and a wine pairing, I nod in agreement. From the table, we can see a few small boats passing along the canal. Daylight is waning and the temperature is dropping by the second, but the lantern light casts a warm glow in the air.

"You sure Daniel won't throw a swing at me for taking his girl out?" Eric asks, and I realize that his old friend is the elephant in the room.

"First of all, I'm not his girl, and second of all, no. I assure you, each of us has moved on."

He nods, still thinking. "How did you two meet, again? I can't imagine he was a bookstore customer. I mean, he's a great guy, but he's not—"

"A reader," I say, finishing his sentence. "And that was, well, part of the problem." I reach into my bag and hand him my treasured copy of *The Last Winter* before telling him the whole story.

He looks at the book, then back at me. "I don't understand."

"It's really a story about me and my mother, actually," I say, explaining our connection to the novel and how I'd found this particular copy with the notes in the margins.

I point out the inside cover where Daniel's name is written. "I just had to find him, and I did." I sigh. "But, alas, though this was his book, the notes inside weren't—and it took him a while to admit that to me." My cheeks feel warm, and I'm suddenly worried that I'm talking too fast, or too much. "Am I making any sense?"

Eric quietly flips through the pages. "You're making perfect sense." His face turns utterly serious, as if he's about to make a confession. "Valentina, this book . . . it belongs to . . . *me*."

My eyes get big, and then I shake my head, laughing. "That's very funny, but I'm afraid I'm not *that* gullible."

"I'm not joking," he continues, his face drawn and serious. "I don't know how Daniel's name got in there—maybe he borrowed it from me, maybe he bought it used at the student bookstore? It was a long time ago. Anyway, I can assure you that the book, and the notes inside, are definitely mine."

My mouth gapes open. "Are you serious?"

He nods. "I am."

"It was *you*, all along."

He nods again.

Our wine and dim sum arrive, and the waiter fills each of our glasses.

"Tell me," he adds. "On a scale of one to ten, how bad are the pontifications of my twenty-one-year-old self?"

I pause for a long moment. "They were . . . beautiful," I say. "Everything you wrote was . . . so beautiful."

Our conversation meanders over dinner, and after Eric pays the bill, he offers to walk me home. I link my arm in his, and it fits like a key in a lock.

"Aha," he says, looking up at the sky as we fall into step together on Prince Albert Road. "Did you feel that?"

"Feel what?"

He touches his cheek. "It just started to snow!"

"Wait," I say, glancing up at him. "Do you like snow?"

"*Do I like snow?* What kind of question is that? Of course I do. Is there any other answer?"

"No," I say, smiling so big my cheeks hurt. "No, there isn't." I slide my grip down his arm until my hand touches his. We weave our fingers together, and it feels natural, like we've done this a thousand times before.

"I'm so happy," I whisper, looking up at him, "that it was you."

Eloise

One Month Later

———

MILLIE WAS HELPING A CUSTOMER WHEN THE PHONE
rang.

"The Book Garden, how may I help you?"

"Yes, this is Dr. Hester. I'm calling for Eloise Baker."

"This is Eloise."

He cleared his throat. "I was hoping to speak with you in
person, but you missed your follow-up appointment. We received your test results, and I've reviewed the ultrasound im-
ages in consult with the radiologist, and . . . Eloise, this is
difficult news, but we found something."

"You found something? What do you mean?"

"Are you with anyone right now?"

"Millie's here, yes," I said, sitting on the stool behind the
counter. "Why?"

"Because I don't want you to be alone after what I'm about
to say."

My heart beat faster.

"Eloise, you have ovarian cancer, and I'm afraid that it has
spread undetected for some time."

As I watched Millie smiling cheerfully from across the room, conversing with a customer beside the new-release section, my heart sank. I wished I'd never visited Dr. Hester. I wished I'd let my body run its course. I wished I didn't know what was happening inside of me.

"You have options," he said, "and we'll get you connected with an oncologist immediately, but I fear that the associated side effects of treatment would be a high price to pay for very little extra time."

I swallowed hard against the heavy lump in my throat.

"I know this is a lot to take in, and I want you to know that I'm here for you. We'll formulate a plan you're comfortable with, one that makes the most sense." He paused. "You must have questions for me. Please, what can I tell you?"

"How long," I whispered. "I want to know how long I have."

"It's impossible to say for sure," he replied. "A few months, or . . . maybe a few weeks. I'm so sorry."

I decided not to tell Millie, choosing, instead, to keep the news to myself for as long as possible. But the burden was too heavy, and on a rainy Thursday morning, I told my best friend that I was dying.

She held me for a long time, and we wept in each other's arms, but after that, she promised me that there'd be no more tears.

"Sorrow isn't what you need," she said. "We'll find reasons to celebrate every day."

Her recent retirement from the law firm allowed her more time to help at the store. We agreed to keep my condition quiet; there was no sense in worrying our longtime customers. I refused to let a cancer diagnosis change the fact that the Book Garden was a place of joy. It was also where Edward found me.

He came into the store one morning and it almost took my breath away. "Do you have any books on eternity?" he asked. "I've waited for you at least that long."

Customers were browsing the shelves, so I did all I could to remain cool and collected, even though my heart nearly leaped out of my chest and straight into Edward's hands. I played along, collecting every relevant book and brought them to the counter. His presence breathed new life in me.

"St. Augustine's *Confessions. Slaughterhouse-Five. The Unbearable Lightness of Being*," I said, showing him my selections.

As I pressed each book into his hands, our fingers brushed lightly. "How did you . . . find me?" I asked, searching his eyes.

"How could I *not*?" was his only response.

"Thank you for the flowers."

He smiled, purchased all of the books I'd selected, then asked if he could take me to dinner that night, and just like that, we continued the conversation that had been broken off so abruptly all those years ago.

But while my heart was as strong as ever, my body wasn't. Dr. Hester's cocktail of prescription pills helped manage the pain. It was enough to conceal my illness from our customers and, I hoped, Edward. We'd only just reunited, and I didn't want my diagnosis to spoil our happiness. I'd hoped to keep the truth to myself for as long as possible, but as it turned out, I didn't have a choice.

One evening, when we met for dinner at Café Flora, I set out on the familiar three-block path from the store, but something strange happened—it was as if my legs stopped working. By the time I reached the café, where Edward was waiting under the awning, I was weak and winded. As I stepped across the sidewalk to take his hand, I felt faint, and my knees collapsed from under me.

"Eloise!" he cried, catching me before I fell.

"Once a klutz, always a klutz," I said, smiling up at him.

But Edward wasn't smiling. His eyes were filled with worry. "When were you going to tell me?"

I paused a long moment, my eyes brimming with tears as I finally told him about the diagnosis. For all those weeks, it hadn't seemed real—like a tragic novel I'd read once, a long time ago, then tucked away on a far shelf. I didn't want to read it again or think about its characters' grim lives. But fiction became fact as Edward stood beside me, his face grief-stricken.

"My darling," he whispered, taking me into his arms. "How much time do you have?"

"Not much," I said as he pressed his head against mine.

He closed his eyes tightly, then opened them again with a burst of certainty. "Then we'll make the most of every moment." He carefully lifted me into his arms and carried me through the door of Café Flora. "Starting now."

And we did just that. Edward took me to the park for picnic lunches, insisting that the fresh air would do me good. He carried me up multiple flights of stairs to the theater and requested the most comfortable booths at London's finest restaurants. It was if he was officially courting me, the way I'd dreamed he would back in 1968. And when my health worsened, Edward remained close, holding vigil on the couch so he could be on hand to make me cup of tea, or find an episode of *Gilligan's Island* on TV.

Millie was equally devastated. I staved off her offers to help, directing her energy to the store, where she took over in my place. I told her that I had a full-time caregiver, which, in fact, I did—one who loved me.

Like it always had in Edward's presence, time passed rapidly, but I longed to slow its pace. I wanted to savor every second. We talked about anything and everything, especially the past. I reminded him of the declaration he'd made the night we'd first met at the Royal Automobile Club.

"Nature, God, whatever you want to call it—it's bigger than us. Bigger and more powerful than anything we can do or dream."

I nodded. "So you're saying what will be, will be, not because we willed it, but because it was a part of a plan?"

"Yes, or a really good novel."

One night, as the sun began to set its sights on the horizon, Edward stroked my disheveled hair. "You can't deny that our lives, apart and together, have been beautiful, in their own strange and stubborn ways."

I looked into his eyes, signaling my agreement.

"Millie helped me prepare a will," I told him.

He looked away, not wanting to talk about the end, but I continued.

"I'm leaving everything to my daughter, Valentina. Promise me you'll find her."

"I promise."

I gestured to a paper bag on my bedside table. "And promise me that when you do, you'll give her this."

He nodded.

"I pray that the store will give her as much joy as it's given me, and that the Book Garden will live on to see the next generation of readers, but what she decides to do with it is entirely up to her. All that matters is her happiness."

Edward held a glass up to my lips, and I took a small sip from the straw. The liquid felt good on my dry throat.

"Please look out for her," I continued, "and Millie, too."

He nodded. "Don't you worry. I'll be there for as long as I can, behind the scenes. They won't even know it." He paused for a moment. "There's something I need to tell you."

I listened as he cleared his throat. "A long time ago, I . . . owned this building. I was all set to sell it when a particularly interesting duo approached my agent with the dream of . . . starting a bookstore."

I gasped.

"You see, some might have considered the venture a losing proposition, but I thought otherwise. Primrose Hill needed a bookstore. *You* needed a bookstore."

I smiled between labored breaths. *It was him. It was always him.*

"Oh, Eloise," he cried, tears running down his face.

"No," I said, reaching for his hand. "I need to see your smile. I want to memorize it, for . . . eternity."

My eyelids were so heavy, but I drew on my meager reserve of strength to keep them open for a few more moments to see the smile that he produced for me.

He squeezed my hand as my eyelids fluttered, then finally closed. I could still see, however—at least, on the big screen in my mind's eye. It was a different sort of sight, but it was crystal clear. And there we were, the two of us. We'd shed the trappings of age and illness leaving only joy, the very brightest sort, radiating from our faces as we ran, hand in hand, through a grassy field speckled with wildflowers. Millie and Valentina were there, too, waving. I was at once filled with the thing I'd been chasing my entire life: peace.

Valentina

Christmas Eve

———

THE TABLE IS SET, AND BING CROSBY IS PLAYING ON Mummy's old record player. I glance at the kitchen, grateful there isn't smoke streaming from the oven, only the savory scent of rosemary and roast beef. I smile to myself, thinking of my first day in London, with Liza holding that smoldering pan. It felt like a thousand years ago, and also . . . yesterday. She might not be gifted in the kitchen, but as I eye the flower arrangement on the table, it's clear that she's found her calling.

"Can you grab that, doll?" Liza says to me when the doorbell rings. "I've got to wrangle this beast." She heaves the enormous pan out of the oven and onto the stovetop, muttering obscenities under her breath. "Bloody hell. Aren't you the devil incarnate. Thought you'd kill me now, did you?"

Millie and Fernando have just arrived. She hands me a tray of fudge, and blushes when I point to the mistletoe, which I hung over the entryway this afternoon. Fernando isn't bothered in the slightest, however. He stretches onto his tippy toes and kisses her.

"Do I have anything in my teeth?" Liza asks nervously

when the doorbell sounds again a moment later. I tell her she looks perfect as I reach for the doorknob again, eager to meet the new love interest she's been unusually tight-lipped about. And there he is, a friendly-looking man in his forties—with a purple mohawk.

"I'm Jiles," he says, anxiously cracking the knuckles on his tattooed left hand. I smile as Liza gives him a quick kiss.

Fernando introduces himself with a firm handshake. "You live or work around here?"

"Both," Jiles says.

"Ah, we're neighbors, then." He smiles. "What did Liza say you did for a living?"

"I'm an accountant," he says.

"But Jiles is also in a band," she adds, giving me a knowing smile. "Honey, tell everyone about Night Shredder." She beams. "He's the lead singer."

"Aww, it's nothing much. Just a bunch of guys with sensible jobs who like to play rock and roll on the weekends."

I watch him wrap his arm around Liza's waist as she looks up at him adoringly. It appears she's found the man she'd been looking for all these years, and so far, he seems to rival any of the best men in literature—at least, in the Book of Liza.

The two couples mingle, keeping a respectable distance from the mistletoe—for now—as Eric arrives next, with an evergreen garland and a bottle of wine.

"Just the essentials," he says, kissing my cheek. He slips out of his coat and I brush away a few snowflakes that still cling to his sweater. "Shall I go uncork this thing?"

"Please," I say, grinning as Millie approaches and links her arm into mine.

"Merry Christmas, honey," she says.

"Merry Christmas."

She catches Fernando's eye across the room, then turns back to me. "Are you happy?"

"Yes," I say. "So happy." My eyes are suddenly misty as I look around the little flat that has become my home. Everything is in place, but one thing is missing. "Millie," I whisper. "I wish *she* were here."

"Oh, sweet girl, but you're mistaken," she replies, her eyes big. "She *is* here."

I let Millie's words sink in until they become truth. And they are—I just didn't know it yet. I'll never again have to look for Mummy. She's been here the whole time—in the Book Garden and on the streets of Primrose Hill; in Millie's smile and Liza's laughter; in Eric's eyes and between the lines of an old favorite book. But above all, she's been in my heart this whole time, the one place where we'll never be separated.

I smile to myself, composing the letter I would send to her right now, with love—with so much love—from London.

ACKNOWLEDGMENTS

——

MY HUSBAND, BRANDON, PROPOSED TO ME IN LONDON ON a chilly late-December night in 2017. I had no idea that he was going to pop the question, or in such a beautiful way. In fact, I was so stunned, I actually dropped the ring on the cobblestone streets of Notting Hill (thank God, I found it and said yes a few moments later). On that night, I knew two things: I wanted to spend the rest of my life with this wonderful man, and I also decided I'd set my next book in London. So, thank you, dearest Brandon, for the inspiration and, above all, for loving me.

The process of writing a book is a roller-coaster ride that's filled with bursts of creativity and zeal, but also heaps of self-doubt and exhaustion. It can be as fun and fulfilling as it is lonely and grueling. I am eternally grateful to the incredibly competent and understanding team of people I work with, who not only understand this but also know exactly how to help an author take a fledgling idea and turn it into the book you're holding in your hands right now. At the top of my list, my two super agents, Elisabeth Weed and Jenny Meyer, who have been with me from the beginning and are the two greatest business partners and friends a writer could ask for.

To my dear editor, Shauna Summers at Random House,

thank you for believing in this book and in me, and for all your wise editorial feedback and encouragement along the way. You could see the heart of this story when my vision was blurred, and it's a thousand times better because you pushed me to go deeper.

I have so many people to thank—for their reading time, feedback, advice, moral support, brainstorming sessions, hugs, wine, and a million more things. This list (in random order) includes colleagues, friends, and family members: Denise Roy, Claire Bidwell Smith, D. J. Kim, Heidi Gall, the wonderful team at Random House/Ballantine, Lauren Vogt, Camille Noe Pagan, my publishers and readers around the world, my wonderful sons—Carson, Russell, and Colby—and my "bonus" kids—Josiah, Evie, and Petra—as well as my sister and brothers. And thanks, Mom and Dad, for being my number-one fans. I love you.

WITH LOVE FROM LONDON

—

SARAH JIO

Random House Book Club

Because Stories Are Better Shared ™

A BOOK CLUB GUIDE

QUESTIONS AND TOPICS
FOR DISCUSSION

1. Valentina experiences two sudden tragedies: Her marriage is over, and the mother who abandoned her has died. What is it about major life changes that spark new beginnings?

2. When she arrives in Primrose Hill, Val is hesitant to emotionally invest in the Book Garden and her mother's carefully curated flat. How can childhood experiences affect how adults experience emotions and change later in life?

3. Val forms new friendships in London that last a lifetime. Explore the themes of friendship and family as seen in the new lives that Eloise and Val build after tragedy.

4. *The Last Winter* is a special book to Val and influences her journey in London. Why do you think the novel resonates so much with her—and with Eloise, for that matter? Reflect on a book or story that has inspired you in a similar way.

5. Eloise finds herself involved with two very different men. What do Edward and Frank represent to Eloise? Discuss the pros and cons of each possible path.

6. What were your impressions of Eric when he first

appeared in the bookstore and as he and Val began developing a friendship?

7. Val embarks on two scavenger hunts of sorts—one to find her mystery book lover, Daniel Davenport, and one following her mother's clues—yet she still carries a lot of resentment toward Eloise. Discuss these two separate journeys and the importance of each for Val.

8. Eloise finds passion in collecting antique jewelry from estate sales, but her life still feels empty. Discuss the social constructs of the 1960s and '70s, the standards set for women at the time, and the drastic change of socioeconomic status that Eloise experiences.

9. Eloise takes Val on a scavenger hunt to all her favorite places in London. Along the way, she shares her story with the hope that Val will understand her better. Map out your own scavenger hunt with places that matter to you.

10. Val asks her Instagram followers, "What's your big life dream?" Discuss the dreams of each character and then reflect on your own. Whom do you share them with?

11. While looking for one of her mother's clues, Val is given the advice to accept the invitation to life's grand second act. Pinpoint this change in the main characters and discuss their evolution. Have you experienced your own second act? If not, what would your second act look like?

12. When Val first arrives in London, it's obvious that her heart is hardened when it comes to matters of her mother's life. At what moment in the book did you detect a shift in Val—anger turning into understanding, pain turning into forgiveness?

13. Why is saving the Book Garden so important to Val? How has her relationship with Eloise changed up to this point in the novel?

14. Frank forces Eloise to go back to London, but it is ultimately her decision to stay and build a new life without her daughter. Did Eloise have a choice? Should Val be more forgiving of her mother? Discuss your thoughts on this difficult situation.

15. Val never receives the letters from Eloise, so she grows up confused, believing that her mother had abandoned her. How do you think their story would have been different if the letters had been delivered?

16. In the end, Val realizes that her mother is all around her, in the Book Garden and the streets of Primrose Hill. They've never been closer. Think of a loved one you have lost or a friend you've lost touch with. What small, everyday moments remind you of them? And if you could choose one person who's no longer in your life to write to, who would it be, and what would you say?

SARAH JIO is the #1 international, *New York Times*, and *USA Today* bestselling author of eleven novels. She is the host of the *Mod About You* podcast and also a longtime journalist who has contributed to *Glamour*, *The New York Times*, *Redbook*, *Real Simple*, *O: The Oprah Magazine*, *Bon Appétit*, *Marie Claire*, *Self*, and many other outlets, including NPR's *Morning Edition*. Jio's books have been published in more than twenty-five countries. She lives in Seattle with her husband, three young boys, three stepchildren, and two puppies.

sarahjio.com
Facebook.com/sarahjioauthor
Twitter: @sarahjio
Instagram: @sarahjio

ABOUT THE TYPE

This book was set in Caslon, a typeface first designed in 1722 by William Caslon (1692–1766). Its widespread use by most English printers in the early eighteenth century soon supplanted the Dutch typefaces that had formerly prevailed. The roman is considered a "workhorse" typeface due to its pleasant, open appearance, while the italic is exceedingly decorative.

RANDOM HOUSE BOOK CLUB

Because Stories Are Better Shared

Discover

Exciting new books that spark conversation every week.

Connect

With authors on tour—or in your living room. (Request an Author Chat for your book club!)

Discuss

Stories that move you with fellow book lovers on Facebook, on Goodreads, or at in-person meet-ups.

Enhance

Your reading experience with discussion prompts, digital book club kits, and more, available on our website.

Join our online book club community!

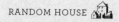 randomhousebookclub.com

Random House Book Club ™

Because Stories Are Better Shared